Cousin! 12-27-[illegible]

IT fe[illegible]ing done This. Now what happens?

Lot of Love

— Jocko

JOCKO

JOCKO

The Last Trumpet

Jonathan Post Magro

VANTAGE PRESS
New York

Bible excerpts are from *The New World Translation*, published by Watch Tower Bible and Tract Society of Pennsylvania. Reprinted with permission. All rights reserved.

Cover art by Gretchen Magro

FIRST EDITION

Published by Vantage Press, Inc.
516 West 34th Street, New York, New York 10001

Manufactured in the United States of America
ISBN: 0-533-14575-9

Library of Congress Catalog Card No.: 2003091945

0 9 8 7 6 5 4 3 2 1

To the One I love and to those who helped along the way

Contents

Preface

Several years ago I met an older man on Cumberland Lake who had several sharpened yellow pencils in his fishing tackle box. When I asked him about the pencils, he said he was writing the end of his book. He said the ending was really the beginning, and he laughed.

This book is the story of a life that gets meaningful toward the end.

JOCKO

1

Home

My sister had a toy monkey named Jocko. She called me Jocko. It stuck.

There was a sign leading down to the place where I grew up that said: MARKIN FARM. Nothing grew there. My mother said *Markin* was a word in the Spanish language that meant “fields.”

My father worked downtown. He left every morning wearing a suit and tie. I always thought I would be like that, but I never was.

There were no other children where I grew up. Another child came over and my mother wanted him to be my friend. When we saw each other he asked me where my shoes were. I asked him what else he was going to say. I went to his house one time.

I spent my summers under the hedges with a group of cocker spaniel dogs playing in the cool, loose dirt with a truck and other toy wheeled vehicles. All my friends had four feet.

The first pony we had was named Snowball. My mother would go on long walks through the fields leading Snowball with me on the pony’s back. I couldn’t ride by myself and my mother liked to walk. I learned to ride that way.

My older sister couldn’t get a dress on a doll named Betsy, so she threw doll and all out the window. When she realized what she had done she burst into tears. The doll broke on the terrace. It happened so fast. She couldn’t believe what she did and suddenly said I threw it out the window. My mother couldn’t imagine my sister could do such a thing, either. I denied it over and over again and again. Betsy’s face was broken.

My mother took me into the next room and tried to get me to confess. She said God knew if I was lying so I might as well tell the truth. I asked if God could see through walls. The subject was changed. I didn't get spanked, and there was no other outcome. The doll's face got repaired.

My parents worried that I was listless and nothing seemed to concern me. My mother, as only a mother does, pointed to a photograph and said I was going to be a preacher. As a young man when I flew over the house in a homebuilt aircraft she said I was going to be an aeronautical engineer.

Soon we got another pony that was mine, but when my sister had a friend over the friend would get to ride my pony. I would whisper in my pony's ear when they could see. Without fail my sister's friend would fall off. Every time my pony went around a certain row of trees in the back field he would cut sharply back toward the barn. If a person wasn't ready for that sudden change in direction they would be trotting merrily along, then they would go straight and downward while the pony went hard left. It didn't happen to me. I was ready.

One time when we were getting Snowball ready for a pony race my pony ran, too, so Snowball would have some practice running with other ponies. An experienced adult rider was on my pony. Her feet were in the weeds. When the practice race was over my pony was still going full speed ahead. They had made the mistake of racing toward the barn. What stopped him eventually was a long farm gate that separated the back field from the barn area. When the lady came back to where we were standing she said she could not stop him. She said she tried to turn, but even with the pony's nose touching her knee he kept running straight ahead. She said as the gate got closer and closer she imagined the pony running through it like in the cartoons, leaving a silhouette of them behind. She was laughing.

Before long my mother's grandmother on her father's side died. After that we got more and more horses and a bigger barn. There were school horses and some show horses, and other people would learn to ride. There was a riding teacher. With the money from riding lessons we would go to horse shows. I had a four-wheel-drive chassis named Morituri. I preferred motorized transportation. My one brother had a motorbike. He felt the same way about horses and transportation as I did, even more so. During the summers we would sit on two rock walls ten feet apart and talk about the most recent motorized scramble around the trails and fields. Mothers taking their children to ride would drive by us sitting on the wall. Several hours later they would go past again on their way to pick up their child. We may have moved while they were gone, but it didn't seem that way.

My mother's stepfather was a very wealthy industrialist. The house we lived in was his temporary quarters while his house was being built. Our families often had Sunday lunch together, and some Sundays we would all go to church. One Sunday when we went to church the sermon was about how it is easier for a camel to get through the eye of a needle than it is for a rich man to get into heaven. We rode back in his most luxurious car made in England, and he said it was a lousy sermon. We did not share any of his fame or fortune when he died, but my mother said he was like a father to her.

My mother's real father wasn't poor either. He died before his mother. My mother's father's father was a well-known architect in New York City. Recently there was a picture of his house in a magazine. A superstar had just bought it and that was why there was a picture. It said who the original owner was, and it named my mother's grandfather. I took it to my mother. She looked at the picture and said it was her grandmother's house. She said she had many Sunday lunches there and her grandfather raised beagle dogs. She never read the story with the picture. It was not as if she did not want to; she just didn't.

My grandmother on my mother's side invited me to her house for dinner. She often talked about dying. That day she said she wanted to buy me a suit to wear to her funeral. She and her husband had just talked with lawyers about their wills. She went on about how she had no money. I said I didn't have any either and then asked her if he (her wealthy husband) would give her some. He was sitting right there, and was amused. A few years before that night I was in a restaurant in New York City with them and some other family people. She said when she married him he "introduced her to the balance book." Then he quickly said that he "introduced her to a few other things too."

At her dinner table in Cincinnati she once told me that adverbs always had to follow verbs and she didn't know why. She said there was such a difference between saying "I love only you" and saying "I love you only." He was sitting at the other end of this long polished table. I was sitting next to her and I said, "The English language is subject to change." There was a long silence and nothing more was said about that subject.

Often when I was a small child she would put both her hands on my head and say it was a think tank. She called me "think tank" when no one else was around.

When I first learned the multiplication tables she asked me to write them down for her. She said she did not know them. She carried those multiplication tables in her purse until the day she died. My mother's half-sister said she found them when she cleaned out my dead grandmother's things.

One time when I was much older they were sitting at either end of a small table of magazines in their library having a drink before dinner. She asked me if I thought it was better to be cremated or buried. I said that when I was on leave from the army just before I went to Vietnam my mother sat on the edge of my bed and asked me if I was killed would I rather be cremated or buried. I told my mother I would rather be cremated.

I said to my grandmother that the whole idea of being in a hermetically sealed coffin and never rotting seemed unnatural. Plus, I said, if buried, there is no guarantee that someone won't dig you up for fun or profit. Her husband was sipping a martini, and he made some guttural sound of agreement. They were eventually both cremated and buried.

Soon after she died her children went to her house to divide up her things. My mother did not go. She sent me and one of my sisters. The table in the dining room was piled high with polished silver. Over on the side of all this was a little glass candleholder. It held four candles and was made up of many tiny glass pieces held together with brass wire. My mother's one full brother was there. He looked at the candleholder and said how different it was from everything else in the room. It had been in the dining room for the last several years. He wondered why his mother put it there, and why she had it in the first place. His mother, my grandmother, had told me about it once when I was there for dinner. I told him what she had told me. She said when she left her first husband (his and my mother's father) she went to live in Paris, France, with the two of them. It was a difficult time, and she said she bought the candleholder to make their dinners a little brighter. When he heard that, he walked into the next room with his back to everyone, and he didn't say a word.

My grandmother's father was a famous American illustrator. The "penny press" and "yellow journalism" were well established where he lived. She said her father often had female models come to his studio and he drew or painted from them. A newspaper reporter tried to get a female model to have sex with him so the newspaper could report what happened. My grandmother said nothing sexual happened. Did the reporter write the story that nothing sexual happened? Or did her father tell his wife and she overheard them? Or did he tell her? I did not ask. It was a nice story about faithfulness.

My father's parents were born and raised in Italy. They came to the United States quietly in a boat full of Italians. They met for the first time in the United States and were married. My father loved music. When he was a small boy he played a cello, which his mother threw downstairs. No one ever said why that happened. He never played a musical instrument, but he managed the Cincinnati Opera and did other opera work most of his life.

He went to college in Boston. He once told me that when he went there his mother told him to shave off his mustache so he would look less Italian. He finished school at the university in 1932.

His first job was mixing concrete. There was an economic depression. Later he got a job in New York City's public relations department. Soon after that he started his own advertising agency.

My Italian grandfather's first job in the United States was concrete work also. The foreman told him and two other Italians to break up a reinforced concrete wall with sledgehammers. The only right they had was the right to quit, and he did. He went to work in a shoe factory and became a foreman before he retired. My father's mother's family ran a corner grocery store in Rochester, New York. My mother told me she and my father were riding around in his raggedy old car when both of them got hungry. He stopped and bought a loaf of bread. That was the meal. She said shortly after that they got married.

When we were children with horses we rode around a ring

with stalls on the outside facing into the middle. There was wire mesh on the front of the stalls. One horse was very aware of the other horses moving around. This horse had its hindquarters close to the wire mesh and it was leaning against the side of the stall. Its tail was lifted to the side. Later the person who took care of the horses explained to me in no uncertain terms that the horse was in season, which, he explained again, clearly, using many four-letter words, meant the horse had its biological urges in mind.

When I went to school I was supposed to show my parents my tests so they knew how well or poorly I did. We had a long driveway with deep woods on one side. I buried many of my tests there. I also ate quite a few. The teacher would always pass back papers beginning with the best and ending with the worst. When the teacher got to mine it was always one of the last ones or the last one. One time she held it up for the whole class to see. It was a standardized test on newspaper-type paper. All through the test I kept tearing off little pieces and chewing them up. It would have made really good spitballs if I were making spitballs. I was really embarrassed when she held it up. I didn't think I had eaten that much.

Another time during recess in the fourth grade, I and two other boys pinned a beautiful third-grade girl down on the ground and kissed her. I had noticed her for a long time before that and I suppose they did also. The one-man disciplinary committee told us if there was a next time we would have to wear the girls' uniform to school. I did not quite see the connection, but it never happened again. That same person was also a teacher who liked to read. When I was in his grade two years later he frequently brought clippings from newspapers to school. Once he read to us about a father and child who went for a walk when it was snowing. The child stopped the father and asked him if he could hear the snow falling. The father realized he had not heard the snow falling, but that it definitely was making a sound. We then talked about sensory awareness and visual bias. That was in the sixth grade.

In the fourth grade the class lessons were about fractions. We were told about pieces of a pie. Meanwhile there was a kid over in the corner with a micrometer who at recess was able to measure the thickness of a person's hair down to the nearest thousandths of an inch. He was always in trouble with the teacher. Plus, his desk was a mess. That bothered and disturbed the teacher very much.

That school was divided into two halves: the upper school and the lower school. The separation was between the sixth and seventh grades. My parents were told that I had to go to another school because the school administration thought I needed a different environment. I was not invited back.

2

School

I went to a boarding school where they planned every waking moment, even when to urinate. After dinner the whole school would form two lines. It didn't matter if a person had to urinate or not. I did well there. The head of the school liked guns and supercharged automobiles. He had both. Sometimes in the afternoon when we were outside on the sports fields we would hear tremendous gunshot sounds. He had a hill behind his house. Someone would look in that direction and say he was doing target practice. He could play music. He was interested in all things.

He was an eccentric man. Sometimes he would read poetry to the whole school, and he was the only one allowed to give us "swats." Swats were physical punishment that involved going into his office and getting smacked on the posterior a certain number of times with a fearsome paddle. That punishment was for the most misbehaved. It was generally known beforehand what behavior warranted swats. I never got any swats, but I heard about them.

There was a teacher who once was a photographer for an acrobatic fighter plane unit that the U.S. Navy called the Blue Angels. He knew firsthand much about fighter planes. He would bring models to our history class and demonstrate for us what a barrel roll was. We spent several weeks on the Battle of Britain.

We were doing a poem in literature class that read, ". . . then felt I like some watcher of the sky when a new planet swims into his kin or like stout Cortés when with eagle eye he stared at the Pacific silent upon a peak in Darien." The teacher asked the class what kin meant, and he said if anyone said it was a relative he would throw up. He called on me and I said something.

Then he launched into a diatribe about if a person had a 400 horsepower automobile in their garage and never took it out it was no good to them. He said it was Balboa who was the first European to see the Pacific, not Cortés, but, he said, it was still considered a terrific poem. One time, off to the side, in a positive way, he told me I was like the continent of Africa, nothing there, but there was something there.

Earlier that same year the entire school one at a time saw a man from outside who conducted an intelligence quotient (IQ) test. Intelligence quotient was a number they put on scholastic aptitude, which was relied on heavily by both adults and children in that school. Everyone talked about his IQ. The results were not made known to individuals, so I wondered how everyone knew what their IQ was. People seemed to make a point of finding out. It was very important. When I took the test it was the first time in my life I could feel drops of sweat running down my sides from my armpits. I was sweating profusely. I had to come back another time and do it once more. Then finally I learned I had no score. I could not be tested. Did they have a code for someone who could not be tested? What would it say on a form that had to be filled out?

On Sunday the entire school walked in single file over to a church where we had a Sunday service. Everyone had to go to church, but there was one exception. If an adult signed a student out before everyone went to church, then the signed-out student didn't have to go to church. The student who was signed out could bring a friend so the friend would be signed out also. I was far from home, but a lady lived nearby whose sons had all gone to that school. One of her sons married my mother's half-sister. His four children were my cousins. He once said, as he was eating one of those delicious Sunday lunches, that there was so much talk about eating less. He said people should do more, not eat less. He said that as he was having food put on his plate for the third time. When she signed me and a friend out, she would stand in the front hall of the school. The faculty room opened into the front hall, as did many other rooms. Teachers would see her waiting for us. She was older and wore thick glasses that made her eyes look big. One day after she was standing there she told me a story that made me wonder if she thought she looked different in that school. She said that when her son was a pitcher on the school's baseball team she went to watch a game. She went up to him to ask where to sit. Friends of his were with him. He gave directions on where to sit like she was just a spectator.

In the same two or three weeks many of the faculty asked me about this person who signed me and a friend out every Sunday. The teacher I had in literature was concerned that I was missing church every week. He asked me if we went to church and what we did all day. I answered that she would put us to work before lunch, stacking wood or something else. Then, I said, we would have the best lunch. One son who always studied upstairs would come down for lunch, and another son and his family would be there also. I said there might be as many as nine or ten people at the table.

Afterward people would go into the next room to watch a football game on television. She had a brown lamp cord leading to her chair and she would switch the sound off during commercials. My friend and I would play with goats she had in pens behind her garage. Her son, who studied upstairs would go on long walks in the afternoon. He always took a dog with him. She would take us back to school late Sunday afternoon, and that, I said, is what we did. Even my friend said his parents asked him about her.

A teacher who had a reputation for being very strict asked about her when I was at his table. I told him I never met her husband, because he was dead. I said her family farm was one of the first ones in the area, but now there were businesses and condensed living spaces as far as the eye could see. I said she worked in a local hospital as a volunteer several hours a day, two days a week, and that getting more money was not her objective. He asked which hospital she worked in and I said I did not know.

I never had this strict teacher in the classroom, but I learned my first year that our birthdays were on the same day. Every time a student had a birthday the headmaster would play the "Happy Birthday" song on a small xylophone he had at the head table. The whole school would sing and someone would carry in a lit birthday cake. The headmaster would then stand up and say the "muse" had visited him. He would read a short poem he had written about the person who had the birthday. This happened at the evening meal. My birthday was during the school year, so this happened to me the three years I was there. Somehow I learned this other teacher had his birthday on the same day as mine. The second year on my birthday I was passing him in the hall and I said happy birthday to him. He stopped and said, "How did you know?"

I said, "It is my birthday also." He and I were good friends for the rest of the time I was in that school.

He ran the "spa," which was a place in the school where a student could buy a candy bar, a soft drink, or some ice cream. Whatever money we had was limited to our school allowance, which was based on our academic performance. He paid us our allowance. The really smart students got to walk to the nearby village and buy candy in an actual store.

When we came back from vacation we were all supposed to turn in any leftover travel money, but I didn't. The single coin I paid with was more than my weekly allowance, so he knew it was outside money that I had kept. He looked at the large coin through his bifocal eyeglasses and said, "What is this?" I realized I had been found out. He sent me back to the study hall, but that was not the end. The next day he called me into his office, and he talked about honesty and deceit. Apparently he told my parents about this event because later that week I got a letter from my mother that said: ". . . when I was a child I behaved as a child, but when I was a man I put away childish things." I guess I wasn't a child anymore, even though I was only thirteen years old.

I went home for holidays and sometimes I would see the person who shod the horses. He would always ask me about school. He jokingly called it an institution of correction, and when a horse he was shoeing relieved itself he would tell me to get rid of those Russians. He loved a song on the radio sung by a lady or maybe he loved the lady. The words to the song were, ". . . if that's all there is, my friend, then let's keep dancing, let's kick off our shoes, and let's keep dancing." He saw me washing windows to earn some money to buy a go-cart, and he yelled to my mother across the way, "It is amazing what Jocko will do for money." Another time he had supper with us. My mother said she would love to meet his wife and he said, "You had better hurry up before the divorce." When he was walking back to his truck after supper he was urinating while he was walking. I was behind him and it was dark. I asked him what he was doing and he said he was, "blazing a trail."

When it was time for me to go to another school I was unaware of the difficulty people were having getting me accepted anywhere. The guidance counselor called me into his office to see if I was experiencing anxiety over that situation. Apparently, the administration of the school was concerned because that school was a "prepreparatory" school. It would prepare children to be prepared to go to another school that would prepare them to go to a university. If I couldn't get in anywhere, they had prepared me for nothing. If I didn't get into one of the boarding schools where I applied I would go to my local high school and live at home. The guidance counselor talked with me a while and learned I wasn't suffering from stress. A few weeks later he informed me that I had been accepted at another "institution of correction" located in the western part of that state.

The Episcopal diocese of Massachusetts ran this school, although that was only a rumor. The headmaster wore a clergyman's collar all the time and so did a few of the teachers. We walked to "chapel" every day. It was in a church that was nearby and off campus. We sat in alphabetical order. On one side of me was a Buddhist from Thailand, and on the other side of me was an American Jew. I was your basic savage in the middle. The school administration said "chapel" was "nondenominational." Students who went there were different from anyone I had ever known. There was an American Indian student. Three students were from the Belgian Congo. There was a person from Harlem. He wore the same tie every day. There were students from Japan, Canada, and Argentina.

There was a time at that school when I got down on my knees and prayed. The custom was that a person upon entering a church would sit down in one of the pews, assume the kneeling position, and commence to pray. I don't remember what I prayed about except often I would pray, *Please, God, don't let me be normal.* The humans in my life were not there and it was nice to know God was. As time wore on I became more acclimated to the people around me. A nineteenth-century Russian asked where was God when a Cossack shot a baby in the face with a pistol at point-blank range while it was in its mother's arms. I would not learn the answers to those kinds of questions until much later in my life. Most people seemed to look the other way when those sorts of things happened. I was no different. My interest in God diminished.

If everything went as planned I would be there four years. My first year I lived in a dormitory that originally housed chickens. It had a slate roof. When the place became a school it was remodeled as a dormitory and named the Coop, as in *chicken coop*.

In the Coop I learned what a bully was. This person mostly just said things that weren't nice. I always remembered the saying "sticks and stones will break my bones, but words will never hurt me." It went on that way with just words for some time. He was popular with the other students. The dormitory master wanted to be popular, so I didn't get any help from him. One afternoon this person pulled my tie, and when he did I spun around with my arm bent. My elbow was pointing outward, and quite by accident it connected very solidly with his nose. Other students were watching. I remember the dazed and amazed look on his face. His image was in question. He put his head down and proceeded to push me against a wall while flaying away at me in an uncontrolled manner. After that he was my best friend. From then on bullies ceased to be a problem. I realized how ineffectual they are.

There was another student there who was on full scholarship, which meant his parents didn't have to pay any money. If he were any smarter he would probably be insane. When he left that school he received a full scholarship to one of the best technological universities in the world. I heard much later that he was working as a carpenter. He must have learned more than they wanted him to learn. In the Coop he and I had felt-tip pen duels. When it was over the person with the most marks on his T-shirt lost.

On the report card sent home the dormitory master, who was also one of the teachers, was supposed to write something perceptive. He said that I was a "loner." I remember being disturbed by that word.

When we were walking from chapel to have supper I noticed one of the Congolese students ahead of me. I ran up to him. I asked him about the United States. He said he liked it, except, he said, "people here think we all live in grass huts." He mentioned one student who sincerely asked him if he lived in a house.

I said, "Most of what we know about Africa comes from Tarzan television shows."

He asked me, "What is Tarzan?" I said he was a European who lived in a tree.

Children in the Belgian Congo must play soccer as soon as they can walk. Two of the three Congolese students played halfback on our school's varsity soccer team. Soaking wet they probably weighed 130 pounds each, which is light for a halfback. They would laugh and jibber-jabber back and forth in Congolese. No one could get the ball past them.

Some Friday nights we would hear music from a high school dance that was nearby. The dormitory I was assigned to that year was the farthest building to the north on the school grounds. It was the closest to the town. On warm nights when all the windows were open we listened to the music. One song said, ". . . she wore blue velvet . . . and I still can see blue velvet through my tears. . . . " Several of us snuck out. When we got there the room was full of people. I don't remember the girls I danced with, except each one said in various ways it was no secret we were outsiders. It is a good thing the adults didn't throw us out or have us arrested for criminal trespassing. We did that only one time and we didn't get caught.

There were other school dances where we would be bused to an all-girl school or a busload of girls would come to our school. We were assigned a partner at the beginning and we had to stay with that person. If anybody "ditched" his partner and that "ditched" person was unhappily standing around, then the person who did the ditching would not get to go to any other dances. At least, in our school that was the case. We were at an all-girl school for a dance and my assigned partner didn't like me or I didn't like her or both. She found somebody else. I went into another room where several other people in the same situation watched television. None of us would be seen standing around.

We sat in front of a TV on couches and heavily upholstered chairs. I started to talk to an appealing girl who wasn't riveted to the television. She was cynical about everything. She had dark hair and beautiful light skin. Later on I wrote to her and she wrote to me. That went on for several years. We always communicated from a distance. I saw her a few times, and soon it faded away with time.

When I first heard the president of the United States got shot it was from a person in a toll booth at the end of an expressway. Several of us were returning from a fencing match in Boston. People got killed everywhere all the time. Even presidents got shot. Everyone was listening intently to the radio and later on it said he was dead.

There are three ways to fence. I fenced épée. The other two ways are the foil and the saber. In practice we spent hours and hours moving quickly forward and quickly backward. The idea of moving backward in the face of an attack is half of fencing. It is when opportunities present themselves. An opponent is most vulnerable when moving forward in an attack. Through repetitious practice we developed the skill to always maintain a striking distance. I was undefeated my senior year.

We had to do some sort of athletics in the fall, winter, and spring. No one in the four years I was there said why athletics was part of our education. Fencing was in the winter. In the fall I played soccer and in the spring I played an American game called lacrosse. I wasn't particularly good in either of those sports. The team that won usually had players who worked well together. If there was one or two good players on the other team we would double-team those people, and that team usually lost.

In the fall the whole school was divided into two groups. Each group fielded teams in each sport and somehow I was made part of a cross-country team even though I couldn't run long-distance. Like all cross-country races this was a long one. Midway through the race I was nearly last. There were many teachers and students gathered in one place to "cheer" us on.

Toward the end of the race the course went up a road, turned west off the road, and continued around a playing field. After people went around the playing field they came back onto the road at the same place where they turned west. The racecourse then went across the road in an easterly direction to the finish line, where practically everyone in the school was yelling for the runners to go faster. A person at the east-west spot made sure everyone ran around the playing field. When I came to that spot I was so far behind, runners were coming back out onto the road and going east to the finish line. All at the exact same time I was at the spot, there was a break in the runners going east, and the person standing watch was facing the other way. I didn't know which way the course went. I only saw the back ends of runners going to the finish line. I turned east to the finish line instead of west around the playing field. There I was at the front of the race when I had been last seen near the end. When I finished, two or three people came up to me and said how terrific it was that I had come from so far behind. I was just glad it was over. A day or so later one of the front runners whom I beat to the finish line came up to me and said he passed me in the very beginning and did not remember my passing him. I said I didn't pass him and that I didn't go around the playing field. He went away somewhat mystified.

In the classroom I first learned I liked the written word even though I couldn't spell and didn't do well on vocabulary tests. I was not a very good student. I wrote compositions. One time I liked a passage in a book so much and thought it was so well done that I copied it verbatim with the proper introduction and conclusion. The teacher read the paper to the whole class as an example of a good composition. I guess he thought it was a good passage also. After the class was over a friend came up and insisted that I had copied it from somewhere. It was rather obvious to him. Also, later on, the teacher pulled me aside and the long and short of what he said was that it would be a much better composition if it didn't have that terrible introduction and conclusion.

Once a year when school closed for a few days in November I would go to an island in Penobscot Bay, Maine. It was much closer than my home. I knew a family there and would duck-hunt or deer-hunt with them. The head of that household worked as a boatman for my mother's stepfather. He and his family lived there all year, and everyone who had a place on that island depended on him to keep an eye on their property. The only other person who lived there all year long was an old man who was a wood boat builder. His houseboat was permanently located above the beach at the boatyard. I doubt it could float. He worked in the boatyard. Often he would come over and watch television. While looking at the TV he sometimes sharpened his pocket knife. He could get it so sharp that it could shave hair on his arm. He showed me how to use a sand stone, but I could never get a knife that sharp.

The boatman would always threaten that he was going to get the backhoe and rip the television out of the side of the house. He would say that when he didn't like the program. That was most of the time. The backhoe was a piece of construction equipment in the tractor shed. It was a yellow farm tractor with a digging arm or attachment on the back.

Eventually, my mother's stepfather bought the boatyard. It was next to my grandmother's property and the owner of the boatyard wanted to retire and move to the mainland. Nearby there was a bigger island where there was a school and many other people lived. Also, there was a ferry service from the bigger island to the mainland five miles away. My grandmother's father, the artist, originally bought the island property, but it was my grandmother's second husband, the industrialist, who kept it up and spent much money there. He loved that place more than any other place. My grandmother always went there in the spring to plant the garden, and I think that is when she enjoyed that place the most. One time my mother's stepfather asked me about my November trips. It never occurred to me that the boatman was putting me up in his house at his expense. Each time I wrote and said I was coming, but there was no doubt I was a guest in that house. My mother's stepfather said I should take them a turkey or something. He never asked me about it again and I went there many more years.

I remember when the boatman first started to work there years earlier. It was in the summer and he was splicing the bowline on a rowboat. I asked him how long he was going to work there. He said he didn't know. He said he always worked around the water, but that his former job was driving a semitruck on the mainland. He said he overturned a truckload of chickens and that was the end of that job. The way he described it, there were chickens and feathers everywhere.

During those days in the summer the boatman and I would go across to the post office on the bigger island. We would go around the corner to a store to get milk and newspapers. Sometimes I would get ice cream. He would always say to the man behind the counter, "Charge it to J.J." When I was little we were on that island for two weeks in the summer. Throughout the summer other members of my mother's family went there for an equally brief time. There was always a project in progress: digging a pond, winterizing the house, building a new dock, rewiring the house. Every summer it was something different. My mother's stepfather wanted anyone there to help if they could. The boatman was involved with those projects, so I was too.

When I went there from school in November I would take a bus to Boston, then I would transfer to another bus that went up the coast to where I was going. School didn't let out until noon on Wednesday. I had to make a connection, and once I missed my bus and had to get the next one, which left hours later.

In the bus depot I put my bag in a lockable compartment so I would not have to worry about luggage during my wait. I sat down, stood up, and looked around. Over and over again I did those things. It had gotten dark outside. One of the times I stood up I was looking through a circular rack of postcards. Another person said something from the other side of the rack of postcards and we started to talk. He told me his name and asked me mine. He asked if I would like to go get a cup of coffee. He seemed like a nice person. He was about ten to fifteen years older than I was. I was sixteen years old and drank coffee. I said yes. It didn't occur to me that there was coffee right there in the bus depot. I didn't think. We went outside in the dark and got inside his car. I explained my situation, that I was waiting for a bus. We went to a place nearby and sat in his car sipping hot coffee. The conversation turned to matters of sexual activity in an all-boy boarding school. I said there was none. I thought the conversation had gone bad. I wondered why I ever left the bus station. I said I had to get back or I might miss the bus. He said, "If you do I will drive you to Maine myself." I could just imagine what the boatman would say if I appeared with this guy. He started his car and halfway back he came to a stop along the curb where other cars were parked. He told me that he wanted to do what he said I always wanted. I said, "What is that?" He said something that made it very clear to me that here was a raving homosexual. I said politely, "No thank you," and I thought, *Here I am in a dark place, in an enclosed place.* I thought I might be in the morning paper if they recovered my body. I was hoping this was not a person who would put a bullet in my head and throw my body in a river somewhere. Or maybe he would simply push me out of his car and I would miss my bus. As it turned out, he let me off in front of the bus station, said good-bye, and drove away. I acted like nothing had happened. I said if I was ever in the area again and I had more time I would look him up. I don't know why I said that except I was thankful he had brought me back to the bus station and I wanted him to think I thought he was a nice person, which, basically, he was. He couldn't control his messed-up biological urges. I went back inside the bus station relieved that it was over.

Very soon after I sat down another person sits down right next to me and starts talking. Right away he asks me where I've been. He knows I was gone. I said I went to get some coffee with . . . and I said the other person's first name, which was the only part of his name I knew. The person sitting next to me throws his head back and laughs like he is amazed and says how he knows this person. He says isn't it amazing that in this whole city this person was in the bus depot, how amazing. Then he asks me if I want to go get some coffee. I say, "No thank you," and soon he leaves. I go to the locked compartment and get my bag out and go back to sit down. Then I look around more aware. It seemed there were some people just standing around, not there to catch a bus. I was there for a long time with no bag, so they probably thought I was like them.

I was glad to be out of there and on a bus going north. When the bus let me off I was the only one to get off and it was two in the morning. There was a pay phone on the ferry dock and I called. I was on the mainland and the ferry was stopped for the night. It was a very clear, cold night, and the water was calm. I stood at the end of the ferry dock looking at how beautiful everything was: the sea, the stars, the moon, everything. I could see the running lights on the boat coming to get me. It was a long way off and it took a long time to get to where I was. I wanted it to take longer.

The next morning we got up early to duck-hunt. We wanted to have all the duck decoys set at dawn when the ducks started to fly. There was one coal oil stove in the kitchen and that was the only heat in the house. The upstairs was brisk. I shared a room with the boatman's son. Three daughters were in two other rooms. The boatman and his wife were in a bedroom downstairs beside the kitchen.

That morning there were four of us who were going to hunt, the boatman, his son, a friend of theirs from a nearby air force base, and me. The two older men were going to hunt together, and me and the boatman's son were going to hunt together.

None of the women in that family hunted or expressed interest in hunting. Hunting and killing animals for food was a primeval working out of men-get-food, women-cook-food.

Their one son, whom I was going to hunt with that day, drowned years later. His body was never found. His lobster boat ran aground on the shore and people said he fell overboard while hauling his lobster traps. He was a lobster fisherman by trade. He was a good swimmer, but he would have had heavy rubber boots and heavy rubber pants over his other clothes. When a trap is being hauled the boat is left in gear and set in circular travel. If he fell overboard at that moment the boat would have kept going in circles until it went up onshore, which it did. His family thinks his rubber clothes weighted him down. He was presumed drowned. His father, the boatman, died a short while later. He died the day before he was to leave the island to retire on the mainland. I was there when he died. The night before he died he said he didn't want to leave the island but he said he was supposed to do that for very complicated reasons. My grandmother and her husband had died a while earlier. When she was alive she called him the "Prime Minister" of that property.

The November day that we were all going out to sit in duck blinds was perfect as far as the weather was concerned. There was a quarter-of-a-mile visibility and it was drizzling. That meant there would be many ducks flying around looking for a place to feed. We took two boats and went in two different directions. The boatman's son and me went to one place and set up our decoys.

A duck decoy is an artificial duck that floats in the water and is anchored by a weight. If decoys aren't arranged properly, no duck in its right mind will land anywhere near them. When the water is coming for another hour or so there are three or four hours before the tide leaves them on the beach. Those tides are extreme. From the high tide mark to the low tide mark might be as much as 200 feet. We built our blind high up on the shore close to trees and other plants. Our decoys were well within range. We had a small flat-bottom boat that we pulled up onshore and camouflaged. Nobody ever had a dog retrieve ducks all the years I went there. The water was ice-cold. If someone was sitting beside a shivering dog they would get cold. People either used a boat to retrieve ducks or they let the wind blow them ashore.

Another year on a bright and clear morning in practically the same place, I was with my brother in a duck blind. A sea gull was soaring back and forth in front of us 100 feet above the water. All the time it was calling out. It did that for an unusually long time. There was no other sound and that made it seem loud. I remember thinking that if it came in range I could shoot it, but later I was glad it didn't come in range. I didn't shoot it. Months later I wondered why I wanted to shoot it and how I could be capable of such a thought.

On the morning I was in the blind with the boatman's son a drake Whistler duck landed about two hundred feet up the shore from our decoys. It was a smart old bird. All morning ducks were landing in our decoys, but that one wouldn't. It started to feed off the bottom. It would dive and be gone for about twenty seconds. Then it would reappear, look around, and dive again. This went on for five minutes or more. The boatman's son proceeded to crawl out of the duck blind and each time the bird went down belly-crawl closer over cold wet seaweed and rocks. When the bird came up he would stop. This went on until he was right where the bird was. The bird went down, he stood up, and when the bird appeared again it got "basted," to use his expression. When we ate ducks that night, that duck was bigger. He knew which one it was and it went on his plate.

My brother told me about another time when the shooting was slow. The boatman's son plucked, cleaned, cooked, and ate a duck right there on the beach. One time when I was hunting with him after hours of nothingness he broke the silence saying, "Jocko, what would you do right now if a duck charged you?"

When we went back in it would be lunchtime. That was a big meal. If anyone asked the boatman to pass the turnips he would say he couldn't reach them.

After lunch people would go bow hunting down island. A person was allowed to hunt deer on an island only with a bow and arrow. A game warden enforced the hunting laws of the state. In all the years I went there I never saw a game warden. If I ever did I wanted to have a camera because I would like to take a picture. I'd put it in a photo album and say, "Here is what a game warden looks like." The boatman made it sound like there was a warden behind every tree.

Years later when I came back from Vietnam I smuggled a Russian-designed, Chinese-made AK-47 into the United States. That same year, the U.S. government allowed people to register any illegal firearms with impunity. I registered the AK-47, which was a semi-automatic or fully automatic assault rifle depending on where the selector switch was. On the registration form I put that I kept it on the island in Maine. When I told the boatman this he was very irate because he thought now there would be more wardens than ever on the island. He was afraid they would think he was hunting deer with a fully automatic assault rifle.

The island had too many deer. They had only two natural enemies: the severe winters and humans. The deer were smaller than most deer and had thick fur. A long time ago quite a few people populated the island. Grave stones and apple trees are in the woods. Fieldstone basements indicate where a house was. A road called the cord wood road went through the north end swamp. Four-foot logs were laid side by side and covered with dirt. Horses and horse-drawn wagons could then travel through the north end swamp. The cord wood road disappeared. The wood rotted away and trees are in the middle of what was the road. Other roads on the island are still traveled. They are narrow dirt roads through the woods.

Late one fall I was bow hunting and walking up one of those

dirt roads. About a hundred yards ahead the trees opened into a sunlit clearing where a house used to be. I saw a deer with huge antlers walk by in the sunlight. I walked hurriedly to the opening. He didn't see or smell me. He went to the far side of the clearing and had his head in the woods like he was feeding. As soon as I stepped into the clearing he looked back at me and disappeared. When I got back I said what happened, and the boatman said I had buck fever.

When I got back to school winter came, and in that part of the country there was deep snow that lasted. The headmaster told us to get haircuts all winter long and one student said it was because he was jealous because he was going bald. When a teacher dropped dead from a heart attack that same student said, "I'm not going to his funeral because he isn't going to mine." I admired his irrefutable logic, sick as it was.

When I was a senior the pressure was on to get into the college of our choice. I didn't really have a choice. I went east one day across the state to interview at the college in Boston where my father went. It was considered one of the best universities anywhere and it was sort of a joke among the seniors in our school that I was applying there. We took a standardized test that put everybody in the same hat, so to speak. It was called the SAT. As I recall, a maximum score was 800. Anything above 600 was a good score that would cause any college to look at you seriously. I had a pair of 400s or something in the low 400s, which was mediocre at best. I was seriously applying to one of the best colleges and that was an insult to everyone's sense of propriety. I applied because my father wanted me to apply there. It was where he went, but when he got accepted it was right after two Italians in that city were executed by the state. It was found out after they were dead and gone that they were without doubt wrongfully accused and innocent. It made national news. The president of that university was on the jury that convicted them. I wondered if a bunch of Italians were accepted that year. My father always was good at public relations. He knew a good opportunity when he saw one. I didn't have anything like that going for me.

I had a nice visit with some person who worked high up in a building under construction. I suppose to him I was another privileged kid from an East Coast boarding school wearing a tweed coat and trying to follow in his father's footsteps. Scholastically I wasn't there, either. We sort of went through the formality of an interview. He said my appointment for the interview was another day and that it was a good thing he was there. I didn't think I had the wrong day and wondered if he said that to everybody to see what they would say. If he was trying to start a fight he wasn't going to get one from me. I just agreed that it was a good thing he was there. We talked about the school where I went and I said, "They give you enough rope to hang yourself." He was amused by that comment, but soon after that, to everyone's relief, I got a notification in the mail that I was not accepted.

As it turned out I was accepted at my home state university, where they had an open admissions policy. Anyone who was a resident of that state who applied, who paid, could go there. I didn't go there right away. I went in the U.S. army, because my senior year I flunked economics. That meant I didn't have enough credits to get a diploma. I couldn't go to college. What I did get was a certificate that said I was there. When we had the graduation ceremony no one else beat me out for last place. There were seventy students in our senior class. Years later I would say I graduated seventy out of seventy and the other person would say, "Oh, you graduated first in your class?" I would say, "No, I graduated last." I would watch the expression on their face change.

The diplomas, and in my case the certificate, were all rolled up the same way so the roomful of people didn't know that I was getting a certificate instead of a diploma. I didn't have to wear a dunce cap or any other visible sign of my achievement, which I thought was big of them considering how competitive everything was. The headmaster said something for every student. When it was my turn he used the word *vacuum*. It was a positive statement in general, but I remember I wanted to cry. I read about a nineteenth-century Russian who said, "Life is everywhere life, I shall not despair . . . not to falter or fail in any misfortune whatsoever, that is life and therein lies its task." He said that to a tribunal after they sentenced him to go to Siberia. He wasn't going there to make a million dollars, so I wondered what was failing to him.

When school was over it was summertime. I could make up the credit for a diploma in summer school. I called my former school to get approval for a course in mechanical drawing at the local high school, but the person in charge said that subject wasn't even close to a substitute for the economics course I had failed. Then I found a chemistry course at a local private school. That course was approved for credit toward a diploma. I enrolled and failed it completely. It was nice that my parents didn't seem to care either way. I would go to and from the school in Morituri, which wasn't street legal. Morituri didn't have fenders, lights, turn signals, or anything that wasn't absolutely necessary to make it go. I never was stopped by the police or saw any police.

That summer I ran away from home and went to live in the woods on Peterloon Farm. It was a large farm of over 1,300 acres, of which probably only 50 acres was tillable. It belonged to my mother's stepfather, the wealthy industrialist. Markin Farm belonged to my parents. It was twenty-four acres in the middle of Peterloon Farm, and before it belonged to my parents it was part of Peterloon. My grandmother came up with the name Peterloon. When I asked her how she got it, she said that she would probably take that information to her grave.

When I ran away from home I took Morituri, a twenty-gauge shotgun, a sack full of clothes, and all the money I had, which was about twelve-pounds of coins. I only fired the shotgun once. In the middle of the night it seemed to me that all the night-life was out sniffing around my campsite. I could hear rustling noises all around me. I crawled out of my tent and fired one shot into the ground to quite things down. My mother's half-sister lived nearby. I heard voices faintly. It sounded like her whole family heard the blast. I didn't think I was that close.

During the day I would drive out of the woods and leave Morituri parked behind a small hardware store about three miles away. I would take the bus downtown and see two or three movies and then take the bus back, walk to Morituri, and go the three miles back into the woods. While I was away during the day everything I had was in a sack strapped to the back of Morituri. I knew the owner of the hardware store, his wife and children. None of the things in the sack were ever disturbed, and that included the shotgun. That hardware store with its galvanized bins of loose nails is gone. Now in its place is a trendy shop selling cashmere sweaters. In the woods I felt very much on my own. I wasn't aware that anyone knew what I was doing except a slightly plump girl I met on the bus. She took the bus every day from the same place to the same place. She went to a beauticians' school downtown. After a few days we struck up a conversation, and when I moved back home we went out a few times. She lived with her father near the hardware store. He was a hardworking, sober man who, she said, didn't trust anyone who wore madras shorts. I was getting gasoline in my parents' car. One of the people who worked there, kind of greasy-looking, came over to the car to speak with me. Never mind about the madras shorts. He said she was his friend's best girl. The whole thing was getting to be more than I could handle. It was taking on the ramifications of a family. The girl and I didn't like each other that much anyway, and it soon ended.

When I failed the chemistry course there was a big U.S. military buildup going on that involved many people. It was a foregone conclusion that if a young male was not in college he would be part of the military buildup. I didn't concern myself with that reality; rather, I thought mostly that I had a good month of summer left and I wanted to go to Maine to get involved with whatever was going on there.

When I left home my younger sister was painting an old field car with a paintbrush. She turned around with the brush hanging down at her side and said, "Are you leaving now?" She was in the distance, but I could see that the look on her face dissolved any differences we had over the years. As I was going up the long driveway it dawned on me that I was leaving. It would never again be quite the same. Then I remembered the words of a poet who said, "Home is the place that when you go there they have to take you in." I would always have a home. I was going to Maine and I took my time getting there. I was driving the car my father gave me. At one point he thought he had the Midas touch and, among other things, bought a failing French car dealership. It soon went out of business altogether, but not before he gave each of his five children one of the used cars. My job wasn't to carry out the garbage but to keep all the cars running. I became very familiar with them. I could make repairs or do engine rebuilds without even looking at the manual.

It was about a thousand miles to where I was going in Maine, and I performed certain preventive maintenance on the way. The term *preventive maintenance* I later learned in the U.S. army means you fix something before it breaks. Before I ever got in the army I was performing preventive maintenance, although I didn't call it that name. As far as I knew, the front wheel bearings had never been packed with grease since the car left the factory. I stopped at what turned out to be a friendly garage, and out there on the gravel I proceeded to disassemble one front wheel and then the other. I took off the wheel and moved the break caliper out of the way and removed the hub and rotor as one piece. That exposed the bearings, and I packed them in grease. A man who seemed to own the garage gave me the grease and said he didn't understand why I was going to all the trouble if the bearings worked.

When I was packing a wheel bearing with grease and holding it in my hand I thought about when I was in school. A teacher said everything that rolls uses bearings and in conventional war if bombers or anything else can knock out a bearing factory it means the enemy suffers a big loss. That was conventional war. Vietnam, where I was soon to be, was not a conventional war. Over there, when the Military Assistance Command Vietnam (MACV) thought the Twenty-fifth Division base camp at Cu Chi was going to be overrun by a bunch of people with garden tools there was a high-altitude B-52 strike one night that I could feel in my feet. Actually, those people had Chinese-and Russian-made rifles called AK-47s and wanted to kill us. The killing from our side was so sophisticated. We were told bombs could be dropped in a rain barrel from way up there out of sight and sound. I think it was from 30,000 feet. The planes flew out of Thailand or the Philippines and were "vectored." They didn't depend on ground reference. On the night when the B-52 strike came, all of a sudden there was a sound like thunder. No one around me had their cold beer interrupted. Also, in broad daylight MACV flew in the Third Brigade of the 101st Airborne Division, which was a hard-core infantry unit and the "reactionary force" for MACV. The attack never came. There was a Vietnam-era song that said, "Oh please, please don't drop that H-bomb on me. If you are going to drop it, go drop it, on yourself." If they didn't drop those bombs that night maybe all of us would have been killed. It was a wicked circle. My son recently heard that song and asked me what an H-bomb was. I hope he only reads about bombs.

When I got to the island in Maine they were digging a pond and I went right to work. The boatman found old dump trucks on the mainland and put them on a scow, and we took them over to the island. They were small three-yard dump trucks that were not going to last much longer. When one broke down, rather than fix it, he would have another ready. Sometimes I went with him to the mainland to find inexpensive dump trucks, but when I worked, my job was to haul dirt down island, dump it, and come back for more. There were three or four dump trucks going at the same time. The idea of the pond was to use it as a source of reliable water to lower fire insurance rates. My mother's stepfather had a transit to measure how much dirt he needed to remove, and I helped him. He showed me how to use a transit, which I learned is a handy thing to have if you are going to dig a pond. When the pond was finished he put freshwater fish in it and made it look natural. The ocean was out there, "water, water, everywhere," and there was a pond where there would be more water. When I left Maine several weeks later the pond was finished. I went to orientation at the Ohio State University. It was scheduled before I flunked economics. I never got any notice saying I couldn't go there. I didn't have to be there for a week, so I took my time.

I stayed in state parks overnight and ate from a box of groceries that I carried with me in the car and replenished from time to time. In one park there was a big U.S. Civil War battle over 100 years earlier. A songwriter sang, "You can please some of the people some of the time, but you can't please all the people all the time." Then, in the same song, he sings, "The President of the United States said that."

Late one afternoon I pulled into a small camping area near Youngstown, Ohio, to spend the night. I didn't have a tent or other obvious camping gear. I slept in my car, so I was unusual in that respect. A park ranger came around to collect money. Only two other campers were there. I got out my box of groceries and proceeded to make dinner. The camper nearest to me waved me over. He told me the night before the same two campers had been there when several runaway teenagers went through the park to get to an adjacent cornfield where they were going to spend the night. He said the other camper was a vacationing policeman who called the local police. When the police took the runaway teenagers back through the park one girl yelled how she would get even.

I never suspected at the time that they thought I was the person who was going to get even. I listened to the story remotely. Then I went back over to finish my dinner and sleep. I was trying to go to sleep when I heard the camper I had been talking to leave. He packed up and left. It was still daylight when the other camper, whom I had not met, rapped his knuckles on my car window and asked if I wanted to sit by his fire. I took him up on the offer. They were some clean-cut, uncomplicated people who were amazed the other camper had told me about the previous night, especially the part about his being a policeman. When I said that, he suddenly went into the trailer long enough to either go to the bathroom or strap on a gun. There were two couples among them, and they loaded me up with hot food. In the course of conversation they learned what I was doing. It wasn't as if they asked twenty questions in a row, but when I think about it, they learned everything they wanted to know. I told them I was coming from Maine and going to orientation at the state university. They were warm, friendly people and their food was extremely good.

There were probably 10,000 freshmen at Ohio State University. The orientation program for freshmen was cycled over and over all summer. Each group wasn't that big, and it didn't feel as if there were that many people.

Three things stick in my mind. First, I befriended one orientation individual with a pipe. Four years later when I went to school there I didn't look him up. Second, there was a get-together for incoming freshmen on the roof of the Student Union. I danced with one girl the whole time. It seemed the song about ninety-six tears played often. She said she didn't understand why I was there.

Any illusions I had about attending the university that fall disappeared when I was summoned to the Admissions Office in the administration building. That was the third thing that sticks in my mind. I waited in an outer office and was soon called into an inner office where one man in a suit sat behind a desk. We talked for a long time. He was aware that I did not get a diploma and said I could not enroll there as a freshman without a high school diploma. I said I would probably join the army. He gave me his card and asked that I please look him up when I got out. Several years later I did go back, and he was still there. I made an appointment to see him. He came out to greet me that time. He shook hands with me and talked like I was there the day before. I said it was amazing to me that he remembered my situation. He must have kept a file.

3

Vagabonding

When I left his office I left that city. I went directly to the federal building in downtown Cincinnati to have my draft status changed. In those days every male who was a U.S. citizen had a draft card. A draft card showed a person was classified for military service. My draft card indicated I was classified as a student and therefore exempt from military service. Since I was no longer a student I thought I would speed things up that were going to happen anyway. In those days anyone who could be drafted was drafted.

When I got to the federal building I had to keep asking where to go. I went from desk to desk looking for the right person. It seemed everyone had a specific job.

The first floor of the federal building was a U.S. post office. They said I should go to another floor. Every draft card had a signature on the bottom, and draft cards from that building had the same signature. Toward the end of my journey in that place it became apparent that I was going to see the person whose name was on my draft card. Her signature was like the signature printed on all the paper money. I expected her to be a dusty lady with a cane and horn-rimmed glasses.

She was in a room with rows of fluorescent lights and rows of steel gray filing cabinets. She had a small wooden desk near the door and on it was a brown gooseneck lamp.

When I got there I stood waiting. I could hear her in the back of the large room opening and closing file drawers. As she walked around the corner of the row and came closer with a file in her hand I could see she was not the person I had expected. She was a very well put together woman. She seemed preoccupied and bothered by my presence. By the setup of that room she was probably not in the habit of seeing people. Her hair was tied up. She had shoes with raised heels, and she wore a skirt and top that went together. It wasn't tight but it wasn't loose either. She told me to sit down in a metal chair that was at one end of her desk. She also sat down in her desk chair, crossed her legs, and asked me what I wanted. She had brown eyes. I said I was no longer a student and didn't have that exemption any longer. I said my draft card said I was a student, which was no longer the case, and I wanted to get on with it, rather than wait for the inevitable.

She explained in a very businesslike way that there were several ways I could go. She said I could volunteer for a branch of the military, in which case I would get my choice of schooling.

She said that was a three-year commitment. But, I learned from her, just because I requested a certain school there was no guarantee that I would use that in the job I did for the rest of the three years. She said I could wait until I was drafted, a two-year commitment, or, I could volunteer for the draft. If I volunteered for the draft my name would get put at the top of the draft list, but I would not get my choice of schooling. All draftees went into the army. I was told the army uses its resources to its best advantage. That includes human resources, and she said I would probably be assigned the schooling I was best able to do.

Volunteering for the draft sounded like the way to go, although she didn't say anything about evading the draft altogether and going to Canada with someone warm like her. She was a federal employee, but it crossed my mind. I would have probably signed up for twenty years in the armed forces if that had been her recommendation. She was so honest and helpful and many other things. She had a wonderful way. I ended up volunteering for the draft and thinking it was my idea. My name and number would be put at the top of the list. She said for me to keep my draft board informed as to my whereabouts.

I stayed in state parks every night, and almost always I was invited to the campsite next to mine to have something to eat. I didn't plan on that happening. I had my box of groceries, but being invited to sit and eat with other people became so predictable that I would buy my canned food and other groceries accordingly. Those evenings were the only time I had any human association. It went that way for about two or three weeks until I ran out of money and had to get a job. Campers I met were older people on vacation without their children. Some of them were retired people going from place to place just like I was. Almost always it seemed campers next to one another got to know one another the way they did me. Some campers would stay in the same spot all summer. To comply with the rules they had to register their campsite in another person's name, and they had to move their camp vehicle or tent a few feet one way or the other every so often. I was all-around different. Maybe that is why I got invited over to their camp so many times. They wanted to find out who was camping next to them.

One place was a large park with a lake and a beach. I could tell the sand was trucked to that place from somewhere else. I got there in the late morning. I stayed the rest of the day. I went to a restaurant on the park grounds. Potato chips, soft drinks, hamburgers, and hot dogs were the main things for sale. It had a screen door like on old farmhouses with a long extension spring to pull it shut. It slammed twice every time one of the children ran in or out. There were eight picnic tables inside, and I sat at one of them. The only other table where anybody was had a group of children standing around an older girl who was sitting down. She was showing them over and over again how flies could be drowned in water and brought back to life. When they appeared dead she would put them in salt, and soon they would fly away. On the way out I stopped to watch. One of the children would catch a housefly. Then she would put it in a container of water and stir the water vigorously. The fly would get caught in the vortex and go under. After a long while she would take the seemingly dead fly out of the water and put it in the salt. Then it would start to move and soon it would fly away. She said she was bringing the fly back to life. I asked her if the dead fly had any vital signs. They all pretty much ignored me and I left.

It was a hot sunny day with no wind. I went to the lake. There were many people sitting on the hot sandy beach. I had learned to swim so I could survive in the water, but at that moment I wanted to cool off. I was wearing shorts and my pockets had things in them.

There was a girl by herself on the sand a short distance from me. She was sitting up looking at the water or something in that direction. She had a very straight back. I took my shirt off and walked over to where she was sitting. I asked her if she would watch my things while I went in the water. I had a wristwatch, some money, a pocketknife, and a few marbles or something. She looked up at me with disbelief. I didn't wait for too much of a reply. I just put those things down on her towel and headed for the water. I was wading around in deeper and deeper water. Once I looked back. She was still sitting up and it seemed she was looking at me. I must have looked silly wading around in circles, but that is all I did. I wouldn't have defied death on a high diving board even if there was one. One time I squatted down in the water and got my upper body wet. When I came up out of the water I was soaking wet and I walked over to get my things. I thanked her. She did not say anything or even look up at me. As I walked away I thought that would be some fine human association, and also I thought about a poem that says, "I have miles to go before I sleep, and miles to go before I sleep."

When I left the next day I was going down the road and my car stopped. It was dead in the water, so to speak, and to make matters more difficult I was in a prison zone. Signs up and down the road said: DO NOT PICK UP HITCHHIKERS. After a long time of trying different things with the engine, I figured out that the camshaft was not turning. A fiber timing gear had worn out between a metal gear on the end of the crankshaft and a metal gear on the end of the camshaft. I wondered why the scientists or whoever they were at the factory ever put that fiber gear in there instead of a metal one. I had my tools with me and I proceeded to remove all the necessary stuff to get the timing cover off. The sun was setting when I finally saw the timing gear. All the teeth were worn off, as I expected. Parts were all over the side of the road. I went to sleep in my car. That night, each time a truck went past the rush of air made the car move from side to side.

In the morning it was a beautiful day. I opened a can of peaches. I had two quarts of water in a canteen. The canteen was an American Boy Scout canteen. I never was a Boy Scout, but they made a good canteen. Where I grew up, one weekend every year hundreds of Boy Scouts from Cincinnati would go to one of the fields and camp. They called it Peterloon Day. I rode my pony bareback and looked at their camp. I was amazed by how organized it was. All the tents were in rows and everyone, even the adults, had the same clothes. They didn't want to talk to me. It was as if I were not there. I suppose an American Indian must have felt like that when he saw the settlers moving west. It is a wonder I didn't get shot.

I was standing by my car eating peaches from the can when someone pulled over and came to a stop behind me. She asked me if I needed help. I explained my situation. I said I needed to get to the next town so I could look up the nearest dealer for my car. She said the next town was Terre Haute and that she would drive me there. Going down the road in her car she said she had been going the other way and turned around to see if she could help. I don't think she cared if I was an escaped convict. She was helping me whoever I was.

I was amazed that there was a car dealer for my car in Terre Haute. I had the worn out gear with me. The parts man asked me the year, make, and model of the car. He looked up something in a book and went in the back. After a short while he came out with a new timing gear.

When I went back outside she was waiting in her car. I told her how terrific it was that he had the part on the shelf and didn't have to order it from some big city. She drove me back out to my car, let me out on the other side of the road, and kept going away from Terre Haute. I was sorry I never thought to offer her any money for gas. I ate a can of beans for lunch, put my car back together, and was on my way.

I drove all day. I got to a park where I could spend the night. It was in Collinsville, Illinois across the river from St. Louis. My money was almost gone, so I got a newspaper and looked at the job listings. I found one in a retirement building that seemed like a job I could do. It was late Thursday. Friday morning I planned to see about the job.

Thursday afternoon I took my wristwatch off to wash my hands. I put it on a shelf above a white sink in a row of white sinks and forgot to put it back on, and when I went back to get it five minutes later it was gone. That park was in an urban area and it was different from the others. People there weren't so friendly.

Friday morning I got up and went across the river to talk to someone about the job. I talked with a Catholic nun who was dressed in the clothes nuns wear. She asked me many questions. I told her I was going into the army in a month or two. She asked me if I could clean up rooms and people. She said many of the people there couldn't clean themselves. I don't think she thought I knew what she was talking about, and I didn't. I spent the rest of the day looking at other jobs in St. Louis. When I went back to the park I noticed once again a horse track. I thought I would look for a job all the next day and on Sunday, when everything else was closed, I would go to the track to make some quick money.

Saturday in downtown St. Louis I came across a gun store. I walked in to look at the guns. A salesman was showing a handgun to someone in a suit and tie (something he needed at the office). When I looked at guns in a glass case the salesman loudly said for me to leave. St. Louis was not going to be my favorite town.

When Sunday morning came I went to the racetrack. I and one other person waited at the gate to the barn area. The guard announced through a microphone that there were two "hot walkers." After a short while someone in an old car came out and got both of us. The car had no reverse. The driver said he had to go in a circle to turn around. He was the only stable boy (groom) for about six horses trained by one person.

After a horse is exercised it comes back to the barn sweaty. The jockey or exercise boy jumps off, and a hot walker walks the horse around the "shed row" until it cools down. A shed row is an area under a roof like a house porch. But the shed row floor is the earth, and it goes around the entire barn. This racetrack was typical. In each barn there were two rows of stalls back to back, about thirty stalls in all, and there were about forty barns.

I was familiar with horses because I had been around them much of my life. I knew how to bandage their legs, clean stalls, tack them up, brush them, and do just about anything else. I could even ride a horse, but I never rode a horse on the track.

After an hour or two the other hot walker was paid in cash and he left. I was leading a horse around the shed row when the person with no reverse in his car asked me if I would work there.

He said they were going to get more horses and they needed more help. I started to work there that day.

I slept in the tack room. I had a cot on one side of the room, and the other groom had his cot on the other side. On the wall above my cot the bridles and saddles hung. The wall was concrete block, and the floor was concrete. Every barn had a tack room and feed room located at each end. They were the same size, about ten-feet by twelve-feet. Grooms who took care of the horses on the other side of the shed row had the tack room and feed room next to ours. All the stalls down the middle of the barn were made of wood, and they had a dirt floor. We had a portable electric heater for cold nights. All my clothes were in a canvas bag. My other things were locked in my car inside the barn area. During the day the cots were folded and the tack room didn't look as if anyone slept there.

In the early morning when it was still dark the trainer would arrive. Quite a few times when he stuck his head inside the door to wake us up he would say, "It's time to get up, girls." We would quickly transform the room from our living quarters into a tack room. We would feed the horses, and when that was done all three of us would go to the track kitchen. It would still be dark outside when we got there.

The other groom told me the trainer had a temper and he was insanely jealous about his wife. He said I should not even look at his wife's face. She was in the barn area only once while I was there and I didn't look at her.

Several weeks later the track season closed and we went to another track in Chester, West Virginia. The trainer and his wife were living nearby in a trailer, and never once did she come to the barn area in all the time I was there. The groom told me he thought she slept and watched television most of the day. He said her husband didn't want her to go out because he was so jealous. Her father owned several of the horses, and he was very involved with their lives. Maybe she thought he would not be pleased if she wasn't married to that man.

The groom told me that several months before I got there in St. Louis her husband, the trainer, went to catch her little dog that got loose. He said the trainer came back with the dog holding it off the ground by its collar. When he got to the barn where she was he threw it at her feet. It was almost strangled to death. It wasn't dead, but he said it just lay on the ground like it was dead.

The track kitchen was a warm place in the cold morning. It was in a restricted area. The people who went there were trainers or grooms who got up early in the morning. Most of them knew the cooks. There were three of us when we sat down, and always there was one empty chair. Often a proper and dapper-looking older man would sit with us. He and his wife lived on a farm somewhere in Texas. They had no children. I imagined his farmhouse was white with a white picket fence and an apple pie in the oven. He always got up and left first. One time when he just left, the trainer said he wished he had this older man's money. The trainer then said to us the reason he kept sitting down at our table was that "he wants you to go with him to Texas," and he was looking at me. I could see myself living securely in Texas the rest of my life hoeing potatoes. The idea sounded appealing, but not seriously appealing.

The races were in the evening. In the late morning when the stalls were cleaned, legs were bandaged, and other things done, there was little to do but wait for a horse to come back from being exercised. When I was waiting I would sit on a trunk full of hoof picks, brushes, and rub rags. It was against the outside of a stall beside a stall door. In the night both the upper and lower half of the stall door was closed, but in the day only the lower part was closed, so a horse could have its whole head and neck in the shed row. The horse in the stall next to the trunk would rest all the weight of its head on my shoulder. I would kiss it and it would nip at me. It started winning many races. The trainer was thrilled the horse was winning so often. Soon the horse was bought in a claiming race and it was gone. Other horses came, but there was none like that one. It never won another race on that track.

There were three women the other groom was seeing, and since I didn't have much to do in the afternoon he took me with him to see them. They were older. One of them had a little boy who walked around sipping a huge bottle of cola. He couldn't talk although he was old enough to talk. One time he walked over to me holding that big bottle. He smiled. I couldn't relate to him. His smile dissolved and I never saw him smile again. His clothes smelled of dried urine. Two of the women said they used that child to collect ADC (Aid to Dependent Children). The third woman seemed the most sensitive of the three. She said she had a gun and would shoot a certain man if she saw him.

There was a bedroom next to the living room. We were talking. My friend the groom and the woman who said she had a gun went in the bedroom. They did it as casually as if they were going to the kitchen to get an eggplant. They shut the door. After a while they came out and sat back down in the living room. Some time passed. One of the women collecting ADC said to the other that they should undress me and do it right there on the living room floor. They were mad because I wasn't going to go nonchalantly into the bedroom with one or both of them.

I had never met anyone like them. They said I was a snob. I didn't go back. The next morning in the track kitchen my friend told the trainer what happened. The trainer said he didn't blame me considering the women the groom saw. My friend didn't say any more. He finished his breakfast.

There were many honky-tonk joints around there. A honky-tonk joint was a bar that had a juke box always playing. It had pinball machines and trashy people all over the place. I played a lot of pinball and got sloppy. I didn't meet anyone I remember, but the pinball machines paid off. It wasn't legal, but nobody seemed to care.

During the day they called my name over the loudspeaker, and told me to go to the track office. I was asked a bunch of questions. In an indirect way the questions were about if I was one of those draft dodgers or if the police wanted me. The man didn't ask me if I was a pinko communist faggot, but it wouldn't have surprised me if he did. Some other people took a photograph for an identification card, which I was told to carry at all times. The main person said the Illinois State Racing Commission held their license, and might take it away if they didn't check me out.

The track provided legalized gambling for people. People went to the races in large numbers and gambled that the horse they chose would win. If it did, they won money. If it didn't, they lost money. The person in the office said he had to get my fingerprints. He said for all anyone knew the police might want me. He looked worried when I agreed no one knew if I was or was not wanted like maybe some Illinois gangsters had sent me to choke him to death.

When the meet at that track was over we moved to a track in Chester, West Virginia. I followed the horse van in my car. The father of the trainer's wife drove the van. He was a tall man who did things exactly the way he wanted. When the horses arrived at the other track I would be there to take care of them. The other groom and the trainer would show up later.

On my way there I got separated from the van. Then in Steubenville, Ohio, I was coming over the top of a hill when another driver going the opposite direction pulled in front of me and we collided. She was a busy housewife eyeing a parking place, and she didn't see me. It was her fault as far as the police were concerned. A state Highway Patrol post was across the street. A policeman, the lady, and I sat in a room while the policeman filled out the necessary forms. Soon the woman's husband arrived.

The right front fender of my car hit the passenger side rear wheel of her car. Her car had a bent rim and slight fender damage. On my car all the lights on one side were smashed. The steering mechanism on that side was bent. The car didn't track very well. Nobody was hurt, but when the two cars, hit my right knee was cut open by a two-speed toggle switch located on the bottom edge of the dashboard. The woman seemed genuinely concerned about that, and her husband was worried about a lawsuit. He wanted everything in writing when I said I was OK. The state policeman informed me that even though the accident was not my fault, I would get a ticket because my driver's license was expired.

When there was silence the woman's husband couldn't take it anymore. He said in a loud and angry tone of voice that many of the people there said I was going fast. I pointed to the policeman and said, "That is his job so why don't you let him do it."

The man gasped and sputtered, "What?"

I repeated, "That is his job, so why don't you let him do it." I looked over at the policeman, who didn't look up from busily writing. When I said it the second time his eyes looked over to the side like he was listening. I was glad he was there because the woman's husband was losing control. Policeman carry guns because people are so out of control.

Since I was from another place I had to post a bond for my expired driver's license or I would have to sit in a local jail until my case was heard by the judge. I had just enough money when I added the change in my pockets to post bond. The state policeman drove me to the municipal courthouse, and then he drove me back to my car. He looked the other way as I left. I was not a valid driver.

Steubenville was not far from where I was going in West Virginia. I returned to Steubenville on my court day. The policeman correctly listed my occupation as "groom." The judge asked me in an irritated way what a "groom" was, since the only groom he ever heard of was a person in a wedding. The woman and her husband were in court, too. When it was their turn he pointed in my direction and said I had an expired driver's license. I was sitting in a mass of people. I slumped down, but it didn't matter. The judge didn't even look in my direction. When it was my turn I was fined and had to pay court costs.

I was delayed by the traffic accident. When I finally arrived at the racetrack the trainer's wife's father was worried that I was not going to show up, that maybe I went to Alabama, where it was warmer. When I saw him I explained what happened and that I didn't have any money left. He gave me a small amount of money. We put the horses in their stalls and he left. I thought he had given me the money, but on the next payday the trainer knew exactly how much it was and he deducted that amount from my pay.

The racetrack in Chester, West Virginia, was next to the Ohio River. A nice place to walk in the afternoon was through the woods along an abandoned railroad that went between the racetrack and the river. A well-worn mud path led there. It went down a hill from the barns. In more than one place there were some bobbers and tangled fishing lines in low branches over the water. People fished there. Those were the ones who must have made the path. It was September and October. I did not see anyone else when I was there. Sometimes I walked balanced on a rail. Trees came together over the tracks with leaves that were bright shades of yellow and brown. The river was wide in that place.

Across the highway in front of the track there was a bar where everything looked cold. The light in that place was called black light. A gin and tonic looked ice blue. On the wall over the bar was a clock. Every so often the big hand on the clock would whiz around, and depending on where it stopped a person sitting at the bar who was playing that game either won or lost money. I was with the other groom and he told me to be careful where I put money on the bar. Apparently he had been there before that night. According to the state of West Virginia I was not old enough to be served alcohol, but as far as the bartender was concerned I was old enough.

The other groom and I walked into a large room with normal light. It had a sliding wall for a door. The room was filled with many people laying their money down. It had the pretense of being a clandestine operation, but a couple of tourists with tropical shirts and cameras around their necks would not be fooled. We were to believe we were getting away with something.

The nights were cold. At that track I had to keep my car outside the barn area gate. It didn't have a heater that worked, and the tire on the side that had impacted in the wreck was wearing out fast. The extreme toe-in alignment of that wheel could not be corrected without some major work.

My friend the groom didn't have a car, so we used mine. One time we went to another bar that was nearby where they had a band with electric amplifiers. Another person who met us there my friend knew. He lived at the other end of our barn in one of the concrete block tack rooms. He was a trainer and a groom all in one. I don't know how many horses he had, but it couldn't have been very many, because no one helped him. He was an older, big man. At the bar my friend left to go to the men's room and the big man said right out loud to me that he was a homosexual and that he wanted to perform a certain sex act that involved me. He said he had never told anyone before that night that he was a homosexual. I told him I didn't believe in the tooth fairy, either. I didn't confirm or deny that I was predisposed to homosexual sex acts. I simply said I wouldn't be able to get an erection. That took all the wind out of his sails. The other groom came back and then the big man went to the men's room. I told my friend what that man had said. I expected he would be surprised, but he wasn't.

A person could be served beer at a lower age in the neighboring state of Pennsylvania. My friend the other groom knew of a place just across the Pennsylvania border that was a bowling alley with a bar and a live band. The way he described the place, it sounded like a good bar with a bowling alley attached. I went there many times and always the same band was there. They played well together. They didn't have fancy clothes or other fanfare. There were no bright lights. It seemed like the music was theirs. They weren't trying to make it sound like one type or another. All the times I went there, the place was packed.

I met a girl there who was very sweet indeed. I went there often to spend time with her. She lived forty minutes away in Coraopolis, near Pittsburgh. She lived with her mother and younger sister. She worked for a gravel company.

All racetracks were the same, like men's rooms, and one morning in the track kitchen I told my employer, the trainer, about her. The next time I went to the bar in Pennsylvania both he and the other groom went too. The trainer wore a light gray suit the color of a shark's skin. He wanted me to introduce him to the girl I always saw there, so I introduced them. She and him were facing each other and I was standing with him on my left and her on my right. I said, "This is the person I work for," and she said, "How do you do?" to him very politely. The music was playing, so it was difficult to be heard.

He asked me to ask her if she had any girlfriends who were there. I leaned over to her ear and said, "He wants to know if you have any girlfriends here."

She said, "What?" like she wasn't sure she heard correctly. Then like a translator I said to him that she said, "What?" He said the same thing again except this time he was looking at her with a glint in his eye and a look on his face that didn't need words. Again I passed the same words to her. She didn't say anything. She moved over to where I was standing, looked down, and hid her face behind me. He left, and I never saw him back there.

I saw her almost every night after work. Sometimes I would drive to her house, forty minutes beyond the bowling alley. There was a main room centrally located with a couch across from a television.

My car tire was wearing thin and the heater didn't work. It was cold at night. I took a large can and filled it with cotton. Then I poured rubbing alcohol into the can. I lit it and that was my heater. At traffic lights it must have seemed strange to people in the other car to see light from the dancing flame.

Her little sister was full of mischief. Her mother was on guard. When I was there we all sat in the center room. I didn't ask about her father. She never mentioned him. He was not there.

Before I left to go into the army we were driving away from her house and she said to me, "Let's stay together all night." Some nights when I got back to the barn area it was four in the morning and the chickens were about to wake up, so being up all night was nothing new. I didn't understand what she was saying. We went somewhere that night and I dropped her off at her house so I could get back to work at five in the morning.

I slept that afternoon. Then I thought about and understood what she said. To her I think it meant closeness, but I was not ready for that closeness. One time before that when we were at the bar the band was taking a break and records were playing. She knew the words to the song. In the end female voices sing. When the record got to that part she leaned over and sang very softly in my ear the same as the record, "So tell me how much you love me. Come near to me and say you need me now." I liked her a whole lot. But I never told her I loved her or that I needed her now.

She wore a coat with a bright green lining. I thought her blond hair looked so beautiful against the green. One afternoon I drove across a bridge into East Liverpool. I found a sweater the same green. I bought it and gave it to her.

She wrote poems. Soon I got my notice that I was to be inducted into the U.S. Army. When I was in the army I got many poems from her, and some of them were sad. When I was home on leave from army basic training I was going to drive from Cincinnati to see her. I couldn't get a car and called her to say I was not coming. After that I got the saddest poem of all. I never saw her again or heard from her. Ten or fifteen years later when

I was going to Maine I went by Pittsburgh on the turnpike. I stopped to telephone her to hear what she was doing or how many babies she had. The person on the phone was amused. I think it was her little sister who would have been grown-up by then. Whoever she was, she wouldn't tell me who she was or what anyone was doing or if I had the right number. I said good-bye, and that was the end of that.

4

The Army

The day I left it was raining and that was good because the wet pavement would cause my worn-out front tire to last longer. I had several hundred miles to go to get to Cincinnati where I would report for induction into the army. I had to correct the steering only a little bit compared to when the wheels were on dry road. I knew the tire was slipping along nicely, and I would make it as long as it kept raining. It rained all day.

I got there just in time to undergo an army physical and other mental evaluation. They were fairly relaxed about who they would take. I thought the fact I even got there qualified me. There were many of us like cattle in lines and we had on few clothes. When that part was over we were put in one room fully dressed. An army sergeant had a piece of paper for us to sign. He passed out paper to the first person in each row of desks. They took one and passed it back. Everyone got one. On the piece of paper there was a list of all the organizations the U.S. government considered insurgent. The list was in fine print and it barely fit on one page. We were supposed to read the list carefully and then sign our name at the bottom where it said we solemnly swore we were not an active member nor ever had been an active member of any of the groups listed.

The sergeant was sitting silently at a desk in the front of the room looking at us. Some people could read faster than others could, and without crowding they handed the paper to him. I read the list and was overwhelmed by the thought that if I said I belonged to one of those groups then I wouldn't have to go in the army. I wondered, *Could it be that easy?* I found the worst group, the most hateful group on the list. I walked up to the sergeant's desk and said politely that I wasn't going to sign because maybe

I belonged to one of those groups. He smiled, like he knew all about my ideas, and he had a procedure for me. He told me to go wait over there until everyone else had signed or not signed. I was the only one in the room who didn't sign. He showed me into another room and he told me to wait there. He said army Intelligence wanted to talk with me and they would be a while because they were on the next floor up.

Finally two people came in and they were both wearing suits. They weren't exactly twins, but they were dressed the same. Physically they were the same. I suppose they were from army Intelligence. They never said who they were representing. They didn't even introduce themselves. One of them said it was the end of the day on Friday and they were going home in five minutes. Apparently, they didn't have time to properly interrogate me. They said the government was obligated to provide me with accommodations until Monday morning. They said they had meal and housing vouchers that were good at local hotels. I said, "I have my own accommodations," and thanked them.

I spent that weekend in the woods on the back of Peterloon Farm. I drove off the road down a tractor road to a clearing where farmers mixed fertilizer and loaded grain onto trucks. All their work was done weeks ago. I didn't see anyone the whole time I was there. I didn't want to go home because there was so much up in the air and I didn't have any reasons for doing what I was doing.

There were large clumps of orchard grass everywhere and a small stray hunting dog passed through with his nose in the long grass smelling for something. The dog seemed as if he was too busy to notice me. I named that dog Freeman. It took me a while to figure out what Freeman was looking for in the long grass. It wasn't rabbits. It was bugs. The dog was eating bugs he found in the grass. I offered Freeman some of my food. He ate it, but not in a voracious way. Freeman would just as soon eat bugs, but he wasn't too proud to eat my food. Freeman was in and out of that clearing all weekend. He always smelled for bugs to eat and he seldom looked at me directly. I figured there were many tasty bugs in the grass under my car, so after a while I moved it over a few yards. I last saw Freeman Sunday morning. I suppose he left as busily as he came. He probably ended up in some humane shelter getting decompressed to death. Even if he was adopted by a human he would have just tolerated them and at the first opportunity would have left to go look for bugs in the long grass. Freeman preferred live bugs, and they weren't sold in stores anywhere.

Monday morning I cleaned myself up and went downtown to the federal building to see those two people from army Intelligence. When I met them we never sat down. I quickly explained that I didn't want to sign that piece of paper with the list of all the groups that the government said were insurgent, because then I would be swearing that I never belonged to any of those groups when that might not be the case. I said to them that if I belonged to . . . and I named the hateful group I had seen on the list the Friday before . . . and I signed their list, then that would be a crime. I said there was nothing illegal about belonging to such a group. I said if they didn't want me in their loving military machine that was their prerogative, but I wasn't going to possibly lie about it. They looked at each other when I named the hateful group, but when I was finished talking one of the two people said signing the list was just a formality. I wouldn't have to sign.

I don't remember exactly how many days it took. In short order the sequence of events was that I put all my things away at home, gave my lame car back to my father, hugged and kissed whoever was there good-bye, and reported for induction into the U.S. Army.

Everyone in the group was told to stand and raise their right hand and repeat after somebody who had been there a long time. He read something someone thought was significant. It reminded me of a song and dance we did in grade school called the "Hokey Pokey." Everyone in the group danced what they sang as they sang, "Put your right hand in. Put your right hand out. Put your right hand in and shake it all about. You do the Hokey Pokey and turn yourself around. That's what it's all about." The song and dance repeated itself over and over again naming different appendages of the body. I couldn't help thinking, *Here are a bunch of grown people who were still trying to learn what it is all about.*

We were put on a bus headed for Fort Knox, a hundred miles

away. Fort Knox was well known in military circles as the place where people learned to drive tanks. I didn't know this until that day, but I did know from movies that tons of gold were kept there. On the bus going to Fort Knox I was sorry I flunked economics where we talked mostly about what makes the world go around. I wondered what the U.S. government was doing with all that gold.

Fort Knox was a big place. We were going there for a few days of orientation. From there we would be split up and reassigned to basic training units at other army bases.

On the way there the bus stopped at a roadside restaurant. The army would always feed us well, especially in a war zone. There were so many armies in history that lost because of cold and hunger. It was a point of pride that we be fed well. If we lost it wasn't going to be because we weren't fed. I got plenty of food the next year, nine months, and nine days. After that I got "early out." When I came back from Vietnam I was discharged rather than re-assigned for three months.

At the restaurant there was a jukebox. We were in that place for an hour. People from our bus put so many coins in the slot that the jukebox probably played most of the next day. The army didn't pay for the music.

At army orientation we learned about living in the army. A new second lieutenant was assigned to our group. We had to clean the barracks every day after breakfast, but one day it was a major cleaning. I was cleaning the latrine. I was scrubbing out a urinal with a long-handled brush made for that purpose. The urinal was cast iron with a white porcelain finish. It was four or five feet long, with one drain in the middle. For some reason the drain cover had to be removed, according to the second lieutenant. I didn't have anything to grab it with and said so. He said, "Use your fingers. It is only piss." The idea of touching an object covered with other people's urine seemed to go against common sense, but I was in the army now where common sense was not relevant. The urinal drain cover I was looking at was covered with fresh urine. There probably wasn't any bacteria on it yet. I reached down with my bare hands, removed it, washed my hands, and didn't die. About an army at another time someone said, "Ours is not to reason why. Ours is but to do and die.

Into the valley of death rode the five hundred."

When I was at orientation we were given written tests. After that we talked to a person who was a permanent military man. He filled in the blank spaces on a form. He asked me where I would like to go overseas. I said I would like to go to Italy. He was amused like I thought he was a travel agent. This was a ridiculous exercise and a game. In so many words he said there were about two GIs in Italy (*GI* was a slang expression referring to one U.S. army soldier, and it stood for Government Issue). I didn't want to be stuck somewhere polishing boots all day and playing soldier. I said, "Just put me down for Vietnam." If there was going to be a game it never got started. I was aware that just about everyone around me was going to do a "tour of duty" in Vietnam. A tour of duty was one year. Many people over there would mark off the days. The expression "I'm short" meant there weren't many of the 365 days left. When a person got short they were very careful not to take any unnecessary risks, but still people would get killed who had only several days left.

Because I signed up for Vietnam I was assigned to a Chinook helicopter outfit that was being formed at Fort Benning, Georgia. It was part of the Vietnam military buildup. Otherwise, I would have probably been individually "deployed" to replace someone who had either gone home on his own two feet or been killed. The assignment I eventually got was a safe one, although there were still many bullets whizzing around the country. Considering my assignments it was as if the only one doing the planning was me. Still, I have never been to Italy.

When I left Fort Knox we were in a bus going to Fort Bragg in North Carolina, where we went through basic training. On the way there we stopped at a bus station in Knoxville, Tennessee. We had a few hours to wait. Several of us went out of the bus terminal to have a cold beer. It didn't seem like there were places of any kind open around there. It wasn't that late, but it was dark. We were standing on a corner looking lost and here comes a man out of the night. We were in our army dress uniforms or "class A's," as they are called in the army. He might have guessed that we were from another city going to another city. Someone asked him if there was a bar nearby. He turned this way and that way to think what was down each street, and then he points down one street and says there is a bar in that direction. Sure enough, less than half a block down one poorly lit side street there was a place we would never have seen had he not told us. It had a varnished wood door with a tiny window at eye level. The bartender hurriedly took a posterboard sign off the bar when we opened the door. We sat in a booth. A woman asked us what we wanted, and we said, "Four beers." The beers came and we paid for them. As we were drinking the beers and talking I saw a horrified look on the face of one of the two people sitting across from me in the booth. He was looking behind me. When I turned around to see what he was looking at I saw two girls embracing and kissing passionately. They were sitting in the booth next to ours. We had asked the man on the street where a bar was and we didn't specify what kind of bar. The bar he pointed to and the one we were in was for people who would rather get sexual with members of their own sex. People went there to meet people who felt the same way about sex as they did, or they went there with people who already felt that way. We took a few more drinks of our beer and left. That is probably what the people in the bar wanted us to do, and it was what we wanted to do.

When we got to Fort Bragg the drill sergeants were waiting for us. It was in the wee hours of the morning, but that didn't slow them down one bit. We were half-asleep. Our welcoming committee was three people whom the army referred to as drill instructors. They were assigned to our unit for the duration of our U.S. army basic training. The moment the bus door opened I could hear the loud, shrill voices of the drill instructors: "You better hurry up and get off my bus, trainee." A trainee was the lowest form of life in the army. The drill instructors were career people or lifers, as we later called them. They were also experienced infantrymen. I didn't hear that from them. They weren't particularly concerned, with what we knew about them. We only had to know they were drill instructors (DIs), and we were trainees. The army wanted us to know about the army. The army's instructors didn't talk about anything but army-related subjects. They were good instructors about army life because they ate, breathed, slept, and drank the army. They were the U.S. Army through and through.

When we got off the bus we had to get our duffel bags from the luggage compartment, and all the time the three DIs were loudly telling us to line up.

One DI kept repeating that we should get our head out of our duffel bag. A duffel bag was a canvas bag four feet long and sixteen inches wide with an opening at one end. In theory when a soldier moved from one assignment to another everything he had could be put in his duffel bag. The one DI who kept telling everyone to get their head out of their duffel bag was saying it in such a way that it was obvious he was substituting the words *duffel bag* for a slang expression denoting a person's anal orifice. DIs weren't allowed to use profane language.

The army wasn't able to hold the idea that a person be limited to a duffel bag. "Whole baggage" developed. That is a collection of a person's "personal effects." The idea that someone has "personal effects" has to be one of the army's best and most thought-provoking ideas.

Eating meals was the same as getting off the bus. The DIs would walk up and down the center aisle telling everyone, "You better get out of my mess hall." Once, a DI leaned over close to the person sitting on the end and started barking at him. The DI kept yelling at him to get out of "my mess hall" and to hurry up and eat. Finally the person was so flustered he couldn't eat. He got up with the tray of food to leave. The DI pounced on that opportunity: "You don't like my food, trainee? You had better sit down and eat my food, trainee." Then the confused boy sat down to eat again and the DI stood right over him and yelled at the person to hurry up, eat and "get out of my mess hall." Would the boy's mother be that way? I never sat in an aisle seat.

A mess hall was what the army called a building where everyone ate. The idea was to eat and get out since more people had to eat there than there were seats. Nobody had a leisurely meal. The DI made sure everyone got that message in the first few days. Outside the mess hall we formed two lines in front of two sets of parallel bars. There were about twenty bars on each set. A person had to go hand-over-hand through them before they went in the mess hall. If they dropped off before the last bar they had to go to the back of the line and try again. Few people dropped off. Inside the mess hall we each took a metal tray and as we moved along people behind a counter would put serving spoons of food on the tray.

When I had to work in the kitchen (KP) the mess sergeant told me to pour five gallons of fresh milk down a drain. I did it for the same reason I picked up the urinal drain cover. After several days the milk was still on my mind. Very little made sense to me, but I didn't think that was something that would make sense to anyone. I asked someone who knew much more about the army than I did, why would the sergeant do such a thing? He said our company mess hall was allocated a certain number of gallons of milk per day and if all the milk was not used the allocation would be reduced. To keep our company's allocation the same the sergeant had to do something to get rid of the milk. He said the sergeant didn't do the deed; I did. The sergeant gave what amounted to an order, but I was the one who actually poured the milk down the drain. Considering I was a trainee it was less punishable, but it was punishable. The army had a system where a lower ranking person could file charges against a higher-ranking person, but they didn't have a witness relocation program. I wonder if a trainee ever had the nerve to write up that sergeant for ordering him to throw away food. Sometimes at home we would not finish all our milk at the table and my father would get upset and talk about how people were starving in other places in the world. Now, there I was far away from home dumping five gallons of milk down a drain, and I wanted to tell my superior officer about all the starving people in the world.

Every day at basic training we had to do physical training (PT). Approximately 120 persons in our company would join other companies to make up a battalion, and toward the end of our training we would compete with other battalions. The group with the highest score would win. Before we went into that competition one DI who always led us in PT exercises told us that we were going to learn which group was the most physically fit. He said the scores would go up to Division Headquarters. He said, "Men, I want you to be honest, but there is nothing wrong with a good plan." The army was his life. He had an insignia on his starched field uniform that indicated he was "airborne." That designation meant he was considered to be hard-core army and one of the best soldiers the army had. The only thing more prestigious to a soldier than being airborne was being in the Special Forces, which meant airborne training and much more.

It wasn't easy to get in an airborne unit. One day while standing in formation we were told that anyone who wanted to try out for airborne should "fall out," which meant go stand over there. We marched to the airborne field. About twenty people wanted to try out and I was one of them. We stood very seriously at attention and looked straight ahead. An officer of captain's rank asked each person why they wanted to be Airborne. Most people said in one way or another that they wanted to be a man. Airborne soldiers were trained as paratroopers. That meant they jumped out of airplanes with parachutes. Surely that meant something. When he asked me I said, "It is something I have never tried before, sir." He stood there silently for what seemed like a long time. I kept my eyes straight ahead, never looking directly at him. Finally he said, "Give me six." That meant right away I was supposed to get down in the "prone position" and do six push-ups. I did it while he moved on down the line. I didn't get accepted into an airborne unit after basic training.

When we were on the PT field, the airborne DI led us through thirty minutes of hand-to-hand combat training each day. It was karate with some additional pointers. One was how to kill a person quickly by striking them in the throat. Toward the end of our training or "cycle," the DI said, "Now, men, don't go into town and jump up on a bar table. You know just about enough of this to get tore up."

Sometimes in the afternoon we would see training films on various subjects and give written answers to written questions. One question was which animal we would least mind seeing killed. I don't remember all the choices listed, but I do remember that I selected the goat. That must have been a popular answer a long time before that, because later we were shown a training film about nerve gas. A goat got gassed to death. It was kind of like a short movie I saw named Godzilla meets Bambi (Godzilla is a green monster and Bambi is a newborn deer). In this movie Bambi is an animated fawn contentedly nibbling on clover grass while music plays. After all the credits roll up, and after it names the people who produced the producer, Bambi is there alone grazing. In a moment there is a great crescendo of music. A big green foot with claws and scales comes down hard and squashes Bambi. Only Bambi's four little black hooves are seen at the four corners of Godzilla's huge foot. The movie is over. That movie is very much like this training film except the training film has no music. The goat is tethered to a rope, grazing. A puff of smoke indicates nerve gas has been released. A gentle breeze carries it over to where the goat is grazing. The goat raises its head quickly, sniffs the air, drops, twitches spastically, and is dead.

In the early morning we would wake up when it was still dark. Outside there were speakers on poles and a bugle tune would wake us up. It was always the same tune. It went back many years. It was named Reveille. We would make our beds, go outside, and stand in formation. The three DIs would be there. We would be dismissed for breakfast. By then we had learned to wolf down our food in silence. Afterward we did whatever cleaning the barracks needed. At an exact time we went back outside and stood in formation. A second lieutenant stood in the background. A DI was in front of the company formation. At one end of each row a platoon leader briskly reported that everyone in the platoon was present or accounted for. Then the drill sergeant or DI in front would say that anyone going on sick call should fall out. Going on sick call meant going to the infirmary. There was one person who went to sick call every time. The right to go on sick call was probably the only right a trainee had. Army policy was that no one could be kept from going on sick call. A person who went on sick call would miss a good part of the morning exercises. If that happened often enough they would be "recycled," which was like flunking a grade in school. It was possible a person could spend their whole army career in basic training. This person was a draftee well briefed on how to get out of the army.

One day as we were getting into formation I asked him why he went on sick call all the time. He wouldn't talk to me. It was like I was talking to a wall. Then later that day the airborne DI pulled me aside in an empty barracks. He asked me what I said to this individual and what that person said back to me. The DI was standing extremely close to me like drill sergeants often do when they are talking to one person. I looked down to see how far apart our shoes were. He said in a stern army voice, "What are you looking at, trainee," and he jabbed me in the stomach. Soon after that the person who went on sick call every day filed charges against the same DI for hitting him. Apparently, the boy's congressman got involved. The battalion commander who was a major in rank told our company commander who was a first lieutenant to have everyone in our company file through his office in the "orderly room" and for him to ask each person if that sergeant ever hit them. If it was found the sergeant hit others then that would support the charge. The drill sergeant could be "busted" in rank from E-7 to E-6. If that happened he would have a loss in pay and his career would take a step backward.

As the line fed into the orderly room there was an outer room where the sergeant was sitting. When he saw me he said something intimidating. I didn't even look at him or acknowledge him. When I went into the company commander's office he told me to shut the door like he had told everyone else. I closed the door, turned around, and stood at attention. I said, "Sir, Sergeant so-and-so probably eats snakes for breakfast, but he is not a brutal man." That may or may not have been factually true, but it was my narrow opinion. Other people said the lieutenant went to the army college at West Point. He leaned back in his chair and said I should get a field jacket that fit better than the one I was wearing. He also said he was looking for a clerk typist. He said he would send me to clerk typist school after basic training. At first I didn't know what to say, but I thanked him. Then I said being a clerk typist and spending my time in the army behind a desk in North Carolina wasn't my cup of tea. I was in his office longer than most people were, and the sergeant must have thought I was singing like a canary. When I went back outside he was looking glumly downward like it was all over.

Later, I wondered why the lieutenant had offered me a job. It was doubtful he offered everyone a job. I wondered if the sergeant had told him I was a person who could incriminate him. I never said the sergeant didn't hit me. I simply said he was not a brutal man and that he was RA army. *RA* means a person chooses to be in the army. They volunteered to be in the army. Soon after that the person who made the charge and went on sick call everyday was given an undesirable discharge. The sergeant stayed at E-7. It was a happy ending for everybody.

After breakfast and before formation we straightened up the barracks. If we were done cleaning there might be a few moments to talk with other people, write letters, or read. The girl whom I had met at a dance in boarding school would write occasionally and say what was happening in her life and ask me about mine. She sent me a photograph of her sitting cross-legged on a rock wall. I put that picture on the inside of my locker door. In the army we each had a steel locker like the ones in gymnasiums. The door of my locker was opened and another person walked past. He looked at the picture and asked me who it was. I said it was a girl I know and he insisted that it was my sister. He was doing basic training to become a National Guardsman. We didn't take the National Guard people very seriously and he was no exception. GIs in the army said the National Guardsmen were "weekend warriors." After basic training they would go home and meet together periodically on the weekend.

Everyone had metal tags around their neck called "dog tags." The tags had our name, blood type, religion, and our serial number. Our serial number had a prefix of *RA, NG,* or *US. RA* meant a person was a volunteer, *US* meant draftee, and *NG* meant National Guardsman. My serial number was US51798734. They told us in basic training that if we were captured by the enemy according to the Geneva Convention we were only obligated to tell the enemy our name, rank, and serial number. We didn't have to tell them our blood type or our religion. I suppose they could figure that out for themselves. It must have been quite a convention.

Then the North Atlantic Treaty Organization (NATO) came up with the idea that no rifle bullet could be bigger than 7.62 millimeters in diameter. No one could put a hole in someone bigger than 7.62 millimeters with a handheld rifle. Otherwise it was a violation of a signed agreement. The other side had AK-47s that used ammunition that was 7.62 millimeters. They designed a rifle that shot a bullet that was to the nearest one-hundredth of a millimeter of the legal limit. We had the M-16, which fired a .223-caliber bullet, which is the equivalent of a 5.56-millimeter bullet. The bullet had a big charge behind it so it traveled at a much higher velocity than any other bullet. People who said they knew about such things said the higher-velocity bullet makes a bigger hole in someone than anybody else's legal military rifle. They also said the M-16 rifle bullet starts to tumble after a 100 yards of travel. If a high-velocity bullet going sideways hits a person, it will really open them up. The people who designed the M-16 figured a way to make a bigger hole than the law allows. They probably got a raise and a pat on the back and felt so clever as they drove home from work in rush-hour traffic.

I was told there were a few infantrymen in Vietnam whose weapon of choice was the Thompson submachine gun. I don't know where they ever found that firearm, but there were plenty of .45-caliber cartridges around since the .45-caliber pistol was the U.S. government standard issue side arm for officers. The Thompson submachine gun shot .45-caliber bullets. That machine gun was often shown on American television being fired by gangsters from fast-moving cars. The Thompson submachine gun was designed more than fifty years before the Vietnam War. A person could almost see the bullet traveling out the end of the barrel it was so slow. But when it hit something that is all she wrote.

That weapon didn't conform to any international agreement, but some people had it anyway. I guess they figured when you're dead, you're dead. Who cares what size the hole is?

We had one hour of instruction in the afternoon about sexually transmitted disease or venereal disease. At that time the most common type of venereal disease was called gonorrhea. The slang word for it was *clap*. Someone spoke and answered questions. A group of us were sitting in folding chairs. He said that we would know if we had gonorrhea when we went to urinate. He said we would want to rip the pipes off the wall because it would hurt so much. He said a male knows right away when he has gonorrhea, but a female doesn't. He asked if anybody knew why. He called on somebody with a raised hand and that person answered in street language that women do not urinate from the same place where they have sexual intercourse. The sergeant said that was correct. He said the beginning stages of gonorrhea in females were asymptotic. He explained that men know they have gonorrhea within twenty-four hours of their infection, but several weeks might go by before a female even thinks she has the disease. In the later stages he said a female would have a pus-like discharge from her vagina that might be confused for a light pus-like discharge that is part of her normal bodily function. A woman might not seek medical attention for weeks and if she is a prostitute, during that time she could infect dozens of males.

Much later I was in a college freshman health class. I repeated what the sergeant said. It was the teacher who assigned me to do a presentation in front of the class on venereal disease. We all had to do a presentation on something the teacher assigned. The health course was mandatory.

During my presentation I looked over at the teacher and her face was buried in her hands. I think she just wanted me to singsong facts and figures from the freshman 101 textbook. There were the faces of girls and boys staring at me wide-eyed. I didn't want to be different from them, but I was.

I added one thing the sergeant didn't say. I said the university health clinic would treat a student for venereal disease but the treatment of that disease became part of their permanent record. I said the public health center downtown would treat them without asking any questions and it was free. I don't remember how I knew that, because I never had gonorrhea when I was at the university. When I looked over at the teacher, she was cringing. Several weeks later I asked a friend to "withdraw" me from all my classes because I unexpectedly and suddenly went to jail for ninety days. When he went to tell my health class teacher, he wrote me, she disavowed I was ever in her class or that she had any knowledge of me. He wrote that her reaction was "far out," which was his way of saying how he thought it was amazing. When I read his letter I also thought it was far out.

There was one huge individual who for one reason or another wanted to beat me up. I didn't think I could prevent him from beating me up. I tried to move away from him, but he and another person who was encouraging him followed me. Finally, I picked up a three-foot broken board that had a sharp point. I remembered a similar situation in a book. I said he should make sure I didn't stick him in the eye. I said besides blinding him it would ruin his supper. He left me alone and several weeks later I heard he was absent without leave (AWOL) and they gave him an undesirable discharge from the army.

I would never have stuck him in the eye with the stick. I learned later how foolish it was for me to produce that stick if I wasn't capable of carrying through with my threat. If he picked up another sharp stick then where would I be? A Military Police (MP) person told me they always carry a loaded side arm. He said they are instructed never to take the pistol out of its holster as a threat. If they draw their pistol as a threat and the other person draws a pistol then where would they be? A split second of indecision might get them killed. He said they are taught to resolve in their mind beforehand, if they take their pistol out of its holster be prepared to use it.

One of the drill instructors was a very colorful person. He had a belly that stuck out on one side and a larger than average posterior that stuck out on the other side. That is the way his body shape was. He was very fit. He could march long distances without slowing down. He could probably march circles around us. He was often the sergeant who led us out in the morning on long marches. One time we were all standing in formation. He was in front facing us, and he said we all looked like we were from the "house of David." He wanted us to shave better.

When we marched to the rifle range it was five miles away. That was a long march in the U.S. army. I wondered about a time when an army marched thousands of miles. In history books it is called the "long march." It would be interesting to hear about it from one of the people who were there. The person who led the long march and later ruled that part of the world said, "Power comes from the barrel of a gun." That statement scared people on this side of the bellicose world.

On the rifle range we used the M-14 rifle, which was the standard issue before the M-16. It shot a 7.62 bullet called the NATO round. We were taught how to take it apart and put it back together. I was reminded of a poem about the naming of parts. It says when the person in the poem was learning the parts of his rifle he saw a butterfly. I looked around but did not see any butterflies. I learned what the receiver group was and other parts.

One anticipated event of basic training was "bivouac." It was the army's version of a camping trip. The idea was that we learn to live out of tents and eat out in the "field." The cooks were trainees guided by people who had been in the army a long time. They knew how everything worked.

The army had an ingenious device that could bring a thirty-gallon container of water to a rolling boil in a matter of minutes. It fastened to the side of a garbage can like an outboard motor. It had two six-inch pipes that went into the water. The pipes were connected at the bottom of the can in a shape that resembled a doughnut lying flat. One of the six-inch pipes coming up out of the water was the chimney. It extended five or six feet into the air. The other six-inch pipe extended a short distance above the water. It had a bracket over the open end of the pipe that held a one-gallon gasoline tank. When a small petcock valve was turned, gasoline would drip down into the pipe. It would splash on a cast-iron grate near the bottom of the pipe. After several drips a person would drop a lit match into the pipe. The gasoline would be ignited on the grate. The heat would travel around the doughnut-shaped configuration at the bottom of the can and exhaust up the other pipe. It was a large-scale version of an electric immersion heater. I doubt it was UL-listed, but it sure got water to boil in a hurry.

There were several of those cans in a row on our bivouac. After we ate, people would wash their metal food tray in hot water. There were long-handled scrub brushes beside each can.

The cans were interesting also. In the army they are mostly used as garbage cans and are called GI cans. They are different from the metal garbage cans consumers usually buy. A GI can is made from heavier-gauge galvanized steel and it has a riveted steel reinforcement on the bottom and top edges. It cost more than the average garbage can. I recently bought one in a very complete hardware store. My wife doesn't like it because it is heavy even when it is empty. I carry out the garbage.

Bivouac lasted for two days and one night. We had two-man tents, and the person I shared a tent with was someone from Cincinnati who was inducted in the same ceremony as me. We went different ways after basic training, but during the time we were in the army together he and I were friends. We talked for a long time before we went to sleep. He was telling me about his family and at one point he mentioned where his brother worked.

It was the chemical plant my mother's stepfather owned and ran. The company had for its name my mother's stepfather's last name. I told him how I knew the person the company was named after. We talked a little while longer and went to sleep. There was a difference in our past, and it had little effect. When I was further along in the army there was a person who was a biker from California, or that is what he aspired to be. He often talked about his "hog," which is an expression bikers use to say "motorcycle." In the army he was just like us and we were just like him. Everyone dressed the same, had the same haircut, and did everything the same. There was no difference between any of us. Rank was based solely on ability.

My next assignment was at Fort Dix in New Jersey. In the last week of basic training we all stood in formation and the drill sergeant passed out pieces of paper that were our orders. Each person's piece of paper showed what their "advanced individual training" (AIT) would be and where they were to go, to get that training. Our AIT assignment spelled out what MOS we would have. Everyone had a MOS. My MOS was 36K20. Any letter-number designation that ended with *K20* was an infantry MOS, and I found out the *36* meant I was to be trained as a "field wireman." At first I thought I was going to blow up many things, but a field wireman is someone who establishes ground telephone communication. Every army unit or company has a list of all the MOSs they are supposed to have. The company I was eventually assigned to had slots for two 36K20s.

It was the middle of winter at Fort Dix. Everyone in our company was a 36K20 MOS trainee. I learned all about the field telephone, setting up "nets," and how to operate the field switchboard. I also learned how to climb telephone poles in the "pole orchard." We had spikes on our feet called "climbers." If anyone hesitated to climb the telephone pole one of the sergeants teaching us would threaten to go up the pole with that person hanging by the collar of their jacket. The sergeant said the hesitant person could either climb down the pole or be dropped. I never saw anyone going up the pole hanging from a sergeant, and I never saw anyone dropped.

An exercise we had to do involved living out in the woods and stringing wires all over the place. All wires led to a switchboard so people at any two telephones could have the wires from those phones connected by the switchboard operator. It snowed the entire night. Many of the trees were conifers. The tree branches hung down with the weight of the snow. The snow crunched under my feet, and I could hear it falling. The bright moonlight made it pretty to see. Everyone talked quietly even the sergeants. No one said we had to talk quietly. It was as if we were trespassing on someone else's land, and everyone knew it without being told.

Back at the company area we ate at a huge mess hall called the "big deuce." Several thousand people ate at the big deuce. We had to stand in line and wait to eat. We filed through a small room sixteen by twenty-four feet. That kept cold air from blowing into the mess hall. We would stamp snow off our feet when we got in there.

Five or six people from another barracks were always together. Each time they walked defiantly to the front of the line. Someone said they were left from a training cycle completed long ago. The army ignored them. They had one floor of a barracks all to themselves. The only thing they did in the army was eat three meals a day. If they were as defiant about everything as they were about eating then they were trying to butt heads with the army. They seemed angry and militant in their own way. What they probably wanted was to be discharged as undesirables. Then they could return to their street ways. What the army probably wanted was for them to be so bored they would go AWOL. Then there would be some crime against them. They were alone in the world. Their strength was from each other. As far as they were concerned acting individually would be like letting go of a flotation device in the water.

On a cold day our squad leader complained loudly as they walked through the little room in the mess hall. One of them, the smallest and probably youngest one, turned to him and said, "What's it to you, dog face?" Our squad leader, who was built like a fireplug, commenced to fight with him. The people in his group continued into the main mess hall area leaving him behind. They didn't stay to help their friend who was in the middle of a furious fight. If they joined him it would have started a brawl, and they were outnumbered twenty to one. Others broke up the fight, and when they did he did not want anybody to touch him like a wild animal fighting for its life. He went outside and probably cried. After that day I didn't see him or his friends anymore. They stood in line or went AWOL.

When we finished our AIT training we were given orders that said where we went next. My orders said I was to report to the 242 Assault Support Helicopter (ASH) Company at Fort Benning in Columbus, Georgia. The army provided transportation and I flew down there on a commercial airline. The 242 ASH Company was a Chinook helicopter outfit. It was being formed as part of the Vietnam buildup and as soon as we were complete the army was going to send the entire unit to Vietnam. There was no one else from Fort Dix who went there with me, but another 36K20 person was assigned to the 242 ASH company. He had been trained somewhere else. He was the biker from California. We worked together, drank together, and shared other routines the rest of the time I was in the army.

Eventually our unit was assigned to the Ninth Aviation Battalion, First Aviation Brigade, in Vietnam. We would support the Twenty-fifth Infantry Division and be located at their base camp at Cu Chi. The Chinook helicopter had tandem rotors. It was primarily used for sling loading artillery pieces and cargo nets. Also, they were used to haul cargo on board. It was a big helicopter. Big enough to carry a jeep and a trailer and have extra room.

As the unit was being formed at Fort Benning we played army much of the time. We marched around, shined our boots, and kept our beds and footlockers "squared away." A footlocker was a wood box with a hinged top, located at the foot of your bed. *Squared away* meant something was neat and tidy.

Our company area was not far from the center of Fort Benning where there was a PX and a movie house. A PX, or Post Exchange, was a general store, and a movie house was a theater where movies were shown. I saw many movies and went to the PX often enough to memorize where things were located.

One night I came back late from a movie. The lights were out in our barracks, but they hadn't been out for long. When I sat down in the dark the legs on one end of my bed folded up and it collapsed. When it went down it pulled a string, and a water bomb on the ceiling over my bed was released. I got wet and everyone woke up. There were about thirty people on our floor in the barracks. One person was quick to say he was the one who did it. He and everyone else had a laugh. I fixed my bed up. The lights went off, but I stayed awake seething inside. About four hours later I got up and carried a GI can down into the latrine. I filled it half-full of water. About that time in comes the biker from California to urinate. He was mostly still asleep. I asked him to get one side of the can and help me carry it into the main room. He and I lifted the can. He was still half-asleep and grabbed the other side as if carrying twenty gallons of water at two in the morning was something I did every day. We set the can down near the bed of the person who had rigged up the water bomb. I waited for the biker to get back in bed. As he got over to his bed he looked back at me like for the first time he wondered what I was doing. I motioned for him to get in bed.

I'll never forget the sight. It was a hot Georgia night. This person was sleeping on his back with his mouth open. He was on top of his bed without any covers, wearing only underwear. His arms were over his head. I lifted the can up, and I set it down gently on its side right between his legs. I saw this great wave of cold water travel up over his body, slap under his chin, and fill his mouth. Then he woke up and rolled the can off him. It made a lot of noise. Everyone else woke up also, and someone turned on the main lights. I stepped back into the aisle and he came out looking wet, dazed, and confused. We stood there facing each other. I asked him calmly what on earth was the matter, and I asked him if he wanted to tango. He then turned away and went back to his bed. Everyone else did also, and the lights went off. The next day no disciplinary action was taken. One person who was not there unofficially said something.

I went home for a short time. The army called that a "leave" and everyone got one in our unit before we all shipped out to Vietnam. We went on leave at different times. We had to get home on our own steam. We weren't supposed to hitchhike in an army uniform. I took a bus a short way out of Columbus, Georgia, and proceeded to hitchhike the rest of the way home in my class-A dress uniform. I made it home faster than if I had taken the bus. No sooner would one ride let me off than another one would stop to pick me up. A person let me off in Paris, Kentucky, on a back road. I got sidetracked. A mother and several children picked me up next, and I sat in the backseat with two children. One of the small children was fascinated that I was in the army, and this child, who was about four or five years old, asked me very matter-of-factly if there were "Negroes" in the army. I never got a chance to answer him because the mother very quickly said the child's name, which changed the subject. My ride across the Ohio River let me off on an expressway exit ramp. I walked to the bus station where I was going to get a bus to Markin Farm seventeen miles outside Cincinnati.

That week that summer the National Guard was encamped in Cincinnati and many other large cities. Some people had gone on a rampage. They thought they were getting a raw deal compared to other people. The National Guard was supposed to keep a lid on things. Unaware of this, I was walking across a desolate part of town in the dark in my army dress uniform. The National Guardsmen were wearing army uniforms, but they didn't go outside alone at night. There were some National Guardsmen in the bus station.

At home I pulled Morituri out of the subcellar of a barn with a tractor. It wouldn't start without being pulled. Then I spent most of my time on trails in the woods.

One of my sisters was home. She knew a boy and also a girl. We went out together to a place where we could buy a drink. Later that night the girl and I were alone. It was late. I drove her home and turned the automobile off in her driveway. Her house was near the street in a new housing development. The automobile was about fifty feet from the house. We stayed there a long time talking. The lights were all out in her house. Before long my pants were unzipped and she was sitting in my lap facing me. We were trying to have sexual intercourse. We didn't have sexual intercourse in the true sense of the word. We forgot to undress. She had a piece of clothing on her lower end that looked like a skirt but had a middle part like shorts. Later on she drove down to Columbus, Georgia. She got a room in a local motel. I got a three-day pass and a series of overnight passes. We refined the process. It seemed, during the three days of the weekend we didn't see the light of day except to eat. The only other time we went outside we went to the motel pool. There was an Officers Candidate School (OCS) at Fort Benning and it seemed all of them were at the pool. We only stayed there a minute or less. It was like being in a monkey cage. There were no other women there. The OCS people were having fun among themselves, but when they saw the girl it was like they turned into a bunch of monkeys jumping up and down making monkey noises. We went back to the room.

After that weekend I got overnight passes which meant she could pick me up late in the afternoon and I had to report back to our unit the next morning. At the time I didn't know she was exceptionally different in the way she naturally vocalized rhythmic sexual movement. I don't think she knew she was making any noise. It was loud. Nobody complained. To the contrary the people above us apparently got fired up. I could hear the bed above hitting the wall. I hopped it wasn't two OCS troops.

She told me that one afternoon when she was alone someone knocked on the door who said he was the motel manager. She said she hated the personal questions he asked. She said he was wrong about everything. They heard about us in the front office. On the last day we had breakfast and there was very little to say. We seemed to both know there was very little to say, but we said good-bye.

Our company commander was a major in rank. He was marching us down a paved road shouting the cadence. It started to rain. Our first sergeant pulled up beside him in an army light utility vehicle and asked him if he wanted a ride. I was marching in the formation near where the major was. The major said, "Not unless you have room for all of us in there." The first sergeant knew the army as well as the major. There was about as much chance of the major getting in that seat as all of being discharged from active duty on that same day. If he had left us we would have marched into a brick wall.

Our unit was complete and we were waiting to be transported to Vietnam. The Chinook helicopters were put aboard a ship on the Atlantic coast. All the other heavy things went on that ship.

Early one evening we were told to get in formation with our duffel bags. It was dark outside. Finally, this was the big move. We got on buses that took us to a nearby runway where there was a large jet airplane waiting. It was a C-141 Starlifter. The wing was on top of the fuselage. We sat along the sides of the aircraft in web cargo seats. The airplane wasn't in the habit of carrying live people. The cargo bay was dimly lit. Even after it was at cruising altitude the engines were too loud for casual talk. It was an effort to talk. We were on our way to Vietnam.

Others and myself spent the first part of the trip dozing in and out of consciousness. The first part was over when the airplane landed at Elmendorf Air Force Base near Anchorage, Alaska to refuel. We must have been catching up to the sun, because it was daylight in Alaska. We stood beside the airplane to stretch our legs while a tanker truck did its thing. Wooded hills were in the distance. The air had a different smell. If a dog was there, it would have sniffed the air with its noise pointing up.

After the plane left Alaska the next stop was Japan. For a brief moment we stood in daylight near the plane while it was refueled one more time. There were many utility poles and wires going between poles. There wasn't much to see from that place. Soon we got back on the plane and departed.

The last stop was Tan Son Nhat Air Base outside Saigon, Vietnam. From there we went by helicopter to the air base at Bien Hoa. For the most part all travel by Americans in that country was done by helicopter. Nobody drove from one city to the other unless they had something heavy and unessential to transport like a refrigerator. Several vehicles in a convoy did any travel over roads. Many precautions were taken to avoid being ambushed by the other side. The opposing army was called either Viet Cong (VC) or the North Vietnam army (NVA). On our side was the army of the Republic of Vietnam (ARVN). They were Vietnamese. I don't know what Americans were called. When I went to Nationalist China for my "rest and recuperation" (R & R) I was referred to in a written greeting card as an "anti-Communist warrior." It made me feel like I had a sword, a spear, and a javelin.

Bien Hoa was a steamy little city teaming with life. We were put in an old French compound at the north end of the city. At the south end of the city was the Bien Hoa Air Base where our helicopters were kept. We were in Bien Hoa for three months while our company area was being prepared at Cu Chi. Pilots from our unit immediately started flying sorties for the Twenty-fifth Infantry Division. Other people in our unit who were not directly involved with the helicopters had little to do. I was one of those people. We marked time. Each of us had one year to be there, and the clock started ticking the moment we arrived.

I helped string a field telephone wire from our company area on the north side of Bien Hoa to the helicopters at the air base on the south side. We spent many of the following days between those two points in the town of Bien Hoa drinking Vietnamese beer and "troubleshooting" the line. The sergeant in charge of our section told us to troubleshoot the line often. That was his job. We found imaginary and real breaks in the line. We kept it operational. It went on utility poles through town, but toward the air base there were no poles or trees. The wire lay on the ground. That is where most of the breaks occurred.

There were four of us in the communications (commo) section of Headquarters Platoon. There was another 36K20 person and two radio teletype operators. The other 36K20 person said we were the heads of headquarters. At that time a "head" was an American who ingested or inhaled mood-modifying substances.

The two radio teletype operators were trained to send messages in code. Code was a series of electronic dashes and dots. The 242 ASH Company was capable of operating out of a field. If that was the situation, we would then receive our helicopter missions each day in code. The other side wouldn't be able to tell what the Twenty-fifth division was doing by listening to radio transmissions. That is why our company had two radio teletype operators.

Learning code was difficult. The army sent the smartest people to that school. Those people had to have a security clearance of secrets. The highest clearance was top secret. Our company wasn't going to use radio teletype so they helped us string wires.

The four of us shared one room that was part of some very nice old buildings built years before by the French people for their army. The buildings had red tile roofs and thick white walls that felt cool in the middle of a hot day. There were louvered wood shutters on the windows. At night they were closed. There was no screen or glass. The floor was six-inch-square pieces of dark red ceramic tile. It continued outside underneath a covered walkway that went alongside the rooms. Each room was about ten by fifteen feet in size with high ceilings. It was unusual for enlisted men (soldiers who are not officers) to have such beautiful housing. The army put us there probably because they had nowhere else to put us and because the place was too remote to safely put officers. Our compound was between two roads that forked together a thousand feet south of us to form the main street down through the middle of Bien Hoa.

On the north side of our compound there was a high wall that was like the walls in the rooms. There was a lightly traveled residential street on the outside of the wall. It connected the two roads that formed the main street in Bien Hoa.

There were quite a few days when the four of us in the commo section would get a ride to the air base several miles away. We would buy a bottle of bourbon at the PX and work our way back up through Bien Hoa. When we got back to our compound the day was over, the bottle was empty, and we slept or read until supper. If we ate anything for lunch it was eaten in town.

There were no restaurants, however along the street there was someone who had a cart filled with the ingredients of a sandwich. We were told informally never to eat the local food because the meat might be from any animal. We were told the Vietnamese people eat dogs among other things. One time I had one of those sandwiches. I was slightly drunk and very hungry. I didn't care what it was made from and as I remember it was very tasty. The bread was a fresh, thick loaf about three inches in diameter. When I thought about it later I was sure I had eaten fresh dog meat, and I never ate one again. We usually drank our lunch.

Other days we wouldn't go all the way to the PX at the air base. We would go to the bottom of town and zigzag our way back and forth from bar to bar. We would end up at our compound going fast asleep. In each bar they served a French beer made in Vietnam. It was always served cold. Each bar had a bevy of young, pretty girls. They spoke broken English. If they sat with us, as they were always welcome to do, we had to buy them a drink. It was their job to get us to buy them drinks. Their drink was always non alcoholic colored water that cost twice as much as a beer. The American GI named that drink "Saigon Tea." Unlike us, they had to remain sober throughout the day.

We went to the same bars often enough and became well known. There was a girl I liked in each bar. The Saigon Tea was an indirect way of paying for a female's companionship. It was sort of a forgone conclusion that we were disgusting sloppy GIs. We didn't disappoint them in that respect. We were always the first ones there. Sometimes we were outside waiting when they unlocked the door. I don't remember what we ever talked about, the girls and me, but I do remember that a bar girl was not a prostitute. There was one girl in one bar I especially liked and when I suggested we go somewhere and roll in the hay she got up and left. Before she left she turned around and verbally scolded me.

When I first got to Vietnam and didn't know too much about what was going on, I and the other 36K20 person were walking up through town with a bottle of bourbon and this small child comes up to us and says, "GI want Puck?" He keeps saying over and over again, "GI want Puck." I wondered what in the world was he talking about. I thought, *Did he play hockey?* Then he says, "Number one French girl." Then I knew what he was talking about. He was tugging on my sleeve and he led us through back streets. I felt like J. Alfred Prufrock. I was glazed over and feeling no pain. We had been to a few of the bars by then. When they saw us walking up the dirt path with the boy in front leading us, three or four women came out to welcome us. They were about as French as my dead grandmother.

One of the women put her hand on my crotch. Then without a word she unbuttoned my pants and put her hand inside in an inquisitive way. We didn't have zippers on our pants. The designers of our clothes must have thought the enemy might hear someone unzipping his pants. Buttons were quieter.

She was not at all bashful. Her directness and her dispensing with meaningless talk were amazing to me. Actually, I don't think she spoke any English. I don't know because I never tried to converse with her. I looked over at the other 36K20 person. There were several women standing next to him. He was paying attention to them. He and I exchanged glances. This was beyond control. When I came back outside he was waiting in practically the same spot where he was before. For a second I wondered if I was the only one out of control.

A long time later I was watching my son's hockey practice at an indoor skating rink. On the other side of the rink there was a big sign that said if a person wanted tickets to see a local professional hockey game they should call ___-PUCK. It made me think of that incident so many years before.

Several of us were sitting in one room. A pet monkey was there. The owner had just gotten it from someone else. I don't know what happened to the monkey, but it didn't go to Cu Chi with us. When a person who had not seen the monkey before entered the room the monkey started screeching and having a fit. It was obvious to everyone, including the one who came in that the monkey was reacting to him. To explain the situation he said, "The monkey don't like me. If you see me running, look for the monkey behind me." This person was the only one in the room with black skin. He was very tall and slender. He had a gold tooth in the front. He talked calmly and distinctly and moved like he was going to get a crown. The monkey's reaction to him could only be a conditioned response. An animal has no other learning mechanism. Two things I knew for certain; One, the monkey had a previous owner. Two, the room was full of people, and the only visible difference in this one was the color of his skin.

The army Corps of Engineers built a paved highway between Bien Hoa and Saigon. I never traveled on it, but I heard about it from my favorite bar girl who lived in Saigon. The main street in Bien Hoa was surfaced with something hard, but it wasn't blacktop. The street was busy from early morning until the end of day. I never saw it at night. In the day there were many bicycles, two-cycle motorscooters, and small three-wheeled vehicles loaded high and wide. There were people on foot and comparatively huge army deuce-and-a-half trucks that lumbered up and down the street. There were a few French four-door automobiles with running boards and headlamps. All of them were black. Those were practically the only automobiles I saw in Bien Hoa.

We entered our living area from the lightly traveled residential road that connected the two busy roads. We entered on the side where the sun sets. Our compound was on the edge of town, and it wasn't unusual to see a water buffalo being led toward town or away from town but never in town. There was an MP standing by the entrance. I suppose he kept people with water buffaloes from taking a shortcut. There was a rice paddy across from where we went in, and there was another one on the far side.

The commo shed was on that far side. When I had switchboard duty at night I could look out across the rice paddy to where people lived. I could see them cooking on charcoal. I could smell the charcoal fires. I would sit back and watch the tiny lizards crawl on the wall. In the light from the window I saw a rat. It was so big that when it moved it bounded instead of scurried. There was a heli-pad next to the commo shed where helicopters landed during the day. They would fly very slowly over the rice paddy and set down lightly. People would get out just like it was a car. Those helicopters were UH-B1 Hueys. I developed an attraction for the helicopter. When I got out of the army I bought an autogiro kit and flew it about ten hours before I crashed it the second time. After that I gave it up. It wasn't a full-fledged helicopter. It was a lawn chair that flies. Informally it was called a widow-maker. I wasn't married at the time.

One of the two radio teletype operators assigned to our unit often read books in the afternoon, and I would read the books after he had finished them. We got in discussions about the books. A book he was reading had a passage he memorized and repeated to me when he thought it appropriate. I, too, memorized the expression. It was, "Dense and unenlightened people are notoriously confident they have a monopoly on truth."

The other radio teletype operator and I were making the rounds in Bien Hoa. We happened upon a pedicab or rickshaw driver who was standing beside his cab. He had a light metal tube about a foot long and a quarter-inch in diameter. Between his thumb and index finger he was rolling something into a ball, which he inserted into one end of the tube. The other end he put in his mouth. He then lit it and smoked what it was. He was wearing a straw hat Americans call a sampan hat. It was round like a small umbrella without the stem. It came to an obtuse point on top and formed a wide brim that kept the sun off his neck and head. He smelled like manila rope.

The radio teletype person with me said to him, "Number one pot. We want number one pot." The man with the sampan hat didn't speak the English language, but he understood what was being said. *Pot* was an American word for marijuana. He motioned for us to get in his rickshaw. We piled in and he trotted off. A rickshaw has two light wheels on each side where the passengers sit. There are two shafts that the person who is pulling the rickshaw holds. It is very much like a pony cart.

As we went down many backstreets and around many corners I became completely lost. I was hoping he wasn't a VC with plans. We were helpless, dumb Americans, in a strange land. Eventually, he came to a stop outside a door. We got out as if we owned the place and knew just where we were. A mama-san came to the door and we all went inside.

To an American GI everyone Vietnamese was a papa-san, mama-san, girl-san, boy-san, or baby-san. This was a mama-san and she spoke to the man at length in Vietnamese. We pretended to understand every word. Then she left the room and came back with a large bowl of marijuana. The papa-san who had brought us was very concerned about his rickshaw. He kept turning around and looking at it through the open door. We weren't very concerned about his leaving because we hadn't paid him yet. Neither one of us was sober. But I was sober enough that if he did leave I was going to look for cover, and take the mama-san with me.

As it turned out, he went outside and smoked. We bought some marijuana and he took us back to the main street. Bien Hoa was tightly controlled by the South Vietnamese, who were on the same side as the Americans. It would have been bad for business if she didn't treat us right.

A war was raging all around these people who simply wanted to brush their water buffalo. Everyone was told all sorts of things about the other side. The enemy would have two heads and antennae. Whoever thought it up would have no eye contact with the dead people.

The Armed Forces Radio was a radio station in English. It would broadcast news events for the American GI. One day when I was lying on my bed reading, the radio had something the president of the United States of America said to the American people. In his own words he said that he was going to step up the bombing as much as was necessary to win in Vietnam. Then, at the same time as the broadcast, a pair of F-4 Phantom fighter bombers took off at the Bien Hoa Air Base. The president was our commander-in-chief. He was the leader of the American Armed Forces. It was strange being at both ends: to hear what he was going to do and at the same time hear it being done. It was very dramatic even if he was talking about another kind of bombing.

It was my turn to do guard duty. At basic training I learned the army's way to make sure a person was who they said they were was called authentication. It worked like this: When a voice came from outside the perimeter in the night the guard would ask them if they could authenticate three words that corresponded to letters of the alphabet. Each letter of the alphabet was represented by a word. For example *z* was represented by the word *zulu*, *b* by the word *bravo*, *h* by the word *hotel*; *c* was *charlie*. Every letter had a corresponding word. The guard would say, "Can you authenticate *zulu, bravo, hotel*?" If the person was who they said they were, they would say something like this: "The authentication for *zulu, bravo, hotel* is *foxtrot, delta, victor*." A person would not know the matching words if they hadn't come from inside the camp that night. The words could be changed for each patrol or as often as anyone liked. The military people at basic said anyone walking around in the middle of the night was "unfriendly." The whole business of authentication, although it sounded good, was not used in Vietnam. We didn't do it that night or, as far as I know, on any other night, in any other place.

Many of the people in our company were being transferred to other units. That way everyone in our unit wouldn't go home at the same time. We arrived in Vietnam on the same day. If no one was transferred we would all go home on the same day. Most of the transfers were people directly involved with the helicopters. The commo section that I was in was nonessential, so we were not transferred. There were four of us, and a buck sergeant in charge. The buck sergeant considered everything serious. The army was his career. He was in for twenty years. We didn't have to salute him, but we always did the best we could to show him due respect even if we were bleary-eyed most of the time. We would make him look good by being very dutiful soldiers. That was especially true when his superiors were in the area. He could have made life miserable for us if he wanted to, but he didn't. The other three and myself in our section were very appreciative that he left us alone as long as we did our job or pretended we had a job. Actually, we didn't have a job that amounted to anything. None of us were called for, and the fact that we were never seen standing still was very important to our overall objective of doing nothing. We stayed out of the way. We always walked fast around the company area as if we had many things to do and so little time to do them. We fit right in, because that is the way everyone else looked. Maybe everyone had nothing to do and they wanted to look busy like us.

Finally, our area at Cu Chi was ready. Bien Hoa was fun, but bottles of bourbon were starting to grow on me. I was anxious to move to Cu Chi. Three months had passed and the longest anyone had to be in that country was a year, 365 days. Many people would mark off each day on a calendar. I had a relatively enjoyable time. If things were different perhaps I would have looked at the calendar more often. Army life was one big blur for me. I didn't have to kill anyone and no one had to kill me. I am very aware that I lived through that "conflict" and the tragedy of life is that many others didn't. They went home in a box.

I wrote to my sister about what it was like to go to Cu Chi and she wrote back. Among other things, she said it was a very graphic description. I wrote to her that I went there by helicopter and going there was like an insect flying a few inches over someone's plush green living room rug. Then off in the distance there appeared a square cracker. That was the Twenty-fifth Division base camp at Cu Chi and the insect was going to land there.

A friend of mine, who worked on the flight line, traveled to Cu Chi in a truck loaded with things. The person driving the truck was Vietnamese. My friend rode along with his rifle, helmet, and flak jacket. The driver was wearing long khaki pants and a short-sleeved shirt. The flight line person said it was just him and the civilian driver in the cab of the truck and that they were in a convoy of trucks. The truck he was in got farther and farther behind the truck in front. My friend said he motioned for the driver to catch up but the driver didn't seem to understand. The flight line person imagined that when the other truck was out of sight the driver of his truck (I don't know if it was the last truck) would turn somewhere and get rich from selling all the things on the black market. That truck carried mostly refrigerators and other American-made major appliances. All the things people would kill for. He said he got scared thinking of all that could happen. He chambered a cartridge in his rifle, which would have made a very audible and universally understandable sound. He said he leaned over and put the end of the barrel against the Vietnamese man's head and told him in plain English to speed up. It is questionable whether the man understood the English language, but he understood everything else, because he radically accelerated the truck.

Our company area at Cu Chi was permanent. All the buildings had concrete floors with one-inch-by-six-inch louvered wood sides. Screens were behind the wood. The roof was the most solid part of each building. It was constructed of very light corrugated, galvanized sheet metal. I had an army cot bed. It was the most prominent part of each person's living area. Twenty or thirty cots were arranged in parallel down each side of the barracks. There was an aisle down the middle. Civilians came on the base each day to clean the barracks.

We got our regular army pay, which was based on our rank plus about a third more money for "hazardous duty." There was no place to spend large amounts of cash in Vietnam, so we indicated on a form to which bank account we would like our money sent. The bank was usually in each person's hometown. What little money we had in Vietnam was in the form of MPCs (Military Payment Certificates). We weren't allowed to have dollars (greenbacks). The Vietnamese economy accepted MPCs, but they liked their own currency better.

Other civilians came on the base each day to fill sandbags. Eventually, each building had a sandbag wall about four feet high all the way around the outside of the building. These people enlarged the bunkers on the perimeter. There was always a need for more sandbags. Occasionally at night our company area was mortared. Rather than run to the bunker outside, we were instructed to lie on the floor. Unless there was a direct hit on a barracks, the sandbags on the outside would stop any shrapnel. One person was killed because he was running to the bunker after a mortar attack had begun.

It turned out that mortars were mostly for harassment. Members of the Twenty-fifth Infantry Division must have harassed the enemy in return, or they practiced with mortar tubes from the perimeter.

One night when I had switchboard duty the radio teletype operator who rode in the rickshaw in Bien Hoa with me was having a party in one of the bunkers on the perimeter. He threw a lit match under the wood boards he was sitting on, and as he later put it, he "got burnt up." Under the seat there were some scattered pieces of plastic explosive used to propel mortars. The infantry people firing mortars carelessly left behind scraps of this propellant. Someone who was sitting on the open side of the bunker said that for a millisecond there was this great *whoosh* sound and a great ball of fire engulfed everything and extended out of the bunker. There was no explosion. The teletype operator got some third-degree burns on his face, but otherwise he was not hurt. No one else was hurt, either. It broke up the party.

My friend went to the base camp hospital for treatment of his burns. The other radio teletype operator went to see him. He said his burnt friend went on and on about how "sick" the wounded were in that hospital. They were mostly combatants. The burnt teletype operator said wounded infantry people joked among themselves about the positions "gooks" die in, and he said they copied those positions in their bed. *Gook* was the American expression for a Vietnamese person, in this instance a Vietnamese person who was either VC or NVA. We named the NVA. They named themselves the NLF, which stood for the National Liberation Front.

The latrines were small buildings where human waste was deposited in a sanitary manner. There was no running water. Our latrines consisted of a front door where a person entered, a concrete floor, and about five feet farther back four toilet seats side by side. Around the back of the building at ground level there were low doors that would swing open. Steel fifty-gallon drums cut in half were placed under each of the toilet seats. Human waste would drop into the steel drums.

Each day a GI with three or four civilians would collect the waste. After the GI checked inside, the civilians would slide out the cut-off steel drums. They would then lift each one into the back of a truck and replace it with an empty one.

The driver would go to a place on the perimeter where the wind was blowing away from the base camp. The civilians would put the cut-off drums on the ground, add a little diesel fuel, and light them on fire. When it was done the drum would be empty inside. The smoke was thick and black.

There was a person who couldn't handle life in Vietnam anymore. He wore little round sunglasses and things around his neck. He was beginning to come apart mentally. He went to an army psychiatrist at the base camp at Cu Chi. We had a resident psychiatrist. This distressed person went to the psychiatrist glassy-eyed and thoroughly under the influence of marijuana. It could be gotten from the civilians. He was hoping the doctor would think he was a lost cause and give him "early out." He said he told the doctor that Vietnam was a godforsaken country. The psychiatrist didn't send him home. He was given the permanent job of "beautifying" the company area, and he was told to quit smoking that nasty weed. The first sergeant added one thing, that the new job classification includes burning human fecal matter; however, the first sergeant and everyone referred to human solid waste with one four-letter word. A three-quarter-ton truck was assigned to this person, and he spent the remainder of his time in Vietnam "beautifying" our company area.

In the United States two phonograph albums had been

released that my older sister sent to me. We all got together and bought a phonograph machine at the PX. One of the records my sister sent was called *Are You Experienced*, and the other one was called *Sergeant Pepper's Lonely Hearts Club Band*. Then she sent another one called *Magical Mystery Tour*. We played those records until we wore them out. We would sit around in the evening, modify our mood with that nasty weed, and talk while one of those records was playing. One evening we got a case of maraschino cherries from S-3 (supply). We ate the whole case. Cherries never tasted so good. We also tortured a scorpion with a can of insect spray. The active ingredient in that can was a great big long scientific word with more than fifteen letters. I knew it was made especially for the army because the can was olive drab. That was the army color. Everything the army had was that color: airplanes, tanks, helicopters, and cans of bug spray. If the army had it, it was painted olive drab.

There was a notice on the company bulletin board that they were seeking an enlisted person to tend bar and run the day-to-day operation of our officers' club. One of the teletype operators and I showed up. We were supposed to wear civilian clothes. We wore our best civilian clothes and neckties. A warrant officer met us and put us to work serving supper in the club. He said we didn't have to wear ties, and please take them off. There were four grades of warrant officer. He was a W-3 grade. He was older than most of the other officers. He had more than 8,000 hours of flying time in a CH-47 Chinook.

Our company had about thirty pilots who were all officers. A warrant officer never told anyone what to do. They were experts at flying, and nobody told them what to do. They did their job and weren't concerned about much else. The younger pilots greatly respected them. Rank meant little.

That night in the officers' club the company Commanding Officer (CO) asked me why I wanted the job, and I said that I knew that I should serve from the left and pick up from the right. He asked if that was a fact. He asked how I knew that, and I said it was something I picked up along the way. He and I were very different, but I liked him. I think he liked me. He was a field-grade officer from the southeastern part of the United States. He didn't have much use for formal education. Sometimes he flew the Chinook. He had an executive officer (XO) who was also a major.

The XO was in charge of helicopter maintenance, which was largely about the availability of aircraft. The company commander oversaw that as well as the daily routines of all company personnel.

I was informed later that I should report for work each day at the officers' club. I reported to a W-1. The W-3 I first saw oversaw the W-1, and the W-1 oversaw me. I officially became the custodian of the officers' club. That meant I was the manager. A civilian mama-san cleaned the club each day. She reported to me. The army had a very clear-cut chain of command. The President of the United States was our commander-in-chief. A five-star general reported to him.

The enlisted men's shower was next to the headquarters barracks. The shower consisted of a large rubber bladder that held about three hundred gallons of water. A gasoline pump moved the water from the bladder to showerheads. I slept late because I worked at night in the officers' club. Most mornings I would wake up to the sound of people trying to start the gasoline engine so they could take a shower. When I got up several hours later I didn't have any easier time trying to start that engine.

One morning I walked into the supply building and told the S-3 about the difficulty we were having with the pump. He issued me an electric motor-driven pump, wire, a switch, and other necessary hardware to hook the thing up. I didn't think anything of it at the time, but now I realize how unusual it was for him to issue me that kind of hardware. I was dressed in civilian clothes, and I worked around officers all the time. I was friendly toward him and explained the problem. He got the electric pump, wire, and everything else. Later I realized how that would have infuriated the first sergeant. I had taken it upon myself to put an electric pump in the enlisted men's shower. I was the equivalent of a private fourth class. I wired the pump into the electric line in the Headquarters Barracks.

We had a 100-kilowatt generator that supplied electricity to our entire company. It was only shut off for periodic maintenance. It was located over by the flight line. Judging by the sound and size of the block, it was probably two or three times bigger than a truck engine. Wires came into each building from poles. On the inside wall there was a panel. In the panel there was a master breaker; then down from there was a row of smaller breakers. I wired the pump into one of the smaller breakers.

It was very nice to simply flick a switch and get water. For several days it was that way, but one morning when I went out to take a shower I saw that all the insulation was melted off the wires. They had gotten very hot. I went into the barracks and when I opened the panel I saw that the pump had been rewired. It was wired directly to the 100 KW generator. I couldn't imagine under what circumstances someone would have changed the wires, but I was certain it had been changed. I went to the S-3 and told him that some fool had rewired the pump directly to the generator. Shortly after that the pump had new wires and was working once more. I never looked to see how it was wired into the building.

There was a traveling United Services Organization (USO) show that came through the Twenty-fifth Division camp at Cu Chi. One night they performed at our company enlisted men's club, and the second night they performed at our officers' club.

They were a small group from Las Vegas, Nevada, and one of their leading members was a physically beautiful woman from the United States. In the middle of the afternoon she and the CO were sitting alone in the officers' club talking quietly. There was a time when I made her a drink.

I never had the opportunity to look into her eyes again, but I was very aware of her presence the entire time she was there. When I was behind the bar I heard the CO ask her to open her blouse and show him her breasts. She had large breasts. Before that he must have been talking about her breasts. A bartender has much in common with a fly on the wall.

That night the USO group did a show at the officers' club. They were supposed to be paid by each unit that contracted a performance. I heard later, long after they were gone, that the CO hadn't paid them. I guess she never did open her blouse for him.

That night when they performed at the officers' club an

enlisted man from another unit came into the club and sat down. He had seen the show at our enlisted men's club and apparently he wanted to see it a second time. He came into the officers' club for that reason.

Many of the hard-core infantry people had faded fatigues that along with the olive drab color were slightly the color of dirt. A "bird dog" reconnaissance plane had reported a large enemy buildup near us. MACV probably thought it was more than the Twenty-fifth Division could handle. For the better part of half a day C-123 fixed-wing aircraft brought planeload after planeload of infantrymen from the Third Brigade of the 101st Airborne Division. They were MACVs reactionary force. He was probably from that unit. Army decorum wasn't very relevant to those people. They did and died. He didn't have any insignia on his fatigues that I could see. Enlisted men were not allowed in an officers' club and officers were not allowed to fraternize with enlisted personnel.

The CO prided himself on being physically strong. He kept his sleeves rolled up higher than anybody else did. He had big, muscular arms that showed. He walked up to where the enlisted man (boy) was sitting and asked him if he was an officer. I didn't hear the answer. The CO then told him he had ten seconds to leave and he raised his arm to look at his wristwatch. The enlisted man didn't move. Then after a short while the CO grabbed the enlisted man by the shirt with both hands and yanked him up. He didn't resist. The CO held onto his shirt with arms outstretched. They whirled around toward the door and went outside, where it had gotten dark.

When the CO came back inside, another officer went outside. I saw the other officer with his arm over the boy's shoulder walking back and forth like he was trying to console him. The boy was wiping his eyes. He didn't appear physically hurt.

The CO had the army Corps of Engineers dig a hole for a swimming pool. They did other work on the pool in trade for helicopter time.

After the hole was dug, sandbaggers stacked sandbags in the shape of the pool. The ground behind the sandbags was backfilled and compacted. The pool was then lined with rubber sheeting used for helicopter landing pads. The pool was about twenty feet wide, forty feet long, and eight feet deep.

After the pool was finished, the army Corps of Engineers dug a well. They positioned a crane with a clam shell bucket over a spot and started digging. The walls of the well never caved in while it was being dug. Gravel was put in the bottom, and then a galvanized pipe was lowered down the length of the hole. The space on the outside of the pipe was backfilled. An electric pump was lowered down into the well. It delivered over 300 gallons of water per day. The major had the only swimming pool in Cu Chi.

One night in the early morning when everyone was asleep, after I locked up the officers' club I took my clothes off and went in the water. It was a clear starlit night. That was the only time I went in that pool.

One day I got a notice that I was to report to the orderly room (the company office). That is where the first sergeant had a desk and the CO had an office. When I went into the CO's office the first sergeant was standing behind and to one side of the major, who was sitting behind his desk. I knew that this was the time to play army to the best of my ability. I marched in there smartly. I came to a stop and executed a perfect square corner. I faced the CO and the first sergeant.

The people at West Point would have been proud of me. I stood at attention and saluted the major. He returned my salute and said, "At ease." I assumed the at ease position. I crisply stepped one foot to the side, clasped my hands behind my back, looked directly at the CO, and acted relaxed. I was there because the first sergeant had said my area was not as neat as it should be. I think he wanted me transferred to the "Russian front."

In the officers' club, officers didn't want to be reminded of protocol. I was told to wear civilian clothes, I suppose, so it wouldn't be so obvious I was a soldier. Now, here I was in a military situation dressed in jungle fatigues. I hoped the CO was impressed with my knowledge of military behavior. He probably didn't know what to expect. He had to know how hard I was trying to play soldier.

Dealing with my messy area was a duty the CO had to handle. The first sergeant made it an issue. The first sergeant was in charge of the enlisted men. I was an enlisted man. According to the army chain of command I reported to the first sergeant and he reported to the CO. My area looked as neat or messy as anyone else's did. He was grinding an ax. I never broke rules, and that kept him at bay.

Several times right after I closed the officers' club we would go to a big bunker. Twenty-fifth Division perimeter guards thought a motor attack was coming. Headquarters Platoon shared a bunker with all the NCOs (sergeants).

I was in that bunker extremely drunk, and there was nothing the first sergeant could do. According to the other 36K20 person, it was obvious I was drunk. He said no one else was talking except me, loudly, about all the Communist interruptions. The bunker was dark inside. It was pitch-dark. Everyone, including the first sergeant, was sitting anonymously in the dark. The 36K20 person told me I repeated over and over again that an American civilian helicopter technician kept buying everyone drinks. The W-3 warrant officer I saw about the job said I could drink as long as I didn't get inebriated. That night was an exception. I got inebriated, but to someone who didn't know any better it may have seemed that's the way I finished off every day.

There was another time in Vietnam when I inadvertently got under the first sergeant's skin. I was walking from the officers' club to the mess hall to get something we needed. There was a Vietnamese civilian at the back door of the mess hall. He was wearing a pair of shorts and sandals. He was just standing there.

I opened the back door of the mess hall in my civilian clothes. I called to the mess sergeant, "What does he want?" The mess sergeant said from inside that he wanted something to eat. The mess sergeant said the man wouldn't leave. I looked at the man. He didn't look at me, but he pointed to his open mouth. Then for a split second our eyes did meet. "Give him something to eat," I said. "Why do you think we are here?" The mess sergeant was giving him something to eat as I was leaving.

That night in the officers' club without mentioning that incident the CO said pointedly to me that we didn't know anything about the civilian sandbaggers who come on the base. He said there might be enemy spies among them. The mess sergeant had told the first sergeant, and the first sergeant had told the CO, hoping to get me in trouble. The glance of that man keeps coming back to me.

From behind his desk the CO said to me, "The first sergeant tells me that you're not keeping your area neat."

"Sir," I said, "if the first sergeant says my area is not neat, then it is not neat. I pay a civilian to keep it neat. I will watch more closely how it looks." There were a few more exchanges, but a potentially ugly situation had been defused.

In the middle of my time in Vietnam I got R & R. All GIs got that once during the year they were in Vietnam. The U.S. Government paid our transportation to one of the big cities in Southeast Asia.

I didn't know what to expect. I soon learned there was a road mapped out for us and a procedure that had been set in motion years earlier.

I put in for several places. A clerk in the orderly room told me that all the airplane seats to all my choices except the last one were taken. The first sergeant authorized a person's R & R trip. Last on my list was Taipei. There was a seat on that airplane. Taipei is the capital city of Taiwan, also known as Formosa or Nationalist China. Western civilization and Western influence were firmly established there.

One other person from our unit was going to Taipei on that airplane. I did not know him before that trip and I never met him again after we got back. When we landed in Taipei there was a busload of GIs from Vietnam. We all went to a processing center where our money was exchanged for the local currency. On the way there an NCO stood up in the aisle in the front of the bus and told us there was a war going on between the taxicabs and the pedicabs. He said the taxicabs were winning and not to travel in a pedicab. He also told us not to wear our uniforms.

From the processing center we went to the hotel of our choice. Me and the other person from our unit went to the same hotel. We each had our own spacious room. Money was no object. Within ten minutes there was a knock on the door. It was a Chinese man selling tailor-made suits. He said he would take the measurements and the suit would be made and back to me before I left. I asked him what I would do with a suit. I said even if they sent me home in a box they wouldn't put a civilian suit on me. I looked at the cloth samples he had. They were glassy. I said there were some people who would wear that stuff, but I wasn't one of them. I practically had to push him out the door to get him to leave.

I went to the street to get a taxicab somewhere. I didn't know where. I said to the cabdriver that I was new in country and asked him where would be a lively place to go. He didn't have to think. Off we sped. I paid him when he stopped. Inside there was a very ornate bar that went down the length of the room. There wasn't a soul sitting at the bar. A bartender was polishing the bar. Across from the bar on the other side of the room a row of girls sat on a hard wood bench like ducks in a row. I didn't look at them. I went to the bar and got a drink. I was sitting there for a while minding my own business and suddenly this girl is standing beside me talking. She points to the bench and says do I see a girl I like? There were three girls bouncing a golf ball on the floor oblivious to what was around them. "That one," I said, pointing to one of the three lovely girls. The girl who was standing beside me said that girl was "going to meet her brother in a few moments." It was definitely a first-time experience to be able to sit on a bar stool and point to this one or that one like I was in a market.

I said I would go outside and come back in a little while, after her brother left. When returning I noticed from across the street an old Chinese man who was squatting down. When he saw me he quickly went inside as if to say I was coming. When I was inside, the same girl came up to me. I asked where so-and-so was. By then I knew the girl's name, or her trade name. The girl I was talking with said that girl had to go but asked, "Do you see any other girl you would like?" It was sad thinking I was never again going to see that girl. Then I looked up and said, "What about you?" She dipped down a little bit by bending her knees.

She led me up a spiral staircase to another part of the bar. She went in front of me. She was kind of swanky the way she moved up those stairs in that little red Chinese dress. We sat down in a booth, and I got another drink. She ordered a Saigon Tea or whatever it was called in that country. A few moments later when the bartender brought her a second one she snapped at him in Chinese. I think it was all for show. She was older and very professional.

When we got up we went over to a baldheaded Chinese man behind a partition. He completed the necessary paperwork. I signed a contract or legal agreement. It was prostitution pure and simple, but it was more. She was a companion, a tour guide, a trustworthy person, and a prostitute all in one. The government controlled prostitution. The baldheaded man recorded my identification so there was a record of who went with whom and when. I paid him some money and the girl and I left.

We went to a nightclub where there was a floorshow. The tables had white tablecloths, and we got Shark's Fin Soup.

Then she took me to a place where I thought she said she lived. She had all the keys. We went into a modern glass-and-steel building. We took the elevator up many floors. The door opened and we got off. It was an office in every direction. She unlocked several more doors and turned on electric lights. Everywhere it was an office. Then she went over to a wall and pushed a button that was not visible to me. A section of the wall silently slid back revealing a big room decorated like a bedroom with a big bed in the middle. She saw I was aghast. I could not conceal it from her. She watched me intently. I didn't think those kinds of places existed, but I saw it with my own eyes. I don't know why she took me up there, but she did.

We left that place. It was late in the evening and we went back to my hotel. In the morning she left. She asked me for some money to get her hair done, and I gave her some.

I met up with the guy from my unit, I got another girl, and he got one, too. We went to a place run by the U.S. government's armed services.

That bar was a big enlisted men's club. To get inside a person had to have military identification. No one wore a uniform. If a drink was nonalcoholic there was no pretending that it was alcoholic. A GI could have nonmilitary personnel with them. Many people in there were with local girls, and many were not. We sat at a large round table with other GIs and their female companions. People got up and left. People sat down. Soon all of the GIs at the big round table had a different color skin than me. There must have been a U.S. military base nearby, because my friend and I were the only ones from Vietnam.

Vietnam and where we were from was never discussed, but by the way they behaved I could tell they didn't come from there. One person sort of took over the table, commenting that so-and-so's girl was so fine-looking. He was doing all the talking. When I said something to him with a big painless smile, he stared at me for what seemed like a long time. The person who flew down there with me quickly piped up, "He is with me." Then the dominant one went on being dominant without replying to what I said. I finished my drink in a couple of gulps, and the girl and I got up to leave. My friend from Vietnam stayed there.

We walked out in the street and she asked me why I kept sitting there. She said the situation back there was strange to her.

I said to her as we walked nowhere in particular, "So why stop there? Everything is strange." I told her there are rays of light everywhere.

She asked, "What is a ray of light?" I told her she was a ray of light.

That night we went to have supper in a place that wasn't very big. She knew about that place. She said it was small and I would like it there. We sat at a cozy little table with a candle in the middle. There was a red-checkered tablecloth. Someone walked around the room playing Italian canal music. A year later when I was living in New York City I wrote some words about that night:

> What they were doing was nothing new to the world, but a Mediterranean man playing his accordion and a candle in a wax-covered Chianti bottle were to him part of growing up. Because he had seen this in so many commercial productions it all suddenly seemed wasted. She was good to look at but a part of the mood, like the candle and the old man. When they finished they went out into the street to think of something to do. They walked and that was something. When she got to her bar she changed her shoes and they walked to the edge of town in the cool night. They took a pedicab back to his hotel. They took a shower and made love into sleep until the phone rang to wake him up. He put on his uniform and went back to the army wondering what would be so wrong if he married a whore.

That night when we went back to my hotel she was very drunk. We stumbled, and I half-carried her down the hallway. There was someone stationed at a desk by the elevator. I looked back at him and saw him starting to get up as if he thought I had abducted some sweet young thing. I also saw him sit back down in the same instant. All the GIs must have been on that floor.

She flopped down on the bed and was fast asleep. I stood there for a while looking at her. I sighed, thinking about spinning wheels in the mud. I lay down beside her and went fast asleep. The next day she took me to a place far from the city. There were no other tourists or anyone except the people who lived there. We were near the ocean and there were workboats on moorings out on the water. As we meandered under the trees a child ran up to us with a well-worn leather coat in his hands. He spoke in Chinese and she said he was insisting I wear the jacket. I asked her, "Does he want to give it to me?"

"No," she said, "he just wants you to wear it while you are here. He wants to see an American wear the jacket."

I wore the jacket the whole time I was there. It fit perfectly.

We walked around, and after that we sat outside at a small round table drinking hot Chinese tea. We sat close to each other. The same boy came over with a camera in his hand and asked her something in Chinese. She said to me that the boy wanted to take a picture of us. She said I could keep the picture, but it would cost some money. She bargained with the child. He took our photograph, and I stuck the picture in my shirt pocket.

When we left that place the boy made sure he got his coat. It was late in the afternoon when we got back to Taipei. She turned and faced me. She said she had to get her hair done. She asked me for some money to get her hair done. I said, "What?" She repeated, looking down now and again, that she needed some money to get her hair done. I gave her some and she left.

I went back to the hotel and banged on my friend's door. He was busy and didn't want to be bothered. I went to my room and in a short while was back on the street again. I was with the next girl the rest of the time I was in Taiwan, which was two days and a night, not counting the night I had to leave. The night I had to leave she sat with me in a taxicab at the processing center until the last minute. She never asked me for money to get her hair done. When I got back to Vietnam she wrote me a letter that said among other things that I "was a nice men." I never wrote back.

She showed me many things in that country. She showed me a classroom where girls were taught English to be companions for the GIs. I asked her, "Why do so many pretty girls want to be companions for GIs?" She said she grew up far away from the city, and always wanted to live in Taipei. She said the older she got the more she realized how easy it would be for her to live in Taipei.

When it was dark outside but still early in the night that girl took me where there were many Chinese people who didn't see many tourists. We walked through a wide pedestrian tunnel several hundred feet long. It was over twenty feet wide. There were bright neon lights inside and people sitting against the wall. There were young Chinese men standing in a group, talking among themselves. The ones standing stopped talking and looked at us when we went past. There were people busily walking both ways in the tunnel. I was the only Westerner. When they stopped talking and looked at us she looked down at the ground and started to walk faster. She was afraid of them. I walked faster also.

When we came out in the night we went a short way to a busy little area with many shops with bare lightbulbs hanging from long wires. We walked into a restaurant and she talked to a man behind a high glass counter. Inside the counter there was a bed of crushed ice and in one place on the ice there was a whole fish over a foot long. They were talking about the fish. I wondered what she was saying, because the conversation went on and on. I paid. He reached in, got the fish, and put it in boiling water. We went and sat down with some tea at a small square table against a wall. Moments later the man came out from behind the counter with the boiled fish on a round piece of wood. He also had two sets of chopsticks. That was the first time I had seen or used chopsticks in China. She showed me the best way to hold them. We didn't have plates or sauce or salt or pepper or anything like that. Just the fish was there.

We scraped back the skin with chopsticks and ate the meat. She ate the fish's eye. She said that to her the fish's eye was one of the best parts. I said to my countrymen and me the fish's eyes, and for that matter its whole head gets wrapped in yesterday's newspaper with the rest of its guts and thrown out. She laughed beautifully, and I said, "It is nice to know not everyone is the same when it comes to eating." She didn't eat the other eye, and we didn't go back the same way. We did other things that night and had a very nice time.

The next day a taxicab drove us down the coast. Across the water in the fog was Mainland China. We traveled on a paved two-lane road. There was thick woodland on one side. On both sides there were no other structures, except every several thousand feet on the ocean side there was a bunker. An overhead wire went from one bunker to the next. Over and over I pointed to the wire. I said it was the same wire we used. I knew its military nomenclature. I was startled to see that same wire there. I couldn't believe that it was there. When I first saw it I thought some children used it to talk between tree houses. When the next bunker went past I looked for the wire again and there it was. It was the same wire that we were trained to string all over the place. I kept talking about it in amazement. She said something to the driver, and we turned inland on the next road. I should have kept my mouth shut and enjoyed the scenery. She was trying to show me a good time.

We turned back to the coast and came to a beautiful place where a hilly peninsula jutted out into the sea. We got out of the cab and walked out on the peninsula. It was a park with paved pathways. We came upon some Chinese teenage girls going the other way on the path. They were dressed the same in Chinese clothes. They were schoolgirls. We stopped, facing each other. One of them said something and they giggled. They looked away and a few of them put their hands over their mouths. I wondered if they said something unkind, because she shot back sternly in Chinese. They put on straight faces and walked past in a hurry.

We stopped once more at a hilly place. Around one hill there were several brightly painted Chinese sailing boats on the ocean.

When we got back to Taipei she showed me where she lived. She said she lived with an older relative, but there was no one else there when she showed it to me. The windows were closed. They blocked out most of the light. They were more like shutters than windows. The room was dimly lit by sunlight that came through the closed shutters. She didn't turn on any lights. I didn't see any electric lights. The furniture and walls were unpainted wood. It was a real Chinese apartment in Taipei.

It was late in the afternoon by then. We stayed together when I got my belongings out of the hotel. We had supper together, and we went to the army processing center. She sat very close to me in the cab. We didn't talk much. I went back to Vietnam that evening.

Soon after I got back to Vietnam one of our Chinook helicopters crashed and burned. It had just refueled at the company's POL area near the perimeter. It was leaving the POL area at about three hundred feet when it started to go down. The word was that a sniper from somebody's window outside the perimeter had caused the crash. The pilot, copilot, crew chief, and door gunner were killed. The pilot was my immediate boss at the officers' club. He was the new warrant officer, and in the other seat was another new W-1 warrant officer whom I didn't know very well. All anyone ever said about him beside the fact he was dead was that he loved his wife. He talked about her all the time. The W-1 who was my boss wanted to do his time in the army and get out. He told me he signed up to fly helicopters because he qualified. The Twenty-fifth Infantry Division maintained the perimeter. After the crash they removed the position the sniper used. I could hear a track vehicle equipped with "twin-forties" banging away for a long time. Twin-forties were two mobile forty-millimeter cannons.

Before the W-1 warrant officer was killed he would have days when he didn't fly. On some of those days he would schedule trips to Saigon to get officers' club supplies. I would go with him so in the event he couldn't go I would know how it was done. He would requisition a jeep. One of the sorties for a Chinook that day would be a trip to Saigon. The ramp at the aft end of the helicopter would lower, and the jeep would be driven on board. The helicopter would put us down at Tan Son Nhat near Saigon. We would drive around front and wave off the pilots; they pulled pitch and were gone.

The liquor supply was at Ton Son Nhat. We always went into

the city of Saigon first, because we learned if we parked the jeep in Saigon, even for a moment, everything would be removed. Tire irons, jacks, anything that wasn't bolted down would be taken. Saigon was a huge city with crowded streets.

The first time we were in Saigon we bought a sack of about a thousand coin-size metal blanks to operate a jukebox at our officers' club. A Korean company run by Koreans supplied all the jukeboxes in Vietnam. At another place we got out of the jeep and I put the bag of blanks in a compartment under the seat. When we came back to the jeep a few minutes later the bag was gone. They were gold in color. They had no inscription on them. They could only work in a machine of some sort that took quarters. The person who took them probably made earrings out of them and is rich and famous today.

A person who wanted to play songs on the jukebox bought the blanks at the bar with MPC. About once every few weeks a Korean would come into our officers' club. He unlocked the jukebox to collect blanks and exchange records. He thought he was the only one who could open the thing, but he wasn't. The CO opened it all the time by jerking up on the lid. He would then play any records he wanted for free. By the time I left a W-1 was authorized to open the jukebox to play a record for free. The CO even told me to ask the man to get a new needle because he thought the one on the machine was worn out. Every time the Korean man came, unlocked the machine, and saw only four or five blanks he stood there looking severely puzzled. When I told him we needed a new needle he looked at me in utter disbelief. It wasn't my place to tell him we were getting into the machine all the time. The CO operated like the NCO in basic training who told us he wanted us to be honest, but there was nothing wrong with a good plan.

Another time getting supplies in Saigon there was a Vietnamese man walking down the street with solid brass bells hanging from his shoulders. The bells rang as he walked. They were the same size, about ten inches high and ten inches wide at the bottom. We drove the jeep over to where he was, and I asked him how much he wanted for a bell. I gave him the money. It was heavy. I brought it home and gave it to my parents. They used it as a doorbell. Now I have it in a building where my wife and I have a mailbox business. When it was a doorbell a faded card next to it said: PLEASE RING BELL. Every year wasps made a nest up inside the bell. It unnerved most people when they rang the bell. They ran away fast as they could. Now it hangs from a long chain in the shop. No one rings it except me to hear it ring.

There was a creek that went through Tan Son Nhat. I was driving the jeep. We stopped and looked. It was muddy water that looked to be a foot deep. It would be a shortcut to go across the stream. After going a few feet in the water the front wheels suddenly dropped like there was an underwater ditch. The jeep couldn't backup. On the other side there was a crane with a boom long enough to reach across the water. I tried to fire it up. My plan was to lift the jeep out of the water. I couldn't start it, and it is a good thing I couldn't. When I was fooling with the buttons inside the crane the W-1 was sitting in the jeep with his feet against the dashboard. The footwells were underwater. He looked like a general sitting in that jeep with sunglasses on his face. The sight of him in that jeep full of water and me in that crane made both of us laugh. Someone pulled us out, and the W-1 called a Chinook. Soon the Chinook arrived. The crew chief drove the jeep inside, tied it down, and we flew back to Cu Chi.

The XO assigned to our company was a major in rank, and he was responsible for the aircraft. How well he did his job depended on the number of aircraft that were available each day. Various parts on the helicopter had to be replaced after a certain number of hours. The helicopter wasn't available to fly during that time.

When a new XO came to our unit he and the CO sat by themselves at the bar to talk in the middle of the afternoon. I was behind the bar. The new XO was concerned because very soon he knew he would have low aircraft availability. The former XO had made his work look good by having very high aircraft availability during his last few months. He accomplished this by staggering aircraft in such a way that scheduled maintenance would not be due while he was there. His record would show that when he was responsible many helicopters were available to fly missions each day and as soon as he left there was low availability. On the surface the former XO's record would show he had high aircraft availability compared to the new XO's low aircraft availability.

Battalion would then put a favorable report in the former XO's personnel file increasing his chances of being promoted to the rank of lieutenant colonel.

The new XO was concerned that Battalion would think he wasn't doing his job. His aircraft availability numbers would be low. That afternoon at the bar the CO was being made aware of this situation.

During the former XO's tour of duty there was a fight in the officers' club between the CO and a husky American civilian who was assigned to the area by a company contracted by the U.S. government to engineer, design, and build things. It wasn't much of a fight. The civilian immediately went down on the floor, covered his face, and assumed a fetal position. He was crying.

It was just a matter of time before the CO got in a fight with him. All it took was a couple of drinks and a couple of words. The place was not big enough for both of them. The civilian never came back.

The XO was laughing at the hulking civilian crying on the floor. The CO was trying to connect with a punch. I suppose there was a look of disgust on my face as I looked at the XO. For sure the civilian's response was unusual, but for a high-ranking officer to laugh at that was more unusual. While the XO was busy laughing he glanced up off the floor at me and then back down to the floor where the CO was still unsuccessfully trying to punch the civilian in the face. The XO's eyes shot back up to mine, and for a second he stopped laughing like something else was on his mind. Then he looked back down and resumed laughing. After that day he made it very apparent he didn't like me. At least once that I am aware of he tried to have the CO remove me, but it didn't happen.

Earlier that year three lieutenants came into the officers' club. It was when the 101st came to town, and those lieutenants were from that outfit. The 101st was at Cu Chi about a week, but their officers appeared at our club only once. They stood at the middle of the bar and loudly had a good time like it was a holiday. Several other pilots from our unit were partying with them.

The bar didn't go all the way across the room. At one end, four feet from the wall, it went ninety degrees and extended toward the back wall. Between the wall and the outside of the bar there was a passageway to the storeroom behind the bar. On that end were a few seats. The CO was in one of them talking to no one. From where he sat he could see the bar from the bartender's side. Often the CO looked long and hard at the lieutenants. It was obvious he didn't like their being there in what he considered his officers' club. They must have picked up on how the CO felt. They left. The CO was a major.

Another time two of our pilots had the day off. They were sitting at the bar. It was late afternoon. They were the only ones there. They played worn-out records on the jukebox. They talked and complained how the CO took himself off flight status when there were hotter than usual Landing Zones (LZ's).

The Chinook was a big cumbersome $5 million helicopter. Compared to a Huey it was a sitting duck. Sorties for the Chinook didn't require it to fly into hot LZs. So an LZ that was considered relatively routine by an infantryman might be a hot LZ as far as a Chinook driver was concerned. Over a one- or two-week period the Chinook sorties involved flying in and out of areas where it was highly possible that the helicopter or anyone in it would take a hit.

The W-3 warrant officer who first interviewed me at the officers' club came in one afternoon after flying and belted down a shot of corn liquor. Then he did another one. He said a rifle bullet had come right up through the seat between his legs and ripped his pants. It was a bad day at the office for him. He looked down between his legs, I suppose to see if the booze was running out.

In the mess hall that week I heard from a door gunner who manned an M-60 machine gun on the left side that a stray bullet hit his flak jacket. He said it hit hard and if the crew chief wasn't in his way on the other side he would have fallen out.

The officers' club was air-conditioned. There was a self-contained refrigeration unit on the outside wall of the building. It was to be installed on a walk-in freezer, but with slight modifications it served well as an air conditioner.

The officers' club was a small club. The building was about 35 by 75 feet. On one side it had a screened-in area twenty-five feet square. Not counting the screened-in area, the club was divided into three rooms. One room had the bar and jukebox. It was about ten feet deep, and the width of the building. The second room was an unfinished storeroom behind the bar. It was eight feet deep, and it extended the width of the building also. The storeroom had an outside door that led to a bunker.

The third room was the largest area. It was separated from the bar by a wooden partition. On each side of the partition there was a wide floor-to-ceiling opening.

The floor had gray square linoleum tiles stuck to a concrete slab. The ceiling was eight feet from the floor. It consisted of textured white pieces one foot square. Above the ceiling, thirty wood trusses held up the roof and the ceiling. The roof was sheet metal. It sloped down in two directions to the sides. There were no gutters.

The main entrance into the building was through the screened area. Then a second door led into the largest of the three rooms. The refrigeration unit that served as an air conditioner was attached to the wall at the far end of that room. I turned it on when I opened the club at 1400 hours (2:00 P.M.) hours and turned it off when I closed the club at 0200 hours (2:00 A.M.), seven days a week. Pilots who were there when I closed the place didn't have to fly the next day.

Very soon after the air conditioner was functioning I realized cool air didn't reach the bar area. I found enough 1-by-12-inch pine boards and fastened them together to make a square air duct. It began at the refrigeration unit. It went straight up from the source of cold air through the ceiling. It made a ninety-degree turn and extended practically the length of the building to a position over the bar where it made another ninety-degree turn back through the ceiling. Then the bar area got plenty of cool air.

A civilian technical representative (tech rep) who worked for the American company that made our helicopters was assigned to our unit. His function was to help the helicopter maintenance people with problems they couldn't solve. He was a familiar face in our officers' club.

Shortly after the air conditioner was operational and the ductwork was completed he looked at the opening in the ceiling above the bar and asked me what it was. I said the bogeyman lived up there. The tech rep was standing at the bar with the battalion doctor, who was a black man. When I said that, the tech rep looked down into his beer like he was embarrassed. Then he looked at me and asked me what the bogeyman was. I walked over to where they were and for the first time thought maybe I didn't know. I said from behind the bar, "The bogeyman is like Boo Radley in the book. When I was a child my uncle would tie up me and my sister and leave saying the bogeyman was going to get us." Then I told him what the opening in the ceiling really was.

After a while the doctor left and the tech rep called me over to where he was at the bar. He said the reason he questioned me the way he did was because he thought the bogeyman was another way of saying a black person. He said I shouldn't say something like that in front of the doctor.

It was after that I got genital herpes, although I didn't know it by that name until years later. It was the result of my loose conduct in and around Saigon. I made several trips to Bien Hoa. The longest helicopter ride I ever made was to a place called Vung Tau, which really was by the sea. Several of us used to say "Cu Chi by the sea" because it rhymed, but in reality the sea was not even close. I was told Vung Tau was the most beautiful place in all Vietnam. In Vung Tau there was a great big sandy beach. The wide ocean was out front, and on land there were no tall buildings. It didn't look like the modern world was there yet.

When I got genital herpes in Vietnam there was a small sore under the foreskin on my penis. I went to the infirmary to see the battalion doctor. He walked up, looked at it, and in the same moment turned around and walked away. He had his face turned up toward the ceiling. He didn't say much of anything. He gave me some white ointment to put on the sore and I left.

Thereafter every three months or so I would get a sore in the same area. Then twenty-six years later when I had a near-death motorcycle crash and was in the hospital three and a half months the herpes went away. That was five years ago. I haven't had a herpes sore since. Recently I asked a doctor if there was a medical explanation. He said there was no medical explanation. I told him the length of the time I was in the hospital and the situation in general. I didn't say I had learned to fly right since then. He said it probably didn't reoccur because I had been through enough.

A few months earlier I asked another doctor who specializes in public health and communicable diseases that same question and she said she had never heard of that happening.

Right after I got back from R & R, I became painfully aware that I had gonorrhea. The cure I received then was a series of penicillin injections. The government in Taiwan required the girls to go to a health facility every so often and get injections to prevent venereal disease. One apparently didn't go.

I got gonorrhea once more in my life a year later in the United States. I never was around any prostitutes in this country. The girl I got it from was the last person I would think had that bug. The cure then was one big penicillin injection. The doctor asked me if I was in a marching band.

There were American nurses in Vietnam. They were treated very well by all the menfolk in the area. I seldom saw them open any doors for themselves, and they never stepped in any mud puddles. They, or any one of them, seldom came to the officers' club. One time one nurse did. She was there and the CO instructed me to escort her to the officers' latrine. I was to stand outside as a sort of sentry, and then when she had done her thing I was to walk her back to the officers' club. After a while I heard the door open and I started walking back. I couldn't see her. It was night. We were on a boardwalk that was built on the mud between the officers' hutches and the latrine. She knew my name and she said my name. I stopped and turned around and faced in the direction of her voice. She said it again and I could tell she was standing still. I said, "What?" And she said nothing. Then she said my name again like she might fall off the boardwalk. I went back to get her, and we marched to the officers' club.

That night when I was talking to her from the other side of the bar she told me her name and that her father was a car salesman in California. I wondered why she came to Vietnam, but I didn't ask that question. I thought she should go back home as soon as possible. She didn't seem very happy. She didn't have a very high opinion of herself. She thought of herself as a living body. Nurses could leave when they wanted to leave.

Back in our sleeping area the other 36K20 person had a small plump pet dog. Another person who ate maraschino cherries with us had a dog the same size. He was in helicopter maintenance and slept in another building.

When the 36K20 person had night duty on the switchboard he slept during the day. I asked him why he taped up the dog's legs and mouth and put him on a shelf. He replied that he wanted to get the dog on the same cycle as him. The dog was on the shelf while the 36K20 person was sleeping and was with him when he had switchboard duty. As I was getting dressed one morning he was there. I said it was sick the way he treated that dog. I said there was enough sickness in the world without his having to add to it. He taped up his dog a while longer, but then he told me that he and the other person took their dogs to the perimeter and let them go. He said when the two dogs were a short distance away they looked back like they were going to return. At that point the person who slept in the other building grabbed the M-16 from the 36K20 person who was telling me this story and started shooting at the two dogs. The dogs must have heard the bullets whizzing over their heads, because he said they turned and ran as fast as they could for cover.

Some of us had small electric fans that we purchased from the PX. The fans blew air on us while we were sleeping. My friend, the same 36K20 person, called those fans matchbox fans. When I was unpacking my "whole baggage" in Cincinnati, Ohio, I looked at the fan closer than usual and the words were written on the base of the fan: "Love get out of Vietnam." I don't know who wrote that or when, but there it was.

When it was my time to leave Vietnam we were sent to Saigon and crammed in a holding area or processing area. A sergeant explained to us the benefits available to us if we were being discharged from the army. One of the teletype operators told me, "The only way to benefit from the army is to get out of it." The sergeant explained a piece of legislation passed by the United States government called the GI Bill. He said how it provided all sorts of educational benefits. Apparently my friend was right.

We were in the holding area for one night. It was like a jail, with concertina wire and high fences around the entire area. I suppose it was to prevent anyone's getting loose in town.

The next day we boarded an unmarked airplane that was fitted inside like a civilian passenger plane. It flew us home to the

United States. The first stop was in Anchorage, Alaska. We went inside while the plane was being refueled. It was very late at night and there were some older ladies sitting at a table providing coffee to anyone and everyone as we came into the terminal from the plane. They were not government employees. We were going home from Vietnam, and that was the first time we touched American soil. They were there to welcome us home, but everyone walked by with sleep in their eyes. The ones who took some coffee didn't even see them.

It reminded me of when I was in Vietnam. A grade school class from somewhere in the middle of the United States sent us a package containing things they thought we would need. One of the items was a can of Band-Aids. I carried one of those Band-Aids with me everywhere. If I got shot I was going to put the Band-Aid over the bullet hole. They must have been very sweet little children to send those things.

When I got back to the United States several of us found ourselves discharged from the army, standing in a commercial airport waiting for airplanes traveling in different directions to take us home. I remember putting on my civilian clothes and how good it felt to be out of the army now. All I had in the way of luggage was what we called an AWOL bag. When I was changing in the airport men's room, my class-A uniform wouldn't fit in the little bag, so I put it in the trash can. I was sure I was never going to wear it again in a hometown parade or anywhere. There was a high-ranking army sergeant in the airport men's room. I wondered if I was going to have to explain myself to him, but he didn't say anything to me. Then I called my parents to say I was in the United States and that my plane arrived in Cincinnati at such and such a time. My mother answered the phone and I could hear her crying. I wondered if she thought I was an anti-Communist warrior.

5

A Time to Read

When I got home I sat on a stool at the counter in the kitchen drinking one glass of cold milk after another. My mother and father sat quietly at the kitchen table while I talked and talked about nothing. They must have thought it strange how thirsty I was, but they didn't say anything about my behavior. I was glad to be home. One of my younger sisters was there sitting at the kitchen table also. I started to feel slightly self-conscious, because I was doing all the talking. Silence would have been awkward. The radio teletype operator who read books told me, "Silence is a trick."

During the few days I was home a carload of friends invited me to go swimming. The husband and wife who owned the pool were my parents' age. They had told one of the people in the car they could go swimming whenever they wanted. If I wanted to go with them I had to drop everything right now and get in the car.

It was a hot day at the end of summer. I didn't like swimming very much, but the idea of jumping in some cool water sounded nice. I told them to hold on a minute and ran to get a towel and bathing suit. I had black engine grime on my hands. I washed them quickly.

I knew the pool was in a wooded area not in sight of their house, but when we got there the husband, wife, and one son from San Francisco were sitting by the shallow end. If I had known they would be there I would not have gone. The one who was invited to swim anytime said hello politely. They had already been swimming and were sitting in bathing suits, talking, and watching us. Even though I washed my hands, they looked greasy enough to leave an oil slick on the water. I mostly went underwater. I came up in the shallow end after going underwater from the deep end. I stood up, and there they were. The lady said she heard I was in Vietnam. I said, "Yes I was."

She said, "Good for you."

I said, "It was good for some." I felt awkward standing there. I wanted to be able to breathe underwater and never come up. They were still there when we left.

I wanted to read more books. One book told about an author who came to the words in the Bible that said: ". . . there once was a time in Israel when everyone did what was right in their own eyes . . ." He got up and paced around the floor smoking cigarettes wondering when that time was. He wrote that when he lived in New York City the company he worked for was fornicating the country. He didn't use that word but a much shorter word beginning with *f*. He followed that example and started fornicating one of the secretaries. It sounded like Vietnam.

I saved most of my army money so I didn't have to work someplace in order to earn more money. I didn't want to sit around home in a fog. I made plans to go to New York City, where they had a very complete library on 42d Street. I had a list of books I wanted to read. The list started with old books like *The Decameron* and *Gargantua* and *Pantagruel*. Dostoevsky, the complete works, was on the list. There were many unheard of books like one named *The Unavailing of Timbuktu*. It was subtitled, *The First White Man to See Timbuktu*. Every book I wanted to read was in that library. For almost a year I went down there every afternoon and read. It was the most reading I have ever done or will probably ever do.

In the mornings I would wake up early and write. That work was eventually named *The Half Book*. The sequel would have simply been called *The Other Half*. It was half a book because that is how far I was when I had a stark realization that in a mechanized world would I be educated? They weren't far from mechanizing the trigger finger. If I was not part of the main event I would be out on the street. If Abraham Lincoln went to a job interview and said he was self-educated would it mean anything?

Sometimes the only person I would talk to all day long was the librarian. I lived like a monk. After a year I left New York City. Jumping into a beehive of activity seemed appealing to me.

I went back to Ohio and enrolled in Ohio State University on the GI Bill.

There I came to know formal education as advanced potty training. That provoking idea was put forth by a discontented college student in New York City. Everything else seemed to reverberate what the song said. "We want the world and we want it now." It was like he and all the others were standing on a soapbox. They were very much like the people with whom they had a problem. One of them always wore a red plaid shirt.

When I left New York my half book and everything I wrote that year went into a very expensive, lockable, leather briefcase that my grandmother gave me. She figured I would need it soon enough to carry papers to the office. Shortly before I got married someone broke into the house where I lived. The locked brief case probably looked like it was full of money. It was taken, and most of the other things stolen used electricity.

When I went to New York City to read and write I went there first to find an apartment. I took a bus. I got a room at the local YMCA. It was the most inexpensive room in town. Each day I looked in the newspaper at the listings of apartments. I mostly looked in lower Manhattan, but after two or three days I found a cold water flat in a rent-controlled three-story brownstone building on West 69th Street half a block from Central Park.

The Frenchman who owned the building was working on the front door when I got there. We talked a while. He was not far removed from France. He said there was an old French saying: "When you plant a potato you get a potato; when you plant a carrot you get a carrot." He showed me the apartment he had for rent on the third floor. It was one room with a bathroom down the hall. The third floor was the top floor. There were two other apartments on that floor. He said he would be around each week to collect the rent. He asked me what I was doing. I told him I was going to write a book and read in the afternoon. He laughed and said he would like to write a book. Rent-controlled meant the building was older and the amount of rent had limits. I paid $17.50 each week.

I paid him for the first week and went back to Cincinnati to get my belongings. An agency that delivered cars to places in the United States advertised for drivers. I delivered a car to New

York City for them. In exchange, I could use that car to move my things and myself. The agency paid for all the oil and gas and turnpike tolls.

There were no places to park when I got there. I parked beside another car that was parked. I had to carry my things up three flights of stairs. I came back down after one trip and a policeman was writing me a parking ticket. I was getting the full flavor of New York City. I didn't have the energy to rant and rave like he was an umpire. I calmly asked him if it was necessary for him to give me a ticket considering my circumstances. He finished writing the ticket and put it under the windshield wiper of the car. He wasn't even convinced I was the driver. He was good at doing what he was doing. He was ignoring me. I asked him if he practiced that routine in the bathroom mirror each morning. He cracked a grin, but it would be more in character if he said, "Does not compute." I settled down to a routine myself.

On the floor where my apartment was there were two other people who I never talked to beyond saying hello in passing. One of them had a tiny apartment that was just big enough for a small bed and bureau. He went to work each afternoon in a tuxedo looking absolutely immaculate. He grew up in France and came to this country fifteen or twenty years earlier. He worked in a French restaurant where he supervised the dining room. Soon after I got to New York he went back to France. He wanted to open his own restaurant in Paris. He saved every penny. When he was gone the man who owned the building said the Frenchman had lived in that room all the years he was here.

In the other apartment was a voice student from Montreal, Canada. Her apartment was probably like mine. In my apartment, the main room was about twenty feet square. There was a kitchenette with plenty of cockroaches that were always hungry, and there was a closet. Nobody talked to anybody else in that building and I didn't break any rules. "Merge yourself with your surroundings and move along with it." That is what Lao-tzu said, and it is what I did.

My mother's half-brother was in the city and he came to visit me. He was like an older brother to me. He taught me to swim. He gave me a single-shot 410 shotgun and a single-shot bolt action .22 when I was twelve. He taught me about hunting and gun safety. He said I should have single-shot guns first because if I got a semi-automatic gun later, I would have learned to make each shot count.

In 1968 the U.S. Government had a period of grace that allowed everyone to register illegal firearms. He called me up in New York City from Virginia where he lived and told me about the law and how it allowed me to register the AK-47 I brought back from Vietnam.

When he came to see me we were in my apartment talking. He let go of a very loud, robust laugh. He woke up the voice student next door. We could hear her heels hitting the floor as she stomped barefoot across the floor of her apartment. He had broken one of the rules of engagement in that building and probably in the whole city.

We left my apartment and went around the corner to a neighborhood bar and grill on Columbus Avenue. When we came up to the door he stopped and said he would buy lunch at another place. He was all dressed up as the well-to-do out-of-towner he was. He went to the curb and the first cab streamed on past. I said to him, "Wouldn't it be funny to have an RPG Rocket and blow that cab out of the water." He must have thought I meant it, because he looked at me very seriously and said I couldn't do that anymore. An RPG rocket was a Russian-made handheld armor-piercing self-propelled device that could go through several feet of concrete before it exploded. It was a much-feared, seldom-used weapon available to the other side. The nearest thing we had to that was the bazooka, and I never saw one of those.

Eventually he got a taxicab and we went across town to a restaurant off Fifth Avenue that was known as one of the best places in that city to get fresh fish. I had been there shortly before with my grandmother when she was in town. She was also his mother. The waiters all looked like the Frenchman in the building where I lived. When I ate there with my grandmother she ordered what she termed a conversational wine.

Soon winter came. It snowed one night and in the early-morning daylight there was a thick covering of snow over everything just like in the woods. To me, the way I lived in New York City was just like being in the woods. I was very alone, but I was not lonely.

I walked a short distance into Central Park. The branches were covered. Nature came there in a big way that night. No other person was in the park. Over treetops I could see tall buildings where millions of people were probably asleep or they were waiting for the city crews to clear away the snow with their mechanical attachments.

I followed the outline of the walkway. I knew it went in a mostly straight direction across the park. Along the way, to one side, there was a large clearing. The trees along the far edge of the clearing gave it no regular shape. I walked off the path and plowed my feet through the snow. When I got near the trees I looked around. No one else was outside. I lay on my back and opened and closed my legs in the snow. Then I moved my arms away from my sides until my hands touched over my head. I stood up. I had made an angel the way I used to do. As I started to walk back across the open field I could see a bundled-up person on the path standing there, watching me. I stopped and stood there. We looked at each other in the distance. After a moment that person resumed walking busily across the park toward the West Side.

My grandparents on my mother's side were in town. They were my mother's stepfather, the wealthy industrialist, and his wife, who was my actual grandmother. Even though they lived in Cincinnati they kept an apartment in New York City. He kept his money in a bank in New York. He liked the privacy. She would go to New York City to buy a pair of shoes or to see a show.

One of the times they were both in New York she called me up and invited me to dinner in their apartment. I wore a coat and tie. The doorman was expecting me. He announced over an electronic device that I had entered the building. Another person who operated the elevator took me to their door. When I was in their apartment I felt comfortable. I called my mother's stepfather my grandfather. He knew what he could do and what he could not do. His word was binding. He probably had lawyers and contracts, but someone who knew him would realize those things were not necessary. I could understand why he did very well in business.

My grandmother was amazing as always. She had small individual-size steaks for dinner. She showed me how to cook them on very high heat in a frying pan without using any oil. She used salt to keep them from sticking to the skillet. She told me that they used to have a cattle ranch in Texas and that was where she learned to cook steaks that way. She said the people who lived there liked tough steaks.

He sat in a bigger room with crackers and a martini. He was talking with another person whom I had not met. When I came into the room he introduced us, and told me to fix myself something to drink as if I had seen him last week. He pointed to a tray of liquor bottles. Bourbon was my flavor. The warrant officers who knew what they were doing drank bourbon. I got some and sat down.

He asked me what I was doing. I tried to sound important. I said I was writing a book and reading in the library every day. As soon as I said those words I realized how unimportant it sounded. He looked at me directly and said many newspapers were slanted. He said a newspaper gets slanted when the publisher lets it be known how he feels about an issue. A reporter who tries to curry the publisher's favor will have that bias.

He asked me about Vietnam. I told him that water sports were big over there. He was amused. I said I didn't have anything to say about that place except that I was there for one year. My grandmother had come into the room. She reminded me that I had written them that it was "pithy."

He told me about what he termed "my Vietnam." He said years before there was no dividing line between the North and South. He said he was in a car speeding along between Hanoi and Saigon. He said they ran over another person. My grandfather was in his twenties at the time. When he finished college his father sent him around the world, and that is why he was in that car. It sounded as if he was swept up in the whole event. He said that when he got to Saigon he inquired of the Vietnamese driver how the person was who they ran over and was told that person was dead. He then repeated the words, "That was my Vietnam."

I said, "Very little has changed since then."

He smiled into his drink and after a moment started talking with the other person.

Two years later in a college creative writing class I wrote a paper titled "My Vietnam." Could a place be different for two people and be the same place?

When dinner was over and coffee was over I left. I walked back to my apartment. I went up Fifth Avenue, across to Central Park West, and up to 69th Street. It wasn't very late and I wanted time to think about them.

There was a large complex fairly near where I lived that was a center for the performing arts. There was also a library at that place where recorded performances were cataloged and stored. A person could sit in a booth and listen to one of those recordings. Some afternoons I would do that instead of reading in the 42d Street library.

There were also many theater performances of mostly modern plays in that city. I walked to and from those plays. One evening I saw a play near Times Square and was walking back to my apartment. I walked up Broadway. It turned into Columbus Avenue.

I was walking along in the bright lights of the theater district. There were many people on the sidewalk going in both directions. I heard a voice very clearly and it said, "Speak to me." I looked over to the side in the direction of the voice. It came from a girl on the sidewalk who was standing almost against the building. She was talking to me and looking at me through the other people who were walking past. I kept on walking like everyone else. I thought that was really a good line in that city. It sounded like a high-powered advertising slogan, and yet it came from a prostitute on the street. Was she a prostitute? I would have liked to talk to her about life in the big city, but would she be thinking the whole time that I wanted to pay her for sexual services? She probably wouldn't have wanted or expected any conversation. She probably thought I had some money and she wanted some. She probably was out there to get some money, and she was willing to destroy herself if that was what it took.

I thought about those words all the way up to 69th Street. The next morning I wrote a story called "Funerals from 25 Cents." It was a fictitious story. It had much conversation in it and an equal amount of Dostoevskian mind travel. She ended up sawed into pieces, stuffed into an overnight bag, and placed in a locked locker at the bus depot. The locker cost twenty-five cents.

The little room in my apartment that served as the kitchen

consisted of two gas burners and a sink. There were no major appliances. Next to the sink there was a freestanding bathtub. I never made anything in there.

All told there was about sixty seconds of running hot water. I pointed this out to the building owner when he was on his rounds collecting rent. He said he would turn it up. After that there was about sixty-two seconds of hot water. The building owner for the most part was European. The building was full of Europeans. No one else complained. One toilet and shower was on each floor. I never was in the shower very long. After sixty-two seconds the cold water made me gasp for breath.

One of my favorite things to eat was eggplant stew. I would chop up part of an eggplant, put it in the top of a double boiler, and add one can of beer. My grandmother gave me the double boiler for making soup. I seldom had soup, but it was perfect for stew. Recently my wife was away and I said to the children, "Do you want to have something that is really good to eat?" I should have rubbed my hands together like the Wicked Witch of the West. I told them when I was living in New York City I made this recipe all the time. I hadn't eaten it for many years. I cooked it for them and couldn't believe how awful it was. They agreed that it was awful. No one ate anything. I told them I was a very tough person in those days.

When there was good weather in the afternoon I would walk down Central Park West on my way to the library. I would walk as far as Central Park South, and near there I would get public transportation. On more than one day there was a raggedy sleepless-looking person standing on the corner. There were park benches nearby with people on them who looked like him. He stood away from the benches and held a large sign over his head. It said: REPENT, THE KINGDOM OF GOD IS AT HAND. He never looked at anyone. I walked past him several days in a row. I always thought he was insane, but now I am not so sure.

I seldom went out on the town. I stuck to my routine. My budget was tight so I didn't have extra money. Computer dating was a new concept. Two people would be matched up by computer. Theoretically, they would like each other. I received several names and telephone numbers. The list was based on a questionnaire I completed and returned. Twice I went on a computer date. The girls couldn't have been more different, and once I got a gun stuck in my face. That was not my date's fault. I must not have been specific enough on the questionnaire.

The first girl on the list and I conversed on the telephone a short while. She said emphatically I should meet her at midday in a famous art museum located beside Central Park on Fifth Avenue. I asked how I would recognize her and she said she would be standing beneath the Raphael painting. She wasn't a Russian spy. When I asked her if he did more than one painting she said there was only one in that place.

I asked a guard where the painting was. He told me and then followed me there. When I found her, everything I said seemed to be an insult to her. She was very proper. I couldn't get into the same mode as her. We looked at several paintings. After that we got some ice cream and said good-bye.

On the second computer date there were three of us. I talked to her on the phone, and later that week I went to pick her up. She wasn't ready. I sat in a main room talking to her roommate, who was the same age. She said they recently came from England to New York City because they had jobs here. She said they were secretaries and had been in New York a short while.

When the other girl was ready all three of us left together. We went to a section of the city called the East Village. We went to a large psychedelic place, which was a trend in those days. There was loud music and flashing lights. If I were more in control we would have left, because the music was so loud we couldn't talk. When I was in their apartment I liked their accents.

At one point I was standing in a group of people away from my dates. A person seemed to stick his head into the middle of the group and swivel it around several times, inquiring if anyone wanted to buy some "pot." I did not know that this individual fed off people who went in that place. They were mostly people who had not come to grips with the world around them. When they grew older ideas of love and peace died and seemed to vanish with them. It was said those people were naive. Now I wonder if people with heads that swivel are the reason it died.

We went outside where he said he would show me the marijuana. I asked him if he had any Vietnamese "weed." *Weed* was another word for marijuana. We went around to the other side of the block. It was a quiet residential street. I was sitting on a railing and he was standing between the street and me. We were talking about his bag of marijuana. He rolls a marijuana cigarette, commonly called a joint. Then along comes a person down the sidewalk from the left side. They seem surprised to see each other and that person stays with us. Soon after that another person comes down the sidewalk from the right side. They all act surprised to see one another. Now three people are standing facing me and I am standing against a railing facing them smoking a rolled-up marijuana cigarette. We talk a while. I said I have just come back from Vietnam and would like to get some marijuana like the stuff over there. Over the course of our conversation his friend who doesn't say much else interrupts three times with the same question. He says, "Were you in Vietnam?"

I was feeling very comfortable with these three people of the street. I took some money out and the other money in my wallet was a 100-dollar bill. I must not have been very discreet with my wallet, because after I put it back in my pocket the guy on the right side says in amazement, "That was a one-hundred-dollar bill." His friend on my left side said, "I saw it." The guy in the center was wearing a long overcoat and his hands were in his coat pockets. He stepped back and looked up and down both sides of the street. I was suspecting nothing. He then steps toward me, slams his closed hand under my chin, and says in a very firm voice, "Shuck it up." I looked down and he was pointing a small .22-caliber semi-automatic pistol up at my chin. I saw the end of the barrel. It was a real gun.

I brushed his hand away and walked down the sidewalk. The moment I moved, his two friends ran in different directions. They moved so swiftly, they seemed to disappear. I walked down to the corner. The person with the gun followed me. There were other people walking back and forth at the end of the block. I stopped and turned around. He looked back and noticed again that his two friends were gone. I was clutching his bag of marijuana in my hand. I still had it in my hand. I threw it in the gutter of the street. He said it wasn't a gun. He said it was a toy. I said, "Yeah, sure. Let's see the toy." He quickly went to pick up his marijuana. He took a small clear plastic bubble gum machine toy out of his pocket and said that was the gun. I told him he had a gun, and I blurted out that he had let me down. After I said that he looked even more remorseful that he hadn't been able to separate me from my money, I walked away from him.

I was distraught. I walked all the way from the East Village to 69th Street, which was a considerable distance. I was a third of the way there when I remembered the two English secretaries sipping their beers amid all the smoke and loud music. I hoped they had cab fare. I never saw them again, I wasn't going to turn around and go back there.

Later on I told my uncle about what happened. He knows much about guns. He said I could easily have been killed. He said the little .22 would do the job nicely. He said it wasn't worth getting killed in the streets of New York over $100. Of course I had to agree.

All the money I had, over $2,000 in cash, was in my apartment. I don't know why I had that $100 bill in my wallet that day. Usually, I never had that much money on me.

When I was walking up Fifth Avenue from the library one sunny cold day I went under an awning that extended from the front of a hotel to the curb. On the metal frame of the awning there were rows of infrared heat lamps that made it warm under the awning. When I was walking along the sidewalk and felt the sudden change from winter cold to the warmth of those heat lamps I stopped, looked up, and was going to stand there a moment to enjoy the heat. I wasn't in anyone's way, but a person hurried out of the hotel and yelled in Spanish and English for me to be on my way. Both his arms were outstretched, and he was moving the backs of his hands forward and backward as if he were shooing away a stray animal that wandered into his china shop. I moved on without saying anything. My old headmaster, who was a pretty good shot, said at least once a year every year I was in that school, "Science can tell you how, but it can't tell you why." Somehow that seemed to apply here. I wondered if he would think so.

When I left New York City I was ready to go. Reading books was getting me nowhere. It was like the time later in my life when I went to Yugoslavia and bicycled around for a month. At first I felt very content, but the longer I was there the more I became aware how little I would know until I learned the language. In New York City I realized how little I knew.

Over the years I had written several letters to the girl I saw years before at a boarding school dance. She had written as much. When I was in New York she was living 250 miles away at an all-girl collage. We got together one time in New York. I didn't spend much money when I was by myself, but when she came I got a big wad of money out of the steel box in my apartment. We had a fine time doing all sorts of things.

Several months later, when I left to move back to Markin Farm, I delivered a former New York City cab that had been painted blue. I was able to stop in the town where she went to college. We went to a place where there were hamburgers, fries, and beer. It seemed very often she got up, left, came back, and sat down. She told me much later that a boyfriend of hers had been moving along the wall in a crowd of people the whole time we were there. That was the place where they always went. I don't know why she didn't introduce us so we could all sit down and get dizzy. I suppose if he sat down with us, it would have been awkward. Would she leave with him or me? It wasn't her way to leave all by herself. I would have been somewhat tormented if she left with him. I suppose he would have been tormented if she left with me, but she did leave with me. Maybe it was the only place in town.

6

To Fly

I enrolled in Ohio State University. I had several months before I started. I went home to assemble an autogiro I bought when I was in the army. I saw it in boxes in a stall at Markin Farm when I got home from Vietnam but didn't put it together. It cost a third as much as an automobile. It was a one-seat aircraft that arrived in many packages. I set up a drill press and a workbench inside an unused concrete block building on Peterloon Farm. It was named the Apple Barn. Apples were processed in that building. At one time there were orchards everywhere. When the apple trees started to die no one planted new ones. No one harvested apples anymore. The building was not used.

An autogiro has a freewheeling rotor that is permanently set at zero pitch. It can't do vertical takeoffs and landings. It cannot hover like a helicopter. The spinning rotor is the wing. *Auto-rotation* describes how it flies. When a seed from a silver maple tree twirls to the ground, that is auto-rotation.

The engine on this aircraft turned a push propeller like an airboat. Propeller thrust gave it forward movement. A 72-horse-power two-cycle engine weighed nearly as many pounds as it generated horsepower. For that reason it was a very suitable engine. The U.S. military originally designed the engine for unmanned "drone" aircraft used in target practice. It was "remanufactured" with longer-life rod bearings and a few improvements that took into consideration it would be a significant part of a manned aircraft.

As it moved forward faster and faster the rotor would spin faster and faster. A person sitting in the driver's seat would change the entire plane of the spinning rotor with a handheld control lever. That created lift. There was rough movement on the ground. Then there was a transition to smoothness. When that change occurred I knew I was flying.

I had about ten hours of total flight time before I crashed the second time. I was like Goofy in the cartoon where Goofy is flipping through the pages of an instruction book as he is speeding down the runway about to leave the ground. The pages are blowing in the wind.

There was no experienced pilot advising me. I learned all I knew from the manual, however I didn't take it with me in flight. It was too windy.

The manual covered all the peculiarities of the aircraft. I understood "pilot induced osculation" and the importance of avoiding a zero gravity condition where the rotor had no load and the engine thrust would invert the aircraft with obvious results. I was aware of these things and many others, but the book didn't spell out the importance of avoiding areas where there were fixed objects on the ground I was preparing to leave.

My first crash happened on takeoff when the right wheel hooked on a pile of pipes in a new industrial park. I spun around and rolled gracefully into a large concrete drainage ditch thirty feet across. That incident destroyed a set of rotor blades. I was in that industrial park because it was after 6:00 A.M., and I had to leave the airport when it opened at 6:00 A.M. At the airport I flew the autogyro with power off like a glider. Some friends pulled it behind our farm jeep. I got the feel of rudder control. Then under its own power I went up and down the runway. I practiced nose wheel steering at slow speed. I had not flown yet, and it was at that point on my way home with the thing on a trailer behind me that I saw the nice wide, straight industrial park road going off to the right. There were no trees or overhead wires or buildings. It was a new development and I was going to fly out of there, or so I thought.

I had to cope with very little regulation. I built the autogiro myself and so it was classified by the Federal Aviation Administration (FAA) as an experimental aircraft. I applied and received an "N" number from the FAA. I requested the number N8300 and they gave me that number, which had very few digits compared to most N numbers. At some point I had to get an "airworthiness certificate." That required that I fly "around the flight pattern" of an airport while an FAA official verified that the thing could fly. Then there was a catch that I never had to deal with because I never got that far. The catch was that to fly for an airworthiness certification I had to be a licensed pilot, but to be a licensed pilot I had to fly a certified aircraft. Meanwhile, I flew out of a field at the back of Peterloon Farm. I was going to get properly licensed after I flew it several hours. I got new rotors and repaired other things. I was practicing "dead stick landings" in that field when for a second time the rotor blades and other things got destroyed. I almost got destroyed too. I gave it up after that day.

The first time I left the ground and went up in the sky I didn't realize I had mistakenly installed the wrong cheek plates. The craft was extremely out of balance. I had the glider cheek plates holding the gimbal head that attached the mast tube to the rotor. It didn't fly right, but it did fly. I was flying out of the little airport where I practiced in the early morning. As I left the ground I had to keep full throttle and the rotor all the way back. My forward movement in the air was very slow. I saw the people that came with me wave. I needed some more room so I kept going. I must have been going up significantly. After a short while I sat back and looked down at the runway. I was so high that it was a half an inch long. I did my first 180-degree turn and started to go down toward the airport.

The only instrument in the kit was a simple air speed indicator located up front by the tow hook. The book stressed the importance of not exceeding a certain air speed. I could tell when I got there because the entire aircraft started to shudder. After I felt that I started to look at the air speed indicator more often. When the little red ball said I was near maximum air speed (somewhere below 130 kilometers per hour) I moved the rotor back very carefully and the craft effectively slowed down.

It so happened I was making what helicopter pilots in Vietnam called a "short final." That was a steep approach to avoid bullets. I wasn't concerned with bullets. I should have been concerned with the dismal prospect of "auguring in," but that wasn't on my mind either.

An autogiro has to have a glide path. Theoretically, I could go around and make another attempt if things were not right.

The aircraft was descending a whole lot better than it went up. It seemed things were either up or down. Level flight seemed to be a very fine line between ascending and descending. I was going to land the first time.

I wanted to avoid gliding past the runway and flying through someone's picture window while they were having their morning coffee. On the other hand, I didn't want to make contact with the ground before I got to the runway. As I got closer the paved surface seemed nice and long. When I got past all the white lines I was going about as fast as an automobile on an expressway.

When a duck lands it glides and then "flares out" at the last moment before it touches the water. Rotor revolutions per minute (RPM) are reduced when flare out occurs. The manual emphasized the importance of being very close to the ground when rotor RPM drops or else being way up there. It takes several hundred feet to regain rotor RPM.

As I flew over the runway I made a series of small flare outs to reduce my forward speed. When I made my last flare out I was still too high and I had no rotor RPM left. I landed hard. The giroscopic effect of the whirling rotor kept the craft upright. The keel tube got bent. The nose wheel hit the ground hard.

Once I came to a stop on the airport apron I reached up and shut the engine off. When the rotor stopped spinning I unfastened my seat belt and stood up. I took my helmet off and looked at the bent tube. Several people I didn't know came up and said how great it looked and one person kept asking if that was really my first flight. He was a traffic reporter for a radio station. The helicopter he used for his job was at the airport. He went on and on about how terrific it looked. Then I showed him the bent keel tube and he changed his tune. In aviation circles they term my landing "a controlled crash."

I knew I had put the thing together with the wrong pair of cheek plates and I changed them. I installed a new tube. The aircraft manual had described a hang test whereby the craft is suspended by the "teeter bolt" and the measurement of degrees from the plum line says something. If I had done that test I would have known the wrong cheek plates were installed. I didn't do that test because I had center-punched and drilled each hole exactly. I thought the test was redundant which it was. I failed to learn beforehand that redundancy is a big part of aviation. When the W-1 I knew in Vietnam forgot something he would joke and say, "Mistakes like that get you killed in combat."

There was a television program by that name, *Combat.* When I was putting the autogiro together I went through the TV room at home and was horrified to see on television people being riddled with bullets. Some of my siblings were glued to the television watching that happen. It was pretend, but it still seemed obscene. As they watched their faces were expressionless. They were being anesthetized. I didn't say anything. It was me alone. I thought it must be OK since it was regular programming. Now I wonder if for the same reason a person in a $20 million piece of hardware has no problem dropping bombs on people?

The next time half-throttle was all that was necessary to maintain a level cruising speed. It was easy to fly. The pressurized fuel tank held enough gas to last one hour. It was red, the type made for outboard motors on boats.

The average amount of time I was in the air was half an hour. During those times I did mostly "contour" flying which means flying close to the ground. I flew higher when I went ten or fifteen miles from the place where I took off.

One bright sunny day there were white fluffy clouds in the sky. There weren't that many of them. One was here and one was there. One small cloud was all by itself. Considering all the clouds it was the smallest one. It was near. I had felt the turbulence in commercial airliners going through clouds, but this one was tiny. It was half as big as a football field. There was no wind. It was just floating up there all by itself. I wanted to go up there closer. I knew how Icarus felt.

I was in a field beside the autogiro eating lunch. I quickly finished my sandwich and carefully poured a can of gasoline into the gas tank. The engine had a magneto ignition. A while earlier I had taken a piece inside the magneto called the rotor to be "charged," which means it was remagnetized. That made the engine start easier. On the first or second turn of the propeller it started. There was no battery or starter motor. Those things were superfluous and heavy. I got in the driver's seat and buckled up for safety. A little gasoline engine got the main rotor spinning so less ground would be needed for takeoff. The whole mechanism was called the prerotator.

The kit came with wood rotors and instructions on how to glue them together (a person had to find their own glue). When I realized everything hung on that rotor, including me, I didn't want the last thing I ever saw to be my rotors coming unglued. I always had factory-made aluminum rotors. The set I had then was the second pair I had bought. They weren't inexpensive. I think they cost about half as much as everything else put together.

Once the main rotor blades got maximum speed from the prerotator I opened the throttle steadily until it was wide open. As the aircraft started to move forward the rotor blades spun even faster from the propeller blast (prop wash).

The push-type propeller was made of wood. It was bolted to a hub made of a high-strength steel alloy. I know it wasn't regular steel because I tried to enlarge the holes in it with a drill bit. I couldn't do it and had to take the hub to a machine shop. They had a difficult time getting it done. That was almost thirty years ago and I have never worked with steel that hard since.

The hub was fastened to a tapered spindle that stuck out the rear side of the engine case. The spindle was an extension of the crankshaft inside the engine. It turned very fast. The idea was to make the shaft turn.

There were connecting rods inside the engine that connected the crankshaft to four pistons. The pistons moved back and forth in a straight line and made the shaft going out the back of the engine spin. Reciprocating movement was converted into revolving movement. Those parts moved faster than the eye could see. The place of connection inside the engine, the journal on the crankshaft and the wrist pin on the other end of the connecting rod, had to be slippery and required constant lubrication. Mixing oil with the gasoline did this.

The aircraft consisted of primarily three square tubes named the keel tube, the axle tube, and the mast tube. I sat in a woven rope seat bolted to the front of the mast tube. The engine was bolted to the back of the mast tube.

After a short distance I moved the rotor nearly to the level position and it continued to spin faster. As the craft was being propelled forward I had to compensate for the engine torque with the left rudder pedal. Steering was done with the rudder pedals. Staying on the airstrip and traveling in a straight line was necessary for taking off.

Pegs on each side of the castoring nosewheel were used to steer the craft when positioning it for takeoff or when moving slowly on the ground after landing.

Very soon after the angle of the rotor was changed I was off the rough ground and into the smooth air. The field had no crops that year. Either soybeans or corn was planted one year or the other. Some years clover was planted because it replenished the soil by putting some nutrient back in the ground that the other crops took out.

My undefined airstrip in that field went in the same direction as the rows. The crop was gone. No-till farming was the practice then.

The short time I flew I stayed near open land in case the propeller stopped turning. Landing with no propulsion wasn't a problem as long as there was a good place to land within gliding distance. When I flew close to the ground I stayed near open space, and if I had to set down in a tree I had plans for maximizing my chances of survival by selecting a soft tree. My options were greater when I was up higher. I could glide longer distances.

The day I went up to see that cloud I spiraled up and up directly over that field. The cloud was as low to the ground as clouds ever are. When I got up there I flew around it one time. It wasn't any bigger than it seemed from the ground. I wanted to fly through it for some reason. I went away from it, turned around, and headed back in that direction.

There was a fraction of a second as I got closer when I had a second thought. Flying into something I couldn't see through was very much like flying into a wall. It got closer and closer then I was inside. I froze on the controls. I had no visual reference. I was in that cloud for four or five seconds, but it seemed much longer. There is an instrument called an artificial horizon that indicates what an aircraft is doing in relation to the ground when the pilot has lost visual reference. I didn't have that instrument or a compass which would have helped some. A person with their eyes closed who is turning right or left on the ground feels centrifugal force. They know which way they are turning. There is no such sensation when traveling through the air in man-made aircraft.

If an extremely radical right or left turn is made in the air a person won't know which direction they are turning but they will know something is happening when they feel the increased gravity straight down through the center of their body. Thankfully, I didn't feel any increased Gs (gravity). I understand this now but I didn't know that phenomenon existed until I became painfully aware of it that day.

When I came out of that cloud I was still traveling in a straight line and my altitude was constant. I thought, *So much for little white fluffy clouds in the sunshine.* I didn't enjoy being in there one bit. I flew back to the ground and trailered the thing home.

Soon after that I moved to Columbus, Ohio, where I enrolled in Ohio State University. At that point the autogiro was still in one piece. When I went home on the weekends I would fly, and it was one of those weekends when it suddenly ended.

I wanted to learn how to land when the engine stopped in midair. If that happens, the only place to go is down. I would have to pick out a place on the ground quickly and land there. The less ground space that was needed, the more places there were. Extreme flare out reduced the ground space required. I read that some pilots can touch down without rolling very much. I was doing that kind of landing repeatedly with the engine on idle. The last time I tried it the rotor deflected when the little trail wheel touched the ground and the rotor blade struck the ground behind me. The entire rotor, gimbal head, control rods, and a broken-off piece of mast tube went whirling fifty feet away. A stranger who was watching from the edge of the field said he saw a burst of aluminum in the sunshine. He made it sound beautiful to see. I would have much rather been there watching with him. The topside of the rotor had rectangular pieces of aluminum fastened to the spar. When the rivets popped he saw those pieces fluttering in the sunlight. The remaining part of the aircraft went over on its side. I was strapped to the seat. When the propeller struck the ground the idling engine stopped. There was silence.

I unfastened my seat belt and stood up not feeling much of anything. I was wearing a motorcycle helmet that belonged to my brother. I took the helmet off. As I was regaining my senses I felt something wet on the back of my neck. I put my hand back there like I was brushing off a fly, and when I brought it back my fingertips were bright red. Then I remembered my head shot forward when it happened. My body didn't move but my chin went instantly against my chest. In my mind I reconstructed what happened. When the mast tube broke off it hit me in the back of the helmet. However I could not understand why the shell of the helmet seemed undisturbed and so did the padding inside the helmet. The place in my skin where the blood was oozing out was strange also. It was like a cut, but it wasn't a cut. It was an opening about ten millimeters long. It was in my scalp in the back of my head just above my neck. I could feel it with my fingertips, and it felt like a break in my skin where the edges were blunt or undefined. It didn't hurt in the slightest bit.

No other person was consulted about what happened. Several weeks later I looked very closely at the helmet again, this time under bright light. When I did that I could see a tiny place in the white shell where there was a crack. I could barely see some exposed hairs used to make fiberglass. They are called fiberglass rovings. I still could not explain the hole in my head. The padding was intact. No matter how hard I looked, the padding seemed intact. If my bare head had been hit I would have been killed instantly. The force must have been considerable.

7

The University

It was necessary for an incoming student at the university to have a high school diploma. When I was in the U.S. army I took a battery of tests and without further ado I received a General Equivalency Diploma (GED). I didn't need any additional schooling.

One thing I learned about college and everywhere afterward is the significance numbers have. A digit identifies every achievement. The numbers started stacking up on my behalf in college. I was oblivious to them.

I had a guidance counselor who was a graduate student. A graduate student was a person seeking further college education after receiving an undergraduate degree. The graduate students were a big part of the educational system at the university. They would be RA if it were the army. When I went to see my guidance counselor he meant to be helpful. After my first grading period, or "quarter" as it was called, he thought it would be good for me to take a three-hour class to learn how to plan everything. According to the grade the teacher gave me I didn't do very well. Also, I didn't do very well the whole time I was in that university when you look at the numbers, but I consider I learned a large amount. When I completed my schooling I had a 2.4 accumulative point-hour ratio, which was below average.

Well into my time as a sophomore (second of four segments) I had not "declared a major." Declaring a major was the selection of one academic field of study that would become predominant over all the others. My counselor seemed concerned, but apparently many students had to be prodded like me. It was not unusual.

I chose journalism. When I began, the journalism school was

in the process of moving into a new building on "west campus." It was called the J-school building by many people. I learned some very beneficial things about writing when I was there.

When I was a freshman at Ohio State University I was like a babe in toy land. As a new student I had to live on campus in a dormitory called Scott House. It was all male. Across the street was a huge building about ten times the size of Scott House called Taylor Tower and it was an all-girl dormitory. Another all-girl dormitory called Norton House was right beside Scott House.

A dormitory and meals contract for each quarter cost $734. An office in the center of the campus took the money. It was called the registrar's office. A full schedule of academic classes cost an additional $218. I had the GI Bill, which paid for the schooling. Then my parents sent me money for food and lodging. I had no financial concern in those days. I didn't realize it then, but that was marvelous to say the least.

When I was walking to the Commons where three meals were served each day I would walk on a well-manicured walkway. One side of Taylor Tower was facing me. I would often look from the bottom of that building to the top and I couldn't help but think how many females there must be stacked in very precise vertical rows. All the rooms were exactly the same. The bunk beds were in exactly the same place in each room.

I had gone to an all-boy boarding school. Because of the absence of females in my daily life I had developed the attitude that they were mysterious creatures. I knew they were classified as human, but to me that is where the similarity ended. I didn't think of females of our species as more or less than males, just vastly different. While initially sexual attraction was a significant factor I became aware I would effectively lose association with half the human race if I didn't put that aside. At the university there were many conflicting attitudes. I was settled with the idea that each person's attitude was representative of them and there were only absolute answers to questions like what is two and two.

The first girl I became attached to sat down on the floor in the downstairs part of the Commons. It was an event designed for the boys to meet the girls and the girls to meet the boys.

I got a paper plate of dessert food and sat down in a plastic cushioned chair. I didn't know anyone there, and I wasn't with anyone. I was feeling self-conscious and looking for a seat more than anything else. She came over near where I was and joined the girls in her room on the floor. The university was geographically located in what was called the corn belt of the United States. Her hair was yellow and long. It was parted in the middle and went thick and straight down each side. Along the entire length of it there were many tiny little ripples. She was radiant. There was a shine about her. When she was sitting on the floor with her friends she glanced at me several times. Under normal circumstances it would have been rude the way I was staring at her.

It was the weekend and there were no classes that day or the next. It was late in the afternoon. That girl and I kept getting to know each other better. I loved her uncomplicated understanding. We walked to the center of the campus where there was a small outdoor amphitheater carved into a hillside. I did not know it was there, and when I discovered it I was excited and imagined it was just like the ones in ancient Greece. An aisle divided the right side from the left side. About four hundred people could sit there. The seats were flat stones. On the same surface behind the stone was a grassy place where people sitting in the next row up could put their feet. There were many green plants behind the small earthen stage. A person could not see through them. Apparently it was part of a large garden. Beyond the last row of seats to one side I could see the second-story windows of the house where she said the president of the university lived. Other than that it was secluded. There was no one else there.

She sat on the end of a lower row, and I stood where the actors stand. I was feeling like Euripides and in a theatrical way said, "Though the boys throw stones at the frogs in sport, the frogs do not die in sport but in earnest." She wasn't moved. I needed something more germane. "Friends, Romans, countrymen lend me your ears. I come to bury Caesar not to praise him . . . Cry havoc and let slip the dogs of war." She watched quietly. I went over to where she was and sat down beside her. I sighed and told her who those people were. She asked me like a doctor if I always did that sort of thing, and I said I never had such a lovely audience.

The Scott and Norton House newsletter had in its gossip column that a certain room in Scott House had one more than four people living there and it was almost true. Then suddenly she just left. One day she was there, and the next day she was not there. It was just like when I was a small child at home and I forgot a parakeet named Blue was perched on my shoulder. I walked outside and the bird took off. It flew way up inside a large elm tree. I could not see it but that is where I saw it go. I knelt under that tree and cried for hours hoping the bird would fly back onto my shoulder. I went out there several more days. That bird could have been half way to South America by the time I stopped grieving. Much later I heard she was married. I couldn't have done that and thought it was probably better she was gone. All my life I never made a decisive decision to do something or not do something. Everything I did was like a force out in baseball. Going into the army was a force out. Her leaving me was a force out. It happened all the time. Going a certain direction whether I wanted to or not was always happening to me.

In the amphitheater we talked for a long time. I was walking around looking things over and talking to her in the distance. When I was standing one row up from the row where she was standing we were next to each other. I was looking down at her, and she was looking up at me. She put her lips inside her mouth and reached up with both her hands to where the zipper was on my pants. I asked her, "What are you doing?"

She said, "I want to turn you on."

I looked over my shoulder at the windows. I said, "Not here. Imagine how it would ruin the president's day." Then I said, "Actually it is me. I do not like public displays of affection. My car is in the parking lot." I jumped down to her level and kissed her quickly. That was the first time we touched in a definite way.

By the time we walked the distance to the student parking lot it was nighttime. I had a banged-up car that always started. A mercury vapor light was at the top of a high pole about fifteen car widths away. It shone down through the side window. I could see her hair. She stopped moving to put it behind her ear. Then she continued. I could see her cheek and the line of her jaw. I watched her passively. She was totally unabashed.

That summer the snack bar was open during the evening study hall. I was trying to memorize algebraic equations and how lithium bonded with barium. We took a break. We sat across from each other in a booth. Each of us had one of those ice-cream cones that come out of machines in a twirl. She licked it and put the whole thing in her mouth. It was vanilla and I couldn't believe what she was doing. I looked to the side hoping no one was watching. There looking right at us was this fat ugly man who probably had rotten tobacco-stained teeth. He was attending an agriculture seminar. They were staying in one of the empty dormitories. He was hunched over the table on his elbows with a cup of coffee. He was still looking at us when we finished and went back to the study hall.

When I was a freshman we had an assignment to read a little book that didn't get the attention it deserved. It was a small reddish paperback written by a teacher in Indiana. In slightly more than a hundred pages the book defined not thinking clearly.

The English class where I was assigned to read the book met two times a week in a large lecture hall. Then it broke into smaller classes of twenty or so students who met three times a week. A TA (teacher's assistant graduate student) was the teacher in the smaller class. We began and ended our discussion of this book in the same week. At the end of the week we had a multiple-choice quiz on the subject of the book. I didn't do very well on the quiz. At one point in our discussion, the teacher said, "When someone sitting in a stadium sees two people kissing in front of them and it is objectionable to the person, why is it objectionable?" Then the teacher answered his own question and his answer indicated to me that he didn't get what it said. His answer was, "He isn't getting any."

I raised my hand, and he asked me what I wanted. I said, "Maybe the person doesn't like public displays of affection." The girl who was so good to me was sitting in the seat next to mine. Out of the corner of my eye I could see her shift position in her chair.

This little book, insignificant-looking next to big hardbound textbooks, said everyone was culturally conditioned and because of that what is beautiful to one person might not be so beautiful to the next. They have different frames of reference.

If a heavy ball is suspended from the ceiling by a cord and it goes back and forth like a pendulum, two people in different positions will describe an entirely different action. One person in one place will observe a forward and backward motion, and another person in another position will observe a left to right motion. They are looking at the same thing. Those people each have a different frame of reference.

That wasn't part of the discussion. In physics in boarding school I learned about frames of reference, and I didn't put the two things together until a long time afterward.

Ohio State University was much like life. There were terrific teachers and terrible teachers. A student had to find out who were the best ones if they wanted to be in their classroom. I didn't make the effort. I plodded through the system passively. Some colleges were in an academic bell jar, but sooner or later the real world was inevitable. Ohio State University was definitely in the real world. It was well defined by someone long ago who said the primary activity of institutionalized education would soon be to feed the already existing military industrial complex with people.

My teacher in that English class was a total product of his environment. He was a good spokesman for his environment. Another time he said to the whole class, "If you get C grades you are going to have a C life. You're going to have a C wife, have C children, and get a C job." That was excellent testimony about the world in which he was immersed. C was a mediocre grade.

The United States' involvement in Vietnam was being protested by university students all across the country. The height of protest wasn't during my freshman year, but it was during the time I was there.

At another state school several students were shot and killed by soldiers who were sent there to restore normal order. Domestic violence between students and university administrations started when the U.S. military dropped bombs on North Vietnam and Cambodia. The government said the bombs were dropped because the North Vietnamese (the enemy) were using the Ho Chi Minh trail to supply their army in the South.

When soldiers shot the students I read that people questioned why the soldiers had ammunition in their guns. Even if the officers in charge never intended the guns be fired it wouldn't have crossed their mind to issue, carry, or produce a weapon that could not be used. It was reported that the soldiers were backed into a corner. So a bunch of eighteen- and nineteen-year-old weekend warriors with loaded guns were scared. It takes a tremendous lack of imagination not to see someone would get shot.

The state police (highway patrol) came and went first. It was said they had to have a legal reason to be on campus. Neil Avenue was the road going through the middle of the university. A gate on Neil Avenue located in the North Campus area of the university got closed. That blocked traffic. Buses full of state police arrived. They wore facemasks. They had shields and wooden mallets.

A laboratory newspaper called *The Lantern* prepared by the J-students and supervised by the faculty reported the gate closing with a photograph that actually showed the gate being closed. A long time later when order was restored the photograph appeared a second time deep inside the paper. A brief statement said two of the adult people shown closing the gate were identified as plainclothes state policemen.

There were more radical students than the state police could handle. They left to make room for the soldiers. The university was state property so the city police didn't come on campus, but during the military occupation their presence on High Street was significant. High Street was next door. It was where all the bookstores, bars, and fast-food restaurants were. The city police were dressed in brand-new riot gear. They had guns that shot nonfatal wooden plugs called knee knockers.

I saw a line of twenty or thirty soldiers standing shoulder to shoulder in front of the administration building. They were expressionless and stared straight ahead without focusing on anything. An officer was moving around behind them. In front of them were many students trying to provoke any or all of the soldiers. One student with long curly locks was going on and on directly in one soldier's face. It looked like the officer went over to talk to that soldier, but without turning his head he very quickly reached out and grabbed a handful of the student's hair. The officer pulled the student by the hair into the building. I saw the student wince in a bent-over position as he was led up the stairs to the main door. Someone said there was a person on the second floor taking photographs to identity people, but I did not see them. Soon after that, the killings happened at the other university and the governor closed all the state-run schools.

I went to the island in Maine for several weeks. I worked there in peace and quiet. It was like being on a mountaintop where hate and violence were foreign. When the university reopened it was as if nothing had happened.

At the university one weekend I went with a girl to her house where she grew up. Her house was in a farming community near Columbus. Big company silos were on the border of town. The grain that went in them grew on surrounding farms. The silos were like tall buildings that I could see long before I got there. We went to a farm where her family raised beef cattle. She said her mother didn't like living on the farm so they moved to town. She also said her father was a director of a local bank. In the driveway of their house in town they had an aboveground 300-gallon bulk fuel tank. There was a single-axle dump truck parked nearby. She said most days her father drove it to the farm.

They were going to have a cookout for friends and family. We were the first ones there and I talked with him outside by the grill. She and her mother were in the house. As he talked he was busy adding more charcoal. The rather large piece of meat from one of his steers had been cooking a long time in the covered grill, and it would cook a long time more. We didn't talk about anything in particular. We just talked. Later, when I was alone with her in the house she asked me what we said. She said he had told her he wanted me to leave. I tried to be amusing and told her I guess I didn't make a very good impression. We were in a large basement room of her house. I heard some footsteps at the top of the stairs like a person was listening. I said again loudly so they could hear that I was leaving.

I drove back to Columbus alone. An intense heavy-duty drama was unfolding back there that would be perfect for television, but not for me. I think her father was shocked to see what his little baby brought home. If I had a rattle, drooled, and made gurgling noises perhaps he would have allowed me to stay. Didn't he know his baby had grown up? He probably thought I was too old for her. I could understand his concern. I was a twenty-one-year-old freshman. She was a corn-fed eighteen-year-old. I had been in the army, so I was always older.

I was sitting at my desk in my dormitory room when she got back. She brought me several slices of beef from their cookout. She said she was sorry about her father. I said she didn't have to excuse him. I thought it was very nice that when she got back she came right away to say what she said and bring me some of the food.

In one of the first classrooms I was in at the Journalism School we were to learn the news style of writing and practice it every day. The teacher was a middle-aged woman who was once a reporter for a large daily newspaper in Iowa. She always walked hurriedly down the hall like she had to get an important story finished. She was a reporter through and through.

As we were walking out of the classroom during the last week she called me over to her desk. She told me I didn't have the grades to pass the course. I would have to repeat the subject. It probably seemed to her that I took the information lightly. I said OK, like she was telling me to take a right turn instead of a left turn.

She was an exceptional teacher and I got to be in her classroom twice. Each day she would give us a short writing assignment to complete right there. It would be based on a list of facts that she would pass out to each pupil. Before we began typing she would take a few minutes in front of the whole class to talk about news writing and that was the best part. The longest part involved typing. I couldn't type very fast. I had to look for each letter, and it took me longer than it should to type words.

She had something different to say each day, but some things she repeated over and over many times. She said for us to save our opinion for the editorial page if we ever got there. She said our job as reporters was to report the facts. She said the city desk would give us assignments so it wasn't absolutely necessary for us to find news, but it was absolutely necessary that we, as reporters, know how to report the facts of a story in a fair and honest manner. She said a reporter who manipulated the facts to support a particular point of view was being extremely unprofessional. Also, she said they were doing a tremendous disservice to the reader.

She said the most important part of the story should be first because the editing department might have to cut the story short to make it fit. She said the news style of writing developed in the days when telegraph lines transmitted information long distances. The whole story was in the first line because the transmission might end at any moment when the wire got cut. She said we still write that way because it is effective. It sells newspapers. If the reader is short on time they don't have to wade through the entire story to know what has happened.

We were instructed to indicate the end of each story with "30." She said that telegraph operators indicated the end of a story in that manner because it was an easy transmission to make and it was necessary to indicate no more story was coming. The custom has prevailed, she said.

She also talked about knowing what news is. She said a reporter who finds news or can see it on their own is a big help and will be recognized as such. She said news is whatever a person in the community you serve needs to know. Human-interest stories or feature stories, she said, were another subject.

Years later I heard she suddenly dropped dead. A new wing of the Journalism School building was named after her so she must have made an impression on other people. I never knew her personally, but when we passed in the hall she always made an acknowledgment of some kind. One time she told me I had a nose for news, which was a tremendous compliment coming from her. She added that I couldn't type or spell worth beans. She said the typing was an acquired skill, but the nose for news wasn't.

A new issue of the university newspaper appeared every weekday. The paper was staffed by journalism students who were selected by the faculty of the Journalism School. There was a new staff each grading period.

I was never on the staff, but when I was a junior and senior occasionally I would get assignments to do stories for the paper.

One time I was given the name of the director of transportation for the university and told to do a story on that department. I went to the man's office, and was waiting near his desk while he talked on the telephone. He was having a long conversation about whether the exhaust pipes on new buses should go on the lower right side or the lower left side, or straight up on the right or left side. I wrote the story as a day in the life of this guy and mentioned the exhaust pipes. The story never got printed and the person at the copy desk where I handed in the story asked me sincerely, "Are you serious?" I replied that I didn't know the answer to that question, but I added that the assignment on that man's job was not a joke to me. I told her I didn't write a self-imposed joke, but if his job seemed a joke, then that is the way it is.

I got another assignment to find out about a professor in the Agriculture School who was doing much study on a method of growing food called hydroponics. In his study a plant rooted in gravel (any inert medium) was flooded several times a day with a water solution containing all the necessary nutrients.

After the professor of agriculture talked to me I went over to a vegetarian restaurant on High Street to get another opinion. I had become acquainted with the owner-operator earlier when I inquired why I couldn't have an avocado with olive oil. His answer was, "Because it isn't on the menu." I liked him. When I asked him about hydroponic plant growing he said he didn't know anything about it, but he wondered how the plant would get the "trace elements" found in every plant and in the soil. He said, "A plant is more than it looks."

When I asked the professor a question about what the person on High Street had said he walked around me like I was a bother to him. I caught up to him and told him it was a real question. He became friendly, but he never answered the question. I suppose he thought it was unscientific and not worth answering. He was very involved in his work.

Among other things, fifteen credit-hours of a language was a requirement for a degree. I had taken the French language in boarding school and that was difficult. The only reason I was able to complete and pass the course was because the teacher took into consideration my effort. At the university I was expecting Italian would be easier because I was half-Italian, but it was equally as difficult.

I wanted to get a degree so prospective employers would know I was college-educated, but a degree became like a bunch of sour grapes. If I couldn't get it no matter how hard I tried I didn't want it. As a last-ditch effort I wrote a letter to the head of the Italian language department asking him to excuse me from the language requirement. I explained my situation exactly. I didn't try to sell or sugar coat anything. I said that to pass the Italian language course I would have to devote so much of my study time to it that I would not be able to do much journalism, which was my major field of study.

I didn't think he would change anything for me. I was told there was a total of 35,000 students at the university. I was mentally prepared to leave. I was very surprised when I quickly got a letter back from him saying that I was excused from the language requirement. I was overjoyed. It amazed me how good I felt when I got that response. I would never meet the man. I stayed there. One of my past coaches said opportunity presents itself to us all. One person is prepared for it, and the other is not.

There was an assignment for me to do a story about the student ID card. Every student had an identification card, with his or her photograph in the center.

When I went to the place where the cards were made the person who ran the place was alone in the room. He was excited to hear that I wanted to do a story for the university newspaper about what he did. He sat down right away and gave me his undivided attention. He talked and talked. I had to interrupt him several times to clarify a point, but other than that he told me everything about his job without my having to ask many questions.

At one point he was talking about a big stationary camera in the middle of the floor. He said it took the pictures that went on the ID cards. By his conservation he seemed to imply that two photographs were taken at the same time. I thought I misunderstood what he said and backed him up. He did say it. I asked him why the second one and he said it "stays here." He added in quite a matter-of-fact tone that the student riots in the past had helped his office grow in importance. He said the camera I was looking at was a special one purchased recently. He said people who ran the university apparently wanted to have a picture of each student on file.

He told me about the laminating process and other aspects of his job. He had ideas all his own about how the student ID card would someday become a charge card. We shook hands and said good-bye.

One teacher explained the legal aspects of journalism. He said an elected official or someone in the public eye has no legal right to privacy. The teacher said if such a person thinks they have been represented unfairly and they bring the newspaper to court, then what you wrote about them better be true, or you have libeled them. He said truth is a defense when writing about elected officials.

He said when a person minding their own lawful and private business is identified without their permission in the mass media and it is thought by them to be disparaging then they could claim an invasion of privacy.

The teacher said most journalism that is contested falls between those two extremes and that is why it is contested. He asked the class if a reporter was invading a person's legal right to privacy if someone was identified in a photograph that shows them throwing a ball on a sunny day in a public park. He said even if the only purpose of the photograph was to show the beautiful day, we would want to get the person's permission. He said we might think a certain representation is harmless, but the person identified might think otherwise.

He said it is not an invasion of privacy if a person is written about and they can identify themselves because of some private knowledge they have. The teacher said as soon as that person is identifiable by a third party then you have invaded their right to privacy.

The graduate students in the Theater Department directed many short one-act plays for different projects that they were doing, and they needed actors. Undergraduate students in the College of Theater got first choice so I got mostly minor parts, which were sometimes the best parts. In one play called *Waiting for Lefty* I became an immigrant union worker. I imagined how my grandfather was although he was not in a union. I spoke with a heavy Italian accent and had great fun. I almost switched my major field of study to theater, but I had to think of eating when I grew up.

There was one play I did that was very serious. It was called *Jean*. Jean was the butler. He and the lady of the house fell in love. That was the story. There was just one other actor in the play, and that was the lady. The graduate student director, the girl, and I got together several times in his apartment, and read over the script to get it exactly the way he wanted. I was amazed how exacting he was. He once said he was doing the play for her. I suppose his doing something for her meant he knew her well. Their relationship seemed personal and friendly. My relationship with both of them was friendly but mostly academic.

They both had escaped the confines of the Theater Department. They were off-Broadway or different from the usual theater students. Their scene in itself was fascinating, but I didn't ask any personal questions. I was grateful that he asked me to be there and be Jean. It seemed like life was a big chore for her, or maybe that was the lady in the play.

Once another person and I ran the "light board," which was where all the lights for the stage were controlled. We had to bring lights up and turn them down on cue. She was very smart and had almost a 4.0 grade-point average, which was the equivalent of straight A's. She was a theater and dance student. We often talked when there wasn't much to do. One day at the light board I asked her what an arabesque was. She had mentioned that word and I didn't know what it was. It was like she transformed herself into a tiny ballerina that goes around and around on one toe inside a glass music box. She stepped back and unfolded slowly in a deliberate way. She stood up on the ball of one foot, and when that was accomplished she slowly turned her hips and body sideways, raising her other leg higher than her hips. She then slowly brought both her hands together in a circle around her head. Her face was looking up in the opposite direction of the pointing foot on the raised leg. She held that position for a second and then she came down on two feet and said very unemotionally, "That is an arabesque." It is a good thing I was sitting on a stool, because if I wasn't I would have fallen on the floor. I turned my head to the light board. I didn't tell her it was practically the most beautiful thing I had ever seen a person do.

The subject in one journalism class was to know when information was an accurate representation of the truth and not a representation of what someone wanted us to say. The teacher said the purpose of his class was to learn to tell the difference between good research and bad research.

We were each assigned to come up with a question and design a survey around the question that would give the answer. At length we discussed what good data was. The teacher said there would be many people who would give us data to support what they wanted. He said as journalists who had the public trust we had to be able to recognize one from the other.

My survey was designed around the question: Is there any difference between the newspaper reader who buys the newspaper on the street and the one who has it delivered to their residence?

My survey design called for a questionnaire to be inside newspapers sold at newsstands and from newspaper vending boxes. The potential respondent would receive a free candy or something else of value if they answered the questions. A similar approach was taken in distributing the questions to people who got their newspapers at home.

When the course was over the teacher gave us a final grade, and that was one of two times I went back to a teacher to get a higher grade. The teacher and I talked for a while about the merit or lack of merit of my work. He asked me why he should raise the grade, and I said my study would get unbiased results. I needed a higher grade so I wouldn't have to repeat the course. I hadn't received a failing grade, but as a journalism student I had to get at least a C in each journalism course. He said he would raise my grade one letter.

During my time at the university I took two courses in political science. Both courses were on the main campus, and I had two different teachers. The Department of Political Science was not part of the school of journalism. Both courses were about American politics. Often, tests were the type that had several answers to each question, and we were to select the best one.

The second time I ever went back to a teacher for a higher grade was in political science. The teacher didn't raise my grade, but he was a living example of one aspect of American politics. One morning he came to class wearing a three-piece suit with an American flag lapel pin. His hair was all slicked back. He looked very different. He said that day he was going to a luncheon right after class where he would meet longtime elected officials. He wanted to become a politician and it was his idea that he had to have the approval of the people who provided the lunch.

When I was a freshman and sophomore I lived in a dormitory on campus. I had a meals contract. A dietitian prepared the menu. They were "balanced" meals. As a junior and senior I lived in an old house a block and a half from the university. It was on the south side of Frames Street. Two brothers, who spoke Greek, owned the house. Their last name was Greek and they looked Greek. I think they were Greeks. I suppose the house was an investment property for them. I seldom saw either of them. I mailed them the rent money.

The first floor was one apartment occupied by a married couple with a golden retriever dog. He was a graduate student. Their apartment was nicely furnished. I never went inside, but several times I could see inside from the front hall. They were busy people who were nice enough when they talked. He moved one day, and I heard he got a job at a bank in California.

On the second floor there was a small two-room apartment where a music major lived. He listened to classical music and played a large wooden stringed instrument. There were three other small rooms on that floor. I rented one. One student who worked very hard and got good grades rented the other two rooms. There was a large attic room rented by a quiet person. He left early in the morning and returned at night. I rarely saw him, but I could hear him come and go. When he graduated he worked in Columbus and continued to live there. On the second floor we shared a room with a sink, shower, and toilet. It reminded me of the one in New York City. A stick of dynamite would have improved the place.

I went to college year-around, but between each quarter there was a break. The dormitories would be closed during the breaks. When I lived in the dorms I would go home, but when I had the off-campus apartment I didn't have to leave. I made fewer trips home.

When I stayed in Columbus during the break I would do "spot labor" to get some spare change. In those days a company that did that sort of thing had a waiting room where people would show up in the morning to work that day. It was called a labor pool. I always got a job because I had a car and I could take other people to work. The agency liked not only my car but also the fact that I was sober and well rested each day.

Usually the jobs we got were the ones no other person would do. Once I went to work for a plumber whose customer had a frozen three-inch PVC sewer pipe under a house trailer. After I got there that was when the plumber described the situation. He was a nice older man, but I told him I wasn't going to crawl under that trailer and fool with that sewer pipe unless he got "Lincoln and Jackson shaking hands."

As I was walking away I heard him say, "No one wants to work these days." That comment struck a nerve, and I turned around. The work wasn't as awful as I thought, and he bought me lunch.

On another job five of us moved mud. We were to make the ceiling of a room in a new apartment building a few inches higher by digging the floor down deeper. The builder had made a mistake. I dug three days with other people, and I think the job went much longer. Five or six concrete blocks were removed from a wall. We put each shovel of wet, sticky mud through the opening and shook it off outside. We walked on boards. If someone stepped in the mud they would sink like it was quicksand. We weren't supposed to go into a large adjoining recreation room, but once we all did to relax a moment and play a little Ping-Pong. We walked across an otherwise spotless linoleum floor leaving gooey footprints behind us. The room was furnished. There was a large cabinet-type television that was gone the second day. So was one of the people who came with us the first day. A uniformed policeman stood on the edge of the shiny floor looking back and forth at the large hole in the wall and all the thick mud. Maybe it could fit through there and maybe it couldn't. He didn't find out that day.

We all talked as we walked back and forth. The person I talked with most of the time said he was in a state mental hospital. He said he and many others were released at the same time when the governor said there was no need for them to be there. His honesty was most unusual. He had this incredible honesty about himself that no one else had.

Four of us went to work at another place where steel drums were reconditioned. The job lasted several days, and each day the same group of us went in my car. Two of the people were older men. They always carried a pocket-size bottle of wine. Several times, another person and myself in the front were offered a drink.

Outside, on the job, everything was frozen and cold. We were supposed to get a load of drums out in the yard and bring them to the factory. We had an old truck with no license plate. The horn and lights were broken, but everything else worked. An old rusted steel drum that had ice and snow stuck all over it was made to look new. That is what they did there.

At the end of the day a foreman would write our time on a piece of paper and we would go back to the labor pool office. Someone there would cut us a check for the day's work. Our pay rate was the minimum wage. We would hurry to a store across the street. A big sign above the door said: CHECKS CASHED. There was a charge for cashing a check. It was a package store too. Two of the people always bought a particular kind of wine. They would look someplace else if it wasn't for sale there. The wine they bought cost a fourth of the money they earned that day, and tomorrow they would do it all over again. I do not know where they slept or what they called home. They didn't expect things would ever be different for them. It was depressing, but they were never depressed. The person who sat in the front was a young man who always wore the same dress shoes. Without a word he would change the car radio station even if it was where he put it the previous day.

A job in the newspaper sounded good, but it didn't say what it was. The person who answered the telephone said there was much money to be made and if I was interested I should show up at a certain place that evening.

When I got there about thirty other people also answered the same advertisement. After a few minutes a person came into the room. He talked with people in the front row. They laughed. Then he proceeded to speak to all of us, and show slides that pictured a large ornate house with palm trees and flowers all over the place. He said the house belonged to the person who started the business and in so many words he said we could have a similar house if we wanted. He still hadn't said what it was we would do. I was beginning to wonder if it was legal. When I raised my hand and asked him what the job was about he said in a moment he would get to that. A few minutes later he brought out this thing and if it wasn't for the hose and a few attachments I would never have guessed what it was. It didn't look like any type of canister or upright vacuum cleaner I had ever seen.

The person who was speaking said selling the object on the desk in front of us was the job. He said he was a dealer and we could be dealers too by getting other people to sell the product for us. He explained that the office would give us names and addresses of people who were prospective buyers.

He went on to say that before we gave a demonstration for real we should practice it on our parents with him watching to see if we did everything right. I went up to him afterwards and explained that I was a student at the university and my parents lived far away. He didn't seem to think that was a problem. He said I could start right away.

I learned how to show what the product could do by watching another person do it for people in their house. When an appointment was made by telephone by an office person they said there was a free gift for them if they listened to the whole thing. I never sold a vacuum cleaner, but I gave out many free gifts. For several weeks I demonstrated the product to about twenty people. I thought I made a few sales. The main person in the vacuum cleaner office told me each time that the credit application was denied. There was no sale.

I got a sales lead from the vacuum cleaner office to go to a house that was near the university. Early one evening I went there. A woman lived in the house with her daughter. The woman was studying English literature in a master's degree program. She was married and divorced as a teenager. The six-year-old child was from that marriage. The mother seemed my age. Her face was pretty. She wore baggy clothing that day, but I found out later she had an exquisite body. I took a black-and-white photograph of her standing against a white wall in Florida with her hands behind her back. She was wearing skimpy white underclothes. She had a disgusted look on her face, but she did what I told her. She had a picture-perfect body.

The free home demonstration called for showing how well the vacuum cleaner worked. I was practically cleaning her whole house. She was sitting up straight on a couch with her arms folded across her knees. She would point at what to do next. The stairs opened into the main room. There was a banister on the open side. Her child was in the middle of the room and when she saw me vacuuming the stairs she looked at her mother and laughed. Her mother laughed and covered her mouth with her hand so I would not see.

We talked for a while, not entirely about vacuum cleaners. When I was ready to leave I was standing by the door with my coat on and she was across the room. I asked, "Aren't you forgetting something?"

She asked, "What?"

I said, "Your free gift we promised you, it is a big part of our operation."

She walked across the room. I handed her the package, and she tossed it on the couch. I told her it might be a doily or a finger bowl or something useful in the kitchen. She pushed me out the door.

We saw each other often, but I was rarely in her house. I never saw her child again and she never saw the room where I lived. When the university was closed between quarters she invited me to meet her in Florida. My job selling vacuum cleaners had fizzled out. Now and again I did spot labor.

I met her near Miami, Florida, in a fancy hotel beside the ocean. It was a very busy time of year in South Florida, and when I asked her how she was able to find such a nice room she said very plainly that her father ran the construction company that built those hotels. She said there always was a room for him. She flew from Columbus to New York City and then to Miami. She was very stylish. I drove straight there from Columbus, Ohio, in the Rabbit.

The Rabbit was the name my mother gave to an Italian automobile that was subsequently given to me. When it was mine I kept it parked on Frambes Street. My mother had bought it a few years earlier when she went to an auto show in Milan, Italy. It was one of the few times she traveled and one of the only times I remember her traveling with my father. They went to Italy because in Italy my father and a few other American investors were trying to make an orange juice mix that required a person add water and stir. The mix idea died on the vine, but in the early stages my parents went to Italy together. An Italian citizen met them at the Milan airport and showed them around the town. That is how they happened to go to the auto show.

There were many sleek cars, but there was one car with headlamps and running boards. It was the Alfa Romeo replica of their 1929 car that won so many races. In the late 1960s there were many replicas being made around the world and they were so garish and awful that the word *replica* when used in conjunction with an automobile was the same as saying poorly done. The Alfa Romeo replica wasn't like the others, but it always carried the stigma of that word. The car didn't sell very well. Only ninety-two were ever made. The one my mother got was the sixty-eighth. It had the number 393068 embossed on the firewall. It was built in the Alfa Romeo factory, and the body was designed by Zagato who obviously had no restrictions imposed on him by the Alfa Romeo people. It was like the 1929 car in concept only. It was assembled on the Alfa Romeo 101 chassis. It had Borani wire wheels with forty-two-millimeter spline hubs and knock-offs. The motor was the normal 1600 cc four-cylinder engine with twin overhead cams and it had a two-barrel down draft Solex carburetor. An Alfa five-speed transmission, deferential and modern rack and pinion steering made it quite an automobile. Even though it was made and imported into the United States in 1968 when this country's emissions laws were in effect the title to the car said it was made in 1967. That meant it was exempt from pages of emissions laws. The car was spared much plumbing, added weight, and reduction in power. The car was light and quick. It had stiff suspension and went around corners like it was holding on to something.

My father told me what happened. He said my mother saw only the way it looked sitting on the floor. She wasn't one who bought many things, but she ordered one of those cars on the spot. I was told the Italian man with them tried to steer her toward something else, but it was no use.

When the car arrived, my mother drove it one or two times. My father drove it more often, and he parked it the last time he drove it, front-end first into a barn. The reverse gear fork was bent. Neither my mother nor my father ever drove it again, probably because they could not back it up. It got covered with dust and bird droppings. Eventually the battery died. Then one year in late autumn a seventeen-year-old boy on his own time pushed the car out in the sun to clean it up. That was the day I got the car.

I was in Columbus. The telephone rang. It was my father and he told me to come home quickly because "Your mother is going to give the Zagato [he called it the Zagato] to the boy who cuts the grass." I jumped in my beat-up car and headed for home. When I got there I told my mother that if she was going to give the car to somebody she should give it to me. I told her I liked the car as much as the boy who cut the grass. She gave me the car.

The first time I drove it a long distance was also the first time I went to Florida. It was warm. The hotel was near the water. People were lying in neat rows on metal frame cots that had plastic cloth stretched across them. She knew just how to get a cot. We went up to a person in a white uniform at a small station under a large parasol. He took two towels and led us to the cots like a person showing someone to a table in a restaurant. After he left we sat down and she took out a plastic bottle and smeared some of the content on her skin. I did the same. Then we both lay back on the cots like two more greased sardines. Soon I sat up and turned toward her. We were both wearing dark glasses. She didn't turn her head toward me when I spoke. It was like her eyes were closed. I could not see them. I said I would rather go north and break ice or wrestle an alligator than bake in the sun like this. I wasn't as easygoing as I might have been. This whole scene was hers. I told her I liked beaches and the ocean. I asked if there was a place where every square inch was not a grid. We went in the hotel grease and all.

She got two towels and a book and we drove up the coast in the Rabbit. There was one traffic light after another, and at one or two intersections young people in bathing suits walked across the street. She said they were college students on vacation. I replied that I had heard about that phenomenon where college students, not entirely unlike us, flock to this area at the same time every year.

We found a public beach. It was about five hundred feet long. It had a paved lot for cars between it and the road. I put some coins in a parking meter. There was a stucco wall and several palm trees. As we parked someone came up to us and said it was a "gay beach" (that didn't refer to the actual beach but meant the people who went there were homosexual and lesbian). She questioned if we should stay, and I said there are no signs to indicate heterosexual people aren't allowed here. I said, "Maybe we won't stay, but I would like to see if people are running around grabbing each other's rear end, or if they have antennae." When we looked there were relatively few people. I didn't see anyone who struck me as overtly offensive. We sat on towels in the sand.

The water was warm, but it wasn't very clear. Neither of us went swimming. She was wearing clothes over her bathing suit, and when she took them off I had to marvel once again how extraordinary she looked. She could not be unattractive if she tried.

That night we heard a well-known actor-writer-comedian at one of the hotels. When the lights were on she left and came back. I saw her on her way down the aisle to our row, and I kept watching her. The way she carried herself looked so good, and then she sat next to me. I told her the way she looked. She didn't say anything. At dinner I had asked her what she would have done if she didn't get into the master's degree program. She said she would have been a stripper.

On the beach I was sitting staring at the horizon. Occasionally a pelican flew along the shore. She was lying on the sand beside me propped up on two elbows reading a thick book she brought with her. She finished it, and I asked her what happened. She asked me if I really wanted to know, because it was a long story. I asked her to tell me the main points.

She said in the story a space ship is broken down on one of the moons of Jupiter. It contacts its base in another galaxy. The China wall is a message that says: "Part is on the way." Then most of the book is the story of the earth and wars that go into the future. A child being held by somebody's hand on the moon picks up a piece of shrapnel and that is the part for the broken-down space ship. Thousands of years of human history have gone by, but it's only been several months somewhere else. I asked her, "People building the Great Wall in China thought they were walling something in or out and all the time unbeknown to them they were sending a message?"

"That is the story," she said. She also said she met the author.

Late that afternoon we went to a hotel bar that was nearly empty. One table was in a nice place in the room and we sat there. Somebody had been there before us. A waiter came over to clear the glasses away and I was passing them over to him. When I held a half-full glass with fairly fresh ice in it I hesitated a moment and drank it all up. Then I handed it to the waiter and said I hated waste. She ordered a drink. I said, "I'll have whatever he is having," and pointed to the empty glass. When he came back with our drinks he said right away how much money it was. I paid him, and he left.

"He charged you for that drink," she said. I looked over to the side. Ten feet away the waiter was resting on his elbow on one side of the bar and the bartender was beside him on the other side of the bar. They both looked at us with big grins. The people in South Florida were so friendly. I grinned back and waved. It was such a beautiful day in the neighborhood. She said they were laughing at me.

"So!" I exclaimed.

We stayed there long enough to have a few more drinks. When we went to our room she was feeling very romantic like there was a candle in a wax-covered Chianti bottle. For one moment I accommodated her. I wrapped my arms around her. I kissed her deeply and turned so that she was leaning over backwards and I was holding her weight entirely. I thought that was the way a knight who wasn't wearing his suit of shining armor would kiss a fair maiden. My white horse was tied up at a hitching post outside. She didn't like me behaving that way, and she got mad. The fantasy was over.

The next day after breakfast we were in the room getting ready to go outside. I turned on a television that had always been there. It showed the funeral of a former president of the United

States. There were caissons. Even the dead person was in a horse-drawn hearse. Remove all the concrete in the background and it could have been the beginning of World War One. The Prussians were like that with plumes on prancing horses. They ran into fully automatic weapons and poison gas. Here was this on television. They were burying a person this time.

I was sitting on the edge of the bed enthralled by the whole thing. She wanted to go and asked me how I could watch a funeral. I said, "Just a minute," and held my hand up without taking my eyes off the screen. She wouldn't wait and said she would meet me in the lobby. She left the room. I watched a few more minutes, and when I got off the elevator I saw her first. She was sitting on a seat that went around a large column. She was leaning back on the column with her eyes closed and she had this painful look on her face. When I got up to her and spoke she opened her eyes. Soon after that I said I was going back to Columbus. She acknowledged that statement like it was a good idea, and I left. My departure was sooner than planned.

The Rabbit burnt the exhaust valves on the number two and three cylinders on the trip down there. It got worse on the return trip. By the time I got back I had half-power. Also, when I got in the warmer weather on the way down there a bushing assembly located where the steering shaft goes through the fire wall caused the car to steer stiffly, and at high speeds it jerked to the right and left. The two front tires wore out. I didn't correct either condition until I got home.

I stopped in Cincinnati and took the head off the engine. I took it to a dealer to have the two valves replaced and all the others lapped and properly shimmed. I fixed the bushing.

When I got back to Columbus the break was over. I saw that girl a few more times, but it was not the same. Finally, when we didn't see each other anymore she sent back a picture I had given her. It was an old faded ink drawing on rice paper. It showed a Japanese woman in a kimono walking along a path in the rain. Her hand was extended and it held a Japanese lantern on the end of a stick low to the ground. She was finding her way down the path by the light from the lantern.

I went to school year-round, and in the summer there weren't nearly as many students attending the university. Still, it didn't seem there were fewer students than any other quarter because the classes were full and the dormitories that were open were also full.

It was between spring and summer quarter after my second year that I moved off campus. A premedical student on Fourth Street advertised for a roommate. He was in school that summer, but the other students he shared his apartment with were not. He needed help with the rent. I didn't have the apartment on Frambes yet. The first place I lived off campus was the Fourth Street apartment leased by the premedical student.

Several of my friends lived in the dormitories during that time. I was there often. In August the Ohio State Fair was happening in that city. It lasted two weeks, and we went there several nights. We never went through the main gate where we would have to pay admission. We went through the exhibitor gate. We looked down at the ground and said, "Hog barn," like it was a matter of routine. We said it exactly a certain way so as not to raise suspicion. We said it loudly, quickly, and with a country twang. The guard there never questioned us. My friend from New Jersey devised this method of entry. He was in college to become a small animal veterinarian (vet).

8

Jail

We went to the state fair one Friday evening, and it started to rain. When I got back to my apartment that night it was still raining. A few minutes after I had gotten in bed the telephone rang and rang.

The premedical student was gone for the weekend. He lived on the other side of Columbus and bicycled everywhere. He was very industrious. The way he bicycled was indicative of him. When he got an A on a paper, which was often, he would call his father. I couldn't help but marvel at the closeness between them. We liked each other, as different as we were. One time I used his frying pan to cook some meat. He was very upset because the meat I put in his frying pan wasn't kosher. He did not ask, but I bought the frying pan from him. He could not use it anymore.

I answered the telephone and it was my friend the vet student. He asked if I would drive him somewhere very important. He didn't want to talk about it on the telephone. He said normally he wouldn't need a ride, but it was raining. I said I would be there in a few minutes.

It turns out he was going to be the middleman in the sale of an illegal narcotic drug. He told me all about it so I knew what he was doing. According to the law I was a conspirator, among other things.

The vet student had a friend or an acquaintance who lived north of the university on California Street. This friend had some cocaine. Several weeks earlier the vet student had picked up a quantity of cocaine from him at his house and passed it on to a third person who got arrested in the rain that night. The vet student explained this to me as we were languishing in jail. The third person agreed to cooperate with the police. He probably made a deal that if he set up his supplier they would go easy on him. He telephoned the vet student and said he had a buyer who wanted an ounce of cocaine that night. The vet student didn't know the buyer was the Columbus Police. It was right after the call from the third person made from a city police station downtown that my friend called me for a ride. It was still raining.

I met the vet student in the room of another student who was arrested with us. All three of us went outside where there was a car parked on the curb. The driver was the person doing the buying, and he held his hands out the window and fanned out six $100 bills, which was the purchase price of what he was buying. My friend the vet student bent down, looked at the money, and said he would be right back. The one student went back to his room in the dormitory. The vet student and me went to get the cocaine. The police were following us. I learned later when I was being questioned that the police thought I was using evasive tactics when I went past California Street on High Street and then turned around in a parking lot to correct the mistake. The police said I was backtracking. I had never been there before and I drove past the street in the rain.

The person with the cocaine lived near the end of the street in one of the row houses. A policeman didn't believe me when I said I didn't know the address of the house. There was no place to park that night so I waited in my car. The vet student jumped out. I didn't see, or attempt to see, which house he entered. We drove back with the cocaine in his pocket, and we went into the dormitory room of the student who was arrested with us. The buyer came in the room also. There were two clear plastic bags. One bag was an ounce of pure cocaine, and the other bag was one ounce of lactose powder that looked exactly like the cocaine. The second bag was provided so the buyer could mix the contents of the two bags together to make two ounces of the narcotic. Then it would be "cut" 50 percent. The buyer put his money down on the desk where the two bags were, and he made several statements one of which was that he was going to sell it in "nickel bags" on Mount Vernon Street. Then he turned around, unlocked the door, and four plainclothes policemen burst in with guns in hand, several of which were pointing at me. They said, "Police; put your hands over your head." The buyer left.

First, they came to me and several of them searched me and handcuffed my hands behind my back. It was like they thought I was an armed guard. People were sleeping in the bedroom. The police rudely awakened all of them. There was a lot of yelling and screaming in there. I heard the police yell, "Police! Get up!" and I heard a girl who was probably naked and not assigned to that room yell for them to get out. All the students came out of the bedroom fully dressed. Some police came out after them and sent the students from the bedroom out in the hall like so many innocent bystanders.

Soon a van with two doors in the back arrived and we went to the police station in handcuffs. Before I went downtown I saw a police tow truck hooking up to my car. The van had two bench seats that went the length of the sides. A light on the ceiling stayed on the whole time. There was a metal partition between the front where the driver was and the back where we were.

The police took a picture of my face that included a row of numbers under my chin. We were put in the City Prison in a room with other prisoners. The room was seventy-five feet by twenty-five feet. One of the short sides of the room was a wall of steel bars with a door. A policeman sat at a desk on the other side of the bars. On the opposite side there were dirty windows covered with heavy wire mesh and bars. On the two long sides of the room were rows of jail cells, each one six feet by ten feet, where we were locked up at night. Each cell had one set of steel bunk beds welded in place, with thin mattresses. Each cell had a toilet, and a locking door made of bars just like the ones on the front wall.

The next day the vet student telephoned a lawyer he knew. When he came back he told us we would be arraigned the next morning.

Theoretically, in the United States everyone who is in jail for any amount of time has to be either charged with a crime or convicted of a crime. To be arraigned meant we would go before a judge and be told what the charge against us was (what law we have broken). We would respond to that charge with a guilty or not guilty plea. The judge would then assign us a trial date, and he would determine if we wanted counsel assigned by the court or if we wanted to get one for ourselves. The judge would also decide if we would be released or put back in jail until our trial. Since we were each from another city the judge might be concerned that we wouldn't show up for our trial. Then there was bail.

Bail is money that the court holds instead of a person. If I was released on bail and I didn't show up at my trial I would forfeit the bail money and the judge would issue a warrant for my arrest. If I did show up the money would be refunded and my trial would proceed.

There were a host of enterprising individuals who sold insurance bonds for anyone who needed money to make bail. The cost of the insurance bond was 10 percent of the bail set by the judge. The 10 percent was the cost of the money. It was not returned no matter what happened. When a bail bondsman put up the money for bail and the person didn't show up for trial it was the bondsman who lost money.

Many other people were arraigned with us. The lawyer the vet student called on the telephone was not present, but he must have talked with someone in the court system. The judge didn't look at us or speak to us.

We were released "on our own recognizance," which meant we didn't have to put up any money for bail. The lawyer later told us the day and time of our trial. He also said that we were charged with five felonies. They were possession of narcotics, possession of narcotics for sale, keeper of a house where narcotics are kept, transportation of narcotics, and conspiracy to sell narcotics. The vet student told us the lawyer had told him a conviction for first degree murder didn't carry as much jail time as a conviction on all those charges. The policemen who arrested us were plainclothes detectives just back from a national training center for drug enforcement. That explained why they seemed somewhat rabid to me. On the evening news we were named; it gave our Columbus address and said we were the main drug suppliers for the entire campus area. The vet student told me about the report. It also said our bail was set at $25,000 each.

The following Monday when I walked into a journalism class (I was unaware of the television news story at that time) the teacher went on for the first five minutes in a high-pitched voice about how young people had too much money. I didn't understand how that related to anything. I thought he was acting like a babbling idiot that day. Later, when I heard about the evening news, I understood why he said what he did.

Two days later at lunch I was sitting by myself in the commons with a tray of food. I was at the end of a long table, and no one else was there. This girl comes over with her tray of food and sits down across from me at the end of the table. I had seen her before many times. She was particularly beautiful looking. She was a beginner and apparently mindless as well.

She had a lot of sparkle, and the people I saw her with were flashy. They didn't cavort with anyone except their own kind. At first I had to stop chewing when she sat down with me. It was like she did it all the time. I never thought I was cool enough for her. It didn't matter that I wore unironed shirts all the time and that I was "wrinkles" to some people. It didn't matter if I was a farm boy from a cornfield in Ohio. Suddenly everything was different.

She was even better-looking up close, but then she started to speak about "uppers" and "downers" and about pills called black beauties and soapers. She knew about the arrest, and she was so impressed with me or who she thought I was. She was mine for the taking at that point.

As she rattled on I said her name (I knew her name) to interrupt her. She stopped in midsentence. I put my fork down, and leaned forward to talk to her intently. I said her beautiful name another time. I said her balloon should be popped. I said there was nothing glamorous about spending twenty to forty years in the Ohio Penitentiary. I said the truth was not what was said on the evening news. I told her how scared I was about what could happen. I didn't give her a chance to respond. I was nearly full, and my food was nearly gone. I left the table. That was the first and last time we ever spoke together alone.

The person I shared an apartment with on Fourth Street came back after the weekend. When he came in I was there cooking in my very own frying pan. He had heard the address of his apartment on the evening news. He asked me what happened. I knew he wouldn't eat one of the hot dogs in my skillet so I didn't offer him one. The cheese was melted. I put a heaping fork of sauerkraut in the pan and sat down at a table that came with the apartment. It had a vinyl top and chrome-plated tube legs. There was a chrome band that went around the top. The pan was on a dish towel on the table.

I put a spoonful of mustard in the pan, proceeded to eat and tell him the whole bloody story. I was finished with both my food and my tale of woe at the same time. He said if they searched the apartment and found illegal drugs he would never get to be a doctor. He said they had his address as my address. He said if he was ever implicated in any kind of drug activity he would be out for the season. I told him there were no drugs in his apartment that I put there. He seemed to know I wasn't the heavy-duty trafficker of narcotics portrayed on the television. I never asked him why he wanted to be a doctor, but everything he did was with that in mind.

Our trial date was several months away. That night seemed like a bad dream, but it wasn't. I wrote a long expository account of what happened for the *Lantern* entitled "The Anatomy of a Drug Bust," but it never got printed. Since I couldn't use the names of real people I used the names of horses at Markin Farm. That is most likely why it never got printed. There were names like Travelair, Rob Roy, Casey Jones, Jumping Jack, Prime Power, Pepi, Little Man, dar dar Da Buchi, Moon Shine, Sea Moon, Resaletta, Electric Storm, Bea Booty, and others. I handed it in to a student editor without any explanation. I didn't ask or hear about it after that day.

The two people I was arrested with left the university and the next time I saw them was outside the courtroom the day of our trial. We were tried together. The vet student paid the lawyer, or rather his parents did. It was a sizable hunk of change. According to the vet student if he were convicted as charged it would end his plans to be a veterinarian. Our innocence would help his guilt, or so he said. In exchange he would pay our legal fee. I paid the lawyer a token amount of $200, and the other person did also. When I told my parents about what happened my father said, "I'll see you through," which sounded good, but he did nothing. It wasn't like the time I was a child and he fixed my three-speed English bicycle. It was one of the first bicycles sold in America to have more than one ratio between the foot crank and the back wheel. I thought it was the most beautiful, sleekest bicycle that ever existed.

One day the bike was by one of the rock walls in front of the Little Barn and I was standing beside it full of despair. The cable that shifted gears was messed up because of some folly of mine. I was sure the bicycle would never be the same. My father was on his way to the office. He diverted his direction and fixed it in two moments. His hands got greasy and he went back into the house to wash them. The bicycle worked perfectly, and as I pedaled away I thought there was very little he could not do. I suppose when I told him about the crime I had the silly infantile notion that he could somehow fix everything, but I was a big boy now. It was like I was naming convictions to him when I said what the charges were.

I sold things to raise money for expenses, but I ended up selling all the things I didn't use anymore. I sold a better than new Western saddle. The thick leather was extremely soft and pliable. I kept it with me because I liked the way it looked. I put a leather conditioner on it every day even though the horse was dead. The saddle had detailed tooling. It looked good.

I rode with an English saddle growing up. That was a very proper way to ride a horse. Then there was the American Western saddle. It didn't promote rider and horse contact the way an English saddle did, but a person could work in the Western saddle all day. It was different.

The only horse that was ever born at Markin Farm was an Arabian stallion named Sea Moon. When I rode that animal with the Western saddle toward the end of his life it was practically the only time that horse was ever ridden, and it was the only time he was ever ridden regularly.

One warm summer night I stood by an open stall door in my pajamas and watched a foal be born. A veterinarian who had become a family friend arrived to make sure everything went OK. My brother and sisters were there. I was a small child. My mother named the foal Sea Moon. In a book the name belonged to an airplane that went back and forth across the Atlantic Ocean. She said the pilot gave the airplane that name.

Sea Moon, the horse, was seldom ridden. He was never bred and he was never gelded. He spent most of his time in an end stall kicking the wood walls that were twice as thick as any other stall. Every once in a while, Sea Moon would be harnessed to a training cart with large wooden wheels and driven around an outdoor ring. Once he went to an Arabian horse show. I wasn't there, but I heard indirectly that he got an erection in the show ring. At Markin Farm, Sea Moon was never with other horses for any reason, because he was a stallion. Sea Moon was only able to relate with another horse sexually (copulating with females and fighting with males). He kicked the walls all the time and acted sexually frustrated. When he was suddenly in a show ring with all the other horses moving around he apparently still had sex on his brain, and he showed all in attendance what an erect horse penis looked like. It was embarrassing to the female rider, and it was educational to all the men, women, and children who were there.

Once I saw Sea Moon do well in the show ring. I was a small child and my uncle who knew about guns rode him in a costume class at the Cincinnati Gardens horse show. I never saw him ride a horse before or since. At that time more than anything he wanted to gallop Sea Moon around the show ring bareback like Arabs did years ago in Arabia. He had a tiny snaffle bit with braided horsehair reins that were from Arabia. He wore flowing robes with cloth wound around his head and face to keep out wind blown sand. In one raised hand he brandished a rifle. It was the first generation of breech-loaded guns. It was long and heavy. He galloped around and around past all those pompous trotting horses with their silly organ music. It was dramatic to see. He should have gotten first place, but he didn't even get a ribbon. Sea Moon moved like an Arab horse, and looked like one. I wonder if the judges would recognize an Arab if one bit them in the aft-end.

When I rode Sea Moon he was fourteen years old and Markin Farm was not the same. The lady who ran the barn was gone. All the familiar horses were gone. Another lady rented the barn and taught riding lessons to a few people. No one in my family rode anymore. Sea Moon was still in the end stall kicking the walls. I bought that Western saddle to ride him.

There was no riding teacher nearby to correct my equitation. I rode him on the trails and I carried a sawed-off shotgun, which also chambered and shot .45-caliber cartridges. I charged down embankments that would finish a thoroughbred horse. They were so steep that Sea Moon slid down them on his haunches and loved it as much as I did. There was no place that horse wouldn't go or water he wouldn't plunge into. There was a television program about a person who had a sawed-off 30-30 and I carried and shot the 410 like he did. That was the best time I ever had on a horse. I rode Sea Moon the several months I lived at Markin Farm right before I went to the university. When I went away to college his grain wasn't cut back. The rich food and the inactivity got to him and one day he just reared up in his stall and fell over dead. When I heard what happened I felt terrible that I hadn't paid more attention. My brother was the only one home, and he called a new veterinarian who said the horse died of a heart attack.

At that time I also sold Morituri, the wrecked autogiro, and the AK-47. I put an advertisement in the paper, and a man with the words BOOT HILL on his shirt came and bought most of everything I wanted to sell. He gave me the name of someone who would most likely buy the assault rifle.

That person was a military man who was never in the military. His business card read: "Licensed Machine Gun Dealer / Buy, sell, or trade any kind of military item or edged weapon." He lived alone in a large old house on the edge of a gravel pit. Rooms in the house and the attic had rows and rows of World War Two "D-Watt" guns. He explained that *D-Watt* meant the cartridge chamber was welded up so the gun could not be fired. He said the government inspected his collection often. He showed me the main bedroom in the house. It was like a museum with a mannequin standing on the rug wearing a Nazi uniform complete with medals. There was a large Nazi flag draped on one wall.

After he showed me through the house we sat down in a small room with the AK-47. He called someone on the telephone and told him about the rifle. After he hung up he said it was a live weapon I was trying to sell and he didn't want to keep it in his house just yet. When I took it back to my car to leave he said he wanted to buy it, but he would have to do it later. He took parts out of it and told me what to say if a policeman found it during a routine traffic violation. Another day I brought it back. He kept it and gave me money. The first day I was there with the rifle I also had an armful of corroded silver that was horse show first place awards. I sold it all to him. The second time I was there we walked out to a shed. He showed me on the bottom of several platters and other pieces where it said: STERLING SILVER. He thought he had something.

Since his card said he wanted to buy any military item, the second time I went there I took a pair of North Vietnamese standard issue shoes. They were sandals made from a rubber automobile tire. They had automobile tread on the bottom of the soles. They were cut in the shapes of a right and left foot, and they were held to the foot by four strips cut from tire inner tubes. The strips were less than an inch wide, and some instrument that pulled the ends of them through the sole fastened them. Two strips crossed over the front of the foot, and the other two went on each side of the ankle. I called them VC Flyers. The man whose card indicated he collected or traded any type of military item wasn't the slightest bit interested in them. They couldn't be polished. It didn't make any difference to him that it was the army with car tire shoes that won.

The lawyer who handled our drug bust was either a former city prosecutor or, once worked in the prosecutor's office. He knew the detectives who arrested us by their first names. All of them were outside the courtroom the day of the trial.

The lawyer telephoned the day before the trial. I asked him if I should bring a toothbrush, and he said no. On the day of our trial we were sitting in different places in the hall. The lawyer came up to me and said the charges would be reduced to the misdemeanor of possession of a hallucinogen, plus we would have to spend ninety days in jail beginning on that day. I wasn't very happy about going to jail any day, especially that day, and I as much as said so. I didn't bring my toothbrush. The lawyer took two $100 bills out of his pocket and held them out to me. That was the amount I had paid him. Then one of the police detectives who arrested us came over and asked the lawyer what was wrong. The lawyer told the policeman, "He doesn't want to do it."

The policeman stepped very close to me, pointed his finger in my face, and said, "I'm going to put you in the Ohio Penitentiary for forty years." I told the lawyer who was standing right there that I just reconsidered. I'll do the ninety days. I asked him if I could have a day to close out of my classes and do other things in preparation for a ninety-day all-expense-paid vacation. He said he would see what he could do.

In those days judges weren't assigned cases by the court. A person or his lawyer could "shop for a judge." We were in the hall when the lawyer came out and said the judge he and the police had just seen refused to hear the case or reduce the five felonies to a single misdemeanor with jail time. The lawyer said the judge was up for reelection that year. He said there was another judge who would see us after lunch in his courtroom.

The vet student and one of his parents had lunch with the lawyer. The other person arrested with us had lunch somewhere else. I had lunch by myself near the courthouse and gnashed my teeth thinking how rotten things were in Denmark. After lunch we met back in the hall and went into the courtroom. There were two or three spectators. On one side of the room were the three of us and our lawyer. On the other side were the police detectives and another person who might have been the prosecutor. The prosecutor didn't talk the whole time. The judge never said what our sentence was, but he gave us a big lecture about how we were "playing with fire." The judge commended the prosecutor and police for being subjective. The lawyer asked if we could have a day to get our "affairs in order." The judge looked at the other side and they didn't object. The judge agreed and reiterated that we were "playing with fire." In the elevator on the way out of the courthouse the lawyer said to me that the police told him I would be back. I looked down at my trousers to see if they were neatly pressed and felt to see if my tie was straight. The only difference between the other two and me was that in the courtroom the other two had their eyes downcast. The police thought they would see me again in the criminal justice system because I looked at the judge when he was talking.

The next day the teacher of a creative writing class said I could finish the course from jail. He said there was one more short story due and I could send it to him. I wrote one about jail and called it "Whirl Pool."

When I told him the lawyer asked me if he could have my student pass to the football games the teacher spilled his coffee. At that time there were no professional sport teams in Columbus, Ohio. Ohio State University had the only football team in town. For several years the parking lot of a fast food restaurant on High Street had a thirty-foot-high football player wearing a "Bucks" uniform. The Ohio State football team was big in that town. When they weren't playing at another college they played in a stadium on campus. Every student could get a free pass to home games. Seats that were left were sold to the general public. When the stadium was full it was full.

I watched the home games in the stadium when I was a freshman, because the person I was with all the time loved watching football games. After that I never had an overwhelming desire to watch the Bucks play and I never got a pass. It was amazing I didn't get a stiffer sentence.

A nutty professor in the School of Journalism proceeded to castigate me when I said why I had to drop his course. Still another teacher denied my existence. It was a very informative time.

The next day we were processed into the Franklin County workhouse along with five other people. We stood in a line side to side without any clothes on, and one of the guards sprayed us with something that would kill any bugs that might find their way into the workhouse. We were told to turn around, bend over, and "spread our cheeks." A guard then walked down the line visually inspecting each person's anal orifice. I was later told that was done to detect and stop anyone from bringing weapons or other contraband into the workhouse via his rectum.

People convicted of a misdemeanor were given gray pants and a gray shirt to wear and people convicted of a felony were given bright orange clothes. We had white undershirts, and no underpants. A guard gave us a razor to shave with, which had to be returned a few hours later.

We were given "bed clothes" consisting of two sheets, a blanket, and a pillowcase and escorted to the top of the stairs on the second floor where a guard sat at a desk. Ten feet from each side of the desk there were two heavy steel bar doors. Each door was the entrance to a "dormitory" that was about fifty feet by twenty-five feet. Each room had five large windows covered with bars on the fifty-foot side. The three of us were put in the west dormitory facing the front parking lot. In the back of the dormitory room was a urinal like the one at the army orientation center. Also in the back of the room were several toilets with no partition around them. There were several bathroom sinks with no mirrors. The room was filled with five rows of bunk beds end to end, about sixty beds in all. The rows were four or five feet apart. The felons wearing bright orange clothes were in the dormitory beside ours. The steel bar entrance door to our dormitory was in one corner. The rest of that wall was covered with steel lockers one over the other. Each of us had one to keep the few personal effects we were allowed to have.

If a person had more than one year of jail time they didn't go to the workhouse. They were put in one of the Ohio penitentiaries. There was the city prison, the county jail or workhouse, and the Ohio Penitentiary. Where a person went depended on the nature of their conviction.

In the Franklin County workhouse there was a cross section of the criminal population. In that place there were people who had done big time in the penitentiary. They were out on parole and were in the workhouse because of some minor offense like a traffic violation of some sort. There were "decrepit old winos" convicted of public intoxication. There were people there who came for the weekend only. One individual there was convicted of "lewd and lascivious conduct."

One of the people who said he spent many years in the penitentiary was out on parole. He said a policeman tried to stop him for speeding and he didn't stop. A chase ensued. I asked him why he was put in the penitentiary, and he said he shot a policeman who was treating him badly. He wrestled the policeman's gun away from him and shot him in the abdomen. The policeman didn't die. This man said the traffic judge was startled when he saw his heinous criminal record.

On visitors day for various reasons almost all of us were peering from behind the windows into the parking lot in an insane manner. The guard at the desk came into our dormitory room. He told us to get away from the windows and called us a bunch of anal orifices, but he used a slang for that body part. The superintendent of the workhouse got a piece of paper we all signed. It said we didn't appreciate being referred to in such a derogatory fashion. The next day our dormitory had to file into the eating area to talk with the superintendent. The paroled individual raised his hand and stood up to speak. He had a heated voice, and in part this is what he said: "I've been in the joint, and one thing we hate in there is a snitch."

A day later the paroled man was told by the guard at the desk to get ready to leave. He went to the window, and when he looked out at the car parked by the front door he said in a matter-of-fact way, "I'm going back to the joint." I went to the window after he left, as did many others. I saw him go from the front door to the car. There were two guards on each side of him. His feet were chained together, he had a chain around his waist, and his hands were chained to that chain. The superintendent revoked his parole.

After the meeting with the superintendent one of the people who was prominent among us made a loud remark about a snitch that I thought was directed toward me. I thought it was odd coming from him. I was in a reclining position on my bunk. He was two rows over on his bunk several bunks down. I couldn't see him. I said equally as loudly, "The only one who ever snitched on me was . . . " and I said his name. He had a reputation to preserve. He got up and walked down the row to my bunk and smacked me in the face with his open hand. I jumped up, and peppered his face with my fists in an equally harmless way. He seemed very startled and went back to his bed after some more words.

Our entire dormitory was the kitchen crew. We never went outside. At one point I was the vegetable cook, and one time I lost my ring in a five-gallon pot of "greens." This prominent guy told the guard who watched us about my ring. I was given a different job. I was made the "Pot and Pan Man."

Coffee Man was in charge of one thing: making coffee. It was exceptionally potent. Since we worked in the kitchen we could drink as much coffee as we wanted. During the first few days I drank several cups in the morning, afternoon, and evening. It made me feel like I wanted to swing from the high trapeze. I asked Coffee Man about his amazing coffee. He said he used to make coffee on a ship in the U.S. Navy and he was doing the same thing here.

Soon the coffee and the amount I drank didn't give me the

same feeling anymore. When I stopped drinking it completely I had severe headaches and tunnel vision for several days. I went a week without drinking any coffee, and by the end of that time I felt relatively normal.

I started drinking multiple cups of the coffee again and it affected me exactly as it did at first. Then I needed constantly more to achieve the same condition until finally I needed to drink it to get normal.

Once again I stopped drinking it entirely, and I had the same prolonged headache and tunnel vision as the first time. That was some powerful coffee.

One person in a gray shirt who seemed to have the run of the place came in the kitchen every morning after breakfast. He was a large jovial man who didn't seem to have a care in the world. I don't know if it is true or not, but he said the police would go looking for him when it started to get cold, because he was the only one who could operate the furnace in the workhouse. He would say with a huge smile that when "the sun didn't shine on both sides of the street" the police would find him or he would find them. He would spend the winter where he was needed and it was warm.

When he came into the kitchen after breakfast it was to eat four slices of bread that were in the bottom of a stainless-steel serving container that had been full of hot bacon before breakfast. After breakfast it was empty. He liked to eat the bread because it was soaked with bacon grease. He would mop the last soggy piece around the bottom of the container to get all that was there. I don't think he could read or write. He was a middle-aged man who although large in size, was not the least bit fat or overweight. The way he was reminded me of the words of a song: "Lucky old Sun has nothing to do but roll around heaven all day."

Another person in our dormitory was a recovering drug addict. He always talked about the "gorilla jones" on his back. When he talked like that he was suffering withdrawal symptoms from drugs. A drug called methadone was given to him to eliminate his addiction. When he received his treatment he was quiet until it wore off.

One "resident" figured out which car in the parking lot belonged to a certain guard and said he was going to do something to that car when he got out. He said he spent twenty years in the Ohio Penitentiary. He didn't tell me why he was there, but he told me about someone he met there. He said that person's wife was sitting on a living room couch beside her mother. Two children were in the room, and so was a dog. He said she said to the man that she wanted a divorce and added, "The children aren't yours. You're not man enough to have children." The man left the room, and when he came back he said to her, "You mean none of this is mine," and he proceeded to shoot and kill everyone in the room, including the dog.

When the addict needed medication he would get anxious and nervous and he would talk crazily. When he first arrived in the workhouse he was dependent on medication. Out of nowhere and to no one in particular he would say, "You so square, man. Decrepit old winos, if you had some good coke (cocaine) you would probably shove it up your ____ (anal orifice). You so square, man."

Then he would start talking about what he considered his expertise. You freeze a ___ (an American word denoting a house cat but also used to describe the female genital area) with a little coke and she can ___ (a common American slang word for sexual intercourse) all night long." He would go over and over about that and about "decrepit old winos."

One time we talked about "decrepit old winos" and he told me again that if they had any good cocaine they would probably shove it up their rear end. I said a drug addict who lived in Tangier wrote a book fifty years ago that said foreign substances in the rectum could be absorbed into the bloodstream.

He kept right on going as if I weren't there. "You nothing, man. You nothing. A decrepit old wino would shove it up his ___ [anal orifice]."

One of the most often asked questions about jail was about sexual conduct. The most often asked question when I came back from Vietnam was did I kill anybody. I developed a stock answer. I would say I didn't have to kill anyone and no one had to kill me. So when I was repeatedly asked about sex in jail I thought about using the expression from Vietnam with a slight modification, but it didn't sound right. How could I say with a straight face, "I didn't have to ___ anybody and nobody had to ___ me." (Then I would have used the slang four-letter word for fornicate.)

The person who didn't say why he was in the penitentiary told me that in the penitentiary he saw three people hold another person still so a fourth person could have anal intercourse with the person being held. He said a guard walked by and after watching a while walked on without doing anything. The person telling me said the guard said the person being held by the three other people was enjoying himself.

It is doubtful that sort of thing would occur in the workhouse, because none of the people were there for more than a year. Many of the people were there for the weekend. The workhouse never became the closed system that a penitentiary becomes. Forcible sex didn't occur there as far as I know.

In the felon dormitory there were two individuals who made no secret of the fact that they thought of themselves as perfect ladies even though they were men. They had nicknames like Buttercup and Lilac, but those weren't their nicknames. One of them requested a douche from a guard.

The third person who was arrested with us was put in that dormitory after several weeks, I suppose, to separate us. He told us in the kitchen that when he went to the urinal without pants, as if he was in a locker room in college, his bare buttocks were visible and he said right after he went back to his bunk to get dressed several people started masturbating in the area of the urinal. The sight of his bare bottom sexually excited them.

There was a person in there for ninety days who was arrested many times before for public intoxication and sent to jail. He liked to drink on Mount Vernon Street, and that was where he always got arrested. He said it happened so often, he had a reputation with the police for being publicly intoxicated whether or not he was. According to him the last time it happened he was sitting on a bar stool. After talking with him they told him to get in the van.

He told me he lost a job that time and when he was in jail his wife had to go to the public welfare office to get financial help. He said they told her in the welfare office that they could only help her if she filed nonsupport charges against him. He was charged with nonsupport and transported from the workhouse where he was serving time for public intoxication to the city prison to await trial on the nonsupport charge. The first time he was told about the nonsupport charge was after three weeks in the city prison. That was when he saw a judge who sentenced him to ninety days in the workhouse for nonsupport. To him it was life as usual.

Several times each week we took a shower. There were two rooms. One room was where we got undressed, and the other was the shower room, with eight or ten unpartitioned areas in which to take a shower. There was a guard who stood in the doorway between the two rooms and told people to hurry up and keep moving. The felon dormitory and our dormitory of mostly long-term misdemeanors took showers at the same time, but we weren't there all at once. Some people were finishing up when I got there and when I left some others were just arriving.

The first time I walked into the shower room I was naked like everybody else. When I looked for an available shower I saw two people from the felon dormitory standing motionless with water pouring down their backs. They were looking at everyone who came in the shower room. I wasn't in the habit of looking at a person's penis, but I couldn't help but notice that theirs was large compared to mine. Those people had black skin too. When I got under a shower I kept facing the wall partly because my penis was smaller and I didn't want anyone else to make that comparison.

Let me say something about the human penis for the benefit of those who do not have one: There is the full erection, which everyone knows about, but there are many stages between that and a shriveled-up penis (the smallest size) which is the way mine was that day and when I would go swimming in the cold water of Penobscot Bay. What determines the stage of enlargement (erection being the stage of maximum enlargement) is the brain. My penis would get larger when I thought in a certain way. Sexual excitement aroused my penis automatically, but there was something else that could occur to make it swell up bigger than normal without its becoming erect. It required a certain kind of brain control that a person could develop if that was something he wanted to develop.

I turned around in the shower to rinse off my back and when I was facing outward I saw the guard motioning people to hurry up. Then in walks this person from our dormitory who was very small in stature, but his penis was huge. I mean it hung halfway down to his knees, and he had black skin too. He seemed self-conscious.

When I first saw him up in the dormitory I thought he didn't seem old enough to be in the workhouse. When I asked him how old he was he said he was nineteen.

After that first day in the shower I talked with him more. He said he was in jail for a conviction of some long words he didn't know about, but he did know about what happened. He said he was spinning a child around in circles. He said he was holding her by the legs in such a way that her ankles were under his arms and his hands were holding onto her legs above her knee. He said they were outside and when the girl's mother saw what she saw the police were called. This person said when the judge saw him and exchanged words with him the judge wanted to dismiss the entire thing, but the police insisted that he go to jail (they were probably white-skinned males who knew about the size of his penis from a routine strip search).

In the shower where everyone was trying to make their penis look bigger than it was this person felt afflicted because his penis was huge. After that day the person who smacked me in the face said it was a "horse ___" (he used a common American word for penis that is also a proper first name, *dick*). Other people started to use that terminology and it became a frequent joke among us.

In the afternoon before we went down to prepare the evening meal there were several hours to spend in the dormitory talking to other people, reading, writing letters, or sleeping. Among all the people in that dormitory there was a tremendous amount of lawbreaking ability. I suppose if you asked any civil authority they would say a prison or jailhouse was the highest concentration of contrary people anywhere. All we had to do when we weren't working is sit around and develop a future with the unintentional help of the other people who were also locked up. Every sort of debauchery grows there.

The third month I was there I had an idea. The vet student couldn't believe I was serious. It involved the person with the huge penis so I told him the idea, since he would have to be an active participant if it were going to happen. When I started to tell him about my idea he grinned his big toothy grin, but as I got further into it he wasn't so sure.

I asked him if he would like to be in a short movie. I said a beautiful princess with many jewels arrives at a splendid hotel in a horsedrawn coach that looks like a pumpkin. There is a footman standing on the back of the coach and the hotel has a doorman. There are many yellow New York City taxicabs in front of and behind the coach. Other cars of different colors, makes, and models as well as tandem trucks are going up and down the street beside the hotel honking their horns to make it all go faster. There is only one horsedrawn coach with a princess in it and a mist is blowing in the air as if there is an old castle nearby. She gets out of the coach with the footman's help, and goes into the hotel in a manner consistent with the time when there were coaches and footman. Inside, in a hallway she goes into an American-style motel room that has two large beds taking up most of the space in the room. She takes off her diamond necklace and other weighty jewels while looking at herself in the mirror by the television. She steps out of her skirt and lies down on the bed. In a private moment she is having sexual thoughts. She touches her genitals. No sooner does that happen than there is a very soft knocking on the door. She looks at the other bed with a disgusted look and says, "Come in," without getting up. She thinks it is the dashing young prince she knows so well. He usually has a sword strapped around his waist and gold things on his shoulders like Napoléon wore.

"This is where you come in," I said to the person with the huge penis, "and it is where the plot thickens." He grinned for the last time, and when I went on with the story his eyes darted from side to side nervously like he wanted to get away from me. "It is you at the door, and when you open it there you are in a bellhop's uniform complete with a little round brimless hat. You have two pieces of modern luggage on each side of you with airport baggage claim checks on the handles. That is why you are there, to bring her luggage to her. She is startled to see you and sits up quickly and even though she is wearing bloomers and a corset that covers her body she crosses her arms in front of her chest as if she is wearing nothing. She tells you, like she is a modern person, to, 'put them over there.' You do so with only a 'yes, ma'am' in reply, and when you put them down beside the television you turn around and stand there waiting for a tip. She doesn't know anything about tips. She thinks you are standing there to look at her. She thinks she is so pretty. She is pretty, in fact.

"Sex is the furthest thing from your mind, but it is the first thing on hers. She asks you to come over to her bedside in a tone that leaves no doubt about her intentions. Like in an old silent movie you point to yourself while mouthing the words, *Who me*, and you look behind you to see if she is talking to someone else. You do all that in a choppy, accelerated fashion. She thinks she is going to sexually abuse some poor child who doesn't matter to the world. When you come close to her, as she directs, she puts your listless hand on her breast. Then she drops your pants and *whammy*. The tables are turned about who is going to abuse who. You are not the poor child anymore. She can see how well endowed you are. What follows is a rip-roaring ___ oree. (I used a slang word that means fornicate. It begins with *f* but is a whole lot shorter. "When you leave she tells you it is an extraordinary hotel."

The person with the huge penis didn't seem very excited about the idea. I said I knew someone who would make a perfect princess and she would do it since it had political and social import. The hardest part would be the beginning. I said it would have to be done right or else it would be garbage. I asked him what he thought about it and he sort of nodded in the affirmative. Right away someone who heard us jumps off his bunk and wants to be the agent of the person with the huge penis. I didn't like the idea of involving more people from that place. The vet student overheard the whole exchange and he told me the person who wanted to be the agent might be working for the police. The would-be agent was the only one in our dormitory who came and went each weekend, and he asked many questions beyond what was normal. So maybe the vet student was right.

I told the person with the huge penis he would be a millionaire overnight because of his penis. He didn't seem very interested. It was like he thought some authority that was close to him on the outside wouldn't like the get rich quick idea. It was probably his mother. Anyway, it never happened.

Motor Mouth Mop and Bucket Man kept things clean in the downstairs areas. He was in jail for as long as I was in jail. He must have been in one of the two dormitories on the other side, because he wasn't in either the felony dormitory or our dormitory. I never asked him why he got locked up. He seemed like one of the people the drug addict would refer to as a decrepit old wino. He didn't seem capable of a crime. He would talk about everything and nothing.

He came over to talk to me, his mop and bucket forgotten. He talked confidently about the universe. He said it keeps going on in both directions. He said what is too big to see is also too small to see. His talk went from one subject to the next. He wouldn't stop talking if someone was listening, and sometimes he would be talking when no one was listening.

There were six old men in the kitchen called Part Three and their job was to "eye" potatoes and cut them up in smaller pieces. That is all they did. They weren't from our side of the building. We had mashed potatoes often so they were there often.

There was a large stainless teel table. When Part Three was in the kitchen three of them would stand on each side of the table talking to no one as they busily took a peeled potato out of a pot of cold water, worked on it, and put it in another pot of cold water. The table looked like a giant insect, on its back.

When I was the vegetable cook it was my job to supply them with peeled potatoes. A vertical cylindrical appliance with an abrasive wall did the pealing. The machine had an electric motor at the base. The top of the cylinder was open, and that is where twenty pounds of unpeeled potatoes would go and where they were taken out when they were peeled.

It was a vibratory machine and a constant shower of water washed over the potatoes when the motor was going. The potatoes would move from the top of the cylinder to the bottom and from the inside to the outside. When they were on the outside they were against an abrasive wall, and it was by rubbing against the wall that the skin was removed. After several minutes all the potatoes would be peeled. If the machine was left going the potatoes would be ground down to nothing.

When I took the skinless potatoes out of the machine I took them to Part Three where any spots or blemishes would be removed and the whole potato would be cut into smaller pieces.

The six old men who made up Part Three were issued a knife when they arrived in the kitchen, and the only time they put the knife down was in the guard's hand when they were done. There were no knives, forks, or other sharp instruments loose in that place. We ate with spoons.

There was a vivid individual in our dormitory, who said things that might be thought of as hateful toward other people, but there was no hate in him. We talked often. He would talk in metaphors about the relationship between people. He said this: "One day the white mens will wake up and grab their gun off the wall to kill the black mens, but there won't be any bullets, because the white woman took them out and gave them to the black mens."

Another time he talked about a man with the same skin color. For years the man's picture and name was on a box of food on store shelves. He said that man would "jump over five white ___ (the slang name for the female genital area also the name for the common house cat) to get at one tight white ___ (slang for the anal orifice, in this instance one belonging to a male)."

I could always understand him, because his imagery was so good. When I once said it was correct grammar to say there was one "man" and several "men" he quickly and deliberately used the word *mens* several times as he always did. He kind of shot a look at me now and again to see how I was taking it. The vet student was listening and he told me later how idiotic it was to correct anyone's English in that place. I knew the vivid person would not take offense. What I said was simply a mechanical statement about the English language. It came from the years I spent in school that we both knew about. His graphic perceptions did not result from how many years he was in school.

The vivid individual was not homosexual, but sex in any form was the only power he considered he could attain. He felt economically impotent. He talked about "breaking people down like a shotgun" and how they would cry "like sissy punk rabbits as they gave it up."

A few years ago on the observation deck of a tall building in Cincinnati a person was forcibly sodomized. The city newspaper quoted the judge when he sentenced the man. When I read it I thought about the vivid individual's remarks. Maybe sexual gratification had little to do with it and power over other people did.

As Christmas Day got near I wondered if anything would be different when it came. I wrote our lawyer asking him if there was any chance of my being released early so I'd be out for Christmas. I never heard back from him.

On Christmas Day we got up in the dark as usual and went down in the kitchen to make breakfast for the workhouse population. When breakfast was over we were told to go back to bed. That is what we did for Christmas. I was amused when I heard that instruction. I scoffed to myself, *Go back to bed just after dawn on Christmas Day, that was just great, divinely inspired.*

Then the guards passed out small packages to everyone. I asked if it was a bomb and the guard said it was a Christmas gift from the Salvation Army. I had always thought of them as a bunch of tent dwellers with runny noses outside department stores. There could be no payback in mind here. I later learned their mission was to save one soul at a time. It wasn't clear to me what they were saving a person from, but I knew God was involved. We were the dregs of society, and they were giving us presents on Christmas. There seemed to be a purity in what they did.

Right after I got out of the workhouse I was let go in downtown Columbus, and when I went around the corner there standing on the sidewalk talking to another person was the superintendent. After I had walked past him I stopped, turned around, and walked back to say hello. I said his name, which interrupted them both. They looked at me. I asked him how he was doing. He didn't seem to recognize me and he didn't answer. I explained that I had just been in the workhouse, and that I was glad he ran the place. There was a look on his face that wasn't exactly friendly. It was as if he were turning wheels in his head about who I was, how I got out, and if I was going to be an embarrassment to him on the street. Before he had time to react further, I turned and was on my way up the street to get a bus to the university.

Several weeks later I saw on the television news that the

mayor of Columbus was taking recommendations for a new police chief. (He succeeded the person who was mayor during the student riots.) I never before wrote a public official, but I wrote him. My letter said the Franklin County workhouse was run by a person I thought would make a good police chief. I explained that more than once I saw him stop and talk with an old derelict who wanted to have a few words with him.

The guards and superintendent of the workhouse had several tables in the rear of the eating area where they would eat food or have coffee in the morning. They would walk the length of the eating area to leave. It was when the superintendent was leaving that sometimes a person in jail would intersect his path to talk. It didn't happen very often, but when it did the superintendent would stop before the individual ever got to him as if he wanted to hear what that person had to say. I thought that was very unusual behavior in the police community, and it was why I thought he would make a good police chief.

I was surprised to get a letter back from the mayor that thanked me for my suggestion. It said this person was not available for the job of police chief, because people wanted him to be the new Franklin County sheriff.

He won the election for Franklin County sheriff by many votes. The existing sheriff had television advertisements about law and order, and his advertisements showed policemen side by side shouldering pump shotguns. They jacked shells through the guns and fired them as fast as they could. What they were shooting at was offscreen.

I learned as much in jail as any three months in college. It wasn't the kind of thing someone who was looking at my résumé would appreciate, but it was something I appreciated. I would never have met those people if I hadn't been there.

Neither of the other two people I was arrested with stayed in Columbus. I never saw the vet student after we were let out of jail. The third person was in Columbus for several weeks, but then he left.

I never met the person on California Street who had the cocaine, but an out-of-state student who had been in several laboratory plays with me knew him well. They both came from the same place. Most of the students at Ohio State University were from Ohio, but there was a tight little group from New Jersey, and that included both of them. I was in the out-of-state student's apartment several times before I was arrested and once afterward. It was a modern two-bedroom apartment with air-conditioning. His roommate was from the same area as him, and there was always a girl with him who was just like him. I never saw either of them have a conversation with anyone. When I was there I would be there a long time before I knew they were there. They would come out of the bedroom without talking much or focusing their eyes on anyone. When they talked to each other it was always in a whisper. They seemed precise about everything from the way they did their hair to the clothes they wore. When they came out of the bedroom it was to go somewhere else.

The last time I was in that apartment it was after I was released from jail. She was not there. The out-of-state student and I went in together. He turned around and locked the door. We stood there by the door. Our conversation quickly went to the arrest and what took place, especially as it related to the person on California Street. I said I did not know that person. Meanwhile I could hear his silent roommate behind me opening a bed sheet.

He asked why the vet student left Ohio. I told him because we were concerned the police would be following us. At that point he unlocked the door, went outside, closing the door behind him, and left it unlocked. The silent roommate and I were alone in the room. I had never talked to him before, and I didn't that time. I didn't even look at him. True to form, he went into his bedroom. I couldn't see the door, but heard him shut it quietly. There was probably a button lock on the doorknob. I think he was scared I would get the gold chain off his neck. When the out-of-state student came back inside, the roommate was still in his bedroom. For a second there was this look on his face as if he was going to ask where I put his roommate. After the door to the apartment closed, the silent roommate came out. He said to the silent roommate, "I didn't see anyone outside." He pointed to the sheet on the floor behind me and said, "Do you know what that is?" I looked behind me and said it looked to me like he was going to cover his furniture.

The out-of-state student said to the silent roommate, "He thinks we are going to cover the furniture." Shortly after that I left.

I saw him once more after that time. The third person I was arrested with and myself went with him to another person's apartment where I had never been. The people in the apartment were friends of the out-of-state student from the same part of the country as him. I had seen them in the cafeteria before but never had any conversation with them. There were many red pills on the table.

I had never gotten familiar with pills. He knew about them and said I and the third person should take two of them. I did, and the three of us left to go to a big place on High Street where there was live music. The third person disappeared before we went inside the place. The out-of-state student got up several times to look for him and make telephone calls. After that night the third person left Columbus. I never saw him again after that night.

Those two pills took away all my self-control. I had no control over myself. It was awful. One of the times when he got up to look for the third person I tried to snap out of it and look in the direction of the music. I couldn't see the band. There was a relatively customary collegiate couple sitting at the end of the table where I was sitting. When I looked in the direction of the music I was also looking at them. He said something to me in a friendly fashion, but I don't know what it was. I couldn't even talk to them or focus my eyes on them.

When the out-of-state student returned to the table he said, "Let's go," and we did. I could hardly walk out of there. Outside when the night air hit me I felt more able to walk. Amazingly, I drove him to where he lived and then back to my place on Frambes. I never saw him again after that night.

I had some time before classes started again so I got a job pushing a broom around the Animal Science Building on West Campus. I cleaned things. One part of the building I did not have to clean was a large room where animals were killed for food.

The processing took place over three days. The three-day cycle didn't happen continuously but about once every two weeks. The room where the animals were killed had two large entrance doors at the end of a hallway. The large doors were always open so it wasn't difficult for me to walk into the room. Most days the room was empty and the lights were off. It had windows at the top of one wall, and a high ceiling.

On the first day of the cycle live animals were put in a small holding area on the south side of the building. There might be ten hogs or five cattle at different times.

I was struck by how lackadaisical the animals looked. The cattle had blank looks on their faces as they chewed hay, and the pigs had their noses to the ground, doing what pigs do. They weren't the least bit aware that their blood would spill out the next day and they would die. The purpose of their life was providing food for people. Generation after generation of livestock was slaughtered, and not one of the animals back on the farm knew what future awaited them. If one told the other what happens to them then there would be some changes. If one animal escaped from a slaughterhouse and informed all the other animals about their future that would change the order of things, but the animals would have to be reasoning, intelligent beings. They weren't.

On the second day the lights were on in the room and it was very busy with activity. The two doors at the end of the hall were open so I went in to see. A pig was prodded into a pen as narrow as the pig was wide. A person with an electronic device leaned into the pen and pushed two protruding electrodes into the base of the animal's neck. When a switch of some kind was activated the animal was knocked out. The end of a chain from an overhead hoist on a track was wrapped around one of the animal's back legs, and it was lifted up out of the pen and moved several feet farther into the room. A person with a long, narrow knife felt for the right spot on the animal's neck and inserted the long knife toward the heart. When the full length of the knife was in the animal the person holding the knife moved the tip back and forth, and when the knife was removed dark red blood poured out of the incision in a steady stream. Then the pig was dead.

I didn't stand there very long watching. There were several pigs ahead of the one I saw die so I could see where it was going. There was a large, long stainless-steel hot water container with rows of flippers on axles. A pig was lowered into one end, and the turning action moved it to the other end. The process served to remove hair from the dead pig. When it was hoisted out of the hot water it didn't look like the same pig anymore. Then its guts were removed.

I watched as I leaned on my broom for several minutes. Then I went back into the hall to do more sweeping. When I was at the far end of the hall I turned around to go back. One of the people in the room came out, and I saw him talking to another person as he looked at me. By the time he was finished talking I was halfway down the hall toward him pushing the broom and some sweeping compound. He walked over to me and asked if I was an agriculture student. He had a friendly manner. When I said no, he talked with me further about nothing in particular. It seemed like he wanted to know if I was disturbed by what I saw. His concern was genuine. I didn't have an occasion to tell him that I had seen animals butchered for food on a small scale. We didn't talk about anything that was going on in that room.

I ate hamburgers in fast-food restaurants on High Street. I was reminded how it got to be. Sometimes when I only saw meat in the marketplace I would almost forget it came from an animal that was killed somewhere. The third day in another room off the hall the meat would be cut up into familiar looking pieces.

The next time cattle were processed, and that time the two big doors to the room at the end of the hall were closed. There was one small square window in each door. I could see the decapitated, skinned animal hanging from the chain hoist. The day before, the same cattle were standing contentedly in the holding area as if it were their barnyard.

Later someone who worked in a big meat packing plant told me how cattle were killed there. I didn't see how they killed steers at the university. He said at the meat packing plant live cattle walk up a chute to what he called the killing floor. He said a person puts a device against the animal's forehead, and a steel rod plunges into the animal's brain, killing it instantly.

9

Moving Around

In the spring of that year a new cycle (quarter) of classes started. I went to school all year long, even in the summer. By then I was taking the advanced-level journalism courses.

I took many pictures at that time. Once I wandered into the Veterinary Medicine Building and at that very minute an operation called a cesarean section (C-section) was being performed on a Holstein cow. The cow was brought to the university that day because she was unable to deliver her calf normally. The owner was in the room also. He was wearing overalls and had mud on his boots.

Later a doctor who was a professor and who was the person who directed the operation called the Journalism School. One of the teachers asked if the person in there taking pictures was me. They said the doctor wanted me to go to his office and explain my presence. I went. He was a diligent man who was concerned because the floor wasn't clean. He wanted to see the photographs. I was directed to show them to him. Also, he was upset because I didn't say who I was. I apologized and said I was an undergraduate student trying to get some grades. That put him at ease.

The photographs were a black-and-white sequence of the whole operation. After it was over I left without saying a word. The best single photograph in that series was one where several people with masks, coats, and rubber gloves were hauling the calf out of the side of the cow. Everybody was bunched together with a singular purpose. One person who was helping in the foreground of the picture had an upturned empty hand that couldn't grab onto anything. The hand was in the light against a black background. Never was somebody's hand so willing to help.

I handed the whole thing into *The Lantern* "city desk" as a possible "photo page." It appeared several days later.

In one course on Main Campus about Elizabethan plays I always sat next to a journalism student who at first I did not know, but I recognized her as one of the mainstream journalism people. I always sat next to her because we had a certain camaraderie. We were the only journalism students in this class far from the Journalism building. The day the C-section photographs appeared in the paper, she asked me how I thought it came out. I said it was very nice, but I asked her what happened to the hand. The photograph was displayed in such a way that the hand was not included. She asked, "What hand?" I told her. She groaned and said they worked on it for a long time. She said I should have been there. It was nice of her to say that, but I knew when they put the paper together there was no other opinion allowed but the staff's in order to minimize confusion. It had to be done quickly.

Soon after that I handed in several photographs and a small amount of words that was titled "Backwoods Ohio." It showed old barns, corncribs, old tractors, cats sleeping on woodpiles, and an outgrown pony. The page appeared without changes.

I went to the University of California at Berkeley that summer. The administration of that university said a person didn't have to be enrolled there to take summer classes. I wrote the people in charge of the GI Bill, and they agreed to pay my tuition. My only expense would be a room, food, and travel. I knew someone from Cincinnati who went to that school. She was renting a big house with several friends on Benvenue Avenue near the university. It had a guest room. I stayed there until I found a place of my own.

I had never driven across the country, and I was looking forward to that as much as anything. I left a week early so I could take my time getting there.

My first overnight stop happened when I had a wreck in St. Louis, Missouri. I exited off the expressway, and the accident resulted when I moved to an inside lane. I was going to turn into a gas station to ask directions. It was during the hour when everyone was trying to hurry up and get home. The person in the other car couldn't stop in time when I changed lanes, and his car collided into the rear driver side corner of my car. The impact spun my car around across the oncoming lanes. Fortunately, there were no cars coming the other way. They were at a stoplight a short distance down the road.

A policeman came and wrote up the accident report. He didn't give either of us a ticket. He said he didn't know who was at fault, and he said that is why there are insurance companies.

The person at the gas station said I could sleep in my car. The next day I worked on the car from dawn until the middle of the afternoon. I had most of the tools I needed to fix the car, but the person at the gas station had whatever additional tools or help I needed.

The day after the accident I called the person whose car collided with mine. He gave me the telephone number of his insurance agent but told me not to call. He said they might come and get me. I only had liability insurance so I had to handle this myself. The insurance agent seemed to know all about the accident. I asked him what he wanted to do. He didn't say anything. I said I would fix my car and he could fix his. He replied, "That is not the way it works." Apparently, his idea was that he wasn't going to discuss it with me, so the telephone call ended.

A year later I got a letter saying that Missouri and Ohio had a "reciprocity" agreement and if I didn't appear in court in St. Louis on such and such a day Ohio would suspend my driver's license. When I got the letter I was out of school. I and two friends from work drove to St. Louis so I could have my day in court. It was hot outside. We had all the windows rolled down in the car.

In court the lawyer representing the insurance company wouldn't let the other guy answer any of the questions I asked him, but when I got up there they let me say what happened. I told them I was on my way to California and I exited in St. Louis because I wanted to go to Gaslight Square. Little did I know that Gaslight Square had been razed. All kinds of unsavory people passing through town went there. To me it was a place I remembered from years before when I worked on the racetrack in Collinsville across the river. The other groom and I went there one time. I was too young to go inside any of the places. The street was narrow and it was full of people walking in both directions. There were many colored lights. One bar had someone out front in a Panama hat with a cane trying to interest anyone into going inside.

That was the Gaslight Square I remembered. The second time I was old enough to go inside. I never got there, and later I heard the whole area had been torn down.

When I was in court and I said why I was in St. Louis I wondered why the person who collided with me tried to contain his amusement. The lawyer with him in the courtroom wouldn't let him talk with me or even respond to a simple question about how he was doing.

I told the judge that I called the insurance agent and that his exact words were, "That is not the way it works." After the court session ended the judge told us to try once more to make a settlement. I went up to the lawyer and said, "I fixed my car; he could fix his." The lawyer was looking over my shoulder at the judge. He didn't say anything. It was just like before.

Several weeks later I got a letter from the court saying the judge ruled in the other guy's favor, and that I had to pay the insurance company for fixing the other car. I noticed that I had five days to appeal starting when the decision was made. It was mailed on a Friday, so the weekend was two of the five days. I called the judge to ask him why, if the police could not attribute any fault, he was able to, and he said, "I call them like I see them." I politely terminated the call without bringing to his attention that he hadn't seen anything. He heard about what happened. That was the way it worked.

After the wreck I took the shroud off the radiator at the gas station. The radiator was in the rear of the car. When I was in Kansas the next day the motor overheated and all the water blew out. I had my trusty Boy Scout two-quart canteen with me. I stood between my car and the road and dangled it by the shoulder strap to indicate I needed water. After a while someone stopped with a big jug of water. I was pushing the motor too hard when it overheated. I didn't go so fast when I got started again, and it didn't overheat anymore.

Things started to look different in a big way once I got to Colorado. The vegetation became thinner and less green. I often slept in my car in a place beside the road where other people were sleeping in their camper or truck. It wasn't the most comfortable place in the world, but it worked as an inexpensive place to sleep that was not far from the highway.

The road wasn't the main east-west turnpike, but it was a major two-lane highway that more or less went parallel to the turnpike. The morning sun shone on cliffs that were far off in the distance. I could see them through the windshield off to the right. They were reddish-brown and were striking the way they appeared in the sunlight.

There was a gravel road that went off to the right. It was just beyond a hillside along the highway. I saw it at the last possible second and pushed down hard on the brake pedal. The gravel road wrapped around the hill and went off into the distance until it disappeared behind another hill. Utility poles marked where the highway went. I could not see the road surface from where I was.

I stopped on the right side of the gravel road, opened my car door, put my feet out on the road, and sat there looking at the cliffs. On the highway a car or truck occasionally went past at a high rate of speed.

Right away another car pulls off the highway and stops a short distance behind me on the left side of the road. Four adult people are inside. I sit there looking at the cliffs. I didn't hear their car on the highway. They must have been traveling behind me and turned after they saw me turn. Their car has out-of-state license plates. I raise my hand to say hello and none of them make any response. They are close enough that I can see two people in the front seat talking back and forth. They look at me. There is a chance they are planning on ruining my day. The only other earthly reason for their stopping in such a lonely place is to urinate, but if that is what they intended why don't they go farther down the road where they will have some privacy.

I decide they aren't friendly. I lean back into my car, hoping they are watching, and pretend to get a gun out of my glove box and tuck it in my belt behind me. I want them to think I have a gun and that if they try anything a lot of us are going to die.

I get out of my car to get the tripod in the trunk. I am wearing a loose shirt that hangs down over my waist. I walk across the road and set up my camera. When I am standing up it is impossible to tell if I have a gun or not, but when I am bent over looking through the camera I am careful not to let them see my back. If they see there is no bulge where the gun is supposed to be, they may carry out their evil deed if that is what they are about.

I go about my business focusing the telephoto lens on the cliffs. The person driving the car opens the door, gets out and looks at the cliffs also. He has a camera like they sell in drugstores and he holds it up to his eye.

He stands there a while beside his open car door looking through his camera. He is to the left and downrange from me. I see him look over at me between the times he holds the camera to his face. Then he walks over to the front of his car and leans back on the hood. He has on a white undershirt. It looks like his belly gets in the way. The shirt is dirty there. He is mostly bald, but what hair he has is slicked back. We aren't close enough to exchange words, but we are close enough to see each other clearly. I don't look directly at him. They might be tourists, but I don't want to find out. I hope they leave.

Then a strange thing happens, considering how desolate that place is. A pickup truck that rattles and is covered with dust turns off the highway. It goes past both of us without stopping. It goes off in the distance down the gravel road. There is one person in the cab who looks like he belongs there. His skin is the same color as the cliffs. He has one hand on the steering wheel and the other is resting in the open window. After he goes past I hear the woman in the front seat yell at the man. He walks around to the door and gets in the car, and they leave. Soon I also leave.

Somewhere on the road going west the highway went through a little town where I stopped for lunch. There was a rack of postcards. One of the cards pictured the biggest ball of string in the world, and that ball of string was located in that very town. It was something anybody could see, and it was something only that town had. The biggest ball of string in the world was there. It was ten feet in diameter.

When some people have a little piece of string, rather than throw it away, they save it in a pocket or put it on a fence post. Then, when it is convenient, they put that piece of string with all the other little pieces of string they have saved. Did one person do this ball of string? At some point did they come to the realization that this was really big? It was a magnificent postcard.

I bought it and sent it to someone I had met several weeks before in Columbus. Before I left for California she said she collected postcards. We first met on High Street. She was sitting in a bar with several girlfriends. It was the end of a hot day. The laughter and fun she was having was what I saw. I was hoping some of it would rub off. She lived in an apartment nearby and grew up in Columbus. She worked for a bank in that city. She didn't look exceptional but she was. One time we played softball with her friends. She would heckle the batter and say, "Hey, batter, batter, batter." The way she ate a cheeseburger was equally captivating. Back on Frambes it was the way she scooted across my bed, the way she reached, the way she turned her head to the side and closed her eyes. It was the way she was.

I was going, more or less, in a straight line to Berkeley, California, when a hitchhiker sitting beside his backpack on the side of the road talked me into going by way of Reno, Nevada. I had plenty of time to get to where I was going, so I took that detour.

The principal business in Reno was legalized gambling. There was one main street through town. I got out of my car, and the hitchhiker and I walked down the street. It was in the middle of the afternoon. The street was busy with people walking both ways. One woman passed me on the sidewalk. She was noticeable. She was dressed in a very tight dress. She was in a big hurry to get down the street like she had just been called and if she didn't hurry she might miss whoever called her.

There was one place with big wide doors and inside on the street level there were rows and rows of chrome-plated gambling devices called slot machines. Into these machines money in the form of a coin was put by a person who hoped the machine would take their one coin and return many coins.

One coin-activated the machine one time. A lever randomly spun three visible wheels on the same axis. When the wheels stopped the machine would do nothing more until another coin was deposited. When the wheels stopped in a certain way, money came out of the machine. That possibility is what attracted people. They voluntarily put their money into the machine with the hope that a far greater amount of money would come out.

I was at the end of two rows of these machines watching many people who were feeding money into them. When I moved a camera up to my face to take a picture they went in the other direction like it was rehearsed.

Seconds later I felt a tap on my shoulder, and I turned to see two large women standing side by side. They were over six feet tall and large in all other respects. One of them said to me without the slightest expression on her face that I would have to leave. She said it was against the law in the state of Nevada to take a picture of people gambling. They didn't say I had to give them the film in my camera, but they did escort the hitchhiker and me out of the building. Soon after that I left Reno and said good-bye to the hitchhiker.

Several years later I worked for a small-town weekly newspaper. The cochairman invited me to a church festival. He wanted the event to appear in the newspaper.

Before I went home I went to the church grounds to the festival. I had my camera with me and I was taking pictures as I walked past all the booths. I didn't think anything except that when I was finished I was going home. I was there to mirror in the paper what was happening so people in the town would know what it was like. At most I thought one picture with a few words would tell it all. I didn't plan to write a story about the festival.

When I was almost ready to leave, the cochairman who invited me there came up to me and said I would have to leave at that moment. He said several people there were upset because I was taking pictures. I said in a rejected tone that I would leave if that is what he wanted me to do. I said, "What exactly is it that you do not want me to take a picture of?"

And he said, "Of the children playing beat the dealer."

I was jolted back to Reno, but this wasn't Reno. It was a small town that, for all practical purposes, was in the middle of a cornfield. Then it hit me that this was wide-open gambling.

I left and when I got home that evening I called a person who lived in that town. He worked nearby on another weekly newspaper owned by the same person who owned the paper where I worked. He grew up in the same religion as the people conducting the festival. I told him what happened and asked his opinion. He said it sounded like I had a good story. We never discussed that this was not the first instance. Gambling at church festivals was a tradition in the United States. They were trapped by tradition. The paper printed more than one picture with a few words. Perhaps the festival was normal, but if I was paid to capture what was happening then that was what I was going to do.

The next day in preparing the story I called the religious leader of the church where the festival took place. The first part of his name was Father. I asked him where the felt tables and other gambling equipment were kept. There was a long pause, and then he said that I would have to ask one of the festival cochairman. I thanked him for his help, and that was the end of the phone call.

I called the town police chief to ask him if what went on there was legal. I liked him. He read comic books at his desk. This police chief was not overly aggressive. He took care of business in a straightforward manner. But when I mentioned the festival he said, "No comment."

Next I called the Hamilton County prosecutor. He was a professional politician who constantly went against the wind, maintaining his own sense of morality. I expected he would give me an answer. I talked with someone in his office. That same person said he would call me back with the answer, but he never did. I thought it was odd that both the local police chief and the county prosecutor would not comment on so simple a question.

I couldn't believe what was happening. I called the state attorney general at the capitol and I explained to someone on the telephone what I was all about and that I was simply trying to find out if it was legal. After a few minutes of looking, this person read me something. He said, "Games of chance and schemes of chance are legal if all the proceeds after expenses go to charity."

Then he said the attorney general was aware that companies travel around the state with all the paraphernalia associated with gambling and some of them take advantage of the law regarding expenses.

Right after the report about the festival was in the paper several people, some of them school-age children in tears, stopped by the newspaper office and said how could I do that. Some adults said I was against that particular religion. People who went to that church school or had children who did told me in one way or another that the gambling and the entire festival generated money to help pay the operating expenses of the school. They reminded me that their kind of school, unlike state-supported schools, did not receive any money from the state.

When I heard this over and over again, as if it changed what was or justified what was, I couldn't help but think that if that reasoning was carried to its logical conclusion then it was quite understandable for a person to do anything they wanted if their objective was to get money. They could even destroy themselves if that is what it took.

One bright-eyed young girl who didn't go to that school said she didn't see anything wrong with gambling. She asked, "What is wrong with gambling? I really want to know, because I don't see anything wrong with it." I didn't know what to say. When she asked that question it was her sincerity that got me, and she thought I was supposed to have an answer on the tip of my tongue. I didn't answer her. I walked back to my desk in the back and sat down.

I thought about that question off and on, and when the next edition came out a week later I put an editorial in the paper that gave an answer. In part here is what it said:

> Gambling is merely trying to make money with money. People probably came up with the which-shell-is-the-pebble-under game, and set out to make their fortune long before anyone came up with the wheel or fire.
>
> Gambling offers a tantalizing and effortless return on one's money. All that is needed is to win. As simple an ingredient as to win may seem, it overwhelms the reality that the simple and needed ingredient is to lose. That is the design of gambling, that a person lose, not that they win. This obvious but forgotten fact explains why there are so many more losers than there are winners out there. Then it is the losers, who having been beat at another man's game, start their own game, having learned well that all that is needed to win is a loser. What their game may be is anybody's guess; another money game, a prostitution game, a mugging game, usually it is anything that goes well with losers or the creation of losers thereof. For gambling to be successful people must lose, and the more they lose the more successful the game.

Gambling doesn't have much caring for anybody else, and that is what is wrong with gambling.

The following year I didn't work for the newspaper any longer, but along the roads where I traveled I noticed signs advertising festivals at different church schools. At all those festivals the primary fund-raiser was gambling. No longer did the gambling booth operators make a pretense about not letting children place bets.

From Reno, Nevada, I went directly to my friend's house on Benvenue Avenue in Berkeley, California. I stayed there for a few days until I found an apartment. During that time I occupied the guest room. It wasn't very big. The entrance was under the stairs that led to the second floor. In all the time I was in that house I never went upstairs. There were two steps down into the room under the stairs. That room was slightly bigger than the mattress, which was a large rubber bladder filled with water. It was on the floor and popularly known as a waterbed. I had seen them many times before, but that was the first time I slept on one. Once the water calmed down it was better than sleeping on the sidewalk or on the floor. When I moved so did the water. It was like sleeping on the floor of a rubber life raft.

That summer four people lived in the house. One person was rather decisive without being overbearing. She took it upon herself to run the place. It is a good thing she did because no one else seemed concerned about details.

After I was there a week the girl I knew from Ohio left for a job in another state. Growing up I knew her whole family. Her father died several years earlier from a terminal disease. Years after Berkeley I had the job of mowing fields and plowing snow at her mother's house in Cincinnati.

Three or four times her mother was there. She would stop me to say, "Don't overdo it," when I was mowing around the trees. She liked some long grass. Another time when someone bashed in her mailbox all she had to say about whoever did it was that they were thoughtless. When I was shoveling snow on her paddle tennis court she was walking in my direction through a field. She stopped a hundred yards from where I was and stood there looking around for a long time. There was fresh snow everywhere on the trees and in the field.

About twenty years later I didn't work for her anymore. When she was in Cincinnati we invited her to visit us one afternoon. I was married by then and had three children. She seemed to know I had big questions about religion. I told her I was struck by the fact that many wonderful people were being misled and that there were some absolute truths after all. It was like she thought I had a particular point of view. She cut me off and said, "When I die they will take me to Spring Grove, and off I'll go." Spring Grove is a burial place in Cincinnati. When she was driving away that afternoon a blood vein in her brain got blocked and she ran into a woodpile. Five days later she was dead. At the funeral I saw her daughter from past days on Benvenue Avenue. She was married and had children also. It was the first time I had seen her in many years. We didn't talk much except to say hello.

That summer at Berkeley another person who stayed in the house on Benvenue was a friend of the girl I knew from Ohio. She was from the East Coast. There was one class we had at the same place and time. After I got my own apartment I would walk to the house on Benvenue, meet her, and we would walk together fifteen or twenty minutes to the classroom. One time I asked her if she wanted to drive to the hills that overlooked San Francisco Bay. It was quite a view. She said no. Once after class we stopped at a store to get ice cream. She got a trendy flavor. She said I was boring because I chose vanilla.

Halfway through the summer she said her car kept overheating. When I looked at it I said her seals were bad. I knew about French cars. When the radiator cap was off, the coolant level would rise and overflow when she accelerated the engine.

I thought it would sway her opinion of me if I was able to reveal to her my intimate knowledge of the internal combustion engine. We were standing by the front of her car. It was parked on the street and the hood was up. I looked her in the eye. I said there is a high-pressure situation created when atomized gasoline mixed in a two-hundred-to-one ratio with household air is ignited in what amounts to a controlled explosion inside each cylinder.

I figured this was my last chance to get to her. I was deliberately making it more complicated than it was. I wasn't really thinking about her car at all. I wondered what it would be like to kiss her.

I said the explosion pushes a piston down. I told her the overheating problem in her car was happening because some of the pressure from the explosion was escaping into the water jacket. I said the cylinder sleeves weren't high enough above the top surface of the block where the engine head is fastened to the block. I told her the head gasket wasn't able to do its job, because the seals at the bottom of the cylinder sleeves were mashed down to much.

I slammed the hood down, and that was the end of that. I could not detect any change in her demeanor. She didn't believe me.

The fourth person who lived in that house that summer lived there all year long. He had a golden retriever dog. I was told by the person I knew from Cincinnati that when he had a girlfriend the dog, although still there, was like history.

When I left California to go back to Ohio I went over to that house to say good-bye. They were all sitting around the table having supper. He and the others hardly broke stride with what they were doing, but the girl from the East Coast put the side of her cheek up and pointed to it in a way that said I was to kiss her good-bye on the cheek. I leaned over and gave her a big Italian kiss on the cheek. The person with the dog looked at her in disbelief. He said her name and exclaimed, "You slut!" No one seemed to mind, and that included the girl from the East Coast.

Before classes started I moved out of the house on Benvenue Avenue. I rented the upstairs front room in a house under shade trees. The woman who owned the house lived downstairs with her daughter. Another person rented another room upstairs. I think that person attended the university, but I never asked her. We seldom talked.

After I was there a while the lady who owned the house gave me a talking-to about how the people I met in her house may not be the kind of people with whom I was familiar. I thanked her for her telling me this.

She was probably referring to the night before when she and several friends of hers were having a little get-together in the main room downstairs. I was invited since I was there. One person I talked to a long time was much older than I was. At one point she asked the lady who owned the house if she thought I would like a certain friend of theirs who was not there. Without replying the lady who owned the house left the room. I think that is what prompted her to talk with me the next morning.

I met that friend of theirs who was not there. She was recently divorced, slightly older than I was, and a very good cook who had gone to a famous cooking school in France. I ate very well when I was at her house. I met her there. It was a large modern building on a hillside. I could see San Francisco and many other areas from the window. Her kitchen was extensive. The refrigerator was a large commercial type. It had a large see-through glass door with a brushed stainless-steel frame.

Many times on the weekend I stayed there all day and all night. She cooked and pruned roses growing on lattice beside the back door. I would watch her. We would talk while she was doing those things. She was extremely calm. We went to a nearby park where a brightly painted merry-go-round was stopped and all the lights off. We went into San Francisco quite a few times. I saw many sights there. One vendor had a sign that said he was selling live Maine lobsters, but when I asked him why the lobsters had no claws he didn't answer me. That city smelt different. I spoke the same language, but it could have been another country.

The woman who owned the house where I rented the room told me that her friend I talked with that night in her parlor was the divorced wife of the person who made LSD (lysergic acid diethylamide) a well-known substance. He and a group of people experimented with it in upstate New York. He was a college professor at the time. Soon after that he lost his job, and he spent the rest of his days in jail or avoiding the federal police. One English-language dictionary says LSD is an organic compound, C^{20}-H^{25}-N^{3}-O, which induces psychotic symptoms similar to those of schizophrenia. I ingested a half a dose of LSD once in my life, and while I saw things I had never seen before I felt like I didn't belong there. It was as if I went right up to the edge of solid ground and looked down. It was as if I could not see the bottom. It was as if I was fortunate not to be afraid of heights and make it back. That is how I would describe the events, however, that was not my trip. My trip was something else. I was with a person who was like a tour guide. That person was experienced with "acid." When I did some he did not.

I was at home. My parents were both gone. It was winter. I was about twenty-one years old. I "dropped" the "acid" sitting at our kitchen table. When I stood up I knew it had taken effect, because I looked back at myself sitting in the chair. The part of me that had gotten up was not touching the ground. I regained my composure. We went outside and got in an old black pickup truck named Jed. I was fascinated by the dirt on the windshield. Jed had one windshield wiper that moved the dirt out of the way where the wiper went back and forth. I could see very clearly through that part of the windshield, but the rest of the glass was covered with dust. I drove around to the back of Peterloon Farm and down the dirt road farmers used. We parked in the clearing and got out.

There was snow on the ground. Most of the trees on the far edge of the field were bare, but several maple trees close together still had their leaves. They were brown. When I looked at them they became a waterfall the color of polished gold in the sunlight. I didn't question it. I simply stood there and looked. It was making spray the same color that rolled up in the air. It didn't stop. It was quite something. I looked away like it was there all the time, and bent over to peer into a thick bush. The bare branches at the base were covered with smooth ice. The branches turned into big stone Greek columns, and in the distance a beautiful lady with a long flowing veil wrapped around her body stepped from behind one of the columns. The veil was pressed against her side by the wind. She raised her arm in the veil and made a wave in a beckoning way. I looked away just like I did with the trees. Those were the two main things I saw that day. We walked across the snow-covered field. Occasionally we stopped in long conversations, about what I do not know.

The next day I resolved never to do acid again because I was so close to the edge. I could have gone over the side very easily. At the same time I remembered the words of a self-proclaimed junkie who wrote books. He wrote about the possibility of people metabolizing their own junk and about being a metabolic junkie. When I was on acid the downside far outweighed anything else, but I was made aware of how acute human sensibilities could be, like seeing the dirt on the windshield. I wanted to develop those isolated perceptions on my own.

When classes began at Berkeley I was enrolled in an American literature class, a theater class, and a criminology class. It was a light load compared to what I was used to at the Ohio State University.

One of the papers I got back from the English teacher had a note in red ink. Even 2,000 miles away teachers use red ink. It said I had problems with fundamentals and if that was a background problem, I should see the teacher. My background was not lack of schooling. It was what it was. I didn't see the teacher.

The English literature class was in the early morning. I always walked there with the girl from the East Coast. We would always sit together in the same seats. Thirty students were in the class, and there were not many more chairs than there were people. Regardless of when we got there, the same two seats were empty. They were toward the front and in the center. She generally got much higher grades than I did. She never voluntarily showed me her paper, and she never gloated over the fact that she always got good grades. She was confident about what she did. I wondered if she ever got a little bit mixed up.

The student riots that swept the country also touched that place. When we walked from the street onto the south side of the campus there was a large sign that said in so many words that the state university was not public property even though it was paid for by taxpayers. It said the campus belonged to the board of regents and trespassers would be prosecuted. It sounded to me like they found a loophole.

Right away the teacher in the criminology class tells us he is a Marxist (a political persuasion opposed to the politics of the United States), and how he wrote this thick book about criminals, which we didn't have to buy. It was interesting what he said day after day. What he talked about was academic.

Our first assignment in the theater class was to walk in front of the class, identify ourselves (name, rank, and serial number), and proceed with a soliloquy of our own choosing. I was terrified. I always felt like that when I got in front of people. In grade school I couldn't recite a poem although I knew it very well. I had to stand in front of the whole class. The teacher told me to go out in the hall and write it out, which I did perfectly. When I went up in front of the theater class at Berkeley I didn't hide the fact that I needed to loosen up both inside, and out. I took some deep breaths and bent over to touch my toes. The teacher was sitting in one of the student seats in the first row. He made a highly audible combined exhalation and laugh. I walked rapidly back to my desk, got my books, and left, never to return. I dropped out of the theater class.

During the time I attended the university at Berkeley the girl I knew from Ohio came back. We took a long weekend drive to Southern California. Her sister was enrolled in a college there.

Since we were going south I wanted to see the state university at Santa Cruz. I don't know why I wanted to have a look. It was primarily known as a school for languages, and I was never any good at learning a language. We walked around the campus, which for the most part was on a hillside. It wasn't open that summer. We proceeded south after spending several hours in Santa Cruz.

Her sister and the man she eventually married and subsequently divorced left soon after we arrived. They wanted someone to watch their house. There were fruit trees in the back. Some of the fruit was drying on screens in the sun. It didn't rain that time of year. The house was in town, and from a window he pointed to a building across a parking lot and said there was good live jazz music there. They were gone for two days. One of the afternoons the girl I was with left to do something. I was alone in the house that afternoon. An instrument smaller than a guitar but like a guitar was there. I think it was a ukulele. When I was in New York I heard a man from India play a sitar. It was different. I sat cross-legged on the floor and plucked the strings with both hands the way he did. I played with it for a while, and soon I wanted to tell a story punctuated by the sound of the strings. On the shelf was a recording machine. Six or seven times for a few minutes each time I plucked the strings. The recording began and ended with music.

The story was about a lone mountain in Vietnam called Lui

Ba Din. Actually there is a mountain by that name in Vietnam. It begins with a girl named Mai Ling who lives in a village at the foot of Lui Ba Din. The mountain sees how much she loves a boy named Lo and it sees how much he loves her. Lui Ba Din is very happy because of them. Then hands covered with blood kill him. Mai Ling walks up on the side of Lui Ba Din where there are no other people. There is water dripping down from the side of a big overhanging rock. She is sitting under the rock with her arms wrapped around her legs. Her forehead is against her knees and she is rocking back and forth. Lui Ba Din is not happy when Mai Ling is so sad. Mai Ling decides she will never go back, and at that moment the mountain opens a great opening. Mai Ling goes inside and the opening closes. Lui Ba Din holds her, and tells her someday everything will be all right when the sadness caused by the foolishness and stupidity of people is over.

That was the end. I left the recording for them in their house. Several years later I saw them in Cincinnati quite by chance. I hadn't seen either of them since I stayed in their house in Southern California. There they were. I said hello, and right away he starts talking about the tape which at first I didn't remember. He talks like I had a lot of nerve using his stuff. Then I remembered that day.

The only other excursion I made from the San Francisco Bay area was to a rodeo in Salinas. There were as many exhibitors as there were spectators that afternoon. I was by myself. There was a barrel race, calf roping, and all the events associated with a rodeo.

There was one young lady on a good-looking gray quarter horse. It seemed like the two of them went together really well. She was in several of the events. I wondered if she ever read about the cowpony named Smoky. The person who wrote that story said that as far as he was concerned a big mistake was made when they said man's best friend was a dog and not a horse. He also said he could always tell most of what he wanted to know about a person by the horse they rode. I wanted to go back to the barns and ask her if she ever read that book. Then I didn't. It was hot out there in the sun. Late that afternoon I bought an iced drink and went back to Berkeley.

When I left Berkeley to return to Ohio the woman who owned the house where I stayed was gone, but her daughter was there. My car was packed, and when I went to get my bicycle I told her through an open window to have a good life. I tied my bicycle down to the top of the car and left.

I went down the California coast with the lady who pruned roses. We went through a small town called Guadeloupe. There we stopped for lunch. The place had a high ceiling. It was large inside, with white walls. There was a Spanish-language song coming from a radio by the window. A Latin-looking person was walking around with a fly swatter swatting a fly every now and then. I really felt at home. There were many fields outside town. In one field there were a dozen people working on rows and rows of full-grown cabbage.

Farther down the road I slept on a beach. She slept in the car. There was a large utility pole on the ground to keep cars from going on the sand. I was sleeping near the pole in front of the car. In the middle of the night a spotlight from a police car woke me up. One of two policemen said I could not sleep there. He said I might get run over. He said if I wanted to sleep in my car it was fine with him. She woke up, and when the two policemen saw her they didn't seem to care where I slept.

She flew back to San Francisco soon afterward. When she was gone I stopped at another beach and went in the water. I was amazed how far out I could go and still be in shallow water. There was one other person there. I didn't talk with her, but when I was in waist-deep water far from the shore I heard her yell to me although I didn't hear what she said. When I looked in her direction she was going toward the shore. She got out of the water and left. Right after that I felt a very solid bump against my leg. All my weight was on that leg so it didn't move. I had never felt anything like that, and I thought it must be an underwater log. But then I had to admit that it didn't stay there. Without thinking about it any longer and for no particular reason I started to walk toward the shore in slow, deliberate strides. Many years later I was watching a television show about sharks and it said that before a shark dines it bumps its prey.

My car picked up a slight ticking noise that could only be heard when standing over the engine and moving the throttle back and forth. When the engine RPM dropped suddenly the noise could be heard. It was what a helicopter mechanic would call a one-to-one vibration. When I got to the city of Los Angeles I wanted to find a dealership to learn what the noise was. I spoke with a telephone operator and she explained that the city was divided into two sections. She could only locate whatever I was looking for in the north half of the city. She said she didn't have information about the other half and that unless I had a directory of the southern part of the city I could not find what I wanted. I was in a phone booth and there was no directory of either kind in there.

There was a dealership for my type of car in that city. It had an open area in the middle and two rows of one-car garages on two sides. The garages were once horse stalls. I stood with two or three people, and asked them if they knew what the noise was. I revved the engine over and over again so they could hear the noise. None the people knew what it was. Then a person with grease on his hands walked up and without hearing it again says it is a rod bearing. The other people moved out of his way, and they didn't interrupt him. He said they couldn't do the work until after the weekend, but he gave me the name of someone who might be able to do the work over the weekend. He didn't have to tell me it was extensive engine repair. I said my destination was Columbus, Ohio. He said it was anybody's guess if I could make it that far. I found the house of the person who could possibly do the repair. It was on a dead-end street. All I could see when I looked at the house was weeds over six feet tall. There was no one there. I decided to continue on and hope for the best.

That engine didn't give me any trouble until I got to Columbus, Ohio, where it started to knock in a big way. It spun a bearing, and a tow truck pulled the broken-down car the last five or six miles to Frambes. It was late at night. I was glad to be back, going to sleep in my own bed.

The next day I took the engine out of the car quickly as I could. There were a few weeks before school started, and I wanted to get to Maine. The car was parked on the side of the street. One journal on the crankshaft was messed up and so was one connecting rod. I took the crankshaft to have all the journals resurfaced. I got a new connecting rod, and on the front porch I put the engine back together. When I got the engine in the car it started right up and was ready to go.

I called the "big house" in Maine to find out who was there and ask if I could go there. Asking was a formality the management liked everyone to exercise. The only person there other than the help was my mother's stepfather, the wealthy industrialist, who was like a grandfather to me. Someone else was about to arrive.

The other person who arrived was not actually a relative, but I called him my uncle. My mother's half-sister and he were once married and they had three children. When they were married my mother's stepfather asked that man to run the chemical factory, and he was still doing that job that summer. He had been divorced for several years. Several relatives, who owned stock in the chemical business, told me that sales grew during the time he ran the company.

I was there a few days before he arrived. The only time my grandfather and I saw each other was at dinner. When my uncle arrived things got down to business. He was a forceful executive. He came in a private plane to discuss business. He was talking about the trip up there, and he told me it was none of my business when I asked him if the plane was his. I didn't mean to be rude, but he did.

There was a big fireplace in the room where we sat before dinner. Having that fire going was very important to my grandfather, not just that summer but always. He didn't ask just anybody to stoke that fire either. We sat in that room until someone in a uniform opened the glass doors and announced, "Dinner is served." That was our cue to get up and go into the dining room. The first course was keeping warm on a table in the corner. The bowls were on a plate warmer. He got one for each person, and put in several ladles of soup. I didn't have to make a point of not eating before he or anyone else sat down. The rule was: eat while your food is hot. Also, we didn't say a prayer. Occasionally over the years I went to church with him, but in all the time I knew him I never heard him mention God. I was not aware of God either so that made two of us.

He had a very strong sense of decency and goodness which he attributed to his upbringing. He didn't concern himself with why his parents were that way. They instilled it in him, he in his children, and his children in their children.

One of the nights the three of us ate dinner together my grandfather asked me if I wanted a job. He was eating his soup with the larger-than-normal spoons he and my grandmother liked. He didn't look up from his soup when he asked. Before I answered, the executive who ran the chemical business said, "I think they should get whatever they can get on their own."

It is not like the executive and me didn't like each other. I respected him because he was operating the chemical company and a man I liked chose him to do that. I don't know what the executive thought of me. Maybe I was an intrusive relative. The fact that I was there might have bothered him. They were the two highest-ranking people in a large company with thousands of employees.

My grandfather didn't look at the executive when he made the comment about how I should find what I could find on my own. My grandfather knew of my assorted past. I don't think the executive had any idea how close we were. There was a mutual respect there.

On a previous night that summer when there was just the two of us he had told me that everywhere he went he knew which way north was. He asked me if I knew which way was north from right where I was sitting. He said one of the most embarrassing moments in his life was when he was an officer on a U.S. Navy warship patrolling Long Island Sound. An enlisted man asked him which way north was. He didn't know, but ever since then he did.

When he said that about the job I put my soup spoon down. He did not look at me. I said my chosen profession was journalism and that I wanted to do something with that training. I was going to graduate soon, at the end of the winter quarter, December 1972. He provided jobs in practically every area of work. One building he owned was the tallest and largest building in Cincinnati. He owned so much property in addition to the chemical operation that he was once reported to be the "largest taxpayer in Cincinnati."

He probably had a public relations department where a journalism major could work. If I had forced the issue of my working for him I don't know what would have happened that night or with my life. I bowed out, and he never mentioned it again.

During the day I went on long walks "downisland," skipped rocks on the water, and befriended one of the maids in the bungalow. She worked almost all day long. She said she had been on the island all summer except on her day off, when she and the other "help" went to the mainland. Sometimes on her day off she went to a place in the woods that she described in an intriguing German accent as a ledge covered with a thick blanket of moss all surrounded by ferns. She said once in the middle of the afternoon she fell asleep there. She said it was a lovely place with severe solitude.

There was a place on the bigger island where people gathered with beer mugs in hand to talk about things. One person knew us both. He lived on the big island all year long. He had a full beard and long hair. He had done some work on the island where she was working, and that is how he knew her. He sat with us in a booth, and we three were having a merry time. I got up to go to the men's room and when I came back I heard the words "money talks." Even if he cared, I don't think he thought I heard those words. After I sat down I tried to pick up where we left off, but it was not the same. She would not even look at him. There were no smiles between them anymore. He got up and left. I asked her what he had said. She said during the summer he asked her several times to go with him to that place. She said she didn't go. She said I was the first one that summer, beside him, who expressed an interest in her.

That place closed one or two years later. I don't know why. My grandfather, for one, didn't like the place, and maybe some other people felt the way he did. Many people from around the country who went there in the summer were like him. He wouldn't have acted alone. It wouldn't surprise me to learn what happened was a group of them simply bought the place and closed it for good.

When I was there at the end of that summer he asked me many questions about the place. It had opened earlier that year. I'm sure if he was that curious he would have asked a cousin or two the same questions, but he was asking me as if it were the first time. I told him I went there, but I didn't say I went with one of the "help."

The fact that summer people were socializing in the same place as local people is exactly what he didn't like. If left to continue, what were to him two very different groups of people, would mix, marry, have children, and that would be the end of the ruling class. That was his upbringing.

He felt anyone not from his background had a different ethics, morality, and code of conduct than him. He felt that he and others like him had a responsibility to take care of people. Years later he had a stroke and was in a hospital in Cincinnati. His son told me he was talking about the past like it was the present. From his bed he looked out the window at the rooftops. His son (my uncle who liked guns) described the sight and made it sound like there were laundry lines between the buildings. My grandfather, his father, told him they had to clean up that area, get rid of those buildings, and build new ones.

The maid and me became very honest with each other. She was not unpleasant to look at so I was curious how my grandfather related to her. In the late summer she and a cook were the only help there. What she said in so many words reminded me of a song: "Had I been made the partner of Eve we'd be in Eden still." That was his upbringing.

I got back to Ohio State University shortly before classes started. My formal education was almost completed. I took some advanced-level journalism courses such as J-641, which was about reporting governmental affairs. The teacher who taught me the news style of writing conducted the course. I still didn't get very good grades. She was a very matter-of-fact tough cookie. I couldn't spell worth beans, and that was a fact.

I took a history course from a full professor on main campus. There were about twenty students in the classroom. The teacher was talking about the trade routes in the days of the commercial European sailing ships. He talked about Europeans this and Europeans that. He had a really high opinion of Europeans considering he wasn't one. I didn't want to seem rude. I had to speak as tactfully as I could. I waited for a break in his talk then I raised my hand. It still interrupted him. He asked me what I wanted. I said I read a fiction book with a story built around how the Western half of the world wanted silks and spices from the Eastern half of the world, but nobody in the Eastern half wanted anything the other half had. I said there was nothing to trade and their money was no good. I said in the story European sailing ships stopped in Malaysia to take on a narcotic named opium. I said in the story there was no central Chinese government only provincial chiefs who were easily corrupted. I asked him, "Did Europeans introduce opium to the Chinese?" I asked him, "Aside from the legal-illegal question, were the European merchants big-time drug suppliers long before the drug cartels of Latin America?"

He said he was getting to that in a while. Several days later I was thinking about something else as he talked. He stopped and said, "Is that what you were talking about the other day?" I had been looking out the window wishing his lecture was over. I said yes, and he resumed talking to the whole class. I wondered what he had said, and then again I thought about something else. A week later before class started the person beside me in the row of desks said she liked what I said. I had to think back to the last time I said something that she heard. It would have been about the opium trade. I said it was a fact. I pointed to the front. He didn't say it wasn't. Did he?

She and I talked some more. She was small, very proper, and young. She was industrious. Her singular intent was to excel in the grading system. To her, going to the university was a golden opportunity to be somebody.

She was serious and smart. She was like the tiger chasing its tail: everything was exactly the way it should be because that was the way it was.

I would guess she thought the university was right through and through, but now she considered we weren't getting the straight scoop.

A few months later I graduated and received a rolled-up piece of paper that said I had a bachelor of arts degree in journalism. The graduation exercise was held in a gymnasium. The place was full of people. My parents were there, although I did not see them until the end. The only other time they came to Columbus to see me was when I was in the Franklin County workhouse. They went past Frank Road on the expressway. The visitation time was almost over when they got there. It was a wet winter day. The guard wouldn't let me have several books they brought. The uniformed person who inspected them probably thought they were rubbish or that hacksaw blades were in them. It was funny talking to my parents through wire mesh with a nearby guard. I don't think they thought I was very accomplished.

When I graduated from the university they thought I had accomplished something. My degree was proof I had traveled through a certain area and paid all the tolls.

10

Work

The reason I stayed in Cincinnati was that my mother was going to give me what we called the side field at Markin Farm. Nobody could beat the price. It was free. I planned to build a geodesic sphere in that field, and that would be my house.

The sphere that I planned was twenty-four feet in diameter. I prepared a building permit that showed the triangle shapes that would make up the sphere. I got a book that explained how to make everything. It says my design was a three-frequency icosahedron. That book says the intricate mathematical shape occurs in nature. It is called Cirognia Icosahedra. In a picture it looks like a tiny hayseed. The book says there are different geodesic shapes and not all of them involve a curved surface. It says the word *geodesic* means "the shortest line between two points on a mathematically derived surface." Right next to that is the definition of the next word in the dictionary: *geoduck*. It says it is an edible clam (*Panope generosa*) weighing over five pounds. That is the informal nature of the book throughout.

I made a model from plastic straws melted together. The model also included the floor. The sphere was fastened to the floor. The main floor was located in the middle of the sphere. It was atop several columns extending through the triangles. Then there was a lower floor.

On the model all the triangles went together to make the shape. There were no walls or roof. It had an inherent strength. I could do it myself. It was possible. I felt like I discovered something.

As it turned out I never built the sphere. I had a permit to build the thing. That is not what stopped me. The side field was always there when I was growing up, but it was not always part of Markin Farm. It was part of Peterloon Farm. My father mowed it and always took care of it as if it were part of Markin Farm. One Christmas my mother's stepfather, the wealthy industrialist, gave it to both my parents. Then it became part of Markin Farm. Soon after that the side field got tied up in the legal arrangement of a loan, and nothing about it could change until the loan money was paid back to the bank. When my mother said I could have it to live on she was unaware of this situation. When it was explained to her repeatedly by a trusted financial person she couldn't grasp why I couldn't live there. To her ownership of the side field was as absurd as saying you own the Nile River and made it for yourself. I didn't build my dome. It was not disappointing. It was what happened.

When I was in Columbus after I finished at the university I needed to make some money because I had none, and at that point I wanted to have some money when I moved to Cincinnati. When I did move I got an apartment on Riddle Road near the University of Cincinnati. I thought that was the same environment I was leaving. It was after I had made the move to Cincinnati and had a job on a little weekly newspaper that the sphere idea ended.

In my quest to save up a little money I got a job as a dishwasher at a hotel near the University on Olentangy River Road in Columbus. An exchange student from Africa and me were the two people in the dish room. We were extremely quick at loading the racks, sending them through the automatic dishwasher, and unloading them. Even during the busiest time the dishes wouldn't get stacked up on the slide.

I loaded the racks and the other guy unloaded them. Occasionally we would trade off, but usually that was the way we worked. There was a waist-high opening in the wall where dishes and glasses were put by people working in the dining room and the bar. The opening was two feet high and six feet long. It had a stainless-steel shelf on the outside of the dish room that went the whole six foot length of the opening. Its width went through the wall and it became part of the slide. The slide was a stainless-steel countertop with a raised edge so liquids and leftover food wouldn't spill onto the floor. When I loaded one of the racks I would slide it into the dishwasher.

When it came out the other side the person unloading would pull the hot steaming rack and unload it in an area designed for that purpose.

When people bringing things to be washed put them on the shelf I could see they were there, but I could not see them. One of the cocktail waitresses who put glasses on the shelf had unusually long legs. Her uniform was comprised of a very short skirt and sheer stockings with visible black squares all over them. One of the times she came back to the dish room with a tray of glasses I bent over and looked up at her through the opening. It scared her. I could see her face. I asked her if she was ever in the Olympics. She left and never spoke. After that we spoke when there was a break in the work. There was no wall between us. She was a student at the university. I could see the whole of her.

Once when the restaurant and bar closed at two in the morning the manager said the workers could have what was left of the ice cream. She and I were friends by then. I extended an invitation to her to have some ice cream with me in the stairwell. She led the way through the fire door, and we sat on the stairs with our dishes of ice cream.

Several weeks later we both called in sick on the same day. We were having a cold beer with lunch on High Street when all of a sudden I saw that manager sitting at the end of the bar eating his lunch. We both got fired the same day. I was losing it on that job. Every week there was a work schedule posted. I was getting less and less time to work. That job was in the late afternoon and all evening. I worked spot labor on days when I didn't work in the restaurant. One time before the rush the manager told me to get some soapy water. Someone had put some graffiti on the wall in the men's room in the front of the restaurant, and he wanted me to get it off. I had never been in that area. He showed me where it was, and as we walked there he said some frustrated journalism major had made those marks. I scrubbed it off. I think he thought I was the one who put it there. I never wrote on walls where it wasn't intended. I wrote with chalk in empty classrooms when I finished studying there. I would write expressions I had memorized. I once wrote: "Though they stand before the magistrate of the people to be tried, tell me my son, who will the magistrate of the people stand before?" The student riots were fresh in everyone's mind, but I wasn't thinking about them. The next day it was still on the chalkboard, but someone had written an answer. They pressed hard, and underlined several times the words, *the people.*

After the incident involving the graffiti in the restaurant my hours got reduced even more. When the manager saw me eating lunch with that cocktail waitress the day we both called in sick he couldn't take it, and we got fired together. For one reason or another I also got fired from almost all of the jobs I had. Later in life I created my own job. I had to provide for a family. I couldn't afford to get fired anymore.

When I lost the restaurant job I spent more time doing spot labor. I got a permanent assignment as a laborer for a contractor building a twenty-unit apartment building on Fourth Street. It was almost finished. The contractor wanted someone to stay in the building all night as a sort of a night watchman. I moved out of the apartment on Frambes and took most of my things to Cincinnati. I put them in a stall at Markin Farm. When the job for the contractor was finished I moved to Cincinnati.

I spent time with the cocktail waitress who got fired alongside me. Neither one of us seemed to mind losing that job very much. She had an apartment by herself a short distance north of the campus. She transferred to that university after her second year at another university in Athens, Ohio. She was doing her third or fourth year of college when I met her. She was a dance major.

My job at the construction site expanded. I would sign for furniture that arrived every day and keep things tidy. The labor pool still employed me, but I only went downtown to get paid.

There was an old five-story apartment building nearby that was going to be torn down. It had stairs that wound up the middle to the top floor. A corridor on each floor led around to the next set of stairs. There was a railing on one side of the corridor. On the other side of the corridor there were two apartments. At the far end of the corridor there was a door to a third apartment. The apartments in the building were empty.

On the third floor in the corridor between the two apartment doors there was an upright grand piano. I asked the demolition job supervisor about it, and he said it was going to be torn down with the building. I asked him if I could have it, and he said I could if I got it out of the building. It was heavy.

The driver of a furniture truck with a lift gate at my job and two helpers agreed to help me. The cocktail waitress friend of mine said I could put it in her apartment. Everyone who helped me was relieved to hear her apartment was on the ground floor. I got two more people to help carry it down three flights of stairs. There were six of us, and it was all we could do to get it out of the building. The piano went in the truck and we drove the short distance to her apartment. The piano and the move didn't cost me a dime.

When I moved to the apartment on Riddle Road in Cincinnati the piano was still in her apartment in Columbus. She came to Cincinnati once. I was trying to find a real job with my degree in journalism. It was an unimpressive process. Several weeks later when I called her to say I was coming to get the piano she implied it was hers. I told her I would huff and puff and blow her door down if she didn't give it up. I spent the weekend up there. I took the piano back with me on a small utility trailer attached to my car, and it was added to my collection of things in the stall at Markin Farm. I never saw her again. We both got busy with what we were doing in different cities.

The apartment I had on Riddle Road was one among fifty that were in an L-shaped building with two floors and a flat roof. It was an urban area. Each apartment opened to the outside on the same side of the building. From any door I could see all the cars belonging to the people who lived there, including mine. Inside my apartment and each of the others there was one main room, a small kitchen, and a conventional bathroom.

My mother's attraction to alcohol and my father's loss of money tormented them both during the time I lived on Riddle Road. I had a good childhood growing up under the hedges, but when I talked with siblings who lived at home much longer than I did it was hard to believe we grew up in the same house.

Several years later I was by myself in a one-room post-and-beam house. It was cold outside. The wind howled. The wood stove was turned up, and logs were blazing in the fireplace. Inside, it was warm. I had a conversational bottle of wine. There was no one to converse with, so I wrote letters. The next time I was on the mainland I mailed them.

I stopped at my brother's house on the way back to Cincinnati. There were several messages for me from the people I had written the night I drank the bottle of wine. In various ways they all said that I had a long family history of people who became inoperative as a result of alcohol consumption. I was told to go to a meeting or meetings dealing with the subject. I was amazed it was so obvious to them that I had drunk a bottle of wine. Perhaps my handwriting was flared. I didn't think I said anything outrageous. I wouldn't have mailed the letters if I had. When I got back I went to several meetings. Those who had alcohol problems attended them. I learned a necessity to solving the problem is admitting there is a problem. I was amazed how person after person told the same story about their plight. There was nothing unique. When I thought about it some of the nicest people I knew were alcoholics. The ones who survived were the ones who got off their high horse and admitted they had a problem. That state of mind made them highly sensible.

Ten or fifteen years before I lived on Riddle Road my father learned about a floundering candle company that my mother's stepfather was going to sell. My father found a shrewd partner, and together they bought it; each of them came up with half. My father got his half of the money from his wife, my mother. The partner oversaw the candle making, and my father took care of sales. The company tripled in size. The factory was moved to a new location in Leesburg, Ohio. Soon after that the partner bought my father out. My father didn't seem at all remorseful about selling his half when he did. After that for the first and only time he wore the brim of his hat turned up in front like a popular Italian comedian with an Italian name. I could hear language records every morning when he got dressed. He went to Italy.

Not long after he got paid for his half of the candle company my mother and father were sitting at each end of the kitchen table. They were the only ones there. I was passing through the kitchen on my way out the door. They were talking about the money he had. My mother cried often at almost nothing it seemed. She had tears in her eyes and said, "We have never had money before." He was going to lose all of it soon, and it was like she suspected what would happen. He once told me she had lots of money, and that is probably why he was visibly amused in an inoffensive way when she said, "We" have never had money before. She said, "We." Her grandmother, on her father's side, left her money. My father always had ideas on how to make her money increase. My mother was advised by a trusted friend to leave everything concerning money the way it was. She never attempted to guess if what he said about money was right or wrong.

Years after the sale of the candle company when I was living on Riddle Road my father called me up one morning before I went to work and asked me to lend him a thousand dollars. He said he could handle the big things but not the little things. I told him I didn't have any money saved up. The money I made from my job was barely enough to pay the rent, put gas in my car, eat, and buy a few beers. By then the money from the candle company was gone. He invested all of it in broken-down businesses like the candle company once was. He never had a partner. He closed every one of them.

One big effort he made different from the others was an instant orange juice company in Salerno, Italy. He got three or four investors. Eventually the whole thing hinged on a loan from the Italian government, which didn't happen. It collapsed. They didn't make the first glass of orange juice. My father put the whole thing together. He said one of the local newspapers had a story about how one of the investors who lost money was suing him. He said it was a "friendly lawsuit." My mother was not one of the investors. She had been advised by her trusted financial friend not to let money come between them so it didn't. My mother's stepfather had sold Markin Farm to both of them for a dollar when they got married. My father used that land to secure cash loans from banks. During the time my father was having financial difficulty my mother had to pay all kinds of mortgages and liens so the banks wouldn't take the property. She ended up owning the entire place and vowed never to give him another cent. It was after that the Salerno deal happened.

It didn't stop there. He got credit cards and used credit cards to pay off credit cards. Finally, his creditors trying to collect money nearly every day on the telephone became so disheartening to my mother that she got the financial person to pay all his credit card debt, and arrange so it could not recur. When they moved to a smaller house and a different environment in Maine they were older people. Before my father became immobile he had an office in town. My brother looked after his affairs, and he said my father was constantly lured into entering cash giveaway schemes that came in the mail.

He did not make anyone in the family aware what days certain enterprises of his closed and went out of business. As usual, he mowed the fields, read the paper, and swatted houseflies. He was good with his hands. He listened to operas Saturday afternoons with his eyes closed.

His mother seldom came to our house. She lived far away, but one of the last times I saw her before she died we sat on the terrace at Markin farm. I was a child. She was staring at two four-foot-high clay vessels. She didn't ask how they got there or anything else about them. They could have come from a department store in Cleveland for all I knew at the time. They were ornaments on the terrace. She looked at them longingly a long time and did not want to be disturbed.

She was old by then. She was a small Sicilian woman with dark clothes, and she always wore her hair tight against her head in a braided circle.

I met her husband, my grandfather, twice in Rochester when we were driving to Maine. One of my Italian relatives was a barber, and I always got a haircut in the kitchen with everyone else in the room. A well-known American writer said, "Italians are the only ones who know when they are having a good time." He easily could have been describing my family in Rochester.

My father's father, my grandfather, died when I was a boy. I only remember him sitting quietly watching everybody else from a large chair in the main room of the house in Rochester. He was an old man. He had thick white hair. He was lean and small in the chair. My grandmother did the talking for them both. He watched her and even when she was in the next room he seemed to be listening to what she was saying.

On the terrace at Markin Farm that day the clay vessels

were to the side of her. She looked at me and said, "In Italy they put olives in them." She grew up in Cerda, which is a small farm town in the middle of Sicily. They looked authentic with chips in them. I found out my mother got them in Italy.

When I was living at home my father directed the Cincinnati Opera. It was a nonpaying job. He liked opera, and he was unequaled at extracting money from the people who kept the opera alive.

I seldom went to the opera with him, and when I did I usually went to sleep after the intermission. He went whenever there was a performance, and in the summer that was often. My older sister knew what each one was about and she knew who the singers were by name.

My father selected singers at auditions held every year in New York City. The ones who came to Cincinnati were all Italian citizens who knew a small amount of English. They stayed in a local hotel.

A few times I went with him to a restaurant where the singers and some of the staff would meet after the performance. It was late. They were the only ones there. They would eat a seven-course Italian meal. Someone who wasn't connected with them would have thought it was ten in the morning the way they carried on. They were a very happy bunch of people.

In those days the opera was operated in an open-air theater on the grounds of the Cincinnati Zoo. The entire place had a roof over it, but the sides were open. During intermission people went outside where there were many plants along pathways. Concession stands were in bright lights. That opera facility was eventually torn down and the opera moved to an enclosed building in the downtown area. My father was no longer a part of the opera after it moved. He kept his interest going. He made two efforts to promote opera later in his life. They ended after a short while.

My father's main income-producing activity when I was growing up was advertising. That seemed to fade away after he sold his half of the candle company.

His advertising agency was in an office building downtown. That is where he would go every morning when we were waiting for the school bus. He always wore a suit and I could smell the same after-shave lotion all those years. I was in his office several times. It seemed there were a number of people there. His secretary always got the airplane tickets and travel money for me when I was going away to school.

When I moved into an apartment on Riddle Road there were two large daily newspapers, and when I didn't get hired by either of them I started applying at all the advertising agencies in town. My father's advertising agency had closed by then.

At a job interview very often the first question was, "Is your father _____?" and the interviewer would name him. I didn't know if the person sitting across the desk was my father's friend or foe. It seemed like it was a loaded first question. I wanted to say, "What's it to you, dog face?"

After a while I became aware all of the people who asked that question were his friends. I never met anyone who didn't like him. They wanted to see what I could do. That is the closest I came to getting hired. I did assignments for them.

I continued to beat the bushes in my effort to find a job. Now and again I worked spot labor. In the evenings I would hang on a nearby college bar in Clifton and watch the same band do a song with the words often repeated, "Out on the street again."

There was a fascinating girl who wound around the dance floor in a very slow and easy way. I stood up straight and spoke to her once. I wasn't very clear about anything. She made it very clear she didn't want anything to do with me.

I got a piece of mail from my grandmother on my mother's side. It said it was "urgent" that they see me as soon as possible. I called her and we set up a time for me to go over there for dinner.

When I got there she left my grandfather and me alone in the library. We sat away from the magazine table in armchairs. We were directly facing each other. I knew this was not the usual visit. He said the executive who ran the chemical company, his former son-in-law, related to him that my mother had telephoned and said the bank was "calling in the note" on the Markin Farm mortgage. Why she called the executive was baffling to him. It made no sense to him. He said this kind of bizarre behavior couldn't continue. He said my mother had to get medical help for her alcoholism.

I told him I learned from others who knew about this sort of thing that if a person doesn't voluntarily want help it is a waste of time and money to force help on them.

He knew my mother had inherited a bunch of money. I told him I would get the telephone number of her financial adviser and maybe he could provide money for medical treatment. He didn't respond, and I never got him the telephone number.

I told him my father had sold his half of the candle company for twenty times what he paid for it and invested all the money, which he promptly lost. My grandfather who sold the candle company to my father said my father and his partner did an amazing job. A black Labrador dog went over and sat beside him. He looked at the dog a moment and started to massage its ear making a contented growling noise like a dog. He said he didn't understand why my father didn't "rest on his laurels."

My grandmother came back into the room, walked over to where I was, stooped over, and kissed me on the forehead. I didn't acknowledge it in the slightest, because I was in midsentence talking to my grandfather. Later it overwhelmed me, what a dear gesture that was.

No great plan evolved that night. I told my mother what had happened. She must have called the financial person, because I later heard an arrangement was made with the bank that the entire mortgage would be paid during the next year.

My mother never hit bottom because she always had money. Over the following years no amount of reason or periodic hospitalization could help her kick the habit of alcohol. What finally did was old age and a series of falls that resulted in broken bones. After that my parents both had nurses attend to them. They moved to Maine. My father had a stroke. He didn't talk anymore, and was in a wheelchair. Nurses were there twenty-four hours a day. She could not drive. All of us children who were full-grown adults told the nursing agency that if they liked being there then do not let her get any alcohol. We finally got our way, and she didn't. The medical people said she had premature dementia. She also had great perceptions.

Before I got my first real job on a newspaper I went to the labor pool. They got me some work at a company that made machines for the machine tool industry. I swept the floor and occasionally had a conversation with a machinist.

On the floor where I worked there were about twenty lathes. There was a partitioned room with bright lights and large windows where the supervisors worked. Some of the bright light from the windows shone on new computer lathes with young people standing by them.

When a piece of metal was lowered into the grip of one of those machines the operator pressed buttons on a panel. After that another button was pressed and a hood would slide over the piece of metal. A carbide cutting tool came in contact with the turning metal and at the same time cutting oil came from a nozzle. There were no metal shavings, just brittle chips that shot away from the turning piece. When that part was finished it would go to another place, and eventually it would be part of a metal lathe made by that company.

On the far wall there was a huge lathe. It was painted black, and most of the other ones were painted light gray. There were no electronic buttons on it anywhere. The black lathe looked very clean and well kept. The machinist who operated the lathe told me he worked on that machine since it was new forty-five years ago. He said he was going to retire soon. When he was talking he took a shop rag and without interrupting himself he wiped some oil off the lathe.

I was on that job for three weeks and during that time he retired. When he left no one else took his job operating the black lathe. Another person told me it was scrap iron. Some maintenance people came and disconnected the electric wires and hung a sign on it that said: NOT IN USE. Another machinist at the lathe next to the black lathe said when the old man was the operator he could make it work right, but no one else could.

It was bigger than any other machine on the floor. The first week I was there I marveled at the size of it and asked the old man if it was difficult to operate. He said it wasn't difficult because he knew the machine so well. He said for anyone else but him it would be difficult.

All the people who worked in that place except me belonged to a national worker organization called a union. The union had an agreement in contract form with the company about everything concerning the workers. My employer was the labor pool, and I was on assignment to that factory. My job was to push a broom around the place, but when I appeared there day after day some of the workers thought the management of the company didn't respect their union contract. One of the machinists was the union steward, which meant he represented the union.

He worked by the bright lights of the supervisor's office. Often he would slide the hood back on his machine just as it was finishing but not quite finished so metal chips would go all over the floor. When that happened I could hear it and I hurried over to his area with my broom and cart to sweep them all up. My job was to sweep up those chips quickly so he could get on with his work. When I was finished sweeping the chips I always had a few words with him about his machine or the weather.

Perhaps twice a day the supervisor would scurry over to an area where there was a big metallic thud from a large piece of steel dropping to the floor. The first time it happened I asked the machinist nearest to me what that was and he said it sounded like someone dropped their watch.

A laborer from another floor talked to me about working directly for the company. He said it was a good place to work. He told me he had been there a short time. He said how much he was making and what my starting wage would be.

The old man had told me before he left that over his lifetime he had always gotten nickel and dime raises each year. I told the laborer I didn't want to work there, that I was interested in temporary employment.

In one section there were steel racks holding long bars of steel. The day after I talked to the laborer, the supervisor asked me to tidy up the racks. I was lifting up bars of steel. A short distance away I saw the union steward and several of the other machinists grouped together peering at me. I learned later the union contract said only union people could handle steel.

The same day a person from the labor pool walked back to where I was and asked me if I wanted to work there, and I told him there was too much ___ing noise.

He walked away. That evening before I went to the bar on Calhoun Street the man from the labor pool called me on the telephone, and said the job at the tool company was over. In the same businesslike fashion I said that was too bad and asked him what else he had. He said he would call me in a few days. I said that sounded like a corporate comment to me. I said he could just tell it to me like it is.

Several days later he did call me. The job was a long-term assignment fixing lawn mowers and doing related work for the Cincinnati School Board. Each day I reported for work in an underground garage. A supervisor and two other people my age worked there. The two other people were U.S. army veterans who knew each other before that job. Their wages were paid by the government as part of a federal program to help veterans find work. They had been there almost a year and were somewhat anxious because when the year was up the government would no longer pay their wage. If the school board wanted to keep them it would have to put them on its payroll. They only had a month or two left, and they said there was no indication the school board would hire them. My presence was a sign to them that they would not be hired. They often sat away from me when on break or during lunch.

The walk-behind lawn mower used to cut grass at all the schools was the same as the old L model my father had at Markin Farm. The person who shod the horses showed me how to braze metal when the exhaust manifold on it was broken. Also, I had watched my father many times take the head off the motor and fix a stuck valve.

When Morituri was still a working farm truck I put the walk-behind mower in the back and left it running while I took it to the farm implement place at the head of the road. I didn't need a driver's license to get there. I didn't tie it down. After I accelerated I didn't hear the engine anymore, and when I looked in the rearview mirror I saw it bouncing down the road behind me. I stopped. I couldn't imagine how I was going to explain this to my father. When I walked back the engine was still running. It was upright on its two wheels. The rim of one wheel was bent. The handlebar was bent, and the exhaust manifold was broken. That was the only damage. I drove it up the ramps into the back of the farm truck. I didn't have any ropes to tie it down. This time I stopped the motor and put it in gear so it would not roll.

My younger brother and I were always going up to the farm implements parts counter to get a small nut or bolt to fix something. Sometimes we paid for items with money we got from turning in empty soft drink bottles.

Once we made a motorized surrey and were there almost every day for weeks getting nuts and bolts. One of those days we were in my mother's car and she dropped my brother off to get something he needed. On our way back we picked him up, and as we were going down the road my brother, who was about nine years old, said the parts man had called him a little ____er (a four-letter slang word beginning with f that means fornicate). My mother turned the car around, drove back up there, and went into the farm implements place. A few minutes later she returned and drove home. She didn't say anything, and after a while I asked her what happened. She said she walked up to the parts counter and asked the parts man point-blank, "Did you call my son a little ___er?" She said right out loud the same word he used. She said several of the mechanics and the owner all of whom we knew by name happened to be standing there in front of the parts counter. I asked her what they said and she said no one said anything.

When I saw all the lawn mowers in that school board garage were the same as the one we had at Markin Farm I knew I could handle the job. The fact that I could do better work than the two veterans, who had been there almost a year, made the situation with them even worse.

One morning the supervisor told me to get in his pickup truck. He said he was going over to one of the schools to get something. As it turned out, he didn't need my help. He wanted to tell me something.

He told me the other two people were bums as far as he was concerned and when the government stopped paying their pay they were finished. He said next year he would retire and somebody new was needed to run the garage. I suppose he wanted to let me know what the situation was. If he had ideas of my being the person to fill that position he didn't say so. I didn't think seriously about what he said other than he was the person speaking. I was enjoying the breeze in my face, and the ride to nowhere. That was the only time during that job I was not in the garage. I never saw the other two leave while I was there.

Several days later we were on our lunch break. There were ten minutes left before we had to go back to work. The two veterans were resting by the ceiling on two high piles of a soft substance covered with canvas. I was sitting a short distance away on the tailgate of a truck. At one point we were talking and something I said irritated one of them. He climbed down off the pile. I didn't call him a bum, but I told both of them what the supervisor had said in his truck.

The veteran was coming at me with his hands clenched into fists, and he was walking fast. I stood up to absorb his forward movement. We grappled for a few seconds, and then I pushed him away from me. When I did he was holding on to my shirt and it got ripped in many places. I felt like a comic book character named the Incredible Hulk. When he stepped back he was in perfect striking distance, and I hit him twice in the face hard enough to get his undivided attention. I felt like a large cat moving slowly through the tall grass. I outweighed him by about twenty pounds, and he didn't know what he was doing. I knew I had him. I told him to step right up like a person in a carnival. The supervisor came out to see what all the noise was. I saw him out of the corner of my eye standing there between two parked vehicles watching us. He was a weak person in all respects. He said and did nothing. I didn't want to hit him another time. It was too easy. I told him I was going to break him down like a shotgun and he was going to cry like a sissy punk rabbit as he gave it up. That finished him. He went back where the other veteran was. After that the superintendent told me to go home.

That evening a person from the labor pool I never heard of before telephoned, and said not to go back to the school board job. That was the end of the call. I didn't belabor the point. I didn't want to go back. I didn't want to work for them. I felt like I was dying. I didn't want to wallow in the mire anymore.

I started looking diligently for a job. I went to all the little weekly newspapers in surrounding communities. Finally I got hired by one of them in Lebanon, Ohio. That newspaper was always in the shadow of another weekly newspaper with a much bigger staff. If the one I worked on had gone off on its own, it might have lasted longer.

The money to operate the newspaper came from paid advertisements that appeared each week on the same pages as the news. Supposedly people would buy the paper for the news content and see the advertisements. Sometimes I thought it had to be the other way around. Although the obituaries really made you think about death.

There was one lady in the front room who handled the advertising department and occasionally she would have a helper who would go out and beat the bushes for new accounts.

There were three of us in the editorial department. That was another name for the people who wrote the news. My boss had a firm idea how it should be. The other person was a retired self-proclaimed newspaperman who did all the main news. I did the stories he didn't have time to do. I took all the photographs for the paper. I also did routine things like emptying the wastepaper baskets and typing up the obituary column. I'd call all the local funeral homes each week. Eventually I got to know the names of some of the undertakers (funeral directors). I'd ask them if they had any dead ones that week. The editorial department was all in one room. When the editor heard me she told me not to phrase it that way.

When I first saw the man who hired me he was sitting at a desk at another newspaper. It was by chance he was there when I showed up looking for a job. I didn't have any idea he owned the paper. There were several people in the room. He was the only one who looked up when I entered. That is why I went over to where he was. He never got up from his chair, and I never sat down. From the questions he asked I told him I was a recent journalism graduate looking for work. I didn't have to fill in the blanks on an application form.

That night he called me and said, "If you are interested I have something on another newspaper in Lebanon." I should have let him finish talking, because I think he was about to say when I should go to work, but I asked him first. We didn't talk about my pay on the phone. We had talked about that subject earlier face-to-face, and I had said I wanted a good job more than anything else. He asked me what a good job was. I said it was one where I could tell a judge I was gainfully employed.

As a reporter I wrote a story about the money policemen earned on various police departments in the county. I learned a rookie policeman made almost twice as much as I did. Mine wasn't subsistence pay, but it was close. Most of the time I wasn't aware how little I made. It was enough to get by, and I was grateful to have a permanent job I was trained to do.

Most of the stories I did were not "hard news." The newspaperman among us did all those. The lady editor who was my immediate boss did some stories she wanted to do plus she read over everything that went in the paper to make sure things were said and spelled correctly. Her husband of many years had died a prolonged death a few years earlier. She said the last years of that time were difficult. We had long conversations. My grandmother on my mother's side died when I worked there, and she seemed to know all about my mother's stepfather. She told me who he was.

My job description wasn't spelled out in words. I didn't know exactly what to do. I did routine things, but that wasn't very much. The man who hired me never said so, but I think he was a little concerned at first that all he was getting for his money was a bunch of photographs. They didn't give me anything else to do so I thought I was doing enough. After a while I realized my job entailed a delicate balancing act. I was supposed to do more without stepping on anyone's toes.

The owner showed up each week to pick up the copy (written words), go over the advertising with the advertising lady, and give us our paychecks. One of those days when I first started working there I was leaving at the end of the day and I saw him sitting in his car parked outside by the curb. He didn't notice me. He was pulling the photographs out of the large brown envelope the editor had handed him. Most of the photographs were of people who had gained some notoriety in that quaint little town.

Several weeks after that he asked me how I get people to smile. I said that just before I took a picture I'd say to the person, "Say cheese." I said they either started to laugh or said the word (when a person says the word *cheese* in the English language their mouth has to make a smile even if they never do).

He took all the copy to another newspaper office. There the typewritten pages were set into neat newspaper columns. Three or four people operating computer machines did that work. Once the type was set the paper would be "paste-up," which meant each page would be "composed" and made ready for an "offset" camera. The pasted-up pages were called flats. Those finished flats were photographed with the offset camera. The next day the owner would take large sheets of film made by the camera to the printer fifty miles away. Then bundles of newspapers would come back. They were addressed and taken to the post office.

Evenings I helped pasteup all four papers and I operated the offset camera. I made more money doing the production of the papers than I did doing words.

One of the photographs I took that appeared in the paper was of a corncrib near the corner of a large field. Two main roads in the county went along each side of the field and crossed at the corner. The abandoned corncrib was visible to anyone who looked in that direction from the road. The photograph had a few words under it (cutline) that said it probably wouldn't be there much longer and to bid it farewell.

The week the photograph appeared the man who owned the field called the paper. The editor told me to pick up the phone and speak to him. He asked me why I said it was an "eyesore." I told him if a person read the words under that photograph and thought it said the corncrib was an eyesore they should be rushed to a doctor. I said to the man on the telephone whatever is put in its place is most likely going to be an eyesore. There was a silence. He said a few other words and got off the telephone.

I wanted to do a story about the 4H clubs in the county. I collected material here and there for several weeks before the story with photographs appeared in the paper.

During a time in the United States that is generally called the "Industrial Revolution" the Department of Agriculture started 4H. That was when the family farm went from feeding the family to feeding the entire nation. When I did the story the Department of Agriculture had an "Extension Office" in the county and through that office the 4H program was directed. I learned there were similar offices in other counties doing the same thing.

4H enabled young people (mostly young people who grew up on a farm but not necessarily so) to develop an appreciation for taking care of animals, growing plants, making things by hand, and doing all the activities associated with farm life. If one of the

4H club members wanted to learn how they were doing compared to others they could do so at the county fair each year where cattle, plants, quilts, honey, and other things were judged.

I talked with boys who proudly showed me what they said were fine steers and they told me why they thought so. Several evenings I went to club meetings in old farmhouses with high ceilings. Each meeting began with a pledge of allegiance to the flag and the United States of America for which it stands. One club met during the day in a farm house kitchen. A group of girls learned from an older woman how to make bread.

I was in the kitchen for most of the club meeting. One of the girls who seemed like she was going to graduate from high school any day had a sweetness and simplicity they all had, but she had more. I don't remember how I got her telephone number, but I did. I called her up. It was a mistake. She couldn't talk, and the next day the older woman called the paper.

The editor and I were the only ones there. The newspaperman was at city hall and the advertising lady was out. I wasn't paying any attention to the call, or knew what it was. Many calls came into the newspaper office. I was hard at work at my desk trying to find a letter on the keyboard. The editor put her hand over the mouthpiece of the phone and said to me that it was so and so from 4H and now she wanted to talk to me. Then she said for me to get it in the other room. She meant where the advertising lady worked. There were two desks there and on each one there was a telephone.

I sat down at the desk that was most seldom used and picked up the phone. I identified myself, and she said how awful it was that I called that "child" on the telephone. She sounded very angry and I listened to her some more. When she stopped for a moment I said I would hardly call that girl a child. I said that without expecting it to change much in her mind about anything, but it did. There was a pause and her whole tone changed. We talked some more. I admitted it was a mistake. She said it certainly was. We wound down on the telephone. I put the receiver down, got up, and walked back to my desk. The editor asked me if the lady was put at ease, and I said she was. The editor told me to do the story and not get any more information.

Even though the newspaper was in the largest town in the

county, its readers and advertisers not only came from there, but also from small towns and townships throughout the county. The township meetings I went to were held in the evening. They were public meetings conducted by three people called the trustees.

The business they conducted concerned maintaining roads and getting some of the more basic public services done. The townships relied on tax money for operating expenses. Township government was the closest government to the people. The trustees in some urban townships had to work with regional planning commissions on complex matters. Sometimes they also had to deal with matters concerning a township police department. Most townships relied on the county sheriff for a police department, but some had their own. The difference between urban and rural township meetings was extreme. One might be as formal as a courtroom, and the other would be people getting together after work to hear a neighbor's request for the township to ditch a road in front of his cornfield.

At one township meeting the trustees voted to have some work done. That was it that month. There were only one or two people there. One of the trustees said it wasn't often someone from the newspaper came to the meeting. He apologized that there wasn't something more exciting to report. He then improvised and told me a story, which he said I could put in the paper.

He said the Ohio Environmental Protection Agency (EPA) "open burning" law was in effect. The statewide law said people could not have any sort of open fire such as a burning leaf pile. Exceptions to the law were fire barrels at construction sites, cooking fires, campfires, fires that melted tar for the work roofers do, and a few others.

The trustee told me that a person he knew was burning a huge brush pile on his farm when the Ohio EPA swept down on him in a helicopter and two people in the back got out to issue him a citation. He said when they said what they were doing the farmer went up to the edge of the flaming brush pile and, barely able to stand the heat, he stuck a smoldering chicken, feathers and all, on the prongs of a pitch fork. He said the farmer brought the chicken to where the EPA officials were standing so they could see it. He told them in all seriousness he was having a barbecue.

In the city of Franklin on the edge of the county up by Dayton there was a "resource recovery" experiment being conducted by a New York City-based company, the city of Franklin, and the federal government. The company, made paper-pulping machinery. I did a story on what was happening there.

According to the company municipal garbage is 40 percent paper fiber. They wanted to learn if it could be economically extracted. The experiment would also reveal if other parts of raw garbage could be separated economically.

The most unique part of the project was its first step. Private contractors dumped fifty tons of municipal garbage per day from the city of Franklin on a concrete slab. A large wheeled machine pushed the garbage down a hole as it arrived. The hole was the top of a modified "hydrapulper," and that was the first step. It went seventy-five feet below the slab. Water added to the garbage made everything inside into a slurry. The hydrapulper was higher than it was wide, and at the bottom blades whirled around making a rumbling noise that could be heard anywhere at the facility. An engineer described it as very big kitchen blender.

Upside-down magnetic conveyor belts, optical scanners, and centrifuges produced the end result. In one place there was a row of large containers under chutes. They were filling up. Into one went all the aluminum from the garbage. Each piece was small, clean, and uniform in size. The second container had pieces of steel. There was no paint on any of the metal. The next three containers were filling up with small pieces of red, green, and clear glass. Not one piece of glass was in the wrong container.

The chief engineer of the project told me that each day he and three people were able to separate and recover nine tons of paper fiber, three tons of ferrous metals, two tons of glass, and one fourth-ton of aluminum. He said the remaining fraction included plastics and other organics that have about half the energy value (BTU per pound) of coal.

The engineer in charge of the project said separation of garbage at the source is the last resort in resource recovery. He said many consumers (in the United States) are encouraged to save their bottles, cans, and paper so it can be recycled. He said this is not the answer to resource recovery from an economical standpoint because there would still have to be an inspection station to determine how well everyone was separating their garbage. He said everyone would separate their garbage to a different degree, making it necessary for a second separation that would cost nearly as much as if raw garbage was separated at the collection end. He said the effort for resource recovery must not be directed at the goodwill of the consumer but at industries' profit motivation.

The Franklin city manager told me that the taxpayer had to pay the bill to get rid of garbage. He said the conventional way to dispose of garbage in landfills was less expensive. Several years later the facility was closed.

I got involved in editorial comment one time. A group of people in the community wanted to take over operation of the animal shelter because they felt it was being run the wrong way.

The animal shelter was where unclaimed animals (primarily house dogs and house cats) were taken that would otherwise roam loose in the county. If an animal was not claimed in three days it was killed.

A citizens group objected to the way animals were killed, the way carcasses were disposed of, the way live animals were kept, and what they said was a lack of effort to find people who might adopt the unwanted pets.

The animals were killed by carbon monoxide poisoning. They were put in an old van kept for that purpose. The engine was started and the exhaust from the engine was directed into the enclosed section where the animals selected to be killed were put. The bodies of the dead animals went into a nearby pit.

The citizen group wanted to buy what they said was a more humane "decompression chamber" to kill stray dogs and cats. They wanted to install a kennel type of area and group dogs according to their size. They wanted to have an ongoing program to get animals adopted. All of those things involved spending money. The county officials in charge of the money didn't want to spend more on the shelter, and they didn't want to turn the operation of the shelter over to a group that was not in county government.

The county commissioners and a group of citizens comprised of housewives were going back and forth month after month.

When it seemed there was no end I wrote an opinion.

The opinion recounted how dogs were killed by the county ten or fifteen years earlier in a shed at the fairgrounds. Their throats were cut by hand. The dead dogs were then thrown in the back of a dump truck and taken who knows where. I said so now there is a van with the exhaust going inside and the dead dogs go into a pit. I wrote that no reasonable person would deny unwanted animals needed to be collected and killed, but it ought to be done with the respect they deserve as God's creatures on this earth. When it appeared in the newspaper the editor had removed the word *God* and it said, "deserve as creatures on this earth."

In the southwest corner of the county the U.S. Information Agency (USIA) operated the Bethany Relay Station, which was one of five Voice of America (VOA) locations in the nation. It had "rhombic" antennae and one huge "curtain antenna" that simultaneously beamed several radio programs into foreign countries.

The director of that place said the Bethany Relay Station began operation in 1943 to "combat" enemy "propaganda" and to tell people why America was entering World War Two. He said then and now the workers there are responsible for the technical aspect of directing VOA broadcasts into "target areas." He said a target area is a place in Europe, Africa, or South America with a government not friendly to the policies or government of the United States. He said for technical reasons the Bethany Relay Station was located where it is. He said the radio signal they produce bounces the right way off the atmosphere. He used words such as *propagation, aurora zone bypass,* and *aurora zone absorption* to explain. He said the broadcast originates at the VOA headquarters in Washington, D.C.

I went into the control room with the director. People were there to make sure the transmitters and antennae were functioning properly. There was a headset and selector switch that made it possible to listen to each broadcast being made.

I heard the English-language recordings of modern American music. When I asked the director about this he said the hunger for American music is the competitive advantage VOA has over other stations trying to reach the same people. He said many VOA listeners around the world understand basic English from listening to American music and from special instruction on the radio.

The director said the songs are followed by world news. He said the news, unlike the songs, is in the language of the target area.

During the time I worked on the newspaper I moved from my one-room modern apartment on Riddle Road to an upstairs room in an old house on Mulberry Street in Lebanon. My mental health improved considerably at that point. I wasn't sick, but the whole scene on Riddle Road was like a jailhouse where people had their own key.

In the house there were two apartments upstairs and one downstairs. The owner was a plumber. He and his wife lived in a modern flat-topped building next to the house. I mailed them the rent money each month. A few times when I was late one of the plumber's employees came to my door to ask for the money.

A man, woman, and small child lived in the apartment next to mine. I think they both worked and the child went to school. I didn't get to know them at all. When someone leaving their apartment was going downstairs I could always hear the child with the exact same inflections in his voice say, "Bye now."

Sounds from their apartment never came into mine, but sounds from mine went into theirs and beyond. I was restoring the Rabbit. It was under a car cover on blocks outside, but practically everything that could be removed from the car was in my room. I hammered bent aluminum strips straight on a table of mine. I didn't have an anvil. I'm sure the pounding could be heard a long way off. No one ever complained about the noise.

Downstairs there was a seedy person who worked nights in a gasoline station on State Route 123 beside Interstate 71. We had the same routines. We became friends. After one year I was working nights also. The man who owned the newspaper in Lebanon owned four others. I got full-time work pasting up those papers and operating the offset camera. I didn't work in Lebanon anymore. My full-time work was done in two towns. They were forty-five minutes away on the expressway.

I drove that distance almost daily. State Highway Patrol policemen parked on the side of the interstate highway were attracted to my car. I had rolled it a while earlier on a two-lane highway outside Charlottesville, Virginia. When I drove it to work in the afternoon they could see the excessive body damage on whatever side was toward them and on the roof. It didn't look so hot. It was combat-ready in all other respects.

The state policemen who pulled me over were always very friendly if I was friendly first. When they stopped me I asked them, "What's up?" I think my car fit the criterion of having a misbegotten driver. Each policeman said, as he handed me a warning, when the work indicated on the warning was done I should sign the paper and send it in.

One state policeman who stopped me said as he handed me a warning that if I signed my name to the statement on the warning that the work was done and I got another warning for the same thing, then a warrant would be issued for my arrest. I never signed any of the warnings. I had no warrants "outstanding" even though I had quite a collection of warnings. I thanked him for the tip. I stuffed his written warning into the glove box with all the others and proceeded on my way.

The seedy person in the apartment downstairs had a friend who drove a domestic automobile. Without any modifications it was known to have much quickness, but this one had modifications that made it still quicker. It was painted a special way.

The engine had a lumpy idle, but when the revolutions per minute (rpm) increased the sound of the engine became smooth and loud. When the engine rpm increased suddenly the side of the car moved as if someone were pushing on the fender. The exhaust system was designed to enhance power more than anything else. The tires on the rear axle were wide. The suspension was changed to prevent the tires from striking the inside of the fenders. Without looking under the car I could see several other changes in the suspension. All the changes had the singular purpose of making the car go faster.

Several months after the seedy person and I became friends I walked in his apartment early one evening when neither of us were working and two girls our age were sitting on his raggedy old couch over by the wall. I had seen one of them before in the automobile that was rigged to be quick. The person who drove it was her "boy friend," and she was waiting for him. I had not seen the other girl before that time. She looked a little bit refined and out of place. They had come together from the city of Fairfield, in the next county.

When I first saw the other girl I didn't know what to say. Then I walked over to where she was sitting, stood over her, and asked her what a nice girl was doing in a place like this. I told her she should be ashamed of herself. She looked at the seedy person and her friend and without looking at me asked what sort of place it was. By that time I was going across the room to an armchair. I said it was a den of iniquity. She asked what that meant and if we had a dictionary. I said I wasn't sure, but it wasn't good.

Outside it was a still summer night. When the boyfriend arrived, he and his girl sank down low in the seats of his car. The seedy person, the other girl, and me sat on the curb beside the car with a can of beer in our hand. There was a perfectly shaped tree across the street. We discussed its merits and decided that if it were a person it would be a president.

The girl was sitting on the curb. I was sitting behind her on the curb. My feet went on each side of her, and I rubbed her back. I put my hands under her shirt and unfastened underwear on her back that was in the way. She didn't move or speak. Our conversation changed from being frivolous. Her arms were tight against her sides. I was rubbing her back, and that is all I did.

The other two in the car looked over the edge of the window on the passenger side. First the girl and then both of them were peering at us. It was because I had my hands under her shirt and I took them away. The girl had her head down. She had stopped talking and never looked at them.

After the girl became quiet it was just the seedy person and me talking. It was almost like the girl wasn't there. Then the others started looking at us. I took my hands away and things got back to the way they were, talking about trees and things.

The Rabbit was back together by then. It was parked nearby off the street under a car cover. We talked about it, and she asked me if she could take a ride. I asked her if she had ever driven a stick shift, and she said she had. When I uncovered it she put one hand over her mouth. I said I would drive it out of town and then she could take a turn. We changed places when I got to a country road. When it came time to find the next gear she had her hand on the gearshift knob. I put my hand on top of hers to show her where it was. I did that every time, and she became the focus of my attention. That was the only way I touched her. When we got back, the party had ended. She and the girl she came with went home.

I saw the girl's friend a short time later and asked about the girl who shifted the gears with me. The girl friend said her friend would probably go "out" with me. I never saw her again, and our paths never crossed.

Nights when I didn't paste up one of the newspapers I went to the gasoline station where my friend worked. The station was open all night. It was privately owned, but the sign and other markings indicated it was part of a well-known oil company. I never saw the owner or daytime manager. My friend was the only paid employee at night. If he was doing a small repair on an automobile inside I would put gasoline in cars, wash the bugs off windshields, check the oil, and handle the money. No mater how rude and hideous a person behaved I would say "yes, sir" this or "no, sir" that, or if they wanted to argue I would say, "Anything you say." It was the mid-1970s. The price of gasoline increased often. When someone asked rudely at two in the morning why the company charged so much for gasoline, I'd say, "Gee whiz, I don't know. Probably they think they can get it." Or if a customer complained about other things I had no control over I would tell them I would bring it up at our next board meeting. There weren't many awful-behaving customers, but when one was about to drive off, nastiness and all, I would say with a big smile and the same delightful inflections as the child in the apartment next to mine, "Bye now."

The sign for the station was on two high poles near the expressway. People could see it when they were far from there. The sign had lights inside and at night it would attract bugs, which would attract bats. These bats were small furry nocturnal mammals that ate bugs in mid air. During the day they hung upside down asleep, probably in nearby barns. Over and over I could see them turn instantly to gobble up large flying insects going in an entirely different direction. It was amazing to watch those creatures change direction. They moved so fast and could turn so sharply.

One of the seventy-five-foot poles on the sign had steel pegs on each side so a person could climb up, crawl through a hatch, and get inside the sign. Once I did that and before I got into the sign I was close to the bats.

As many as five or six people would congregate at the gas station at night. There was an all-night restaurant we could see across the street on the same side of the expressway. Around midnight several of us usually went over there to get something to eat. If I was still there at dawn when the seedy person got off work we would get breakfast there.

We were familiar faces. When one of the waitresses got fired we would learn all the details from the other waitresses. We also knew the manager by name. Most of the waitresses were recently out of high school or in school. It was summer.

There was a massive amusement park several miles down the expressway. When it closed, many cars going north would get gasoline at the station. After that it wasn't busy the rest of the night. Sometimes when no one else was there we would sit outside in two chairs tipped back against large glass windows.

During that time the idea of a character named the BF'er started. The BF'er was unattractive in appearance but faster than a bullet, more powerful than a speeding locomotive, and able to leap tall buildings in a single bound. The BF'er inadvertently and unwittingly became a defender of justice for people everywhere.

We thought of it as a daily cartoon in a newspaper. As we sat there ideas would come. There were infinite possibilities. The last picture would show the BF'er going out the door tucking in his shirt. In one cartoon the BF'er is leaving a restaurant like the one across the street. In the background everyone is humped over counters, the upright parts of booths, tables, on the floor, everywhere. Everyone has little *X*s in their eyes, their rear end is propped up, their pants are down, and a little wisp of smoke is spiraling straight up from their bare bottoms. The title is, the day the BF'er didn't get served. In another cartoon called the BF'er Vs. Kung Foo, the second-to-last frame shows Kung Foo trying to karate kick the BF'er. The last frame shows the BF'er going under the ropes tucking in his shirt. In the background

Kung Foo is in center ring with his pants down, smoke is rising off his rear end, and there are little *X*s in his eyes. The referee is standing there in awe of how swift and sure the BF'er is.

We laughed about other ones; the day the BF'er makes King Kong come down, the BF'er gets a warning from the State Highway Patrol, the BF'er pumps gas, the BF'er is falsely accused. In that one the last frame would show the BF'er leaving a courtroom. In the background the judge, the prosecutor, the bailiff, false witnesses, and everyone else involved has learned not to trifle with the BF'er. Innocent bystanders are amazed. They don't know who the BF'er is. Nobody does. He has no name or identification number. His alias is the BF'er.

After a year the man who hired me to work on the newspapers made some sort of a deal with another person who owned and operated one small weekly newspaper near Cincinnati. That person took over the operation of all the papers. I still had the job of pasting up the papers, and one evening when I was doing that the editor from the biggest paper of the group came over to help me. She was a mainstream journalist and apparently efficient at getting things done. In an announcement in the newspapers about her it said the man operating the papers appointed her to oversee each editorial department. That announcement was the only indication I ever had that she did anything more than be the editor of the one paper.

I didn't think anything was out of the ordinary when she came to help me paste up the paper. We talked about our personal lives. She was sincere about everything. We were pasting up the paper while we talked, and when I looked over at her she was crying. I didn't say anything. She cried and at the same time was pasting up the paper. It was natural as could be. We could both have a good cry if I knew why she was crying. I didn't ask. That same week the new man who operated the newspaper group came back to where I was and said he wanted me to be the editor of the little weekly paper he once owned before it became a group. I got the same money, but it took a whole lot more time. Several weeks later he called me up at my new job and wanted to know the month and year I got a degree from college. I told him and wondered if he was going to cut my pay any further below the poverty level if I had never been to college. Meanwhile the office where he worked was modernized, air conditioned, and the ceilings were dropped.

When I was doing the job of pasting up the papers I would return to Lebanon when I was finished. It was dark. I never got a warning from the state Highway Patrol at night. It was a matter of routine in the day. One evening when I got back to my apartment I turned on the radio and an accelerated voice with fast background music said the station "salutes Jonathan Margo, grand prize winner of the Feeling Free Photo Contest." The grand prize was a ten-speed bicycle that had a lightweight steel alloy frame. I later read an article on the subject that said it had excellent "geometry." The bicycle was made in Nottingham, England. Later a company in the United States bought the company in England, and after that the bicycle was made in the United States. The name was the same, but it was not the same bicycle.

The knowledge I had of bicycles before then was from peddling up the road at Markin Farm to exchange empty soft drink bottles for money. To get there it was uphill all the way. I was glad when the day came I got a gasoline powered go-cart. When I won the expensive new bicycle I thought I would ride it once, and then sell it in the large daily newspaper in Cincinnati.

I went downtown to pick it up and after a publicity photo was taken I strapped it on top of my car and took it to Lebanon. There I took it off my car and rode it up a hill into a cemetery on Mulberry Street. That day I decided to keep the bicycle. I was amazed what a fine machine it was and how little effort was needed to make it go. It wasn't like any bicycle I had ever ridden.

To enter the contest a person was to send in a photograph of what made them feel free. I figured most people would send in a photograph of their naked girlfriend. I sent a black-and-white photo I thought would be the only one that exemplified capitalistic values. My photograph was taken with a large telephoto lens across two fields. The first field was clover hay, and the second was corn. All the white tassels were out on the corn. In the middle of the first field there was a huge white oak tree. In its shade were two apple wood chairs. In one chair two people were sitting together facing the cornfield. The second chair was empty. Under the photo I wrote the words "I feel free watching my corn grow." The words were probably half the reason I won.

The new job of being the editor of a small weekly newspaper in a small town left no time for anything else, including spending nights at the gas station thinking up new episodes for the BF'er. I moved into an old farmhouse closer to work. The big oil company took over the station. The seedy person lost his job, and soon after that the gas station closed completely. The building became a place where someone could buy a tomahawk or something else of value.

Before the station closed I wrote a letter to the big oil company saying they made a big mistake letting the seedy person go. I said he often would finish working on a customer's car even if it was after he was off duty and he wasn't getting paid for his time. I identified myself as the editor of a weekly newspaper. I didn't say I used to hang out there, that I unofficially pumped gas there, or that I carried a big wad of their money in my shirt pocket. I wanted to command a little respect.

A person at the oil company corporate headquarters called the newspaper office on the telephone. I answered it, and they asked to speak to me. The person on the other end said my letter was why he was calling. I interrupted him to say he didn't have to explain. I told him I just wanted to say they fired a good man. He said since I took the time to write he wanted to take the time to reply. He said the location had become a trouble spot. He said all sorts of unsavory people were loitering there all night.

He may have been right about that, because I learned later that one of us had been arrested and convicted for stealing CB radios from trucks parked across the street in the parking lot of the all-night restaurant. If the authorities had us under surveillance they probably thought we were on drugs or were selling more drugs than gas. The person who was arrested for stealing CB radios told me that once when he was pumping gas two people with a Hillsboro bracket on their license plate pulled up to the pump and asked to buy some drugs. The person who stole CB radios told me that he was startled, and said they better go back to Hillsboro where they belonged. Hillsboro was a rural city two counties over. I never saw any drugs or alcohol when I was there. I don't know why a person would drive up, having never been there before, and ask that question. He probably worked for the police who wanted to find out what we were doing night after night.

Another time two total strangers walked up and one of them wanted to sell a chrome-plated handgun. The one holding the gun was wearing no shirt, and the other person who came with him stood about twenty feet to the side. They were older. They looked well fed and had recent haircuts. The chrome gun was cheaply made. I held it and saw it didn't have any serial number. I said it looked like an exhibit in a murder trial. They might have been from Hillsboro also.

For a short period of time two girls showed up at the gas station. The one who always drove had an older car with a big engine and a yellow sticker on the window that said: HURST. I asked about the sticker and she said it had "four on the floor." When she left the station she always spun the tires to get up to speed.

The gas station had one "bay" which is the area where a car drives inside. Two red car-length steel channels were fastened to a large hydraulic column that when activated lifted up a car.

One evening most of us were in there. No car was inside. The girl with the fast car was a well-coupled young lady. She was kind of like a hornet. She was standing on one of the channels and I was between them. Her leg was bent. There was a rip in her blue jeans above her knee. Her skin was pressing against the rip, and it was a golden color. She saw me staring at that place. Later, when no one else was around she came up to me. Between her thumb and forefinger she was holding a tiny locket fastened to a necklace around her neck. She was sliding it back and forth on the chain. She was looking down at the ground some of the time when she asked me if she could ride in my car. I had the Rabbit parked outside. It was a delicate car compared to her car. I was surprised. We sat in it and she said she could relate to the headlamps and running boards. When we drove out of the gas station I stopped and asked her which way she wanted to go. She said she wanted to see where I lived so we turned toward Lebanon. I asked her if she was from Hillsboro. She wasn't.

Another night a person driving around on the grass with people sitting on the car hood bumped into a light pole. Everyone went flying. Fortunately, no one hit the light pole. The bumper of the car was bent. The driver was concerned that the insurance company wouldn't pay for the damage. He and the people he came with made a plan to drive the car into a big steel bridge located down the road a short distance. They thought the insurance company would pay for that damage. I never saw or heard what happened.

One night somebody climbed into the sign to look around. I don't know if the company thought the seedy person was responsible for any of that, but it happened on his watch.

A state agency called the Bureau of Criminal Investigation (BCI) had my arrest and conviction in their computer files. That information was available to any employers or insurance companies doing a background check on me. I wasn't aware that my criminal record had any effect on what I was doing, but when I learned of a new law passed by the state assembly that enabled people to "expunge" a conviction I wrote the lawyer in Columbus the same day. If my record was expunged it would be "sealed," which meant no one could learn about my arrest and conviction except a police agency or a judge doing a presentencing investigation.

A politician who was in the Ohio House of Representatives sent the newspaper an occasional report about what was happening in state government. That is how I learned of the law. I called her on the telephone to learn more. The newspaper was circulated to people in her district and that is why she always sent information about what happened in the state house. At first she assumed I had a certain opinion about the law. She said, over and over again, she didn't vote for it as if I was doing a story for the newspaper. Finally, I thought it would put her more at ease if I said it was for personal reasons I asked. When I said that she became disturbed and terse. She asked where I lived, implying I didn't live within the political boundary she represented. I was mistaken that I could simply talk to her. The conversation didn't last very long.

When I wrote the lawyer I said I could probably get letters from the city police chief who read comic books at his desk, the city manager, the mayor, members of city council and others that would substantiate that I had rehabilitated myself. I sent him a little money and he wrote back that I was the first person to use the law. He said it might take longer than I expected. Several weeks later he wrote again to say my record had been expunged. I didn't have to get letters from the people I had mentioned. They went on without knowing I was convicted once.

I was the "managing editor" of the newspaper. My job was to carry on the tradition of the newspaper, not start a new one. The owner of the newspaper oversaw the whole group of newspapers. He had an office at the biggest one, but he considered the newspaper where I worked his baby. He wrote complex opinions about government that appeared each week. He didn't do that in any other paper.

I rarely had anything constructive to say. Once I wrote an opinion about bread. I grappled with that one for a long time. It was as difficult an issue as I ever wrote about, except the time toward the end when I saw wide open gambling at a church festival. I wrote an opinion about that sight. In so many words it said people were sinking. Apparently, no one cared, because nothing changed.

An always-friendly old lady delivered a hand-written gardening column to the newspaper office on the same day and time each week. In her last column she said it was terrible to throw out leaves after they were raked into piles because they made such good compost. She said leaves in autumn were like "gold" which I thought was a great conception. When that column appeared in the paper the word gold was among others in large type in the headline. The man who owned the paper called me on the telephone, which was not a regular occurrence, and he said that was a poor choice of words.

The town was actually a small city named Loveland. It was divided in half by the Little Miami River. The half on the East Side was informally called old Loveland, and the other side was called new Loveland. She lived outside the city limits on the old side. On the new side there were progressive shopping centers. Most houses on the East Side were up in the hills in new subdivisions. They all had two car garages and manicured lawns.

After the one about leaves being like gold she didn't bring her column to the paper. The owner called her to say he didn't want the column anymore. I never asked her why she stopped. She was a casualty. I didn't know it, but I wasn't far behind her.

All anyone could do was continue to march and keep their mind about them as everyone was losing theirs.

In new Loveland there was a large furniture store that placed a full-page advertisement in the newspaper every week. The man who ran the store and determined when and where his advertisement appeared called me on the telephone. In a perturbed tone of voice he said photographs in the paper always showed old Loveland, and when there was a photograph of the new side it more often than not had to do with something like getting the utility wires out of sight.

I was apologetic and conciliatory. As I listened to him I was thinking about his place of business. I assumed the man was sincere about his thoughts. Likewise, I asked him sincerely why, if he was concerned about the look of new Loveland did he park his truck with big lettering naming his store on the edge of the parking lot beside the roadway at night? The furniture store man exclaimed, "What!" I repeated myself. He never did provide an answer. Soon afterward the owner of the newspaper, who I seldom saw, walked in and asked me about the conversation. I recounted what was said. He didn't say anything. I asked him what I should have done. He just listened to me and walked out without saying anything.

There was an old farmhouse on the edge of Peterloon Farm. I had gone by it many times. One of the two people who did all the work associated with farming on Peterloon lived in that house. He was the foreman's helper. The foreman lived in a newer red-brick house on the other side of the farm. A farm management company in London, Ohio, a hundred miles away decided what went where, and they determined what the two people were supposed to do.

When I was driving from Loveland to see my parents at Markin Farm I drove by the white farmhouse and noticed the grass was over a foot high. I drove my car in the gravel driveway and walked up to the door. No one was there. I looked through the window and saw bare floors. The house was empty. Each windowsill was over a foot deep.

I went over to the brick farmhouse where the foreman lived and knocked on the door. The helper's wife opened it and explained that the foreman had died. Her husband was the new foreman. I asked her what was going to happen to the place where they used to live. She said she heard the fire department was going to burn it down as some sort of exercise. She said the management company wasn't going to get another helper. I asked her why the windowsills were a foot deep, and she said because the walls were log. Under the plaster and lath there were logs. It was a log house. She said the roof leaked and the wood box gutters were rotten. The farm management company said the house wasn't worth fixing and was going to be burnt down. No one but the person who used to live there knew the walls were solid logs. The wife of the helper talked about other things pertaining to vegetation. She said she liked "anything that grows."

My mother's stepfather owned the house. He lived in the main house at Peterloon. His wife, my real grandmother, died several years earlier. After she died he had two strokes a year apart. The second one left him a speechless invalid in a wheelchair. Not long after the second stroke he died.

He bounced back from his first stroke. Physically it didn't seem to affect him much. It was during this time that I called him from my place in Lebanon and he told me he would discuss the farmhouse with me on a specific afternoon at his house. I went on that day and time, and rang the buzzer. A lady in a black-and-white uniform who had been there for years answered the door. She told me to wait in the front hall. She left, and when she came back she led me into the library where he was. He was in the process of standing up when I walked into the room. I walked over to him. We shook hands. He smiled and said, "Hello Jock. What are we going to do about that house"?

Ultimately, what was going to happen to that house was entirely up to him. His putting me on parity with him concerning the farmhouse was awesome. It made the entire event something other than business. We sat down in those two armchairs facing each other, and I told him I wanted to rent the little white farmhouse. He asked if anyone was living there, and I said no it was empty. I said the management company was going to have the fire department burn it down. I said I would like to live there, and fix it up. I asked him if I could deduct the cost of materials from my rent. I told him it was a real log house and whatever happened to it, I said, please, do not let anyone burn it down. I said it would be the equivalent of burning art.

Without further talk about the house or his telling me what he had decided, we talked about other things. I was there several hours. The time went fast. When I got up to leave he got up too, and he brought up the subject of the house. He named his secretary of many years, and told me to call her. We never talked about money. When I called her I named the rent money that I thought was fair and something I could afford but mostly what I could afford. She told me where to send it each month and that was all.

I lived in that house a long time. I still live there. The area changed faster and faster. Long before I was born the man I would call my grandfather bought six farms that became Peterloon Farm. At nearly the same time several other people like him moved near there also. Soon afterward they set up a political boundary around their property and the connecting land. It was called Indian Hill Village. Their idea was to establish an environment that insulated them from what was different from them, or what was different from what they wanted.

The people who established Indian Hill were not speculating on a payback. It was where they lived. Their concern was that it be a certain way.

Indian Hill became a desirable place to live. When I was a small child it took nearly an hour to get downtown from Peterloon. When Indian Hill was started it probably took much longer. Now with expressways and turnpikes it takes twenty minutes, and that includes the elevator ride. Not only was it close to Cincinnati, but also it was protected by zoning laws from anyone who might be at cross-purposes with the intent of the people who started it. As time went by, more and more people built houses there. The outsides of some of the houses were lit up all night long by outdoor floodlights. It was not long before it was visibly apparent to anyone driving down the road any time of day or night that it was an affluent community.

The little white wooden farmhouse where I lived was in Indian Hill. It was not demolished. It was very different from all the other houses nearby. It is an anachronism is what it is.

One day a few years after I moved in I was outside cooking

on a charcoal grill. A large van went past very slowly. I could see all the people looking toward the house. Then the van came back going the other way just as slowly and again I saw many faces looking in my direction. I waved. The van stopped, and the driver shouted, "We're just looking at your house. My father was born there and his father built it!"

I shouted back in a slightly frantic manner and gestured for him to back up to the driveway. I took the food off the grill and went over to greet them. Many people got out, and some of them were small children. One of the people was a ninety-year-old man. He was the driver's father who was born there. The driver told me they were from another state and were having a family reunion. He said they wanted to see the house once more.

They all came inside. The old man who was born there told me his name, and said his father was buried in the cemetery at the end of Hopewell Road. He said his father built the house after the American Civil War. We talked about the dirt floor in the basement and I said how I planed to make it a concrete floor. He said when it was hot it was always cool in a basement with a dirt floor.

I was using wood stoves for heat in the winter. He saw them and we talked about wood. I asked him how many cords he used. It seemed he didn't know, and I said it took me about eight cords to heat the house in the winter. Then he said that was how much they used.

We talked about the construction of the house. By that time I had taken all the plaster and lath out. Large hand-hewn beams were exposed downstairs. The customary way to build a house at that time was wood frame. That meant houses had a skeleton of wood with an exterior and interior surface put on that frame.

His father, who was born in Germany, personally built the house with several other people who helped him. The land was named the Hog Back Farm. When the house was built there was plenty of wood. The beams were not meant to be exposed on either the inside or the outside. On the outside there was white clapboard siding, and inside there was wallpaper over plaster and lath. The method of construction represented the end of one era in building and the beginning of another one. The solid log walls went as high as the first floor. The walls on the second floor were wood frame with vertical four-inch-square pieces of oak on twenty-inch centers.

The old man's father didn't trust building a two-story house on sticks. Oak studs were sticks in comparison to the solid oak beams on the first floor. He thought it was all right to have wood frame construction on the second floor holding up a roof, but there was no way he was going to have studs on the first floor holding the upstairs plus a roof. The floor joists were full dimension two-by-twelve sawn lumber.

When the old man was leaving the house he saw a chain saw in the corner. He turned around and said they cut those eight cords of firewood with a crosscut saw.

The man who owned the newspaper in Loveland and who took over the operation of the other six newspapers hired a person from Loveland to be the comptroller for the whole group. That person was also on the Loveland City School Board. Not long after he had the job of comptroller he called me to his office at the biggest newspaper. When I went in he was sitting behind a desk.

He had a copy of the newspaper folded in such a way that a recent story about a school board meeting was facing up. He said it was not correct. Basically what he was saying was that I should have made the report so that his position as president of the school board, and therefore the board's position, as a whole, would be reflected more positively. The implication was that it might go well with me if, in his eyes, I was a better reporter. He was the comptroller of the entire newspaper group.

When he was finished I proceeded to talk standing there in front of the desk where he was sitting. I told him how difficult it was to have public trust. I put it in terms he understood. I said if there was no public trust there were no readers, and, if there were no readers there were no advertisers. And, if there were no advertisers there was no money. I said readers of the newspaper will see his name on the "mast head" and if they think the reporting is slanted because of him then the public trust will be shot.

The masthead was a space in the newspaper that identified the publisher and where the paper was published. It was a requirement for bulk mailing in the United States. Also, although not a requirement of law, the masthead usually included the names of the key staff.

Many teachers who wanted more money for their work attended the school board's meetings at that time. The Loveland Education Association (LEA) represented them, which was part of a much bigger teachers' union. The newspaper reported what happened at the meetings.

There were no bad guy's. This man and the entire school board, as well as the teachers who wanted a union, said, first of all, they wanted to provide an education for the children. Their disagreement was over how it should be done.

When I was finished we talked a little more. I told him it would probably happen again, and quoted a dead American president who said, "If you can't stand the heat get out of the kitchen."

I rarely communicated with the "main office." There was no need to, and they rarely communicated with me. I went about my business making sure all the copy and photographs for the next edition of the paper were ready to go each week. That time was called the "deadline."

The typed pages of copy were taken to a place in the building where the main office was, and people operating computer machines would "set" the copy into neat columns called "galleys." Each galley would be pasted on a page that looked like a newspaper page. A page would be photographed on one sheet of film by an offset camera. All the developed sheets of film, each one representing a page of the newspaper, would be taken to the printer. The printer would make a "plate" from each piece of film. The metal plate would be fastened to the printing "press," and with great speed the press would make the finished newspaper.

The owner-operator used the newspapers to get bank financing to buy a greenfield site to build his own printing facility. When completed it would be worth more than all the papers combined. While it was still an empty lot the state of Ohio forced everyone in the development to sell the land so that a huge automobile transmission factory could be built there. The governor of Ohio reportedly wanted to move fast because the automobile company was also considering locations in neighboring states. Ohio's interest in making the land available was that it would provide jobs and tax money.

In the room next to the Loveland newspaper there was a young man who ran a press that did small printing jobs. He had worked for the owner-operator when he had only the one paper. The young man told me that when he first heard about plans to build the printing facility he thought he was probably going to work there. I asked him how much money the owner-operator got when the state forced everyone to sell. The young man said he didn't know. He said the owner-operator told him the selling price was high and that "they were crazy to take it." They did take it and every other piece of land necessary for the transmission plant to locate there. It covered many acres when it was built.

The first time I ever wrote a formal letter to the owner-operator was the time I asked him for more money. I didn't think a nickel or dime would be enough. After several weeks I still had not received a reply, and so I wrote another letter. This time I said that I could not afford to work there which was a nice way of saying I quit. Again, I received no reply, and after a week of trying to get him I telephoned his house hoping I could find him there. His wife answered the telephone. I knew her well from her involvement with the newspaper. I told her the news about my leaving. It wasn't news to her. She knew all about it and my two letters. She asked me what I was going to do. I said I hadn't given it thought. I remembered I needed some firewood so I said I was probably going to cut some firewood.

The week before I left that job someone appeared who was going to be the new managing editor. She was full of vim and vigor. As I went on down the road I doubted I would ever go back.

Not long after I left that job the owner-operator left and the old man who hired me to work in Lebanon had to come out of retirement to run the newspapers.

When I quit my job it was my third winter in the farmhouse. That one was both colder and there was more snow than any other winter in my life. I heated the house with wood. I was allowed to cut any dead or fallen trees on Peterloon Farm. In old English law I had what is called "Stover's rights."

During the first winter there was no heat. The farmer who lived there before me had a large kerosene heater connected to the flu in the kitchen, but when he left so did the heater. The house where he now lived had a fuel oil furnace in the basement so I don't know where the heater went. Without the kerosene heater the house had no heat. When it was there heat from it would rise through a register above it and go into the rooms on the upper floor. Some heat would go into the front rooms, but not much. The two ground floor rooms in the front got very little heat. There was a brick chimney with a flu in each of those rooms. In the years before me they weren't used and got clogged with bird nests and other debris. The house had three chimneys with five flues but no hearth or open fire place. I was able to clean one of the front chimneys all the way, but the other was so packed I was only able to clean it out to the second floor flue. After the first winter I put a cheap light-gauge sheet metal wood stove in each of the front rooms. The stovepipe where the clogged chimney was went through the second floor into the flue in the bedroom. I hooked up a better stove in the back room, which was the biggest room and where the kitchen was. A few times on cold winter nights when I had all three stoves going the heat drove me out of the house. The cheap stoves in the front burned too hot. The air could not be regulated enough, and that is what made them cheap stoves.

The one in the kitchen had a cast-iron top and bottom. The sides were one piece of sheet metal. The air control was a cast-iron piece fastened to the front. A cast-iron lid covered an opening on top where pieces of wood were loaded. It burned slowly all night and gave off even heat, which is the mark of a good stove. On most winter days it was the only stove I used.

During the severe winter I found a part-time job working for a market research company. A hundred other people and me did telephone interviews. I went three days a week and worked from the late afternoon until late at night. When it was late we telephoned the West Coast of the United States, where it was three hours earlier.

We would read questions from a questionnaire and write the "respondents" answers in the spaces. After we started an interview if the person in some way ended it before it was completed we circled the word "terminated" on the top of the paper.

There were four or five rooms with a supervisor and twenty or thirty people in each one. Some of the bigger studies lasted several days and might be conducted in several rooms. At the beginning of a study the supervisor stood before everyone in the room and reviewed the questions. Then we got a stack of interview copies, a list of telephone numbers, and we went to work. Everyone in a room did the same study. The people who had been working for that company a long time were seldom terminated, and they completed many interviews. Somehow we all knew who they were. A successful interview was one where we were able to get answers to all the questions. A telephone call might last anywhere between five and twenty minutes.

Every study was designed to get unbiased answers. Marketing people who were the equivalent of scientists prepared the questions. After looking at all the responses they knew the prevailing attitude about something like chewing gum in a market area. Or from a study they would know what the awareness of a product was after test advertising was done there. Studies would find out what a person recalled about a specific advertisement they saw.

We were told to always use one of the "clears" to answer any question the respondent may have. A clear was a scientific reply that would both answer the question and not bias future answers. We were instructed to terminate the interview rather than say something other than an established clear.

Often someone would ask, "Who is the survey for?" The clear answer to that question was, "We are not given that information." That was the truth. It was never obvious from the questions what company wanted the information, and no one told us.

When someone asked where I was telephoning from I answered, "For the purpose of this study I can't answer that question right now, but I will try to answer any questions you may have at the end of the interview."

The proper clear for the question "How did you get my number?" was "All our telephone numbers are computer-generated."

During the day I cut firewood. The hardest part about firewood was not cutting and splitting it but getting it out of the woods. To do that I made a trailer called my French Guiana trailer. I got the idea for the trailer from a photograph in a magazine about a religious cult of Americans in French Guiana who had just committed mass suicide. In the photograph, off to the side, was a trailer hooked to a farm tractor. It was different from any trailer I had seen. Its wheels were far to the rear. Half its weight was on the drive wheels of the tractor. The tractor when pulling the trailer would have extra weight on the back wheels. That would give it traction superior to that of a tractor pulling a conventional trailer with its wheels directly under the load. I got a rear axle from an old car and made a trailer. The wheels were located just like the ones in the picture. It had an area in the middle big enough to hold one cord of firewood. A cord was equal to 128 cubic feet or a stack of wood four feet wide, four feet high, and eight feet long.

I hitched it to the red tractor my father gave me years earlier. I had never done anything with it except go on tractor rides around Peterloon Farm. It wasn't good for much else. It had a flat head four-cylinder engine that developed slightly less than twenty-horse power. The company that made it ceased operation shortly before my father bought it new from the farm implements place at the head of the road. What he paid for it was less than what it cost me for a new rear tire when it was mine. The farm implements people attached a seven-foot sickle bar. My father used it to mow the fields at Markin Farm. He cut the grass around the house with a walk behind reel-type gang mower. The red tractor lasted a few summers, and then my father got a more powerful tractor with a sixty-inch rotary mower. The red tractor went in the subcellar of the Little Barn where it stayed for several years until I pulled it out with Morituri. My brother and me pulled it up and down the road. The pistons were rusted to the cylinder walls. Finally after almost giving up, the pistons broke loose and the engine turned. Soon it started, and hunks of rust came out the exhaust. At first it didn't sound too hot, but after a while it sounded better. I didn't dare get off for fear it would stall. My brother disconnected the tow chain, and I drove it around in circles.

There was no formal declaration or exchange of paper to signify it was mine, but after that day I sort of took it over. A tooth on the first gear was broken off. That had happened when the gearshift lever broke. It shifted into first and second gear at the same time. Something had to give, and it was that tooth on the gear. I took the gear to a company that cut large industrial gears.

I had been there several times over the past years. I had first been there to buy a two-foot-diameter sprocket for a surrey my brother and I were making. The second time, years later, I wanted to get bigger holes drilled in a propeller hub. The third time I went there was with that broken gear. An old-timer looked at it again and again through his bifocal eyeglasses. After a while he said the way to fix it was to put weld metal where the tooth was and then grind it down. He said he would grind it down, but he could not build it up with metal. He gave me the name of a person who could and told me to tell him who sent me. The man who was going to put the weld metal on it turned it over in his hands several times. He said it had to be "preheated" and that I could pick it up the next day.

When I took the gear back to the old-timer he looked closely at the glob of metal where the broken tooth had been. He asked me what the other guy charged me. It was next to nothing. He said he would have the grinding done in a few days. When I put the tractor back together the first gear didn't knock anymore and it functioned properly.

Not long after that it became apparent the "spider gears" or "planetary gears" in the rear end were destroyed. Almost all the teeth were severely damaged. I didn't think I could get new ones. The company that made the tractor was gone, and parts for it were not available.

If I welded those gears solidly in place so they would not move it would be the same as having permanent "differential lock." Differential lock was an added feature on bigger farm tractors and some off-road cars, but it was something that could be turned off and on. It wasn't permanent. The spider gears allowed one of the two-drive wheels to rotate independently of the other one, which was necessary when making a turn. I was getting ready to weld them in place so at least the tractor would go when a person looking over my shoulder says, "Those look just like the gears in my car." We took them to the parts counter of a large car dealer and the parts man was able to get the exact same gears. When we were driving back I asked the person who went with me how could his car have the same spider gears as the tractor when the tractor was made ten years earlier? He said the spider gears were part of a twelve-bolt rear end assembly made by a third company.

At night I worked for the market research company with others doing the same thing. Each night a few hours after we went to work we stopped to eat supper. The area where we ate was one large room with long rectangular tables and metal chairs. It was on the second floor of a modern steel-and-glass cubical building. The rooms where we worked opened into the large room. Some people brought their own food, but most of us got together and ordered our dinner on the telephone. A deliveryman would bring it soon afterward in an insulated carrying case. When he arrived everyone would stop what they were doing and eat the food while it was hot.

One lady I talked with while we were sitting at a table in the large room told me she lived on a farm across the river in northern Kentucky. All of her children were grown up. She took that job to get some extra money. She said she had some puppies and asked me if I wanted one. I agreed. Very soon after that she brought it to work in a cardboard box. Not long after I lost that job, and when the dog was still a puppy it died. I don't think it would have died if I handled it differently.

Several days in a row I was hitting it with an open hand in an effort to get it to stop urinating and defecating where it pleased in the house. The day it died, the puppy was lying down after I was hitting it, and I couldn't understand why. I wondered what was wrong with it and decided it needed some high-energy canned dog food instead of the dry food it was getting in the fifty-pound bag. I went to the store, and when I walked back in the house it was lying in the same place. It was dead. Then I figured out what probably happened. The dog died from shock. I learned in the army that shock kills. With people the body simply shuts down when death seems inevitable even though, in reality, the wound by itself may not be fatal. Death certainly was not inevitable for that dog, but it thought it was. Rather than deal with me or what was happening it died. I felt terrible. That afternoon I buried it by the split-rail fence.

When I was finished but with the shovel still in my hand a car pulled in my driveway. It was a girl I spent time with named Jenny. She knew I had a puppy, and I told her it was dead and buried. I said remorsefully, "It just lay on the floor. When I got back with a can of dog food, it was dead." She said it probably had distemper (a disease common among puppies). That was not why it died, but I didn't say anything.

I got phased out of the marketing company the same way I got phased out of the dishwashing job. It started right after the manager called me into her office to inquire about a disturbance that happened the preceding night. She must have been told about the incident from a supervisor because the manager wasn't there when it happened.

The other person in the disturbance wasn't in the office with me. There was a rule that when supper arrived anyone with an interview in progress was to finish that interview before going to eat. I had just started a long interview when the pizza man arrived.

The interview was designed to find out attitudes about a number of "fast food" restaurants grouped together in a small community in California. I was especially hungry that night. The supervisor had left the room. For a moment I entertained the idea of terminating the call by simply hanging up the telephone. I stuck with it, reading each question. I asked the respondent about one of the restaurants and he said, "I never eat in those places." I put a check mark in the appropriate box. Then I read him the next question about a fast food restaurant next to the first one. He said, "Didn't you just here what I said? I said I never eat in any of those places."

I made up my own clear. I understood that a clear did not bias the person's opinion. He could bias me, but I couldn't bias him. If he categorically didn't eat in any of those restaurants he was probably fairly literate. I said, "Sir, whether or not you eat or have ever eaten in one of those restaurants does not disqualify or qualify you from the interest we have in your answers. We want to know what earth people eat."

Then he asked, like it might be someone he knows, "Who is this? Where are you calling from?"

I looked up again to make sure the supervisor had left. I thought he would definitely terminate the interview. I said, "I'm in another galaxy."

It was like he got those calls all the time. He said, "Go

ahead. What is the next question?"

It was a fifteen-minute interview and he did the whole thing. When I got near my pizza it was like I was trying to get the last seat on a lifeboat. I sat down only concerned about eating. Then I became aware of someone standing over me. She was furious. Before then I had not talked to her. She looked like a politically militant college student. She asked me who I thought I was. She was mad. It was like she was saying here was one of the social ills we have to deal with every day. My mouth was full. I was still feeding. My forearms were on each side of the pizza protecting the food from anyone who might try to take it away from me.

I should have apologized for being crude and rude. When I swallowed the food in my mouth I looked up at her smiling and said, "'You can do anything you want to do, but don't you step on my blue suede shoes.'"

When I said that her face got all wrinkled up. She looked at the shoes I was wearing and said, "What?" Then one of the big mamas who heard that song told her to back off, and she went away.

After I left that job I spent more time sitting around the wood stove keeping warm. Practically every day I cut wood so I would stay that way. Jenny shared an apartment in Mount Adams with a girlfriend. I went there often, and every fireplace there was so small most of the firewood sold would not fit.

Mount Adams had narrow hilly streets with old houses close together in rows. Twenty years earlier it was a residential community also, but then it had broken-down houses full of people who seemed content to get through the day. Barefoot, raggedy children with big smiles played in the street.

As large companies grew in Cincinnati highly educated young people came, and they needed a place to live. While many people from Cincinnati couldn't imagine Mount Adams as anything other than it was, it appealed to people from other places who were hired right out of college. It appealed to them because it was tucked away from the rest of the city, but it was part of the city. Also, it didn't cost very much to live there, and it was close to the downtown area where most of them worked. Once the change started, people who grew up in the Cincinnati area became attracted to that place also, and they moved there. All the old houses got repaired, and the barefoot children playing in the street weren't there anymore.

A new group of people lived in the old houses with the little fireplaces. They had little cars that were parked up and down the street. Bars on the corners of the street were redone by new owners who wanted to attract people from all over the city. On the weekends Mount Adams was packed with people and cars.

A friend of Jenny had a coffee shop in Mount Adams that had all kinds of different coffee drinks. Before I went there I had never had a cappuccino. That same friend also published a small weekly community newspaper that was delivered to the residents of Mount Adams. I placed a small advertisement in it that read: "Firewood, custom cut to fit your fireplace."

That winter I hauled many loads of firewood to Mount Adams. The trailer I used had no brakes. I pulled it full of wood behind my car on those hilly streets. I never wrecked.

I delivered a cord of wood to one person, and they opened this tiny closet under the stairs and expected me to fit it all in there. That sort of thing happened many times. Once a person paid for the load and told me to take the rest home.

The wood I sold in Mount Adams came from cut your own ads in the big daily paper. There was always someone who wanted to get rid of wood. Their advertisement would read "cut your own" or "free firewood." Also, I knew a builder who let me cut wood on a lot before he built a house there. All the wood I took to Mount Adams I got that way. Some of it I used where I lived, but most of the wood I heated with at home came from Peterloon Farm.

There was an area that had never been logged behind the lake on Peterloon Farm. It was what forest people call a "virgin forest." The trees were huge. Those trees had clear butt logs several feet in diameter that went up forty or fifty feet like giant arrow shafts sticking in the dirt. Far off the ground they spread into a tremendous array of branches and leaves. It was like standing beside a dinosaur or like seeing a spectacular burst of fireworks that didn't go away. There was a majesty about them.

One had been blown over. Close to the wall of torn roots where the tree had parted from the ground the dirt was pressed down in an oval shape. A deer had slept there. No undergrowth was on the forest floor. Young trees were growing, and if left alone someday they would be like the one that fell.

Near there a giant limb was on the ground. Lightning might have made it come down. Between the two there was enough firewood to last a winter and a half.

When the ground was frozen I went back again and again as I needed firewood. Each time I would cut, split, and stack as much wood as the trailer could carry. If the tree or the branch had fallen in a ravine it would have been lost to me. Carrying one arm full of split wood up a steep hill then returning for more was exhausting and impractical. If I could get the red tractor and trailer beside whatever wood I was going to cut I would have a good time.

I put tire chains on the tractor. That, plus the trailer weight made it possible to go anywhere except into ravines. When the trailer was loaded with wood and the tractor was pulling up a grade the tongue weight on the tractor plus the torque from the rear wheels lifted the front wheels off the ground. Each rear wheel had its own brake pedal and I steered by holding the brake on one wheel or the other. I made a special hitch that kept the tractor from turning over on the trailer. When the wheels were lifting up and the tractor was pulling a load I always kept my foot on the clutch pedal. There would be a split second to act and no time to think if the hitch broke. A major accident would result if I wasn't able to disengage the clutch immediately.

Jenny and I spent a lot of time together. There was seventeen miles of road between her place and my place. I traveled that distance many times with and without firewood. She worked downtown in the front office of a company that operated a real steam-powered riverboat. The passengers who went on that boat came from all over the country to enjoy the kind of river travel that existed a long time ago in the United States.

The company's office and the boat moved to New Orleans, and it wanted her to move there also. It was then we decided to get married, and she stayed in Cincinnati. We didn't decide about marriage all of a sudden, but any reluctance I had disappeared when I realized she might move to New Orleans without me.

When she left that job neither one of us had one. I sold some firewood and that was the only money we had. She would marry me, she said, because “There is never a dull moment.” If volatile living is what she liked I didn’t disappoint her in the years that followed.

If there was reluctance on my part about getting married it was because, unlike everything before, it was not something I was going to do for a while and then not do. I was ready for the change, but it was a deliberate and permanent change in my life that caused me to hesitate.

The ceremonial words that we would be one person were both frightening and exciting. It was frightening because her problems would be mine. It was exciting because my problems would be hers. The whole idea sounded nice.

I had plenty of notions floating in my mind about faithfulness and how my great-grandparents had enough to spare. Years after I got married I understood the meaning of faithfulness. Up until that time I didn’t consider faithfulness a necessary ingredient of a happy marriage.

How our marriage survived in the beginning is much like a person who survives putting one bullet in a six-shot revolver, spinning the cylinder, and pulling the trigger with the end of the barrel pressed against their head. It survived by chance.

I was thirty and she was twenty-six. I didn’t consider the big issue of the lifetime responsibility we would have for each other. I’m not sure I was capable of that thought.

It was the right time to get married, and Jenny seemed the right person to marry. We clicked. I always thought I would marry some exotic creature from the other side of the earth. What made us click was probably that we grew up in the same place. She grew up where I grew up. Her father and my mother knew each other. Jenny came to Markin Farm several times with my sister, but we never met.

When I did see her for the first time it was in a bar. The bar was in a building twenty miles outside Cincinnati. A friend of hers who lived in Mount Adams renovated it. It had once been a stagecoach station. The friend made a restaurant out of it and invited Jenny and others to the opening. She came with her parents. I worked for the newspaper in Loveland, and the building that was renovated was in the newspaper's territory. Her friend who owned the building invited me to come because he wanted to have the grand opening publicized.

Jenny was talking with the girl who introduced us. Jenny and I talked the whole time. The other girl left. We sat down at the bar and were still talking when I realized everyone had gone home. We went to another place together.

She was physically beautiful to me but more than that, and one of the reasons I stuck with her so long was she never said anything bad about anyone. I kept waiting for that to change, but it never did. I thought it was most unusual. I wondered if she was aware of all the grief that existed. When I mentioned it she said I was too practical. Without saying anything more I tried to be less practical, and copy what I saw as a quality. For the better part of a year it went on that way, and then we got married. Getting married did not result from analyzing our situation or looking at a long list of pros and cons on the subject. It was kinetic more than anything else.

Getting married the way we wanted to get married was not easy. The closest we ever came to deciding not to be married was when we were planning to get married. Other people wanted to control the event. We both were older and had been living on our own for some time.

The man who married us was a longtime friend of mine. Jenny knew him also but not as well as I did. He had married and buried more of my family than I cared to think about, and now he was an old man. When I was a child he was the preacher at the Indian Hill Church. He wore white robes. Jenny liked his voice. She said he always had a beautiful voice. Two other people became the main preachers at the church. He still put on his white robes to bury a friend, marry the children of friends, and their grandchildren. He traveled with his wife to visit his own children, and he went to a summer house they had.

He met with us several times before we got married. Once in conversation I made the expression, "if I die" and he abruptly interrupted me in a startled way and said half amused, "What do you mean, if you die?"

He talked to us about the table china and the difference of opinion Jenny and I had on that subject. On one of his trips he sent us a postcard. It was about his thoughts after talking with us. He mentioned the china. He wrote that as we went through life we should be aware that "my ways are not your ways." The next time we saw him was when he married us.

The marriage ceremony was in Jenny's house. Neither one of us went to church so it didn't seem right to be married in one. The only people invited to the wedding were immediate family. About twenty-five of them were there. Afterward we got in the rabbit and went downtown to a big hotel where we spent the night in a large ghastly room with mirrors and a free bottle of champagne.

The next day we drove home to the farmhouse. I still had plaster and lath to haul out, but the house was cleaned up. I told Jenny we would take our "honeymoon" later when we could afford it. We mailed a letter to people who knew us explaining that we were going to have a small wedding in Jenny's house and they were not invited. We asked them to come to a party at the farmhouse the next day. It was bright and sunny when we drove home that day.

A friend who owned a wine store gave us a discount on many cases of good red wine. I made five gallons of spaghetti sauce with much garlic, and boiled long noodles. We had loaves of fresh bread that had not been sliced. Many people said it was tasty.

The red tractor was hooked up to a hay wagon. It was loaded with long sweet-smelling fresh-cut hay, and the same friend who helped me get the spider gears gave hay rides in the field behind the house during the party. When people left they talked about having a fine time.

I had a large pot of duck soup on the wood stove. It had been cooking for several days and was for anyone who wanted some at the party. A few people with an inquisitive look asked me what it was. I said, "duck soup."

After we got married there were always fresh flowers around the house. Jenny got a job in the office of a company that did dinner cruises on the Ohio River. The company had several boats. Most of them had a paddle wheel that didn't churn the water into a white froth when the boat moved. It turned listlessly as it was dragged through the water. The paddle wheel on one of those boats probably looked real through a periscope, but the boats were propelled underneath by one or more propellers.

The money Jenny earned from that job was the only money we counted on having. One afternoon I was moving plaster from a pile inside the house to a pile outside the house with a shovel and a wheelbarrow when the telephone rang. A man at a big company near Cincinnati said he had an application about a job. He was one of three managers of an in-house advertising department at the company. On the telephone he said they were in need of a copywriter, and he asked if I would go there for an interview.

11

The Big Company

If they had an application from me it was one sent to a newspaper box number that didn't identify the company. The man who called on the telephone was the same one who interviewed me. He glanced at my work and said advertising copy writing was different from newspaper writing. We talked for a while about the company.

The first day, the zipper on my pants broke. They were going to take a photograph for a card that identified me as an employee of that company. Thankfully the picture only showed my head and shoulders.

That same day I drove to the factory area, where a doctor did a physical examination of me. He asked me a few question pertaining to my health, got a urine sample, listened to my heart, and took a blood pressure reading. It was a formality only if the person being examined was healthy. The physical examination prevented someone from working there whose medical condition would require extensive treatment and cost.

The building was full of copywriters, artists, and others who made all the printed material detailing what the company did and the products it made. We were part of the commercial division at the corporate headquarters. The man who was the head of the commercial division was the stepfather of a childhood friend of Jenny. Her mother came to our wedding party with another lady and was probably one of the people who didn't have any duck soup. After a few days I became aware that the head of our division was her second husband. There were only about five or six divisions in the entire company. He reported directly to the president of the company.

The manager who hired me seemed very surprised when I

asked him if that was why I got the job. He replied emphatically, "No," and said it wouldn't make any difference if it had. He then went on about the company and how good it had been to him in the many years he worked there. His grown child didn't work there, but what he was saying was that the employees were one big family. So according to him it was natural for a family member to work there.

My boss was the advertising manager for the steel-making division. Soon I was switched to another manager who oversaw printed material and the production of visual aids for the company's "profit centers" located throughout the United States. Several months after the head of our division retired the other manager fired me. The sequence was curious. After I was no longer with the company the former division head was at a home and garden show in the Cincinnati Convention Center where I was pedaling mailboxes. He was going up and down the aisles with his wife looking at things. He died of cancer soon after that day. I expected the company to look me up, give me a box of animal crackers, and put me in a pyramid with him. The animals would plow the fields in never-never land.

The advertising manager, another person, and myself went to a profit center outside Chicago. We traveled to Chicago in a commercial airplane and rented a car. During the drive I asked the manager how he got started in the advertising business and he said his father did public relations in Chicago all his life. He didn't like talking about his personal life, and he never asked me about mine. He was as brief as could be about how he got started in advertising.

We went to a company that made paper speaker cones. We stayed there most of the day talking with people who worked there. They showed us how the speaker cones were made. We were going to make a printed sales aid that told about the product, and to do that we had to know about it firsthand. That is why we went there. We drove the car back to Chicago and returned by airplane the same day.

The advertising manager who hired me asked me to do a brochure about pipe fabric for a marketing manager in Kansas City, Missouri. The company had a facility there called the "Kansas City Works." We didn't make the pipe, but we sold pipe fabric. *Pipe fabric* was a technical term for the steel reinforcing in concrete drainage pipe. When someone sold concrete pipe they sold steel.

The selection of pipe fabric for a given size pipe was technical. When an engineer described the process to me it sounded as if he were talking another language. The marketing manager from Kansas City said he wanted a brochure a salesman could leave with a prospective customer who would then be able to show a government official why spending more money for concrete pipe was a better choice than buying other kinds of less expensive drainage pipe.

I made the rough draft and sent it to an engineer in an office building next door. After a few days he called me on the telephone and we arranged to meet. He had nothing good to say about the brochure. With a red ballpoint pen he highlighted all the mistakes. He didn't want a good brochure as much as he wanted to belittle me. Whether or not he was counterproductive didn't matter. He had been there a long time. The advertising manager and him were like brothers. I put the rough draft, which had gotten much rougher-looking, at the bottom of the pile of things to do. It stayed on the bottom. Weeks later the manager who gave me the assignment asked me how the brochure on pipe fabric was coming. I said the engineer was apparently incapable of saying what he wanted only what he didn't want. The manager didn't act surprised. He didn't say anything. He left and said to the other manager in the office next to mine, "Did you hear that?"

A few weeks later the marketing manager from Kansas City was in town and the manager who gave me the assignment said the Kansas City manager wanted to meet with me to go over the brochure. He was youthful and wanted to get things done. The two of us sat in a room with a large oval table and we worked out how to design the brochure and what to say. It took several hours.

Later that afternoon the advertising manager, the marketing manager, and me were talking about the highway to the Cincinnati airport. I said the stretch of I-75 from Galbraith Road to the bridge was the "killing zone." We were walking to the parking lot. The Kansas City manager started to turn around like he was going to say something. He looked at the other person beside him and at the same time decided not to say whatever he was going to say. When we were working on the brochure he never talked about his personal life, but I knew by the way he reacted to those words that he had been in Vietnam. The people who were put in that environment, with the exception of my first sergeant, quickly shed ideas about the differences between people. What difference did a difference make when everyone had a singular goal: to go home alive? When he was working on the brochure there was the singular goal of making it an effective brochure that would sell pipe fabric. Little else made any difference.

The advertising people worked in a long rectangular one-level brick building with no windows. There were clear glass entry doors on the ends. Inside were two rows of offices along the sides with a metal door to each one. The offices were separated by high partitions. There was twenty-five feet across the middle. In that section there were twice as many work areas as offices. A work area was defined by a four-sided five-foot-high partition with an opening on one side. In each one there was a desk, some file cabinets, and a few personal effects.

The people in the middle were hourly employees who helped the salaried employees in the offices along the side. I got an office, but I was an hourly employee. The director had a large office at the end of the building with four walls that went to the ceiling. He leaned in my door and said a mistake had been made. From then on I would be a salaried employee. He was gone before I could ask anything. On pay day, the money was the same, but a salaried employee was considered more important to the company than an hourly one. The money was the best part. When I worked on the newspaper I had lots of fun and made no money, and when I had a big company job I had no fun but made lots of money.

When the assistant to the head of the commercial division retired there was a small ceremony in our building. Everyone stood around him in a chummy way to present him with a gold-colored deep-sea fishing reel as a token of appreciation. He took it and shook a few hands. After more than thirty years of service, when he left he got a gold fishing reel. I wondered if he liked fishing or if there was something more like a Swiss bank account. It was discouraging. A handshake, a pat on the back, and maybe something made of gold didn't seem enough. Little did I know I would soon be leaving with nothing but my unemployment compensation. I wouldn't have left on my own volition. I broke away like an object breaks away from the gravitational pull of another object.

There were three bare walls in my office. I put large pictures on two of them. The photography department made one for me. It was a poster-size enlargement of a picture in a company book that depicted an artist's conception of a strong-looking worker, and in the background there were tall smokestacks. It was done long ago, before the company became a billion-dollar corporation. In the lower right section of the picture there was a remark by the founder of the company. It signified that personal virtues made the corporation. After a while I wondered if virtue ever existed there. What made me wonder if it ever existed resulted from an assignment.

The assignment was to make a script and select photographs for a slide show that would tell how well two companies worked together. The company where I worked was the exclusive international distributor for welding equipment made by a second company. Long ago the founders of each company had gotten together and made an agreement that was still in effect. When I was there the people at the welding company didn't like the agreement, but they lived with it because they had no choice. The slide show was to be given at a dinner for people from the two companies. It was intended to show what a profitable relationship each company had.

I got to rummage through company histories. At the welding company the founder promoted welding when it was a new technology. He demonstrated welding to an admiral in the U.S. Navy who thought the only way two pieces of metal could be fastened together was with rivets. The account said the admiral told the welding company founder that he (the admiral) could kick a weld off with his toe. At that time many ships were being made all over the world. A global war was starting. At the company where I worked I read that during those same years tons of welding exports were sent to São Paulo, Brazil.

When I was getting information at the welding company for the slide show they knew I was not from the international division. A person with a big office asked me to sit down in a chair while from behind his desk he said the company I worked for was asleep at the stick in Mexico City. I asked him why he said that, and he proceeded to tell me about a situation where a big contract sale was lost when it didn't have to be lost.

The manager who hired me told me there was a saying in that business that you could criticize an employee's daughter or question the fidelity of his wife, but you never criticized the company.

When I reported what the man said, the international division already knew the people at the welding company wanted the international business directly. That is why the international division asked for the slide show and invited the group from the other company to dinner. Someone debriefed me from a corner office. He told me the right way to think.

When I traveled to the welding company I went there in a company plane with the head of the natural resources division. We were going to the same airport. I was on that plane because the profit center advertising manager's assistant put me there. When she made travel plans she always checked first to see if there were any seats available on company planes. I told my manager about the trip. That was the first and last time I went on a company plane.

On the plane the natural resources man and I talked about chain saws. Two other people were with him. They carried papers. When we flew back I told him what the man at the welding company said to me. He listened and said, "Who do you work for?" He took another drink. One of the people with him made him a third whiskey drink and he said he had just made a deal with the Canadian government about taconite and needed to relax. Nobody could relax with him.

The head of the photography department wouldn't let me pay for the enlargement of the picture about virtue. He said I could contribute to the coffee fund. One of the first assignments I had was to go to one of the profit centers with him. He worked for the company many years, and on the airplane he told me I could put anything on my expense account but a horse and buggy. In a brochure about signposts some of them were chipped and needed touch up paint. He said it would be easier to retouch the photograph even if the touch-up paint cost fifty times less.

The other picture on my wall was an oil painting. It showed a cold and quiet place just above the tree line on a mountain. A biplane is stuck like a dart in the snow. Another airplane is flying away in the distance. It is barely distinguishable in the haze. The head of the metal products division asked to use the telephone on my desk, and when he finished he said it was a morbid painting. I said, "Some people think the plane is a rescue plane, and others think it's the one that shot the other one down." He and I met at a Christmas party a few weeks before. Jenny was with me. I was feeling kind of loose, and when the three of us were standing together, unknown to her, he shot me a look that said, *Watch it, buster; remember who you are*. In the corporate world he was the head of the metal products division, and I was a word merchant. At the party many of the people from our building were standing along the side of the room talking among themselves as if the other people spoke a different language.

There were many things I did not understand. Not only that, but each payday the building emptied at lunch as managers and everyone else went to deposit their money in a bank. I could only imagine it was because they had so many urgent bills. When I asked another person who did not go to the bank if that was why everyone else did, he laughed and said it was a habit more than anything else.

The day after the Christmas party there was a story in the local newspaper about how someone had stolen some cattle from a nearby field the same night. I thought one of the copywriters was pointing a finger at me. I told him it wasn't me who rustled the cows. I told him I had witnesses that I went straight home after the Christmas party.

During that year Jenny had our first child. It was a boy. No one had to tell me, but when he was still in diapers more than a few people said he was a cute baby. We named the cute baby Whit after Jenny's father. He grew from a cute baby, to a good-looking child, to a handsome and strong young man. As he grew older, I told him several times good looks and a dime would get him a cup of coffee.

A short time after he was born I got fired from my big company job. Whit usually went with me to install mailboxes. When he was a few years old he would play in the back of my truck with tools or whatever was there. More often than not he would pass the time pounding 20-penny hot dip galvanized nails into a block of wood with an eighteen-ounce claw hammer. At first I didn't notice it, but one day a customer's teenage son came out to where I was working. He said, "Look at that kid drive nails." I looked up. On the other side of the road my flat bed truck was parked in the driveway. From beginning to end we watched Whit hammer one of those large nails into a piece of wood. With both hands took long swings with the hammer and he didn't miss once. Before Whit was born Jenny and I both worked and were gone all day. After he was born Jenny stayed at home. She took care of him and did strenuous things like talk on the telephone to her sisters. She would go to a garden club meeting now and then.

At first, the idea of a garden club sounded repulsive to me, but it wasn't. There were quite a few older ladies who set the pace, and they were extremely knowledgeable about plants. One knew everything about the daffodil flower. In her backyard she had many different species from all over the world. Jenny told me her father collected them. Her father was long gone, but in spring I saw hillsides covered with daffodils that he planted. When I put in a mailbox for that lady I knew about her connection to the daffodil. I almost forgot the bill in my hand. She led me around to the back of the house where the daffodils were growing. Each species was identified with a marker. They were all in bloom. It was quite a sight. I didn't know so many different ones existed.

Jenny was still in the garden club when I got unemployed and she went back to work in the middle of downtown Cincinnati. The first thing I did was get rid of the giant wood stove in the basement. That winter it almost burnt the house down while we were in bed asleep.

The wood stove in the basement was more like a wood furnace. It was made from a steel 300-gallon fuel tank. It was cradled above the dirt floor by pieces of angle iron bolted together.

There was a thirty-inch-wide, eighteen-inch-high door at one end where wood was loaded. It was hinged at the top so if blown open by a sudden puff of smoke it would close again by itself.

The air inlet below the door was made from two six-inch-long pieces of two-and-a-half-inch water pipe. One end of each piece was screwed onto a flange fastened over a hole in the tank. The amount of heat could be regulated by partially or completely obstructing the air opening.

The furnace was located in the middle of the basement where a rotten staircase had been. Access to the basement was no longer from stairs inside but from storm doors outside the house. I took a wall out on the first floor so there was one room instead of two smaller rooms. That and the removal of the rotten stairs left a large opening in the floor three feet wide and six feet long. The furnace was right below that opening. In the winter when the air inside got dry a cloud of steam would billow up when I poured a full pan of water down on the furnace. The house could be instantly humidified.

Directly above the opening in the floor was a set of stairs that went to the second floor. There were two bedrooms up there that had white stamped sheet metal ceilings, wallpaper, and windows on three sides. A third door at the top of the stairs went into a bathroom over the kitchen. On one side of the room there was a bathtub, a sink, and a freestanding toilet. The center of the room was seven feet high, but it sloped down to a knee wall four feet high on both sides. The toilet was a foot away from the wall. Behind it a tropical plant was flourishing with big dark green leaves on vines. Sometimes I felt like I needed a machete to sit down. It wilted and died a few years later. At the far end of the room a chimney came up from the kitchen. On each side of it were windows. When I sat on the toilet amid huge tropical leaves I could look across the field. I did some of my best thinking there.

The four-foot walls had a hatch that opened to the area behind them, and that was the only place to store things in the house. Over the years Jenny said numerous times she needed more shelves and places to put things. I told her to think of the house as a sailboat: take only what you need, and don't throw disposable plates overboard even though the ocean is deep. Each time the issue of shelves came up I would recite an adage: "However much space you have, you will fill it and need more." If we had an airport hangar out back we would fill it and need more space.

The advantage of having such a big stove in the basement was that in the early morning I could load it with enough pieces of wood that had not been split to last until I got home that evening. Before the furnace was there I split so much wood with an eight-pound maul that I could always hit the bell in the sky at county fairs and win a prize for Jenny. Splitting wood was time-consuming, and when I had the big company job there wasn't much time for anything else. Sometimes the pieces of wood that went into the furnace were so big I could barely pick them up. I would roll one to the back and then roll another up against that one. The furnace was full after three or four pieces. The wood would smolder and give off even heat all day. It was almost gone at the end of the day when I got home.

It worked very well except it wasn't maintenance-free. The chimneys were a constant source of trouble. The farmhouse was not designed to have a wood furnace in the basement. There were three brick chimneys. Two were in the front, and one was in the back.

The two front chimneys were nearest to the basement. I connected the furnace to them. The cheap sheet metal wood stoves that had been in the front rooms were gone. Two six-inch single wall elbows were connected to holes in the back of the furnace. From there, stovepipe went in opposite directions to each end of the basement. It hung by wire from the floor joists. On each end there was another elbow that went up through the floor. On the west side of the house the pipe went up into the flue on the first floor. On the other side the pipe continued straight up into the bedroom on the second floor. There it went another ninety degrees and three feet in a horizontal direction into a flue.

I had to clean out the long lengths of stovepipe often or they would clog. That was especially true for the stovepipe on the east side of the house. The wood inside the furnace steamed and smoked all day. There wasn't much flame. The smoke cooled and condensed on the inside of the pipe, forming a brown glassy substance. At least twice a month I disconnected the elbow in the basement, put a crumpled-up piece of newspaper in the vertical end, and lit it on fire. The brown glassy substance on the wall of the pipe burned like a fuse. Dark gray crusty material fell out of the pipe.

When the condensed material burned it not only changed its form, but also its thickness expanded four or five times. One time the pipe clogged right after I lit the newspaper and I ran up to the second floor and disconnected the elbow up there. A heavy, yellow smoke spilled down over the open edge of the pipe. I dropped an eight-pound broken sledgehammer down through the inside of the pipe. In that way I planned to unclog the pipe, but the piece of steel got stuck in the expanding material. When that happened I opened the windows. I felt dizzy from breathing some of the smoke. I sat down on the floor and waited for things to air out.

That incident didn't scare me. What scared me was the night I woke up from a sound sleep, and lying there fully awake I could hear the creaking noise of metal expanding. The fire in the furnace was growing. At night caps were screwed on the ends of the air intakes. I listened some more and the stovepipe that came through the floor in our bedroom was making the creaking noise. Something was definitely wrong; the fire was getting all the air it wanted.

I got out of bed and went downstairs to look through the opening at the furnace. It was going full blast and getting hotter. It wasn't red-hot, but it felt that way. The door to the furnace was tightly closed and both caps were covering the air inlets. The only other place where air could get in was the opening for the chimneys. The stove pipe on the east side of the house was hot, and the one going to the west side of the house was as cold as winter. The furnace was getting air through the chimney. In the middle of the night the furnace started ingesting air through one chimney and exhausting it through the other. The fire was wide open, uncontrolled, and running away. When I blocked the cold pipe the intense heat died down. The metal made the creaking noise again, but this time it was contracting as it got cooler. I stood there until things calmed down, and then I went back upstairs. I was wearing shoes but no clothes. Jenny woke up and asked me what I was doing running around stark naked. At that point everything was just ducky, even though it was a little warm in our room.

My job was forty-five minutes from the house. Another person and I shared the driving. His first job after graduating from college was at a company near where I worked. He said his job wasn't very exciting. He worked in a room full of engineers sitting at drafting tables in neat rows busily computing "moments." A short time after I got fired, he quit and went to law school.

He got a new car the year we took turns driving to work. My car ran good (sic) despite the way it looked. When he got the new car he let me take the luggage rack and other things like the radio from the car he was replacing. I would have stripped more stuff off it, but he said he had to drive home. The next day when we drove to work I told him about a new theory I developed called the crumb theory. It says that whenever a big deal goes down there are always a lot of crumbs. Practically everything I had was an example of the crumb theory at work.

The new car he got was a sporty luxury car. It was still on the new car warranty when he wrecked it at a dangerous intersection. The insurance company delayed in making a settlement. They could take their sweet time as far as he was concerned. After several days he got tired of waiting, went out, and got another one like the first except it was a different color. When we took his car to work we traveled in style.

The big company owned a company that made and sold wire mesh containers used to move things around factory floors. The customers were people who operated factories. The profit center advertising manager said the containers were going to be the subject of a series of full-page advertisements in a nationwide material-handling magazine. In the next few weeks he wanted me to think up a theme for those advertisements.

My name was the last one on the routing list of a well-known business newspaper. By the time it got to me the newspaper was four or five days old. It told what was going on with the nation's businesses. An advertisement for rental trucks in that newspaper showed a truck with a chicken on the roof and a few others pecking the ground. In the foreground the owner looked directly at the reader, and the print in his own words said how the truck helped him increase the profitability of his business. The manager who gave me the assignment looked at the page without interest and asked me, "What about the advertisement?"

I said, "Don't you believe he is the owner of a company that sells chickens and the truck helps him the way he says?" I said the container advertisement could be like this: A factory person in factory clothes standing on the factory floor would look directly at the camera, and the printed message in his words would explain how our wire mesh containers helped him. In the background there would be a large stack of the containers so someone could see he was not just whistling "Dixie." I said a testimonial is what it would be.

The manager didn't say yes or no. Later that year the corporate advertisements in a popular consumer magazine were exactly like that, except in each one the person up front was a different profit center executive. He didn't give me any credit. One day I was out in the corridor singing a song, or the part I remembered, "Remember why God made your eyes. Don't shade your eyes, plagiarize, plagiarize, plagiarize, only, please, remember to call it research."

The container advertisements that eventually evolved showed a picture of it with words describing its features. In large type over the picture every time it said, *Look into it.* The magazine that it appeared in sent a framed glossy copy of the advertisement with a little inscription at the bottom that explained it won something like the Golden Gloves award. The framed picture was leaning against a partition on top of a filing cabinet. Every time someone went to the art department they went past where it was. The first time I leaned it back up without thinking. When I went that way again it was face down. That happened several more times, and it made me wonder if the magazine sent it to us because of all the money it cost. If that was true why was it put there in the first place. The first time I knew anything about it was when the framed picture appeared on the filing cabinet. No one said anything to me. I called a person who worked for the magazine. The long and short of what he said was that the magazine's intention of sending the "award" was not to thank us for the money even though it might seem that way. He said the advertisement helped the image of the magazine because it was not dreary. Over the top of the partition I could hear the manager slapping his desk repeatedly, except it sounded like he was using his hand, not his shoe.

There were people in the personnel department who prepared a newsletter. I wrote a response to an article that pointed to all the foreign steel in the parking lot. Our director went by me in the aisle, and he made some sort of brief, barely intelligible remark about how a letter had gone out of his department. That was the only acknowledgment of the letter I got. He smiled the whole time. It wasn't a jovial matter to him even though it seemed that way. When I wrote a letter to a person at the international division about what the man at the welding company said our director saw that letter first. I didn't think a response to an article in a newsletter had to be handled that way.

The article about foreign cars first appeared in the Ashland newsletter. The management there wrote it. The company had a limestone mining operation in Ashland, Kentucky. The people at headquarters thought the article was so poignant that they reprinted it in its entirety for everyone to read.

In those days for the first time steel made in foreign countries was coming into the United States. Previously, several large domestic steel companies had the entire market here and all price changes and employee benefits were the same. That changed when companies from other countries saw the opportunity to compete. It was of little concern to the foreign companies how domestic steel companies set the price of a ton of steel and determined employee benefits. In my letter I said the article about foreign cars in the parking lot at Ashland was a futile attempt to keep things the way they were, and rather than sulk about foreign steel they should sell steel to foreigners.

The Kansas City operation was part of the steel division. The profit center advertising manager whose office was next to mine didn't normally do work for them, but he was doing a billboard that he said was near both the Kansas City Works and a busy highway. He said the management there wanted a public service message.

After thinking a while I stood in his office door and said, "Why not simply have the words Kansas City Works?" We talked about it a little longer. He was busy with something else. I do not know if those words or any other words ever appeared on a billboard there. Several years later when I was doing mailboxes I went to an exhibition of hardware store things at McCormick Hall in Chicago. I drove there and the words "Chicago, the city that works," were said on the radio. I had the long-standing impression the billboard in Kansas City never got made. Maybe it did after all, and I wondered if the people in Chicago got the idea from there.

Two of the other copywriters were made managers. The profit center advertising manager assigned me to the one who a few weeks earlier had freaked over me. An internal memorandum announced the promotion/change. The day I saw him emote freely he was standing there waiting for a secretary's attention. I didn't realize what he was doing. I went right in front of him and asked the secretary if she would type something for me. He made a high-pitched noise. This got the attention of everyone in the building, including the two of us. His face was red. He was having a fit. It was then I realized I rudely butted in front of him. I apologized, but partly with disbelief that I had been the cause of such an outburst. The profit center advertising manager's office was across the aisle. Later that same day I could plainly hear him asking the secretary what happened. He never asked me.

When he was promoted to manager I was assigned to him. The door to his office was open so I walked in and sat down in a metal cushioned chair to congratulate him and have a friendly word with him. Sitting behind his desk he looked at the open door as if to say he would have liked me to knock. He puffed on a pipe. Everything was well lit and clean. His responses were polite. I had to make all the overtures. When I got up to leave I said since he was a full fledged company man now I would ask him where the ropes were. I felt like a worker bee in a huge hive where another layer had just been added.

Several weeks later I sat down with the profit center advertising manager and the new manager in one of the conference rooms for my "job review." The new manager sat there with his arms folded while the other one read something from a piece of paper as if he had been told exactly what to say. In the corporate world the review statement was a necessity for my being fired later. What he said was true, and that was the sickening part. He read that I could not spell and that I was severely lacking in numerous other technical abilities. I wanted to cry when I heard how little they thought of my work. I tried to conceal how bewildered and hurt I was. The last line of the review statement was about how I was good at research. In response to that I said I was gifted in that area.

They probably expected me to say I wanted to improve. What I did say was that the review was a real "hatchet job." The manager who read the words on the paper asked me to repeat myself. I said in newspaper work a "hatchet job" literally refers a murder where someone is not only killed, but their corpse is hacked. Again I said the review of my job performance, although true, was a "hatchet job."

For the first time the other manager piped up. He leaned forward, took his pipe out of his mouth, put his arms on the table in a professional manner, and said I had a strange way of wording things. That wasn't on the script. He didn't open his mouth again and probably got kicked under the table for the one time he did say something. The review was so vehement. I was like a naive child not to see they wanted me out of there. Nothing I could have said would change that fact.

I only did one interesting assignment for the new manager in the last weeks I was there. The company made metal buildings in a small town in Ohio called Washington Court House. The person in charge of the metal building factory located there wanted a brochure that would show what they did. It would be given to interested persons before they went on a factory tour. All the other work I did for the new manager was rewriting directions, which wasn't very thrilling. When I did the brochure on the metal buildings the man in charge showed me what they did step-by-step. When I first got the job at the big company I went to a stamping plant in Detroit, an electric motor factory in St. Louis, and a printing company in Lawrence, Kansas. They were customers that had bought the fork-truck size wire mesh containers we made in Plymouth, Michigan. In each place someone proud of what they did showed me first hand the entire operation.

The day I got terminated I knew something was up when everybody got their paycheck but me. The director's secretary who had a desk up front by his office passed them out in the morning.

I took my personal effects out of my office and put them in my car. The two pictures on the wall were the biggest things. When I went past the open door of the profit center advertising manager he looked up to see what was in my hands. As I walked across the parking lot with the two pictures I saw the other new manager. We stopped and talked. He said in a short while he was permanently going to Houston, Texas, where the company manufactured oil well casing. My hands were full and as I continued on toward my car I said how it was nice knowing him. I could talk to him.

At the end of the workday the profit center advertising manager told me to meet him in the director's office. I got right up, and when I went out in the aisle he was already there at the far end of the building, turning into the director's office. When I got there the director was sitting behind his desk and the advertising manager and I sat down in two chairs.

We weren't there so I could get a pay raise. The director didn't say anything the entire time. He nodded for the manager to begin his soliloquy, and the manager began to read from a paper that was probably prepared by the personnel department. Every so often I politely made an audible acknowledgment noise like people often do. It isn't two words but a sort of two-part sound that shows a person is listening.

The first part was about my performance and it set the groundwork for the second part. The "therefore" in the second part was about how I was getting fired. I continued with the same perfunctory acknowledgment noise at appropriate intervals. The director had a sense of humor, and I could see out of the corner of my eye that it all but cracked him up. The manager sounded so serious and remorseful as he read. You would have thought he was the one getting fired.

The third and last part was the best part. It told about all the benefits I would get. The government would give me money every two weeks and the company paid another company to find me a new job. When all was said and done I stood up and said it sounded like a good deal to me. I wanted to give the distraught manager a hug and tell him everything was going to be all right, but he never looked at me. Instead, I shook his limp hand. He gave me my paycheck. I bid the director farewell and walked on down the hall. Unlike the manager, who looked undone, the director was trying very hard to maintain his dignified composure.

I left a box of color slide film on my desk with a note for someone to return it to a person at the Washington Court House factory. He let it go only after I promised he would get it back. I carried one more batch of things to my car. When I came back in to make the last trip the other person with an office next to mine was out in the aisle leaning on the partition where his secretary worked. His arms were folded on top of the partition. He stopped talking to her and looked at me the whole distance I walked to what was my office. He was an older man who worked in a marketing capacity for the metal products division. I never knew exactly what his job was, but he was a permanent fixture in that company. By the self-satisfied smirk on his face he wanted me to know he knew I had been fired.

I got in my car, opened all the windows, and fired it up. I went over to the engineering company where my friend worked to give him a ride home. When he got in I told him it was all over for me in that town, that I got terminated. I expected him to call me a poor thing or something like that. I was late picking him up.

12

Self-Employment/Roadside Mailboxes

It wasn't long before I left the big company job I made a mailbox for a neighbor whose mailbox got ruined one night by two teenagers trying to outrun a policeman. The mailbox was on the outside of a slight curve in the road. It was a regular mailbox with a steel liner. The liner was welded to a 300-pound I-beam that had six-inch webs and flanges three-eighths of an inch thick. The night it got destroyed the post was twisted and torn from the ground. The car that hit it went out of control. The tires screeched as it went sideways. The loud noise woke me up. I rushed to the window to see what was the matter. The car had come to a stop across both lanes right in front of our house. I heard the sound of a police siren. The policeman was going fast to catch up. He didn't see the other car until it was too late. The siren stopped abruptly two or three seconds before the two cars impacted. I could hear one of the boys screaming when he realized the speeding police car didn't see them. The sound of the crash was loud. The baby started to cry. Soon there were many other police cars with flashing lights in front of our house. I got dressed and went out. No one was seriously hurt.

The next day my neighbor went to get his mail and saw his mailbox and post in the weeds across the road. It was very heavy and had not been moved. His house was far from the road. Several days later when we talked about it he said he didn't hear the commotion. He asked me if I would make him a new one. That was the first mailbox I made. The second one was for my mother's stepsister who was building a new house farther down the same road. The architect of that house lived in another township. He ordered one and right after that four people who lived near him did also. The lady who was building the new house told another lady who mentioned the mailbox in the last paragraph of a column she wrote for a Cincinnati daily newspaper. The column was about hard-to-find things. Many people called to get one. By then I had lost my regular job. I started making mailboxes full-time in the Apple Barn.

There was a seventy-year-old industrial-size woodworking band saw that had been in the Apple Barn for several years. It had thirty-two-inch wheels and weighed over 1,000 pounds. When my uncle who liked guns lived nearby he bought it to make duck decoys. When he moved to Charlottesville, Virginia, he left it there. He said the decoys he made were too big. He said a drake would have to be crazy to land near one of his hens. The band saw didn't have a motor.

The red tractor had a spline shaft coming out the back and it became the power source. The band saw was used to cut the rounded shape of the mailbox door and back.

All the square pieces of steel were sheared at the steel service center that sold me the steel. The first time I went to that place an inside salesman came to see me in the lobby. He heard my ideas and recommended the kind of steel to use. He made arrangements for me to get a few pieces to learn if they were the right size.

There was also a seventy-amp. 220-volt electrical outlet in the Apple Barn that the Peterloon farmers had installed years earlier for a welding machine they had. The least expensive welder at the welding store was a little red unit that was informally called a "buzz box." It used stick electrodes. The instruction book said, properly done welding should sound like eggs frying. It also said a "6013" stick was an all-position electrode that could weld through paint and grease. The mailboxes were made from new steel, but if a 6013 stick could weld through those kinds of things I thought it had to be good. I called it the "farm electrode." At the local home and garden show an accomplished welder was amused by the weld drips on the back of the mailbox. I told him it sounded just like eggs to me. Another person looked at the mailbox and then at me. He said, "I could make one of them," and I said to him, "That is only half the battle. The other half is selling it."

With a welding machine, the band saw, a handheld disc

grinder, several locking pliers, and other hand tools I had all I needed except a way to bend steel. To make a mailbox that didn't look like a battleship the metal had to be bent, and that required twenty tons. I remembered someone real or imaginary said, "If you build me something to stand on I can lift the world." That made a lot of sense. Twenty tons of pressure was easy to get. A hydraulic jack would do it, but if that much pressure was exerted in one direction there would be an equal amount going the other way. That week near where I lived a thick wood utility pole got hit and broken by a car. The utility company replaced it and left the old one on the side of the road. When I asked the utility company man in charge if I could have it he said if I wanted it I could have it for nothing as long as I removed it entirely. Four four-foot pieces of that pole, twelve six-foot pieces of three-quarter-inch threaded rod, and a twenty-ton hydraulic road service jack were put together to make a contraption that would bend steel.

I set up a playpen for Whit in the Apple Barn. If his diapers were dry and he had a bottle to feed on he could cry all he wanted, because the only way I could get work done was do the work. When we had lunch he would play outside in the long grass. He would go with me to install mailboxes. He learned the meaning of work at a young age, and to this day he is a good worker. He gets it from his dad. One day after several years had passed I looked over at the playpen and it was empty. He had climbed out and was looking around the outer room. That was the last day we used the playpen. The Rabbit was under a car cover. He would take naps in that car on blankets bundled across two seats. Once he found a nest of newborn mice. He tried to get them going with warm milk and an eyedropper. They all died. They got a very elaborate funeral such as no mouse ever had.

When he was up and around, which was most of the time, he was constantly told not to touch the mailboxes. They were on the floor in the outer room. The paint was from a hardware store. It took a day to dry. I said, "Don't touch it," so much I suddenly realized he had practically never touched one in his life and I was touching them all the time. Several hundred mailboxes had gone out of there by then. The neighbor who had the first one traded up and got one that was new and improved. With a fresh coat of paint the old one became Whit's mailbox. He could put a saddle on it, grapple with it, hit it with a hammer, drool on it, and in general do anything with it he liked. In a short time it looked as used as any mailbox ever did.

Whit's nickname at that time was Wiener Schnitzel, which soon became Veeders. At the very beginning I cashed a U.S. savings bond that was given to him at birth by a grandmother on Jenny's side of the family. That and my unemployment checks bought enough hand tools and other gear to start making mailboxes. Without knowing about it, Whit paid to start the business. I named the business Veeders Mailbox.

A company paid by the big company to find me employment sent me to an interview at another big company. At the interview the interviewer asked me a simple question about my former job. I rattled on and on about the people there and what a mind-altering experience it was. I didn't get the job, and they never again contacted me. They probably scribbled in the margins of a form that I was chronically unemployable.

At first making mailboxes didn't take much of my time. I got a temporary job as a laborer at a building under construction. The building was more than half-done. Often the superintendent was away at another construction site and he would tell me what to do until he got back, which was mostly keeping things clean, dig a hole here or there, or stack things. Much of the time I and another person who drove an earthmover were the only ones there who worked directly for him. There were independent contractors all over the place who did things like install electrical wires, hang ceilings, and paint, but they didn't work directly for the builder. One time the superintendent drove in just as I was walking from the building with an armload of trash to put in a large container. He called me over to where he was and said I walked "like a slew-footed nigger." That was his way of saying I should move faster.

One of the electrical contractors threw an old screwdriver covered with goo out on the floor, and I swept it up. He said he didn't want it anymore. I cleaned it up like new. It became my screwdriver. He knew I worked for the builder but not much else. One day he said, as if he just found out, I was nothing. A few days later when I didn't do something correctly the superintendent fired me. After that I got a lot more serious about mailboxes.

Jenny quit working at the riverboat company several weeks before our second child was born. Her health insurance was going to expire not long after that. If the child was born before midnight on a certain day it would be free to us. After that we had to pay for it, and if there were complications it would be even more. We didn't have that much on hand. If the cost did come to us we would have to get in debt. Oddly enough, the insurance agent who sold the health insurance policy to the riverboat company was a childhood friend of Jenny. He explained the situation to us. The doctor knew the situation. The night before the insurance expired, Jenny went to the hospital and labor was induced. A boy was born who we named Samuel Langhorne. Sam was a name we picked out of the blue and Langhorne was a family name on my mother's side. Neither of us knew it at the time, but it was also the first and middle name of a famous American author who was born in Hannibal, Missouri.

Making mailboxes didn't provide us with enough money. On some weekend days when it was sunny I would put a few of them on a trailer and take them to an outdoor market where anyone could display something for sale. Many people walked past in both directions to see if there was anything they wanted to buy. The mailboxes were expensive compared to other mailboxes. Some days no one would buy one, but most days I sold at least one. I took other things to sell like old starter motors, tow chains, or carving knives.

One time I displayed a cheap reproduction of a famous painting that hung in a museum in Paris, France. No one even stopped to look or ask what it was. I could have been the artist himself sitting there in a folding chair with bright yellow webbing. A hundred years later my painting would be in a museum. I didn't feel so bad on days when I didn't sell any mailboxes.

Making mailboxes was like going through a meadow after being in a tunnel. The customers were the same as a boss, except if they were awful I could tell them and they could not fire me.

All the financial responsibilities were mine. Paying bills was difficult. I got into debt buying things I didn't have to have like new outdoor furniture and a boat. The attraction to those things was strong. If the person selling the item said it was possible for me to have whatever it was, that was enough for me.

Time flew past. When I saw Whit in a welding booth putting a mailbox together it seemed like yesterday he was happily sitting in a playpen while I made the mailbox.

Several years after I started making them the maximum shipping weight of a package was raised from fifty to seventy pounds. That meant the mailboxes could be sent long distances as easily as small packages. A few months before that I went from brush painting to spray painting. That saved much time and made them look more professional. I then got a letter from an executive at a large mail-order company located near Cincinnati. He saw the mailboxes at a local housing show, and in so many words he wrote that his company was considering selling them. The mail-order company put a picture in their catalog and sold them to people all over the country.

During that time our third and last child was born. That one was a girl we named Gretchen. When she was older I had to be careful what I said to her. I sometimes spoke gruffly to the boys. If the same comment was directed in the same way to Gretchen she would cry, and it wasn't a female affectation. She was different from the boys.

The farmhouse was small. When the third child arrived I began to feel like I lived in a shoe. The attic went the length of the front part of the house, or about twenty-five feet. It was about ten feet wide. That space became a child's room. The ceiling sloped down to a knee wall that was less than three feet high. Along the center it was slightly over six feet high. The entire area was already surfaced with tongue-and-groove pine boards. The space behind the boards and behind the knee walls got filled with cellulose insulation. I sanded all the boards, puttied the cracks, and painted clear polyurethane coating to bring out the color of the wood.

A neighbor who was replacing the carpet in their house gave me their old carpet. I put the best of it wall-to-wall in the attic room. The entrance was through one of the bedrooms. On both sides of the stairs the walls were painted a light aluminum gray color. I made a galvanized steel railing to go around the floor opening at the top of the stairs. There was a small window on each end of the room. It was a good child's room.

In the spring of every year there was a "home show" in the

convention center downtown. People who lived in houses would get ideas on how to improve their home situation. The mailboxes were on display in a booth. At first I would talk with everyone who came into the booth. By the end of the night I was losing my voice. An experienced person selling central heating and air-conditioning units said I should "screen" first by asking the individual if they had a roadside mailbox. When I asked that question more than half didn't even have one. The people who did unfolded great tales of woe. It sounded like there was a war or a contest between the home owner and the mailbox vandal. As time went by I learned most mailbox vandalism was casual vandalism done on through roads where the mailbox cannot be easily seen from the house. If someone on a short residential street with houses close to the road has mailbox problems they are being picked on. Statistics show they are a schoolteacher or there is a teenage girl living in the house. When the police catch mailbox vandals usually it is Friday night and they are juveniles driving their mom's car.

One person at the home show told me a story about a man who lived on a farm and happened to see a car stop at the end of his long driveway. He stood there watching and moments later his mailbox burst into flames. He jumped in his car, the other car sped away, and there was a chase. The car being chased crashed. A parent of an injured passenger sued the farmer for causing the injury.

The most damage from mailbox vandalism happens when someone takes it personally. One man new to an area thought his mailbox was getting repeatedly hit because of his interracial marriage. I told him mailbox vandalism was a fact of life and that everyone on his road had that problem. He bought a mailbox from me and said he would see what happened. I said I would like to hear from him, but I never did. After a while I went to where he lived and drove past his house. I could see the marks on the paint where the mailbox had been whacked many times. Whoever did it continued on their merry way, and the mailbox stayed in fine shape.

Another person said once a week he would take his garbage cans to the end of his driveway. A large truck would come the next morning before dawn to pick up his garbage and everyone else's on the road. This person telling the story said several weeks in a row during the night a car would knock over one of his cans and send garbage flying everywhere. He said he finally filled the garbage can closest to the road with concrete. In the middle of the night he awoke to the sound of a crash. It was his best friend's son in his best friend's car.

One man was full of ideas. He said he had given it a lot of thought and as a result he wanted to put coils of sharp wire like the kind on prison fences all around his mailbox. Another person took a ballpoint pen and a piece of paper out of his pocket. He drew a picture of a World War Two tank trap. He said his idea was to make a modified version of a tank traps for a mailbox post. The picture he drew showed a vertical piece of steel coming out of the ground. Under the ground three other equally heavy pieces of steel were welded at right angles to the vertical piece. He said when a car pushed over the mailbox post one of the pieces of steel under the ground would come up through the bottom of the car.

Several other people said a person who couldn't destroy their mailbox might come up to the house looking for something to destroy. These people were resigned to replacing their mailbox several times a year. They left it there to appease the appetite of the mailbox vandal. Others unscrewed their mailbox and took it in at night.

A lady who grew up in India bought one of my mailboxes. She said she didn't understand the mailbox vandalism phenomenon in the United States. She said it was as if there were ferocious lions that came out at night.

I did the home show four years in a row. In the first two years many people asked, "Will it rust?" I would say, "Yes, if the paint is damaged by a tire iron or a baseball bat the metal will rust." Practically none of those people ever bought one.

The third year, one of the mailboxes on display was made of totally nonferrous stainless steel with a gleaming finish. That mailbox was expensive compared to all other mailboxes. I planned to eventually give it to my grandchildren to use as an anchor. When someone asked I was ready: "Yes, but here is one that will never rust. You could throw it in the ocean and it won't rust." I waited for them to ask how much it cost. When I told them there was a long silence. At first I though that would be the end of the conversation, but it didn't slow them down. Many people ordered a stainless steel mailbox.

The last year the mailbox was on display at the home show there was one with a picture painted on both sides. A person wanted to buy the mailbox if the picture was removed. The woman never asked if the picture made it cost more. She seemed to think it didn't cost any extra. That woman was like the other people I talked with at the home show. If they wanted a strong roadside mailbox they didn't want a picture on it at any cost. There was an established company that sold "personalized" mailboxes through gift shops. Not only could a person specify a street address on the mailbox, but they could also choose the picture they wanted from among more than thirty shown in a colorful brochure. Their customer was not my customer.

Before I enacted the pay as you go policy someone wanted me to install one of my mailboxes many miles away in a neighboring county. When I got there she wanted it to be another color. I went back home, brush-painted it the color she wanted, and then returned several days later when the paint was dry, all at no extra charge.

There had to be a certain inflexible quality to doing the business of installing a mailbox. Otherwise the householder would find some reason not to pay right away or I'd be there all day for the price of one mailbox. Upon first arriving I would go to the door and hand over the bill. It would be understood the bill would be paid when the job was done.

At one place when I asked the householder if there was any place in particular she wanted the mailbox located she said to put it where the old one was. When the posthole was half-dug (that is the hardest part) she came running out of the house and told me to put it six feet farther down the road. That kind of behavior in various degrees was not uncommon. I said to her, "Ma'am, I'll bore holes in your yard all day long, but it is twenty-eight dollar a hole." Then she said, "Leave it where it is."

When all my business was local a busy week was when I made six mailboxes and installed them on Saturday. When I got in the mail-order catalogs sometime it took all night to fill the orders. Mailboxes were selling. There was no grand plan. Each day I went ahead and did what had to be done in order to keep it going. The business grew; not in leaps and bounds, but it grew.

Eventually I got someone to help me. I didn't pass economics in school, but I remembered "the law of diminishing returns." It said the more you make of something, the less it cost to make that thing. Unfortunately, that law didn't work for me to me. I had to come up with a paycheck every week, and often there was no money left for me. The problem persisted. I think it was because the price of the mailbox wasn't enough. Sometimes it felt like a nonprofit organization.

13

Midlife Crisis

The magazines that came into our house had titles like "How to Deal with Your Man During His Midlife Crisis." The understanding I got from those articles was that a traditional midlife crisis happened to males who thought their life was half-over.

A midlife crisis was evidenced by a radical departure from daily routine. In the most extreme example a man might run off with a strange woman. The articles were jovial and chummy. I liked where I was. To abandon my family for something else to my way of thinking was badness to the core. Still, I had to admit there was an allure in doing something by myself that was entirely different. I was almost forty years old and by some calculations my life was probably half-over. Even if I wasn't in the right income bracket, I was captivated by the idea. The notion of striking out on my own was there.

In those days, I read the newspaper each day. The same week that I was having many thoughts about having a midlife crisis there was a big story in the paper about Yugoslavia. It was written in 1986, prior to the ethnic fighting that erupted there. It was when post–World War Two Yugoslavia was still functional even though the political leader from that time was gone. The government he set up forty-five years earlier was beginning to end, but it was still together and the countryside and the cities were peaceful.

I was there most of the month of May. I took the sleek bicycle I won in the photography contest and spent almost every day pedaling around that country. That trip was the "midlife crisis" I was supposed to have. I was determined to do something vastly different, and I did.

Yugoslavia appealed to me because a person from the United

States could travel there with a small amount of money. I was prepared to sleep in the woods, but at the end of every day there was always a town with lodging and hot food. Between towns there were numerous places to stop, rest, drink bottled water, or eat lunch. Even with the cost of transportation to Yugoslavia I probably would have spent more money jumping on my bicycle at home and pedaling around the United States for a month.

The interior of Yugoslavia was less traveled. One old building where I stayed had whitewashed walls inside and out. At that place when I stood outside in front and looked up I saw a white curtain from a window on the second floor blowing in the breeze. All five sleeping rooms were on the second floor, and there was one Turkish toilet among them. Many places away from the coast were like that, but on the Adriatic coast it was like the time I woke up in a huge glass-and-steel building. That place was a modern hotel. Breakfast in the dining room was full of noisy people from Germany on a group tour. They were having fun. I stopped the person who moments earlier inquired if I wanted the package deal for breakfast and asked him, with the usual linguistic difficulty, if the others were on a forced march or what. I understood him to say they were groups of Dutch and German citizens jibber-jabbering back and forth in their respective languages. Then I remembered the day before seeing the great big stainless-steel buses on the coastal highway.

That morning at the checkout desk a hotel employee told the man ahead of me how much he owed in Deutsche Marks (German currency). Eventually he moved over to sift through some papers, and it got to be my turn. The clerk said I owed so many Deutsche Marks. I conjured up just enough rudimentary French to say, "Que c'est Deutsche Mark?" (What is a Deutsche Mark?) He looked at me in a puzzled way and then looked down, making no more visible or audible utterances. I repeated myself: "Que c'est Deutsche Mark?" I thought maybe if I talked a foreign language he would understand me and if he thought I was one of the fun bunch maybe I would get a package deal. The man who had moved over to shuffle papers looked at me. Just as he was about to get involved in the conversation the clerk looked up and said what I owed in the local currency. Being on the coast was like being in another country.

I got there on a Yugoslavian airliner. At the airport in New York City I spoke with a man who was going on the same airplane. He said he was born in a small town outside Belgrade, Yugoslavia, and for most of his adult life he lived in the southwestern part of the United States, where he worked in the control room of a nuclear power electrical generating facility. He was going back home to spend some time with his family.

He had gone back and forth many times. He told me in the first few years he was nervous that the Yugoslavian government wouldn't let him return to the United States. He said he was more relaxed now, but he still worried. To him the fact that he was a Yugoslavian citizen first meant he would always be one.

He said he sent some faucets to a friend in his hometown who was building a house. He said the faucets here were better than the ones made anywhere else. He said the way they turned on and off without washers made them better. We were waiting for the airplane. He said the tourist bureau was strong over there and that if I was being treated unfairly just mentioning that arm of the government by name would instantly set matters straight. Then he told me about a newspaper story that appeared everywhere in that country shortly after the Winter Olympics in Sarajevo, Yugoslavia. He knew about it because his parents sent the article to him. It was about a well-known American movie actor who was entertaining a group of friends in a restaurant there. The next day the celebrity called the tourist bureau, and said the bill at the restaurant was much higher than it should have been. The tourist bureau investigated the matter and as a result permanently closed the restaurant. The man sitting beside me in the airport said the celebrity was a U.S. citizen but a Yugoslavian by birth like him.

Twice I invoked the name tourist bureau. Once at a restaurant in the mountains a short distance above Kraljevica and once in Virovitica, where I told the waiter the bill was too high and if he didn't agree to call the police or the tourist bureau and let them settle the matter.

The time in Virovitica was early in my travels, but I had eaten enough meals to know how many dinars (local currency) one should cost. That one was typical, but it cost three times the usual amount. The manager made a telephone call, but I don't think it was to the police. I could hear him talking in Croatian back and forth with someone he knew. He didn't know any English. When I ordered I pointed to words on a notepad: "Sta mi reporucjete?" (What do you recommend?). That is what I did most places. I could not communicate any other way. After his rather long telephone conversation he returned to the table and said I could pay the amount I said. After dinner I pedaled back to the hotel where they said there was no room. It was the end of the day, and I didn't know where I was going to sleep.

Virovitica was the largest town I was in not counting Ljubljana and Zagreb. It was where two major roads crossed near the Danube River and the Hungarian border. When I got there it was at the end of the day. I went straight to the hotel and asked for a room. It was a big hotel with an elevator. The room had no hot water while the price was quite high. I went back down the elevator with my bicycle and all my things. My habit was never to let the bicycle out of my sight. I was tired and hungry. I must have been the ugly American when I complained. The man gave me back my passport and indicated they had no rooms. I thought he was going to give me another room.

I turned around at the front desk to think what to do next. Close to the front desk there were four people on two dark red vinyl couches. A young man and woman sat on each one facing each other. The two men had button-down shirts, open collars, and military haircuts. They spoke a Slavic language to each other. It was not clear to me if the two girls understood everything they said.

They were looking at me trying not to be rude. I thought that was decent of them to make the effort. I must have been a sight standing there holding that two-wheeled machine, wearing black and blue synthetic fiber bicycle clothes. The girl on the couch closest to where I was knew some English and probably told them about my noisy dialogue with the hotel clerk.

I wasn't staring at them either, but I was aware of their presence. The girl was wearing a small short black dress. She turned her head and looked at me. Then she turned back around and leaned over to the man sitting next to her in such a way that I saw her long legs, her shiny brown hair, her thin waist, and her voluptuous lower end. Then she straightened. I felt tired and hungry at that point, and I thought that was going to be the first night I was going to sleep under the stars on a haystack.

I turned back around and asked the clerk where there was a restaurant. He made no effort to understand me. I got my pad of paper out and pointed to the Croatian word *gastonia* (restaurant), he looked, and then he went on about his business without looking at me or saying anything.

When I realized there wasn't any help coming from him I again turned around and stood there. The four people were talking among themselves. I walked to where the girl with all the softness was sitting. The four of them looked my way, and I nodded hello. I said to her, "Excuse me; could you tell me where there is a restaurant?" She said something to the others. Then she stood up and told me where one was in broken English. When she was waving her hands in the air, telling me the rights and lefts she no longer thought of me as a prospect. For those moments I could see who she was.

The restaurant where the bill was going to be so high was on the top of a slight hill southwest of the hotel. On the way there I noticed some soccer fields to the left. I thought if there was no place else I would sleep there. That hotel was the only lodging place in Virovitica.

During that trip the idea of being with another person the same way I was with Jenny was not going to happen. Distance plus being alone, more than ever made me aware I was one of five people in a family. Being loyal was easy, although I didn't consciously have that thought.

Jenny and I talked a long time about a baby-sitter I took several hours to take home one night. It was I who brought it up. She brought it up again and again over the years. She always said how she blamed the girl for what happened when actually it was more me.

In front of the hotel there was a concrete terrace with round tables where people were sitting. The government made it as nice as it could. I got a table to myself, ordered a beer, and sat back. When my glass was almost empty I thought again how I didn't have anyplace to stay. Some people were chatting busily at the table next to mine. I leaned over and in Croatian asked them if they spoke English. If they did, I was going to ask them if there was any other place to stay. One of them indicated they didn't. At the same time a man in a white suit turned in his chair and spoke in English. He was sitting at a table by himself with his back to mine. I had not noticed him. I told him how grateful I was that he was sitting there. He was a young person and reminded me of the man who comes in at the end of the opera *Madam Butterfly.* I turned my chair half-around and explained to him my conversation with the hotel clerk and my overall situation. He was from Dubrovnik visiting his parents, who lived in Virovitica. He said he would ask them if I could stay there. We walked down a residential street away from the hotel. He talked about the many tourists in Dubrovnik and said his parents lived near the hotel. We went past doors, windows, and solid wood gates in a continuous row of houses. There was an occasional streetlight suspended by two wires that came from each side of the street. They were off. There was daylight. The streetlights were open underneath, and I could see bare lightbulbs in them. We went through one of the gates. Inside, it was a beautiful enclosed area with trees, grass, and other plants. A house was in one corner, and in another there was a corncrib.

I knew about corncribs even though they were part of history in the United States, where now giant machines on wheels picked and shelled the corn. At home kernels of corn were stored in silos or in smaller round corrugated steel structures. Powerful electric fans pushed heated air from the bottom of the structure to the top. In that way moisture was removed.

Before then, a corncrib did the same thing. A corncrib was a small building with a floor several feet off the ground. It had a roof, and vertical boards on the sides spaced several inches apart. Wind as much as anything removed moisture from whole ears of animal corn stored there.

When I saw the corncrib in the corner of the yard I pointed to it and said, "Oh, you have animals." He didn't speak. His parents used that corn for food. The corncrib held the corn they would use that year.

Inside the gate he told me to wait while he went to talk with his father. His mother came outside to greet him, and before he left he introduced me to her. She and I stood there on the grass fifty feet from the house. She was an older woman in dark clothes. I was holding my bicycle dressed in synthetic fiber. It was obvious we were not from the same place. I became painfully aware we could not communicate by words. Whenever I talked there was a blank look on her face. She didn't understand a word I said. She looked toward the house to see if her son was on his way back. Then I reached into one of the canvas bags on my bicycle and took out a photograph of my three children. The picture showed all three of them looking at the camera, smiling. It was taken in our backyard in Ohio. They were sitting close together holding three manila ropes connected to a tire swing. The three ropes went into three evenly spaced holes around the side of the tire. It was a thick fourteen-and-a-half-inch house trailer tire. Overhead, out of sight of the camera, the three ropes were tied to a long rope that was fastened to a tree branch. It was a swing, but in the photograph it was just hanging there, still.

I held the picture halfway between us and pointed to those three happy faces and then to me. When I looked at her I knew we were communicating. She knew they were my children in the United States. She took the picture out of my hand to look at it more closely. She said the same word over and over and repeatedly pointed to Gretchen. Gretchen had rosy cheeks and was wearing a new dress and a perfectly round straw hat with a ribbon. I wondered what the woman was saying and if she had a girl.

Neither of us saw her son in the white suit coming. He walked up to us and said to me, "He doesn't want you to stay here." Then he spoke to her. She was still holding the photograph. She handed it back to me and said something to her son. She went toward the house. I noticed her husband busily doing something near the house. He never looked in my direction. When the woman left I turned and stood talking to the son. He abruptly left when his father called, and again he told me to wait there. It was starting to get dark. I could still see the lushness of green things growing everywhere inside those walls. After a short while the son came back, and he said if I went to the hotel they would have a room for me. I asked him how that could be, and without looking at me he quietly said his father worked for the government. They must have had a telephone.

When I got back to the hotel the same clerk was there. I

asked for a room like it was the first time I was ever there, and like it was the first time I was ever there the clerk gave me one. It had hot water.

Waiting in the airport in New York City the man from the southwestern part of the United States had not talked for a long time. He was diligently going through a newspaper. When he folded it up and put it down he said it showed the most recent winning lottery numbers. Even though he lived and worked several thousand miles away, he regularly participated in the New York State lottery. He didn't win that time, but by the way he talked, soon he would. There was a meticulous way he played the game.

We talked about someone who won the New York State lottery back in the days when that lottery was practically the only one. This someone won an enormous amount of cash and was on the news everywhere. Before that his job was changing lightbulbs in a New York City skyscraper. Three years after he won he was asked how it was going. One of the first things he said was, "At least I knew who my friends were."

People who flew the airplane arrived, and soon after that the rest of us were told it was time to leave. Someone who worked for the airline stood by the door and looked at each person's ticket. Before that another airline employee inspected the ticket and wrote down where to sit. An adorable girl was assigned to the seat next to mine.

The airplane was big. It was an American-made wide-bodied jet owned by a Yugoslavian airline. I had never been inside one that big. There were many empty seats. Few people were going to Ljubljana from New York that night. The plane was almost empty.

I thought the empty plane might have something to do with what went on a short while before. American fighter-bombers flying from British air bases bombed a building in North Africa where the political leader of Libya was thought to be sleeping. The American government said he was using "terrorist" means to achieve political goals. In the latest terrorist effort attributed to him a bomb went off in an American passenger airplane. It managed to land, but not before a tiny baby was sucked out the blast hole. When the Americans bombed his house they didn't get him. He was reportedly sleeping in a nearby tent. Probably, he stood there in pajamas holding back the tent flap with one hand and with the other rubbing his eyes in utter disbelief as he watched bombs bursting in air and rockets' red glare. I doubt he went back to sleep that night. His vulnerability must have become apparent to him. He and the Libyan government faded from the news.

The United States didn't consider Yugoslavia a terrorist country. But it wasn't in the same political camp. The two governments were friendly toward each other, but in that part of the world I didn't think it would be prudent to wear a U.S. army uniform to lunch. A political zealot might open fire on me with a Thompson submachine gun.

Also at that time there was a big industrial accident in the Ukraine region of the Soviet Union. That might have been another reason the airplane was nearly empty. Radioactive particles went high into the atmosphere. Some people died instantly. Many people died slowly. It was termed a disaster. Numerous reports said radioactive particles were invisible and if one entered a human body or the body of any living thing sooner or later it would die.

Yugoslavia wasn't exactly far away from the Ukraine. I asked a person who worked around radioactive medical supplies every day if there was a hazard. She said I should drink only water bottled before the accident and not to eat any salads.

The girl in the seat next to mine on the airplane was on her way home to Venice. That summer she worked for a man and woman in America taking care of their small children. She was flying to Ljubljana and going on the train through Trieste to Venice. She told me she met an Italian family at the airport. She said they were returning to Venice from a vacation in the Caribbean and were on the same airplane.

I never saw them except from a distance going through a baggage inspection station at the other airport. On the plane she got up, and when she came back she said the father in that family had said she could sit with them and that she didn't have to sit where she was. I think he was being protective of her. I understand why. The two of us were put in two seats together on a practically empty airplane. I was sitting by the window overlooking the wing on the left side. She was in the seat next to mine. When I walked back to my seat I noticed the whole airplane was dark. The only bright light came from two little reading lights above our seats. There were no people sitting near. I could see a few people sitting in the middle of the aircraft and along the other side. The Italian man probably thought the airline employee who assigned us those two seats should be court-martialed and shot.

I thought the lights should be on because we occupied the seats under them. I didn't think they should be off with the two of us there. People with lights off sleep better. I was half-asleep when she said she was going to another seat. She had turned back and forth the last time. In the morning she came back and we talked about where we were going.

I was beginning to be apprehensive about being alone in a strange land. I told her she could stay with me and I would take her to the train the next day. She said she had to check with the Italian family because in New York the father had said he would take her to the train station in their car. She went back to where they were sitting, and in a few minutes she returned. She said he was going to take her all the way to Venice, which meant she didn't have to take a train at all. I could tell she didn't think it was a very good idea to stay with me in Ljubljana.

At the airport the girl and I said good-bye in an offhanded way. A few moments later when I was waiting for a bus I saw them all zoom off in a little foreign car that didn't look so foreign over there.

All the money I had was in the form of international certificates guaranteed against loss. When I needed money during the trip I cashed them in for the local currency. The first place I did that was at the airport. From behind a half-open Dutch door a big friendly man who spoke some English made the transaction. I asked him how to get to the hotel, and he told me. He said the name of the hotel meant "elephant." I waited for the bus to arrive. When it let me off downtown I had to walk a long way to the hotel. My bicycle and a few things were inside a cardboard box I carried.

I reserved a room the day I got in the country and the day I left. The eighteen days between I had no plans to be at a particular place at a particular time. The room I got was in the front of the hotel. Two people were working on the roof of a building across the street carefully repairing some terracotta tiles. There was a bicycle race that afternoon. I watched the race from one of the open windows in my room. Many people were lining the street and cheering each time the racers whizzed past. I went out there. I had never seen speed and endurance like those contestants had. I didn't understand a hotel clerk when several hours earlier he looked at the box and asked if I was going to be in the race. In that race there should have been a clown riding an old - fashioned three-speed bicycle equipped with a chromium-plated horn and a wide motorcycle seat.

Late that afternoon I walked along the street. There was a small restaurant on a corner near the hotel. People in line were holding the door open. The people who really knew what they were doing ate there. The line went past a menu taped to the other side of a glass panel. When I was looking at it I understood nothing. I was able to convey this to a person in line behind me and he pointed to one item on the menu. Suddenly three other people got involved in my selection. However, none of them spoke English and I didn't speak a word of Croatian. The line was moving quickly. When it was my turn a person in white restaurant clothes spoke. I assume he was asking me what I wanted. I didn't have the slightest idea what to say. The person behind me said something. I paid some money, got change, and moved to the side like everyone else. I couldn't recognize what was on my plate when it was handed to me by one of the people fixing food behind a glass case, but it was very good. It could have been unborn octopus for all I knew. There were small tables nearby and I ate there.

In the confusion I forgot to get something to drink. I did not know the words for beer or bottled water. I got up and went back to ask someone for something to drink. On top of the glass case there was a large pitcher of amber-colored liquid. It looked just like beer to me. I pointed to it and asked one of the people busily preparing food on the other side of the glass case for a beer in English. He pointed back to it and I got the impression he was telling me to help myself. Finally from seemingly endless talk by the people who worked there I learned that place had no beer, and that the clear glass pitcher on top of the case was full of vinegar for anyone who wanted it. I wasn't used to seeing vinegar in such a large pitcher. I didn't try to communicate anymore and went back to my seat with nothing to drink. I felt like a completely helpless fool, even though the people in that place wanted to be helpful. Being tired didn't help my chagrin. I went back to the hotel, took a bath, and went to sleep. The bathtub was on four legs in the middle of a large, luxurious bathroom with a dark polished floor. I didn't request anything special. That is what I got. During most of the night loud marching music was coming from loudspeakers in the street. It must have been a holiday. When I stayed there on my way back there was no music blaring in the street.

The next morning breakfast was in a second-floor area of the hotel. Other people who were not staying there came to have coffee and read the morning paper. Outside, in front, there were parallel parking places, and in the morning all of them were taken. A few of those cars were luxurious cars with chrome horseshoes attached to the grill. It signified the car got too close behind a horse and got kicked. Away from the cities I frequently saw horse-drawn traffic.

People mixed their own morning coffee from two small ceramic vessels. One had superstrong, almost concentrated, hot coffee, and the other had warm thick cream. It was exceptionally good. There were several rolls that tasted like they were baked that night. They had a hard crust. A person could order other things, but that is all most people got.

After breakfast I put the bicycle together. I had bicycle tools with me. Plus I had a spare folding tire, two spare tubes, a tube patch kit, and some spare spokes inside the frame.

The inadequate feeling I had about language went away when I got on my bicycle and started moving. I went to the tourist bureau office and a man there gave me a map of Slovenia that showed every road in detail. I planned to leave the next day on the road to Ig. The remainder of that morning I rode up and down streets. At one point I was on a hill overlooking a residential part of the city. I saw many irregular tile roofs in the morning sun.

It got to be the middle of the day. On a narrow side street

people were sitting at round tables under large parasols. I didn't need a clock to know it was lunchtime, but I went past that place. The street opened into a park. A man with a large stainless-steel cart on wheels just like the ones in New York City was selling food there. When I rode my bicycle up to where he was I thought maybe he would have roasted chestnuts, but no, he was selling American hot dogs with bright yellow mustard and red ketchup. I had no trouble getting a hot dog.

I was standing there straddling my bicycle eating the first one when three people came up to me. One stood in front of the bicycle, and the other two, a young man and woman, were on each side of the front wheel. The one in front was a young American from Boston. He had long, loose dirty blond hair and looked sweaty and content. He said they were sitting at a table on the side street I passed. "You're American, aren't you?"

I said yes and asked how he knew. He said the valve stems on my bicycle were the kind only Americans have. We got into conversation. Meanwhile the other male said something in Italian to his lady friend. Apparently he considered I was properly distracted and directed her to go ahead. She commenced trying to open the handlebar bag. She was doing it in a coy sort of way. I looked down at her hand on the zipper. It never was easy to open. She couldn't get it opened. The American said he was by himself bicycling to Northern Europe. He didn't have a bicycle with him. I never asked him what he was doing with the two Italians. I suspect they were fugitives from Italy unsuccessfully trying to amend their wicked ways. The American said he started pedaling in Turkey. I asked him if he knew the language in each country he went through. He said he didn't. I told him about the vinegar. I asked him how he managed to communicate. He said I wouldn't get in a deep philosophical conversation with a Yugoslavian about the meaning of life, but that I could get whatever I needed by pantomiming. After that I didn't worry about communication anymore.

Just before I went to bed that night I made a telephone call home. I could make it from my room. One other time I telephoned home while in Yugoslavia. It was from a post office. That was the only place I could make that kind of call. It was unusual that I could do it from the room. It was nine o'clock at night in

Ljubljana, and in Cincinnati it was early in the morning. I was sure everybody would be out of bed in our house. The school bus was about to come. When the telephone rang it must have been a little bit early, because I could tell it woke up Jenny. She wasn't a person who jumped out of bed and hit the floor running. After she picked up the receiver I heard a raspy voice say, "Hello." After I identified myself I said what a great time I was having, she said in the same sleepy voice, "I'm glad *you're* having a nice time." She put emphasis on the word you're. That and her tone of voice clearly said she wasn't having any fun. She said the children were behaving badly and the night before she took them to her father's house to "talk it out." I quickly understood it wasn't a good time to call. She didn't ask me about any of the goings-on at my end. As soon as I could, I terminated the call. After I did I lay there in bed and thought what she said about the children's conduct. I thought it was all a bunch of toro feces.

That morning I moved down the road with all the things I needed. Two canvas bags hung from each side of the back wheel. In front there was a handlebar bag where maps, a camera, money, necessary papers, and other things were. In the bags on each side of the back wheel there were dry socks, a rain suit, an insulated vest, one change of bicycle clothes, one set of civilian clothes, a hairbrush, Chap Stick, and other personal effects. My bicycle tools and parts were in a small pouch attached to the back of the seat. Moving, self-contained, from one place to another was a fantasy I enjoyed. I would need a moving van to transport all the stuff the five of us accumulated at home. I was aware of the difference. I have seen pictures of the past. A long time ago people on horse back traveled long distances across vast plains dragging all their possessions behind them on litters, some with papooses.

Late in the morning a front wheel spoke broke. It was the same spoke that got bent during the airplane ride. It broke close to the rim right above the threads. I had the tools and parts to make the repair. There was a nice rock to sit on in the shade beside the road.

I drank a bottle of water and rested. During that time not one car went past. It was a quiet road. In the distance there was a wooded hillside where a chain saw "rattled and snarled." It stopped, and then for the first time I heard a real cuckoo bird. It sounded exactly like the clock. I didn't think a creature like that existed. The bird was far away on the wooded hillside. It was loud like an owl. Over and over again it made the cuckoo sound. I heard that sound for the next fifty miles until I left that region.

At the end of each day there was a town, and each town had a hotel, some with as few as three rooms. I would eat, go upstairs with the bicycle under my arm, and sleep. Most times I was the only one having supper. I found out why there were so many tables where I ate. A few hours after I went upstairs and fell fast asleep the place filled up with Yugoslavians. The town folk met there after the sun set and talked with friends over a beer.

The first time I knew of this was when, instead of going to bed, I went out to see the sights on my bicycle. When I returned I stayed downstairs to have a beer and review maps. I was sitting at a large round table with empty chairs. Soon the place was full of people. When one of them spoke to me I said the word *English* in their language, thinking it would explain everything. It was unknown to me that I was saying "British."

A little town I came to had a hotel operated by several people who were like a family. There was an old spinster who took care of the rooms. There was a cook who ran the place, a waiter/bartender, a musician, and possibly a quasi-prostitute. The people there didn't see many foreigners. The musician spoke some English. He came from Zagreb each day. He filled out the necessary papers on his knee. Then he put his leg down and looked a long time at my passport. On there it was written: "The United States of America." He said, "OK, I put 'Born in the U.S.A.'?" About that time there was a popular American rock-and-roll song with that title. The musician knew it well and all the other American rock music. When he was finished I asked him about the town. He told me the person who put Yugoslavia together after World War Two, and governed it for the rest of his life was born here. Other than that he said it was just like any other place.

Before I went upstairs to see the room I met the spinster. She was a small older lady with a piece of cloth wound tightly around her head. She came around a corner while the musician was writing. She talked to him in Croatian. Her manner was forceful and it didn't change when she turned to me. It wasn't her concern that I didn't understand anything she said. She spoke to me at length, and while this direct woman went on and on I asked the musician what she was saying. She stopped and looked at him. He said she was saying the room had two beds and not to mess up the other one. In English I assured the woman I wouldn't touch the other bed, and I bowed to her graciously. She seemed satisfied with that response and busily went back around the corner from whence she came. The room was longer than it was wide, with a high ceiling. The two beds were narrow with the side of each one against opposite walls of the room. Near the door there was a small white enamel basin with a drain, one faucet, and a mirror. I shaved there and washed the bicycle clothes I wore that day. They were fast-drying. The socks were not. The next morning when I left I pinned them to the outside of a canvas bag on the bicycle. I wore loose-fitting clothes to supper that night.

There were round wood tables in the dining room. The finish was varnish, but it was worn off from use and repeated cleaning. Someone came out of an adjoining room tying an apron behind his back. I was the only one there. He walked to the table and said something. I said the word for beer and then pointed to the words on a card I carried. "What do you recommend?" That method of ordering food worked well for me in most places, but not there. The door to the kitchen was propped open. The cook, the musician, and the waiter were conversing in Croatian. The cook sounded exasperated. His voice was loudest by far. The musician must have told him Americans like to eat fried food, because that is what I got. When my beer was almost gone the waiter came out with a plate of food. I asked him to please bring me another beer, saying everything in English except the word *beer*. The plate of food was predominately fried mutton. When I was waiting for it and after the conversation in the kitchen died down I heard the thud of a mallet striking something soft ten or fifteen times in quick succession. After I saw the food I knew what it was. The cook was tenderizing the meat. I ate everything on the plate.

In the wee hours of the morning I had the worst diarrhea imaginable. The toilet down the hall was a Turkish toilet. I squatted over a hole in the floor. I never contacted any surface. I had to make several desperate trips there and each time my "trumpet was a trumpet." The only other time I heard a noise of that kind with that magnitude was from a horse named Casey Jones when he was jumping high fences in the show ring. The first time I squatted over the toilet I heard a door opening downstairs, rapid footsteps, and the cook's voice. I was safely in position over the toilet and had time to wonder what anyone was doing awake at that hour. Otherwise, the place was silent. The noisy Yugoslavians had gone home, and as far as I knew there was no one else upstairs. The first time I made a mad dash for the toilet the cook must have been startled awake by the American upstairs. Once he learned from subsequent sounds I was suffering from nothing more than "irregularity" he went back to bed. I felt fine that morning when I had coffee and bread for breakfast. I heard the cook again, this time in the front room. In his usual loud voice with great laughter he was telling some others about the previous night. I knew that because every so often he would force air through tight lips to make the gastric distress noise.

The night before when I finished eating the waiter removed the plate and everything but the glass of beer. The food wouldn't take its effect for six or seven more hours. The musician came in the room and went to a platform where there were some electric guitars. After that he sat down at the table where I was and got a beer. Soon someone else sat down with us. That person was friendly, but unlike the musician, he spoke no English. At first they talked sporadically back and forth in Croatian. Then the musician got his friend a beer and said to me they were going to perform that night. He said there were others in the band who might show up. The sound of conversation and laughter was beginning to fill the room. The musician asked me where I lived in the United States and said someday he would go to that country. He didn't know where Ohio was. The best I could do was describe it as being in the middle. He didn't say it, but I think he wanted to go where the music was like it was in a special place.

He knew the basic parts of the English language. I spoke deliberately and slowly so he would understand. In that way I said, "When you go to the United States come to Cincinnati, Ohio, and you have a good time, number one American girl." As it turned out I never saw the musician again after that night, but when I said those words a big smile came across his face. A moment later he talked in a serious tone to the friend. There were long pauses in the conversation. They were thinking. After another exchange the friend got up and left. A few minutes later he came back, and talked to the musician like something had been accomplished.

We were sitting amid loud conversation. The musician was to my right and his friend was across from me. Someone sitting in the empty chair would be facing the platform across the room. When I turned my head in the direction of the platform I did not see or hear the girl who sat in the empty chair. She didn't converse with the other two and they didn't converse with her. She just sat there looking cute. The musician never said who she was. She never smiled or emoted freely. When I said something to her she made no audible or visible response except to look at the musician, who said nothing. She was not one of the performers. They were in regular clothes. Her clothes would be regular in another part of the world. She didn't put a glossy aqua colored purse on the table, but it wouldn't have surprised me if she had. When I thought she was the musician's idea of a counterpart to the number one American girl, the thought embarrassed me. There was a big misunderstanding.

When I was in college it was awesome to hear a stadium full of people shout over and over in unison, "Number one!" Even a small boy in Vietnam knew the meaning of those words. It was a widely known American expression. To an American if something was "number one" it was not surpassed. The first day in Ljublana the sweaty American from Boston said language would be no obstacle to getting food, water, and lodging. He said any other discussion would have less certain results. I wanted to ask him more, but like the white rabbit he had to get where he was going on time. The longer I was in Yugoslavia the more I became aware I could not sit down and talk with anyone. When I said "number one American girl" I meant a date so he would have a good time when he visited. It was a casual remark, and I suppose in a general way he understood what I meant. At the time it didn't seem significant that he knew the details, but I should have spelled out details. We would find some music, and he would have a better time if a female were with him. I wouldn't be able to describe her specifically. How do you say in Croatian if he wanted to paint a tractor over and over again, a different color each time, she would never say what the color should be?

The musician and his friend got up to sing and make music. Two others joined them. The girl and I were alone. Once more I tried to talk to her and got the same blank expression. I looked at the tables behind me. There were beer mugs. Old and young people leaned forward in deep conversation. Everywhere in that room it seemed so wholesome except where I was. I didn't know what she was doing there or who she was. It never occurred to me to buy her a beer. I didn't, and she never got herself one. I don't suppose it was very nice to leave her there, but that is what I did. I finished my beer and went to bed. Next, I ran to the toilet at 3:00 A.M.

In the little town of Lipik there was a place to stay that was connected to the house of a very wealthy duke or count who lived in another time. There were wide tile walkways with arches and arbors. It seemed many people, when they got there went no farther. Behind glass doors children silently jumped in a large swimming pool and adults with white rubber caps on their head moved through the water without disturbing the surface.

Not long after the sun went down a musical group played in a great big room. Once it must have been the grand ballroom. The entire ornate ceiling was illuminated, but the musical group and the people listing to them were all at one end of the room. When the count was alive, whirling people probably filled the place. I sat by myself at a small table drinking a wondrous beer made in Zagreb.

No matter what kind of music the band played the people dancing held each other. I drank three beers in rapid succession to take away the agony of not being able to talk with anyone.

There was a large group of eight or more people at one table having a fine time among themselves. Occasionally some of them got up to dance. There was a young woman at that table who never danced even though she seemed to be having a good time. When people beside her got up I could see there was nothing ornamental about her. Her dark clothes didn't exaggerate any part of her. I don't know if they were silk or rayon, but it could not be denied she was a lovely sliver of a girl. I walked up to the table and had no trouble convincing everyone there I was a dumb tourist from America. A young man sitting where I was standing popped up. He probably had three beers also. He slapped my back affectionately. He was feeling about as good as I. He said twice, "boom-boom Gadhafi." He was referring to the leader of the North African country the Americans bombed several weeks earlier. Apparently, he was speaking for the others. All faces but the girl's seemed in agreement. She could have had an automatic rifle hidden somewhere outside, but not on her person. I could not tell if she was shy or just unfriendly. Since the person standing beside me was instantly my buddy I pointed to the girl, to myself, and then to the dance floor while saying in English, "Would she like to dance?" He spoke to her, conveying what I said. At first she didn't move. He said something again and she got up. She was shy. We walked to the dance floor, and when I said something it was clear she understood nothing. When we danced I was overwhelmed. The custom was that I could hold her body close to mine. My one arm could go around her waist, and the other held her hand out to the side. Her other hand was on my shoulder. The sides of our heads were close, but they did not touch. I spoke to her, and when I did we looked at each other. Her eyes were dark as coal. I forgot we could not talk. Her head went to the side. I held her as close as I dared and we moved to the slow and easy rhythm of the music. When the music was over we were near the band. People crowded the dance floor. Before we parted I kissed the side of her head in a way no one on earth could see. That was not the custom. She did not look at me. We returned to our respective tables in a methodical way. We did not speak. We did not dance anymore.

In Zagreb I met a spy, or a counterspy, or a thief, or a plainclothes policeman, or someone related to the order of things. The Tourist Bureau in Ljublana gave me a superb map of Slovenia that showed every road no matter how small. In Zagreb, which was in a different political region, I tried to get a similar map. A lady behind a desk in that city said no such map existed. She looked at my bicycle several times when she was talking as if to size up what sort of tourist I was. She repeated herself to be certain I got the message, and then I said twice, "Someday when I come back you have map like this." I was shaking the folded Slovenia map in my hand. Soon after that I became aware someone was following me. That person was watching when I ate lunch. I don't know who sent him or if in fact he was sent, but when after several hours he was still behind me I didn't think he was a common thief looking for an opportunity. On my way out of the city I went down a long, straight hill. There were some trolley cars, but overall it was much less crowded than anyplace I had been that day. The road forked. I stopped, turned around, and looked up the hill. Here comes the spy. He looks off to the side like I am no concern. At that point it is obvious we are both aware of each other. I wave hello as if he is simply another cyclist. He then stops beside me and we converse. He speaks fluent English. I don't ask questions. I say I am on my way out of the city going no place in particular. Shortly after that he turns his bicycle around and pedals slowly up the hill. I watch until he disappears. He never once looks back to see which way I am going. I suppose he wasn't being paid enough to follow me any longer, or maybe from our conversation he understood I had no political design.

There was a tendency in me to get to the next town without paying much attention to the countryside in between, but along the Rijeck River there were places where I looked a long time. It might be a quiet main road high over an equally quiet river or a shaded place beside the ruins of a building where huge stone blocks were half-sunk in the ground.

It was drizzling, and it started to rain harder the day I went into a place that had a sign hanging outside. It wasn't mealtime. There was no disguising I was a foreigner riding a bicycle. When I went inside and didn't buy anything I might be a vagabond too. I bought a bottle of water. Sometimes being a foreigner was no fun.

In another place I stopped to rest on a bench located against the outside of a building. On the other side of the front door there was another bench. On it four young men were conversing. To the side, beyond them far off in the distance I could see a bright sphere above the trees. I got their attention and, pointing to it, asked them what it was. My manner more than anything else helped them understand what I was saying. They all tried to answer at once. I understood none of them. After what seemed like a long time of my being unable to comprehend, I heard the word *Sputnik*. That was the name of an object reported to be the first one propelled beyond the earth's atmosphere, returned, and retrieved in one piece. Their side did it, and the shiny sphere out there was a memorial of that event. When it happened I heard much rhetoric about which side was the more technologically advanced. Years later a bunch of Yugoslavians and I were looking at it over the tops of the trees.

Everywhere I went it was a common sight to see a line of twenty or thirty people cultivating a large field by hand. Each of them always used the same tool. I bought one in the town of Kocevje the last day I was on the road. There was only one version made so I had no trouble finding it in a store. It was a combination garden hoe and pointed shovel. I also bought a wooden handle to make it complete. On a bench nearby I whittled and sanded to make the two pieces go together. At home when the tip got bent from some sort of misuse I hammered it straight. It was made of very high-quality ductile cast iron. When I realized how well made it was and that it could not be replaced, the Yugoslavia tool, as it became known, was retired.

On my way home in Ljubljana the Yugoslavia tool was strapped to a canvas bag on my bicycle. In the big hotel where I started it seemed out of place in the lobby even if it was a familiar sight to anyone living in that country. The manager of the hotel saw it and started talking in Croatian. He pointed to it several times. He never spoke to me but to the other employees. They momentarily looked up and quickly went back to what they were doing.

Along the sides of country roads I saw old people mowing the grass with scythes. Their bodies turned slowly back and forth as the long blade cut effortlessly through the long grass. A sweeping sound was the only sound. None of them were in a rush. They had done this many times before and would do it many times again. It was always the same. There might be ten of them altogether. Some would be standing where the grass was cut, holding their scythe upside down, moving a sharpening stone across the blade in just the right way.

A man was sawing a log into boards in front of his house. I

stopped on the road to watch. The log moved automatically back and forth, and each time another board was cut. A noisy gasoline engine powered the saw. After a long while he signaled for me to have a beer with him. He did that by waving his arm and then tipping his head back, holding an imaginary bottle of beer bottom up. I replied by making a pedaling motion with my hands and pointing down the road. He acknowledged that he understood and continued busily tending the saw. I was fascinated by how such a small saw, crude as it seemed, could do so much. Maybe he figured I stopped to see it work and that was why he offered me a beer. Space-age reflective cloth was attached to the bicycle bags. I was wearing synthetic fiber space-age clothes. It was a pity I couldn't go see his sawmill up close. He didn't seem like a nut case, but under the circumstances I didn't go in there.

Along the coast between Novigrad and Rijeka there was a line of mountains that went behind the villages and the highway. Out in the water there were three islands that extended practically that whole distance. They were named Pag, Rab, and Kirk. For several days I went from one island to the mainland then to the next island.

While the ferry was unloading and loading on the mainland I was on the upper deck looking at the sky, the land, and the water. One piece of human fecal matter was floating beside the ferry. The water was flat calm. On the deck below a crewman came out a door. I looked at him and he at me. He went to the side looking at what I saw in the water. Then he went away grinning at me and to himself.

Going from the island of Pag toward Karlobag on the mainland I could see it was green where the ground was flat, but where the mountains began there was no evidence of there being a single speck of soil up there. On the upper deck of the ferry I asked someone standing beside me why that was? The barren appearance of those mountains was common around there, but I had never seen such a sight. I hoped to understand just enough of his words to get the answer. I was surprised when he responded in perfect English, "Phoenicians came here and took the wood." I leaned on the rail and looked at the mountains. I remembered learning that long ago Phoenician sailing ships dominated the Adriatic Sea. When I turned around to ask him when that was, he was going down metal stairs to the deck below where all the cars were.

On the mainland a group of people from France did a play in French. The audience of a hundred people sat on folding chairs. I was one of them. The other people understood what the actors said and laughed often. I suppose it was a good play. Afterward, outside, on a rock wall I sat talking with a Frenchman who came with the others. He knew a small amount of English. Neither of us really knew who the other person was, and for some unknown reason we talked about international spies. When the conversation ground to a halt we each got up. I went to get another beer, and I saw him no more.

Unlike the interior of the country, on the islands there were many people who spoke English, and they weren't necessarily from English-speaking countries. There were "car camps" where people on vacation lived in trailers or vans equipped with beds and running water. They went to sandy beaches during the day. I met a group of young Germans who said they were all going to a dance club that night. They invited me to go with them. It was like the places at home with loud amplified music. The lights were turned down low. It got crowded. I was having a fine time hopping down the bunny trail. In the late hours of the night I went to get another beer. Four huge Yugoslavian males stood shoulder to shoulder in front of me. I would guess they had been there several decades. It was rather obvious I wanted to get through. When I came up to where they were they turned around in unison and deliberately blocked my path. An altercation with local people wasn't my idea of a good time. I stood there looking at the backs of those four monsters, amazed at their size. I did an end run around all of them without exchanging words or stating a purpose. Afterward, I didn't want to admit to myself there was some hostility in the room directed toward me. Somehow it was not the same from then on, and soon I left. Double doors were opened, and outside there was an empty terrace. The only light on the terrace came from the room where everyone was. A low wall bordered the terrace. I went to the far side and sat on the wall. A manager-type walked a few feet beyond the doors and looked back and forth like he was checking on something. He saw me but didn't look at me. He went back inside. Those four people and the night put me in a defensive mode where all the little men inside me were running to their battle stations. After a few more moments when no one else came outside I spun over the wall and slipped into the night.

When I got off the ferryboat on one island I saw a lone sheep standing on a rock the size of a table. By all standards it was a very odd sight. All the cars had gone ahead of me. The land was semiarid. There were rocks like that one everywhere like it was a crop. From the ferry landing the road went straight between two low hills, and then it curved around the next hill. I was almost to the turn when I saw this animal standing motionless facing in my direction. It was a stone's throw away from the road. I stopped to make sure it was real. Why hadn't anyone seen it? Maybe they did and the thought of touching it or getting involved with it would be too much disruption for them. It didn't show any sign of distress. I looked back in the direction of the ferry thinking help would come from there. It was far away and if I went back, even if I was able to explain help was needed, even then, they would not leave what they were doing to help a dumb animal. I pedaled away perplexed as to how that sheep got there. It couldn't have got up on that rock by itself. Did a misguided shepherd put it there? It would slowly die in the hot sun. Was the animal diseased? Why wouldn't the shepherd kill it quickly? Why put it up on that rock? The whole thing was strange.

Five minutes later the road got flat, and I was moving along at a good pace. Up ahead, close to the road a woman was standing amid a small number of sheep. I stopped to tell her about the one sheep. She didn't speak English. After putting my arms in the shape of a boat bow and baaed like a sheep I think she understood the basic what, where, and when of what I was trying to say. She said the word "Kaput?" I understood that to mean "dead" in German. I shook my head no and said the word "no." I then proceeded down the road. Did she understand me correctly? It probably wasn't her sheep. She had no transportation that I could see. The whole thing about that sheep was strange.

Going away from the coast toward Ljubljana I pedaled uphill for more than half a day. Before that a strong wind blew without letup. The rushing noise was the only sound I could hear. I asked someone how long it would last thinking they listened to the most recent weather report. He answered, "A few more weeks." He said two mighty gods caused the wind. The story was legendary. It had been the explanation for centuries. The truth of the matter was not a concern to him.

The sprockets on the crank and the cluster of sprockets on the rear wheel did not come with the bicycle. Before I left Cincinnati I installed new ones that provided lower gears. Lower gears meant easier pedaling. A small third sprocket up front was the most noticeable change. It was developed for the off-road "mountain bike." It was so low a gear that when pedaling fast, the bicycle would move slower than a person could walk. I named it the "wimp gear." I was in that gear the whole time I went up that mountain. The road went back and forth, but it was still steep. It was like none other I traveled.

A few cars went past. One of them stopped a short distance ahead of me. It was a tiny European car with an equally small utility trailer. I remembered seeing that rig at the bottom of the mountain when I got water. This time the driver came around a curve in the road, passed me, and jammed on the brakes. I didn't like the idea of getting a ride from a stranger on a lonely mountain road, but I could use the ride. When I got near to where the little car was it left. The whole time he was stopped he was looking back over the seat. All that time I kept pedaling the same speed without making any acknowledgment of his presence. I should have made some salutation of some kind.

On a busy road away from the coast, trucks were rolling back and forth. In the middle of the afternoon I stopped at a restaurant beside the busy road and ordered a bottle of water from the waiter. Direct sunlight came through high glass windows and covered the table where I was. In the main area there were no windows. In there six truck drivers in one booth were the only ones in the room. Their trucks were parked outside. I could not see them, but they could see my table. On it was a large greenish-colored glass bottle of water and a drinking glass. There was no mistaking bottled water for something else. It was the same everywhere. They weren't near where I was, but because we were the only ones there, when one of them spoke loudly the words "Engliski" and "pevo" I figured they were saying something to or about the only other person there, me. They were like American cowboys in a television drama about cowboys. I'd get off a stagecoach from the East Coast wearing an English suit. I walk into the Dodge House Saloon holding my round felt hat, sashay up to the bar, and order a sarsaparilla.

When I got up to leave I went inside where they were. There was a question on a few faces. They didn't expect I would come back to where they were. I pushed my stomach out and patted it with both hands. I said, "molto pevo, Molto pevo, m-o-l-t-o pevo." *Pevo* was the word for beer in Croatian. *Molto* meant "many" in Italian. Then I made the pedaling motion with my hands and pointed straight ahead. That was an explicit way to say I was on a bicycle. Again, I said the word "pevo" while putting my two palms together and holding them against my cheek like I was sleeping. They seemed to understand. I was one of the boys. Without further words I left. About ten minutes later down the road one of the trucks passed me. The driver honked his horn twice and looked out the back window. He waved at me as he passed.

I had a room in the big hotel the day before the plane left Ljubljana. The people there saved the bicycle box I brought with me. Late that afternoon I packed the bicycle and other things.

Earlier that day I rode around streets in Ljubljana. An art gallery with fieldstone stairs had a piece of driftwood for sale. An ice-cream parlor where people were standing beside high, small, round tables had an announcement on the wall that seemed to name the time and place of some artful event. A young woman with short dark hair, wearing black silk pajamas, who probably didn't speak a word of English, leaned on one of the tables. One of her arms was lying flat on the table, and the other was holding up a melting ice-cream cone. The elbow of that arm was on the table. She turned her head sideways to lick the drips around the edge.

There were no big stores, only little shops, and the one I went into accepted the American credit card I had. I bought one thing for each child and a few things for Jenny.

That night I walked to a movie house and saw an American movie with Croatian words on the screen. The movie was in English. Not to need to read the words, and understand what was happening was an odd feeling. The movie was about an American who left his home in America. The last words are he is going home to America. In the movie a coal miner says to him after being pushed from the path of a runaway coal car, "Who you trying to save?" And in another place the American says, "It is easy to be a holy man on a mountain top." And in still another, "I got another chance at life. I don't want to waste it on a big house, and a new car every year, and a bunch of friends who want a big house and a new car every year."

In New York the taxi driver was looking for the terminal of the airline that would take me back to Cincinnati. He zoomed around the circle and at one point rolled down the front passenger window and yelled to someone, who was working a short distance away, "Where is TWA Domestic?" The person responded with some direction, and again away we zoomed. If the taxi driver asked for directions like that in Yugoslavia he would probably be ignored. Every encounter began with some sort of expression indicating personal regard. To speak so directly would be thought of as rude.

The first day at home I tugged on Jenny's bathrobe in a direction that led into a room where I had lit more than the usual number of candles. We both sat down close to each other on a small sofa. I was half-facing her on the edge of the seat. Within reach on a low oval table were two wineglasses and a bottle of wine. I took a gulp, and she did too. She was sitting back on the sofa. I leaned toward her and kissed her lips. Our lips were the only parts that touched. One of my hands was on the arm of the sofa, and the other hand was on the other side. I carefully pushed the table farther away and got down on my knees between her knees. Again I kissed her the same way. Both of us tried to get more out of that kiss than any other one. I told her to slide down farther on the couch and put her arms over her head. I untied her robe and opened it to each side. I pulled her down farther by her bent knees. Her legs held up that part of her that was off the sofa. I held her head between my hands and kissed her many times. I began moving my mouth and tongue over her breasts and at the center of them. She was warm, but the warmest place of all was between her legs. I sat cross-legged on the rug, put both my hands on her rump, one on each side, and lifted her up. I moved my tongue where it caused the most excitement. We stopped, sat up, and took more gulps of that wine. She asked me if I was going to take my clothes off. I stood up and kicked off my shoes. I popped a few buttons on my shirt. It took me a few seconds to get naked. When I sat back down her robe was on the floor. I said my favorite point of view was to see her beautiful heart-shaped bottom in the air. To accomplish that I told her to turn around, put her knees on the sofa eight to twelve inches apart, fold her arms on the back of the sofa, rest her head sideways on them, and arch her back. I leaned over and kissed her everywhere, including the hot place. A short while later we both got on the floor. Her back was on the rug and I was on top of her. We moved with such vigor, it seemed the whole house shook. Finally I got up on my knees. We sat back and drank the rest of that wine.

14

Back to Work

As fast as mailboxes were made they were taken to the mail-order company twenty-five miles away. Sales from the catalog were so great, the people who worked there had to tell customers the mailbox was "back ordered." That meant they had to wait. Mailboxes were shipped all across the United States. A product in a catalog had the most demand when it first appeared. Sales would then decrease until the people in charge of the catalog found something else to put in its place. Mailboxes weren't a typical product. Sales continually increased. What happened with mail-order was probably the same as what happened with local installations. One person would get one, and when his neighbors saw how it withstood the slings and arrows of time they also would get one.

The business started with a broken telephone pole. It took three hours to make one mailbox. Over time a new press and better methods were found to do nearly every procedure. The time to make one decreased to an hour. Our in-house motto was "There has got to be a better way," and our outside motto was, "We aim to please." The first hired person had the job of sweeping the floor and making mailbox parts. I spent more time welding. Soon it was like the song said: "The thrill is gone." It was the same work day after day. Needing money to get by and being my own boss kept me going. Many mailboxes went out of there, but there was always a pile of overdue bills on the table. I must have been doing something wrong.

The parts man died from some disease he tried to torment out of existence. The doctor told him one thing and he did the other. He looked gaunt all the time. I asked him if he was suffering from malnutrition. He had more to say about his latest gas and electric bill. He stopped coming to work and a while later I heard from his wife and a government agency that he died. The disease won.

Two more people came to work in the Apple Barn. There was a new parts man and someone I taught to fabricate mailboxes. Once they got familiar with the work I left for Yugoslavia to enjoy my midlife crisis. When I got back there were nearly a hundred mailboxes for me to paint. I told the purchasing agent at the mail-order company you couldn't rush a good thing. Years later they copied the mailbox and passed it off as their own. They had many justifications for their action. They probably would have found a reason either way, but I gave them one. An insider told me when the catalog company first started selling the mailbox the owner of the catalog sent one to a college friend who had a metal fabricating company in North Carolina. His purpose was to find out what it would cost to have the friend make the mailbox. The insider told me when the owner heard the friend would charge twenty dollars more he scoffed and said, "How can he [me] make them for that?" The catalog company began as a one-man operation on a folding table in an airport. By the time I sold mailboxes to them it had grown into a multimillion-dollar company. People who worked there were easygoing, but collectively as a company they were not the same.

Years later the insider and another person started a new mail-order company. Two big outfits were selling the mailbox. The new company quickly became a financial success. It was then the first company copied the mailbox and no longer bought mine. The price of the copy was the same, but not for long. The insider who was now doing the new company had his assistant telephone and say a copy was on the scene and we should meet to discuss "strategy." Jenny and I went there. The assistant was there. We all sat at one end of a large oval table. I said to the insider in an amused way what he had said to me years before about how the owner of the first company sent a Veeders Mailbox to a sheet metal factory to learn if it could be done cheaper. I hadn't talked much to the insider since then. The insider had become the top executive of a financially successful company. When I said what I said about the owner of the other catalog he looked at his assistant, then at me, and said I was mistaken. A pure business meeting was all that remained. If I had a seat belt on my chair I would have buckled up. He wanted to know if I could lower the price so he could sell the mailbox for less. He said the volume of sales would increase with the greater number of catalogs they planned to send out. I told him what we needed in the way of money to pay bills and put food on the table

During the months that followed we made more mailboxes and less money than ever before. The price was too low. The price of the Veeders Mailbox was much lower than the copy, but after a year the price of the copy was made lower than the already low price of the Veeders Mailbox. I knew what it cost to make them. They were trying to starve me out. When I was gone their price would go through the roof. The Veeders Mailbox and the copy looked the same. They even copied the shape of the flag. The flag was a required part of a roadside mailbox, required by the U.S. Postal Service, but ours had a unique shape. I wrote a letter to the head man saying it was business as usual to copy the mailbox, but I didn't think it was business as usual to copy the shape of the flag. I said I always thought he was, if nothing else, a fair-minded person and not to stop being one now. In my own sweet way I was asking him to dream up his own flag. He never replied, and nothing changed. In his catalog he was quoted as saying other mailboxes were "imitators." That took a lot of gall. It was as if the Veeders Mailbox never existed. Jenny and I realized there was a need to get protection from someone passing his work off as ours. We came up with a logo, or mark that went on everything we did. It was like a fingerprint or a DNA test. Gretchen drew it at camp in Indiana. It's on the cover of this book.

For the first time Jenny and I started getting money from our parents. The tax department called it unearned income. The first year it was just enough to get a shiny new motorcycle. The mailbox business was breaking even, or so it seemed. The first and last winter I had the motorcycle I kept it propped up on the kickstand in the Apple Barn. I shined it up and sat back to admire it under the lights. Among motorcycle people it was a "full-dress touring bike." That year ABS antilock brakes were on two models made by that company. No other motorcycle had that feature. I didn't buy it for the brakes, but that might be one of the reasons I didn't get killed when a small truck went left of center, causing a head-on collision.

A few years after the motorcycle wreck the second mail-order company stopped buying the mailbox. There was no money to spare. Any unearned income either of us got went into the bank and it was rationed out as needed to keep the business going. It always needed some extra cash. Money wherever it came from made it possible for me to come down to this dry, heated, air-conditioned, well-lit room in the new mailbox building and write this book. I would do it under a bridge if that were all there was. It scares Jenny when I talk that way. She thinks mailboxes are our life, and when I try to convince her otherwise I can see the look on her face that I might have hit my head too hard on the road.

The mailbox that replaced ours in the second company's catalog was a copy made in Sandusky, Ohio. That mailbox had its own flag shape and weighed much less. The bracket on the bottom fit a four-inch-square post. I never considered they copied the Veeders Mailbox the same way the other guy did, although many design elements were the same. They copied the concept of a heavy-duty, high-end mailbox. When I started making mailboxes there was the Veeders Mailbox and on the other end of the spectrum there was the regular soup can mailbox. Nothing was in between except possibly one type of mailbox with cardinals that went to a different market. All sorts of copies of the concept have evolved. There are plastic ones and metal ones, ugly ones and pretty ones, pliable ones and rigid ones. The Veeders Mailbox never appealed to a mass market. It is clean-looking, strong enough, simple enough, and more expensive. When people on the telephone ask what it looks like I say it is "lean and mean."

At one end of the Apple Barn on either side there are two big doors. Back in the days when orchards surrounded the place a tractor and wagon could drive in one door, deposit a load of apples, and continue out the other door. In the middle of the building on each side there were two smaller doors. One was shut permanently and one was our entrance and exit door. It took muscle to slide it open, and if a person wasn't familiar with it they would think it was latched. There was no buzzer or bell. A knock was futile. The door was made of tongue-and-groove wood. Occasionally, someone who wanted to get in would pound on it with all their strength, and then we would hear.

Before the mailboxes were copied and when we were making them as fast as possible, two people came to see us. They were trim and proper-looking. Each one of them had a satchel.

That day sparks were flying in two welding booths. I was spray painting in an area designed for that purpose. It had an exhaust fan. I wore a paint suit and paint hood over my head that had a remote air supply. The parts man was standing by a drill press making hinges. It was winter. A 350,000-BTU furnace went continuously when we were working. At night a heat lamp kept the water pipes from freezing in a tiny insulated room where there was a toilet and basin. Those things were always there, but the furnace wasn't. It came from an automobile service station that was torn down to make room for a housing development. The paint hood was connected to an air hose. When I wore it I could only go as far as the hose reached. I had just walked out of the paint room with the paint hood off my head when I saw the entrance door move. I went over, opened it, and there were the two people. Much racket was behind me. One of them said. "I see you're busy. We'll come back at another time." They turned and left. When they said that, all I had time to say was, "Bye." It was sunny outside; the snow was melting off the roof. I rolled the door shut to keep out the cold. They didn't ask about an overdue bill. They didn't say what was on their mind. They just said what they said and left.

The average time someone worked for me was three years. When I wanted to find a new worker I couldn't do it by simply putting a job description in the newspaper and finding a person the next day. Sometimes teaching someone how to make a mailbox took a month or more. My job went from making mailboxes to managing people.

We took breaks from work, and in the course of the conversation I'd hear about cars that didn't work, bills that were overdue, and women who ran off. I had my own problems. Early on I decided when we didn't have any problems it was when we were dead. How we dealt with the problem, not the problem itself, made us what we were.

The people in the Apple Barn were paid well. They had only one benefit, and it wasn't exactly a customary one. An employee could take a day off for no reason. One job didn't depend on another job like in a production line. If we were busy they had to make up the work. At other companies the customary benefits were health insurance, a retirement plan, paid vacations, paid sick days, and paid holidays.

They didn't get nickel and dime raises, either. A worker earned what the work he did was worth on the job market. If they wanted benefits they could buy them themselves. When I became aware how much benefits meant I was more graceful about how I talked like a ballerina with tutu and toe shoes.

A good time to try benefits came when two people quit simultaneously. After that each person got benefits that were paid from their paycheck whether they liked it or not. The take home amount was less. After a year I decided benefits had little to do with a person leaving or staying and they were dropped. When a person was ready to quit they quit. A job in a building with barn doors and a big cornfield outside didn't have the same allure that a real factory job did for a young man who had never been there before.

People with raw ability and little else were the easiest to teach. That was not true for someone with all kinds of certification papers and welding experience. An accomplished welder sooner or later always said they knew a better way to do something. The first few times I heard that I let them do it the way they wanted, but after two or three times it became clear they were wasting their time and my money. I took a new approach. I'd say, "There might be a better way, but since I was making them when you were in diapers give me some credit. Learn my way first. When you are comfortable doing that, then show me the better way."

The inexperienced welder was the easiest to teach and to have make the mailbox. Within three years they were experienced welders. I tried not to mind when they left for the big factory job. Everybody had a responsibility to better themselves. It got so when I had a production problem there were many people out there who could make the mailbox and one of them was always available. They worked weekends or nights until I got things straightened out. They had a key. Theft was never an issue.

The number of mailboxes a welder was supposed to get done each day was based on eight hours of work divided by the time it took me to make one mailbox. The worth of each mailbox was determined by what it would cost for an experienced welder to do the same job. If they needed more money all they had to do was make more mailboxes. Everyone, including me, was happier. I never said they had to start before dawn, but usually when I got there they didn't even look up, they were working so fast. By lunchtime they were done and went home for the day. If there was a mistake, a welder could identify himself by the welds and had to fix it on his own time.

At the beginning of each week I painted all the mailboxes made the previous week. Wednesday I packaged them and delivered them to the shipping dock of the mail-order company. Thursday and Friday I took care of any essential nonproductive business.

The little insulated room with the toilet and washbasin was by the entrance door. We cleaned it by first scrubbing the plumbing fixtures with a plastic abrasive material, and when that was done the entire room, the floor, and everything in it got power flushed with water spray from a high-pressure nozzle on a garden hose. Water on the floor was then swept out the entrance door. On Friday I also cleaned up the paint room and carried in the mailboxes that were going to be painted the next week.

For some reason I wasn't going to be there one Friday. There was only one welder at that time, and I asked him if he would power flush the little insulated room. He was working when I asked him, and he didn't answer yes or no. I thought that was because he was busy. On break the following Monday I said no one cleaned it out, and I told him to do it the following Friday. It was a thrill to clean that way, and I wanted him to experience the feeling. Also, I was afraid he thought he was beyond cleaning a toilet. His work was good. He hardly ever had to make corrections. He made a good mailbox. For a year and a half, like clockwork, without any interruption, he came to work, finished his work, and went home in the early afternoon. He had never cleaned the toilet room but knew enough about how it was done to figure it out. It wasn't very complicated. I asked him if he'd rather do it some other day and without waiting for a reply told him by the end of the day on Friday if that room wasn't cleaned then that would be his last day. I told him if he acted on the assumption I didn't mean what I said it would be difficult for both of us. I didn't take any more breaks that week and had no occasion to talk with him.

When I was teaching him how to make a mailbox we sat down to drink some water and he told me he was a Jehovah's Witness. I knew that was a religious group. He said very soon Armageddon would happen. The story about Chicken Little came to mind, but I didn't say anything. If his religion made him who he was, then it couldn't be complete foolishness.

It seemed all of the young people I worked with had problems of one kind or another. When I kept hearing them my first impulse was to give advice or help. A few times I would hold up my hand and say I had problems of my own, and couldn't get involved in their personal lives. Then I realized they didn't expect or want me to get involved in their lives. I was hearing about it because I was sitting there. We worked close together. I heard about a parent who cheated at bingo and got caught, a girlfriend's child, a father who left. I'd hear about wives who ran off with truck drivers, guns, bar room fights, police, and jail. One person who was an exceptionally good worker had a drinking problem. I bailed him out of jail and told him the only reason he was having a problem keeping a job was that every few months he got all drunk and missed over a week's work. One time he put his fist through a glass fish tank.

The Jehovah's Witness lived in a trailer park in Milford, Ohio, with several children and a rosy-cheeked wife. In comparison to the others his situation seemed rather wholesome. She worked in a nearby dairy store. The one time I met her she was wearing a handmade dress. He often talked about a congregation near where he lived. The day after we talked about Armageddon he gave me a book called *Revelations, Its Grand Climax at Hand.* He was serious about giving it to me. It came with a remark about how it would tell me more about Armageddon. I thanked him. Talking about Armageddon was not why I went over to his workstation. I asked him how much welding wire was left on the spool in his machine. A few minutes later when I got in my truck to do an errand the book was still in my hand. I flipped through the pages before putting it down on the seat. The Jehovah's Witnesses printed it. There were many illustrations in bright colors. Jesus Christ never posed for a painting and cameras didn't exist then. The pictures of him in the book weren't my idea of what he looked like. In the Cincinnati art museum there was a painting of him dead being taken down from the cross. In that painting he appeared to be a very ordinary and common man. That image stuck with me and when I saw another idea of what Jesus looked like in that book I thought the whole book was another idea. Anyway, to me books were a thing of the past. Now I had no time for idle pursuits. I had more pressing things to do, such as paying bills and raising a family. I didn't read books anymore. Some people could do that, but I wasn't one of them. I put the book away on the back of a shelf at home.

It was Friday and the toilet was still not cleaned. I was there at noon to get a head start painting the mailboxes made that week. I had the paint suit on and as I was about to put the hood over my head stopped and went out in the shop area. I told him I was going to start painting and didn't want to stop in the middle of what I was doing to see if the little insulated room had been scrubbed and power flushed. I said for him to tell me if he was going to do it and, if not, then go home now. He said he wasn't going to do it; he hung up his welding jacket and left. That was the end of that. I started painting and thought how there are plenty of good fish in the sea.

Our children went to a school operated with tax dollars. In the United States it was known as a public school. Each day they went there, played with other children, learned to read, write, and do arithmetic. Children were required by law to be educated so they would hopefully become useful members of society. The law said as long as they got educated, it didn't matter how it was done. Public school didn't cost any money. All we had to do was get them there on time. Private school cost money, and when thinking about doing it ourselves it didn't take a whole lot of imagination to see teaching our own children would take professional quality plus lots of time, neither of which we had. The school where our children went, like every other public school, was locally controlled. Some of the people who oversaw how the money was spent had school-age children. Everything about public education was a function of money. Constantly decisions were made about things such as whether to start a new soccer team or use the same money to give teachers a pay increase. An involved parent was a welcome sight, but ultimately it was the elected school officials who decided where the money would go. What they said before the election determined if they got elected.

From talking to children, parents, and other people I was convinced my children were in a good public school. My own personal experience with formal education was somewhat tumultuous. Just walking down the halls of that place made me sweat. I didn't get very involved with what went on there. Maybe that isn't the way it should be, but that is the way it was. Jenny got involved. She knew the names of all the teachers and talked to them often. A few times I went to a concert or a school play. Some students did a musical solo or were able to recite all of their lines without help, but most of them sang songs with hundreds of others. My children were always goofing off in the back. Once when parents were filing out of the auditorium in an orderly manner I saw some vaguely familiar people and asked them in a critical way if they were starved for entertainment. Our three children were at an age when they thought their parents could do no wrong. It was a formative time. I became aware how much influence we had. There were five years separating the eldest child from the youngest. They did what we did.

It only lasted a few years. After that each of them made deliberate attempts to do things their own way and have their own opinions. They started to question what I said. Until then, their unconditional adoration made me especially aware of the parental responsibility I had. They were like a sponge soaking up whatever information was around them. One time I was watching television and Sam came into the room and sat down on the edge of the sofa to see what was so captivating and entrancing about the cathode ray tube. An automobile commercial showed a particular type of automobile suspended in the air revolving around in a futuristic setting. The announcer said this and that about the car and then in the same important, authoritative, booming voice he said it had four doors. Sammy looked at me with a startled expression and very seriously and loudly exclaimed, "Four doors!"

They lapped up exposure to things like four-door cars, but they weren't getting any spiritual exposure. The law of the land said state-run schools were not to sponsor prayer. That resulted when someone who insisted God didn't exist went to the highest court in the land and got a decision in their favor. It affected everybody. The ruling wasn't about the existence of God but the guarantee of religious freedom. In effect the ruling said the government could not legally mix itself with religion. It made sense to me. One person's God might not be the same as another's, and what government of and by humans could presume to say who God is or is not. So where my children went to school no spiritual matters were discussed.

I didn't have a pronounced spiritual part in my life. Spiritual thought was always around me, and by osmosis I got some. It was not something I could deposit in a bank, and on a worldwide basis I was aware that religious conviction was the cause of much grief and human suffering. I didn't know if it had to be like that, but it was like that. I wanted my children to have religious understanding.

We all got dressed up on Sunday, packed ourselves in the family car, and went to the "family service" at the church where I went with my father so many years ago. Back then my mother refused to go and never said why. She always asked about the sermon when we got back. It was not as if I had never been there since I was a child. Over the years Jenny and I went for baptisms, weddings, and funerals, but when we went to the family service it was the first time in all those years I went for a regularly scheduled event. It lasted forty-five minutes.

At that service once a month the preacher, who was not the same one as before, asked all the children with birthdays that month to stand up front and face the congregation. Then he went from child to child asking some key questions. The month of Gretchen's birthday she went up front. When the preacher got to her she did not know the answer to his question. He asked her what the date of her birthday was. He didn't stop asking her. It was a simple question. He asked her a third time. All the other children said when their birthday was. She couldn't take the humiliation anymore. She broke ranks with the other children and walked down the whole length of the aisle to where we were sitting. Her face was beet red, and her shoulders were raised up as she tried to contain herself from crying. Afterward someone came up to us and sympathetically said that was just what she would have done. In turn I talked to the preacher. He was friendly toward me. I suppose it was that he didn't know any better. I had a hard time understanding how an adult could be so insensitive and unaware of making a child feel so stupid.

The family service was informal compared to the other two services. The preacher walked up and down the aisle. He instructed everyone to clap their hands in an exact cadence. Hard as I tried, I never got the number of claps correct. Sometimes the only sound was me clapping. We weren't the smartest people there.

Once someone asked me why we went each week. That was a question I could answer. I said we wanted to learn about Jesus Christ. The next week and for several weeks after that the preacher took a moment to review where Jesus Christ was from, where he was born, and a few other facts even the Roman Empire wouldn't deny. Also, each week someone told a Bible story. The family service was geared toward children. Someone said if I wanted more I should go to one of the other two services. I never did. My efforts sort of fizzled out, and we stopped going.

15

The Truth

It wasn't long after that an elderly lady came to the door and when I asked her what she wanted she said something about mankind's hope and God's purpose. My wife and children were running around the floor. I invited her into the room. She had a Bible in her hand. She had gray hair and was wearing a warm coat. The sun was shining. I said in a friendly way that she picked a nice day to talk about religion. She agreed and said she also picked some not so nice days. Jenny came over and listened to her also. She said mankind's hope was everlasting life and God's purpose was to restore paradise conditions on earth like in the Garden of Eden described in the Hebrew Scripture of the Bible. She held the Bible in her hand and said twice, "This is the truth."

I didn't say it, but when she said that it reminded me of a philosophy class I took in college. One week the idea was that nothing was true and everyone did what was right for them. I wrote a paper about that, but it said there was possibly one absolute truth, that s___ (human excrement) stinks. When the lady with the Bible in her hand said the Bible was the truth several times I also thought about the expression "dense and unenlightened people are notoriously confident they have a monopoly on truth." I didn't want her to talk anymore. I didn't want to be rude to this well-meaning lady, but I was trying to think of a tactful way to get her on her way out the door. The conversation started going in circles. She read something from the Bible that said Jehovah (her God) would crush all the other kingdoms and set up a kingdom that would last to time indefinite. I didn't argue with her. I asked her what made her so sure the Bible was the truth, and then I realized I was just leading her on to say more. I wanted her to leave. After a few more minutes she did leave. The next day Jenny said the woman stopped at our house long enough to leave a bright orange little book with instructions that Jenny should read it and give it to me. It was easy to read and titled *The Bible, God's Word or Man's?* Jenny gave it to me when I got home, and I flipped through the pages. Then before and after supper I read it entirely. I remember thinking, *Wouldn't it be the story of all time if on the evening news they said there were some absolute truths after all, and, unknown to us, our self-important activities were nothing more than getting a spare part for a broken-down spaceship on one of the moons of Jupiter? Did an absolute truth exist?* I couldn't waste my time with such thoughts. I had "miles to go before I slept and miles to go before I slept."

I couldn't figure out the meaning of life. Thinking about that didn't do anything for mailboxes. Nobody else seemed terribly concerned, and like them I had bills to pay. What would the judge say if I told him modern civilization was no more than a fuzzy mold on a peach? I would rather spend my free time polishing the motorcycle that nearly killed me.

The older woman became a familiar sight at our door. She belonged to a religious group named Jehovah's Witnesses. One time after dinner I was in the other room engulfed in a meaningless television program. Jenny came in the room and said the Jehovah's Witness lady was at the door. I told her to tell her I was busy. I wanted to see how the half-hour program ended.

Another time when the Jehovah's Witness lady came to our house she asked us if we would like to study the Bible. I said we meant to do something like that as a family but got sidetracked. She got two books out of her bag. The yellow one was titled *My Book of Bible Stories* and the red one was *You Can Live Forever on Paradise Earth.* She said she would come to our house each week at a time that fit everyone's schedule. We decided upon Tuesday at 7:00 P.M. She suggested the entire family do a story or two from the yellow book and then Jenny and I do the red book. She explained that no book was in place of the Bible and that the two books in her bag were Bible-study aids. Sitting down once a week and going headfirst into the Bible seemed highly concentrated and worth more than any weekly television show. Eventually I came to realize there is a reality that is the same for everyone whether they like it or not.

Before it sank in and I was carried away by the enormity of the situation I was lukewarm about efforts to learn what the Bible said. It was definitely nice for all of us to sit down as a family and read a Bible story. We would each take a turn reading a paragraph, and then the Jehovah's Witness lady would ask a question. The questions she asked were in small type at the bottom of each page. The stories in the Bible dealt with a person like Rehab, who was a common prostitute in a fortified city. She helped some Israelite spies. After the Bible story the children would go upstairs and do schoolwork. Jenny and I would go through part of the red book. It dealt with subjects like the nature of death, what hell is, what heaven is, and the meaning of many other terms in the Bible.

We read that the widely held belief that God, Jesus Christ, and the Holy Ghost are three persons in one is not a Bible teaching and that it most likely began at the Council of Nicaea in the third century, where Constantine, the emperor of Rome, wanted to solidify his empire.

Years later when I was able to talk about it I put those facts to a person who led a congregation of people in a popular Christian religion. Her reply was, "What difference does it make?"

When I first studied, little things kept piling up until finally it was just like a break in the dam. I wanted to leave it alone. On some days when the Jehovah's Witness lady was coming if there was a button to push to have her not come I would have pushed it.

She brought me an article about someone who dropped bombs on people living in Dresden, Germany, during World War Two. That someone was from England, and between the times he dropped bombs he asked a chaplain, "Whose side is God on?" The chaplain said God was on their side. The man wondered to himself why the German soldiers had the words "God is with us" inscribed on their belt buckles. They also thought God was on their side.

The man became an atheist, and long after the war two Jehovah's Witnesses knocked on his door. He asked them the same question, expecting the same answer. He asked, "Whose side is God on?" They flipped through the pages of the Bible and read these words spoken by Christ to his followers: "I am giving you a new commandment, that you love one another; just as I have loved you, that you also love one another. By this all will know that you are my disciples, if you have love among yourselves."

Also, she told me a story she heard from what she called a spiritual sister. The sister was talking to a woman at the woman's front door. The woman said, "The name Jehovah doesn't appear in my Bible." The sister said, "Maybe it does. Why don't you go get your Bible and let's see?" The woman left and returned with her Bible. The sister knew in that translation the name Jehovah appeared three times. She found one of the places in the Eighty-third Psalm. The woman took the Bible back, ripped the page out, snapped it closed, and said, "Now it doesn't say that." Later on I was with a spiritual brother who said it was a general rule that if a person wasn't humble, honest, and hungry they would believe what they wanted and no amount of reason would change that fact. The weight of time has caused many ideas to become traditions. The origin of the tradition is of little concern.

The Bible was first written in Hebrew and Greek, and while there are no original manuscripts that exist, the earliest known copies give almighty God a proper name, which first appeared thousands of times in the earliest known transcripts. In South America the name Jehovah was on a building block of a church constructed long before there was a religious group called Jehovah's Witnesses. After a photograph of it appeared in a Jehovah's Witness magazine it was removed, presumably by the hierarchy of that church. In recent years many translators have completely deleted the name of the Christian God. Why is a matter of speculation. Ask a Jehovah's Witness and without much hesitation they will answer in one way or another that Satan makes them do it. The Bible says much about Satan. Mainly Satan is misleading the entire inhabited earth.

More than anything else what happens after death was different from what I had heard. Most of my questions at first were about what happens after death. When it became overwhelming I put the issue aside. What was going to happen was going to happen. I was more interested in living day to day around here. I saw no sense in getting worked up thinking about what happens after death. If I was in the next life, that would be icing on the cake, or maybe this is the icing and "that which is to come" is the cake.

The only time I had these thoughts was when the Jehovah's Witness lady came, but I kept them to myself. I didn't think there were any easy answers. I didn't think any of what I was learning had any tremendous importance, simply because no one else did.

When I bought the motorcycle I was in a club of people who had one or more motorcycles made by the same company that made mine. A newsletter from them said there was going to be a two-day meeting the last weekend in April beside the Snake River near Cape Girardeau, Missouri. That was several hundred miles from where I lived. I was itching to travel on my motorcycle. It was shined up under a cover in the Apple Barn. Spring was coming. I made plans to go.

16

Wake-Up

The day finally came when I went down the road on the motorcycle. Jenny said she looked out the window and watched me leave. She told me a few months later that she never liked "that thing." The previous autumn right after I got it we took it out for picnics in a cow field or two. It seemed like we had a good time then. When it was gone, a wreck in my parents' barn, was the first time I heard her come out and say she never liked that thing.

I packed camping gear in three rigid carrying cases on the motorcycle. There was one on each side of the back wheel, and the third one was over the rear wheel. In them were clothes, a small tent, a cook stove, food, water bottles, and whatever else I needed. There wasn't enough room in them for a pillow and a sleeping bag. Those things were in a heavy waterproof bag tied on back. A small lockable compartment near the handlebars was where things such as maps, money, a driver's license, and paper were kept. There were recording tapes in there also. The motorcycle had a remote-controlled tape player. When I listened to songs they were about being strange, about riders on the storm, and about how "into this house we're born; into this world we're thrown."

Downstream from Cincinnati I took a small ferry across the Ohio River. From there I went on Route 8 past Louisville, past the entrance of Fort Knox, back across the Ohio River, and on practically the same bridge I went across the Mississippi River into Missouri. After going a few more miles I arrived at the campgrounds beside the Snake River. There were hundreds of motorcycles.

It took all day Friday to get there. I stopped only once by a rock wall along a road in Kentucky. I sat on the wall and made a cup of coffee. I wasn't dying for the coffee so much as the excuse to make it right there.

At the campground I set up my tent and made supper on the one-burner stove I had. There was still daylight. Afterward I walked the full length of the campgrounds and looked at all the motorcycles. There were some old ones. The only two times I spoke was, first, a conversation I had when I signed in and, second, with the owner of an old motorcycle. I camped in a place across the road from the registration table where there were no other campers. The motorcycle experience had been one of solitude, and that continued. Saturday morning I awoke after the sun had risen, fired up the stove, made a big breakfast, and went to see the area. I saw the Mississippi River up close for the first time. It was moving very fast.

When my mother's brother came down there several days later he saw the Mississippi River up close, too. In a letter a year or so later he wrote how mighty it was. It was tremendous compared to all else. I got back to camp late in the day, had some dinner, and crawled into the sleeping bag. Sunday, I got up at the crack of dawn. That was the last day for the motorcycle and almost for me.

Sunday morning I packed the bags and left. I remember driving onto the paved road and making a concentrated effort to be careful of the gravel. I don't remember anything else or what happened during the next month. My plan was to go north in the state of Missouri, cross the Mississippi River at the first bridge, and go home on the highway. I didn't get far.

According to the accident report and what an eyewitness said, at 7:30 A.M. a sixteen-year-old boy fell asleep while driving home from working the third shift at a popcorn factory. The pickup truck he was driving went left of center and hit the motorcycle head-on.

A nurse traveling in the same direction was in the car behind me. She said what happened. It was a straight section of road. The person driving the truck weaved over the centerline several times before he got to me. I was not going very fast when we hit. The motorcycle never went down. On the initial impact the open-face helmet I was wearing came off. I was catapulted up in the air. I never impacted with the accident vehicle. By the time I came down both motorcycle and truck had gone past. I landed on the pavement.

The nurse got out of her car and went to where I was. There were broken bones sticking through the skin on my legs. My face was cut from hitting the pavement. Doctors later described one of my problems as a "closed head injury." Much later my brother told me the nurse told him I was irate because she would not let me go see if the motorcycle was all right.

In Cincinnati the previous autumn I rode with a motorcycle group who called themselves the Over-the-Hill-Gang. After the accident a few of them went down to Cape Girardeau to get the motorcycle. It was in a junkyard. They took it back to Cincinnati and put it in a barn at Markin Farm. Five months later, hobbling around on crutches. I stood at an open stall door and saw that it was beyond repair. I telephoned the man who sold it to me and told him he could have it if he did the hauling. He was there with a trailer that night. When he saw it he shook his head back and forth. He said he had never seen one that bad where the guy lived. The next time I saw him he told me the only part on that motorcycle he salvaged was the rear mono-shock. Everything else was destroyed.

The odometer said it had 3,000 miles. One of the Over-the-Hill-Gang members had traveled more than 200,000 miles on a motorcycle. He told me there were two kinds of riders: those who have had accidents and those who are going to have accidents. He said most of them were either under eighteen and didn't care or were over sixty-five and it didn't make any difference.

My brother talked with the nurse at length about the accident. Months later when I asked him what she was like he said I would like her for all the wrong reasons.

The ambulance would normally be far from the accident scene, but on that day and time it was nearby on another call. In a few minutes it arrived. The boy and me were taken to the hospital. I don't know if I was conscious or unconscious.

When we got to the hospital emergency room a doctor recognized stitches in the boy's head. He put them there a week earlier, only then when the boy fell asleep the car he was driving went across the road into the woods.

I was what a nurse back in a Cincinnati hospital would term

"a mess." I broke more than twenty bones. The number varied depending on who was asked, but no one said fewer than twenty. In the same way I was told the number of medications I was taking in the Cape Girardeau hospital exceeded twenty. No wonder I was delirious. Jenny wrote down what the doctors said and the few things I said.

Like a person of the "nations" I was immediately hooked up to a blood supply.

That day a doctor telephoned Jenny to say what happened and what he needed to do. I was like Humpty Dumpty in the children's story. It says: "Humpty Dumpty sat on a wall. Humpty Dumpty had a great fall. All the king's horses and all the king's men couldn't put Humpty together again."

In Cincinnati long after the accident a friend told Jenny that when she was sitting beside an orthopedic surgeon on the bleachers she said to him, "Remember the X rays of that guy who you said would never walk again? Well there he is," and she pointed across the soccer field to where I was walking to retrieve a child.

She was not the sort of person who readily accepted something that was not explainable in a scientific manner. Months earlier at a gathering of people where she was I asked her how her certification to be a schoolteacher was going. She said she was learning about evolution. I asked her, "What about the possibility of everything being created by a supreme being?" She said she'd rather believe what could be proved, and she went away to talk with someone else. So who did put Humpty Dumpty back together again and, more importantly, why?

There were two doctors who kept track of my progress. One of them did a second operation to reconstruct my hip. After the operation he told Jenny the next seventy-two hours would be the most critical, and during that time I went into a coma. Somewhere along the line I also had a stroke caused by all the broken bones. Jenny needed comic relief. During the first few days the only one she talked to for any amount of time was the doctor. She joked with him, and on Friday in the course of conversation she asked him, "When is Jocko coming out of his coma?" In his reply he named a certain person who at the time was the vice-president of the United States, and who went to college with the doctor at Vanderbilt University. The doctor said, "When ——— is president." That weekend it was reported in the news that the vice-president was president for twenty minutes while the president underwent surgery. I came out of my coma the same day. On Monday Jenny questioned the doctor, and she said he said like he was scared that he wasn't going to say that anymore.

In the following weeks at different times all of my siblings came to Cape Girardeau. Also during that month a cousin, one aunt, one uncle, Jenny's father, and a few of her friends came there for a few days. I must have been expected to die. One sister was convinced I tried to kill myself. Jenny was there the whole month. Our three children were with her parents in Cincinnati. The weekend of my accident my parents left Markin Farm to live permanently in Maine. That might seem like strange behavior, but as always they were extremely pragmatic, particularly my mother. What could they do at my bedside except gum up the works? What they did do was buy airplane tickets for my three sisters and one brother.

Jenny said of all the people who went, my brother was the most helpful. It wasn't anything he said or did; rather it was his being there. He came twice. The first time was right after the accident, and the other time was before the second operation. Jenny said he walked up to the bed, lifted the sheet, looked at my black-and-blue body, put the sheet back down, and said, "At least your d___ is OK."

Without opening my eyes I replied, "Butt out." Jenny said I mumbled a few things earlier, but that was the first thing I said that was a sign I was mentally all right.

Earlier in the day she wrote down that I told her to put the letter *A* on my forehead. Months later I read for the first time about marks on foreheads. The Bible describes a mark on the forehead of Satan's people and God's people. In Bible times the owner of a slave often put a mark on the forehead of a slave to show whose property they were. At the time I didn't know anything about the subject of foreheads or marks as they are represented in the Bible. I don't know why I mumbled those words, but I did.

The whole time I was in that hospital I was in the intensive care unit (ICU). The way Jenny described it to me, the beds were in an arc around a nurse and from where she sat she could monitor the vital signs of each ICU patient. A nurse was there day and night. Each bed was separated from the next one by a curtain. Jenny said there was an "aura" around my bed. She said it wasn't just her, because one of the nurses said something about it also.

It was reassuring to be told I was heavily medicated, because that explains a poster I saw every day that Jenny says was not there. It showed a soldier wearing a helmet and holding a small dog. I always thought at some point they were going to give me one of those dogs. A month after I got there I was transported by air taxi in a bed to another hospital in Cincinnati. When I left I expected to get a little dog. Also, I thought the hospital was adept in handling trauma victims because there was an army base nearby. Jenny was so polite when she said neither of those things existed. Why I had delusions about the military I don't know. I never considered when I was in the U.S. army or anytime afterward that I was any kind of a military man.

There were people who went out of their way to make Jenny feel comfortable. Traveling from St. Louis to Cape Girardeau she was on one airplane and then another that had mechanical problems. Both airplanes while speeding down the runway suddenly decelerated, turned around, and came back to the terminal. Finally the passengers took a bus. While they were waiting, Jenny sat beside two people who were on the two airplanes but whom she had not met. Jenny described the woman as tall. She never described the husband. They had been married a long time and belonged to a motorcycle group that called themselves the Christian Motorcycle Club. The husband and wife traveled extensively, usually on one motorcycle. Jenny said the woman showed her around the town and where to get a room at a motel within walking distance of the hospital.

Many mornings when Jenny got to the hospital Christian motorcycle people with leather jackets were already there. They weren't allowed to go into the ICU. I was hallucinating in there. Jenny saw the tall woman and her husband practically every day, and when there was no family she went to their house for supper. The tall woman gave her a photograph of the motorcycle people standing in a circle. Each one was facing toward the center with their head down. They appeared to be in the woods. Jenny said she was told it was a "prayer circle" and that the motorcycle gang was praying for me. When I saw the photograph back in Cincinnati and heard what it was I was amazed, because I never met any of those people.

At home I heard at the church where we clapped hands the preacher during the early-morning service asked everyone for a moment of silent prayer as he did every Sunday morning. The Sunday after my accident when he said that, the name "Jocko" reverberated around the congregation in a barely audible way. I knew some of those people by name only. I didn't know much else about them. They were mostly my parents' generation and/or people who got mailboxes.

The Christmas following the accident I was on crutches looking at Christmas trees for sale. Someone I hadn't seen for a long time, who sold industrial coatings in fifty-gallon drums, drove past, stopped, rolled down his window, and with a big smile on his face said how it was good to see me. Then he abruptly said, "I prayed for you." By then I was well aware there was more going on in this world than modern science, although I didn't know much else. I thought it was nice of him to say what he did. I said to him, "I'm sure every little bit helped."

At the Cape Girardeau hospital there was an old man who volunteered to work there without pay. He and Jenny became dear friends, and for several years afterward, at least once a year, they wrote back and forth. My aunt met him at the house where he and his wife lived. Jenny said he was a wise man.

The month I was in the Cape Girardeau hospital the Jehovah's Witness lady in Cincinnati fell. She had to have a hip replacement. Before she went in the hospital she telephoned a congregation of Jehovah's Witness near Cape Girardeau and spoke of my situation. Jenny said a Jehovah's Witness doctor came there, talked to her, and said I was in good hands. It could not be denied that the thoughts and/or prayers of so many people were real.

A doctor in Cincinnati said the doctor there did exceptionally good work. A relative and a few others used the words *miracle* and *miraculous* to describe my recovery.

When Jenny went to settle up with the husband and wife

who ran the motel one of them said the bill was already paid. My cousin paid for the whole month.

The first memory I have of that time is leaving Cape Girardeau. There was much discussion near the plane. Jenny said later the pilot wanted payment. My aunt who was there paid him. He must have wanted to make sure it got in the bank. That would explain why I saw him hand paper to someone who was not going on the airplane.

We flew to a small airport in Cincinnati. Jenny and the pilot sat up front. A nurse and I were in the back. Even with folding wheels on the bed, getting it into the airplane was difficult. It was a tight fit. The airplane had a piston engine on each wing. It must have had radar too. We flew at night in the pouring rain. Jenny said the pilot was flying up, under, and around clouds the whole time. Rainwater was coming through the side window where she sat. The pilot told her to squeeze repeatedly a rubber bulb that pumped air into a space between the glass. She had to do that every few minutes.

I was feeling no pleasure or pain. I could fly if the plane became inoperable. Whether I could have carried passengers is another question. It was a rough ride. The pilot must have been practicing aerobatics. There were many jolts and he made a few evasive maneuvers. The rain stopped when we landed. The tarmac at the Cincinnati airport was shiny and wet.

I went through the entire medical system without paying a dime. When it was over a doctor explained it this way. He said a person (in the United States) would be taken care of in an emergency without consideration for their ability to pay.

I often read and heard how a person would be "stabilized," but if during that time it was learned the person could not pay then every effort would be made to move them elsewhere. I had no health insurance and no money. During my time in the hospitals no one spoke of money. No one asked if I did or didn't have money or health insurance. I had neither. But for five months I received the royal treatment. I don't know if the state police cited the boy for a traffic violation. He must have been, because his insurance company paid all the insurance he had which was the state minimum. That, plus the underinsured motorist protection I had on the motorcycle, totaled half of all the medical bills. A year later a federal judge determined those who wanted money would get fifty cents on the dollar.

I don't remember ever seeing the boy. If I were dead I wouldn't say the accident helped me, but it did. Years later when people asked if I was fully recovered I'd say, "I am not sure I want to be fully recovered. My wife says I am a nicer person now than before." I was made aware of "the more important things." The authorities determined whose fault it was. That was their concern.

Even though I remember something about transferring from the airplane to the ambulance I don't remember being wheeled into the Cincinnati hospital where I spent the next three months. I was put in the ICU on the eighth floor for several days. After that I was moved down to the rehabilitation floor where I learned to walk with crutches and talk. There were three parts to the rehabilitation process. They were physical therapy, speech therapy, and occupational therapy.

I was in bed most of the time. When I got therapy I was in a wheelchair. I couldn't transfer from the wheelchair to a toilet. A tube was clamped to my penis, and it was connected to a bag where my urine was collected. A second tube went through my abdomen into my stomach. It was connected to a plastic bag full of brown liquid food. Soon after I started eating solid food I also started having bowel movements. I had to ask a nurse for a "bed pan." That was a shallow metal container with a toilet seat type design on the open side. She would draw the curtain between the person in the next bed and me. Most of the time it was open. I would roll on my side, the nurse held the bedpan in place, and then I would roll back. When it was positioned correctly she left the room.

The first few times I just did it like throwing up in school. Once in school when we were sitting on the floor all facing the same way learning how long the human intestine was I didn't say how sick I was until it was obvious. I threw up on another kid's hand. That period of instruction ended early that day. Everyone but the kid was appreciative. They thought I did it deliberately to avoid the boredom. I felt much better out in the hall. The teacher told me to report to the infirmary. In there I vomited several more times into the proper receptacle.

The bedpan seemed shallow, but it wasn't. When I finished the nurse came in and held it again while I rolled onto my side. The hospital gown was around my waist. I could hear her wash it out in an adjoining room where there was a shower, sink, and toilet. Then she returned and proceeded to wipe my rectum. The first time that happened even though I was delirious from all the drugs I was acutely aware of my pitiful condition. I was humiliated. I couldn't even do that myself. I didn't cry, but I could have.

When I realized I could not even wipe my own rear end I knew how helpless I was. Months later people on the outside would talk to me about my self-determination and they would say how wonderful it was. I would try to tell them it wasn't like that at all. I didn't tell them I couldn't even wipe my own rear end, but I did say I was quite a lot like an animal with a ring in its nose being led through a field or down a road. I would tell them I did what I was told and there was nothing in me. People heard what I said, but I could see and hear from them that they thought I was being modest and gracious. They wanted to think it was me. It seemed futile for me to keep saying it wasn't that way at all. I couldn't bathe myself. Two or three times a nurse with a washbasin and a cloth would draw the curtain and wash my entire body including my crotch. I couldn't do that either. In the hospital it could be said they were paid to be the way they were, but I don't know. Several weeks after I got out the main day nurse telephoned. I recognize her voice immediately. She didn't say who she was and asked; "Do you know who this is?" I asked her about her trip to Hawaii with her children and grandchildren and if she was enjoying her retirement. It was nice that she called. I never learned the names of complex medical procedures, but by the time I left I knew everyone's first name.

Another nurse whom I knew remotely lived in a small town just beyond where I lived. We had talked about that and I told her to visit after I was released. One day on her way home from work she showed up. I was preoccupied with something else, and it must have seemed that way. She said as if to explain herself, "You said I should stop by." I realized what she was saying and how time had had its effect. I told her I was glad she did. In a short while she left.

A few months after I got out, Jenny's father invited his children, their husbands, and a few other friends to have a meal on a riverboat parked along the Ohio River in downtown Cincinnati. We were all sitting at a long narrow table. Many other people were there also having a meal. One of them was a nurse from the hospital. She said she saw me before I sat down, and when I did sit down she came over to where I was to say hello. She asked me why I didn't go to a special party at the hospital. I didn't tell her I never received an invitation, probably because a method of payment to the hospital had not been made. I didn't want to talk to her about money right there.

I was aware the person two places down from me on the same side of the table had recently been in a treatment center for alcoholics. I knew firsthand the way an alcoholic thinks. I said, "I didn't want to go back there, because I was afraid if I did they wouldn't let me out." I could not see the person sitting at the table with me, but the nurse who was standing on the other side of the table could see her directly. When I said that, the nurse looked over at the other person who must have been visibly reacting. The nurse's main job was in the ICU on the top floor. A few times she worked on the rehabilitation floor where I was and we talked. She told me she remembered the night I arrived in the ICU. Her last name was the same as the last name of the city manager of the political subdivision where the farmhouse was. She said she knew him but wasn't related.

A great kindness came from a boyhood friend who shaved my face two or three times each week when I was in the hospital. I was too weak, uncoordinated, and unable to do it myself. At the time I never thought about it one way or the other. It seemed very ordinary that he do it, but now I realize how exceptional it was.

We grew up together in Cincinnati. For a short while he lived in Monroe County, West Virginia. Quite a few years before my accident he and his wife moved back here to live, work, and raise children. Our routines were different. We seldom saw each other, but that all changed. That summer he was taking architecture classes at the University of Cincinnati across the street from the hospital. The first time he came, a nurse was shaving my face. After that if I needed a shave and the nurse wasn't doing it, he would. It was an elaborate process compared to normal shaving. I was propped up in bed; there was plenty of water, and the sheets never got wet. The nurse must have seen what a good job he did, because the rest of the time I was there he was the only one who shaved my face. It became a perfunctory matter for both of us that he arrive and shave my face. Sometimes he was in a hurry looking for this basin or that towel. As time went past the things he needed appeared more and more quickly. Once, midway through my time there the nurse stood at the foot of my bed and asked if I wanted to see the man who shaved my face. I made an affirmative utterance. She went out; he came in, got the stuff, and proceeded to shave my face. Every other time before or after that no nurse asked if I wanted to see him. Months later it made me think.

He shaved my face because I needed a shave. The nurse asking like that must have thought it was strange. Was it strange to her that a grown man would regularly shave another grown man's face? It was not his job. He was not my brother, but it could best be described as brotherly love.

I was in a daze most of the time but apparently not all the time. One day Jenny told me the two people making mailboxes in the Apple Barn wanted to get a third person to make parts. She said one of them told her the time they spent making parts was taking away from the time they could make mailboxes. I said, " I too once lived in Arcadia." She came to the hospital every day. Another time she said they wanted more money to paint, and that the hourly rate they got for that work was nothing like what they made welding. A month or two before my accident I taught one of them to paint. Until then I was the only one who could paint. Also a second person learned how to do it while I was in the hospital. I replied to her automatically without any thought or hesitation. I said they should get whatever is greater: the hourly rate or a certain amount of money per mailbox. The amount of money per mailbox was based on how much I would make if I painted at the hourly rate. They must have thought I wasn't that bad off when they heard that, because that week both of them came to see me in the hospital for the first and only time. Their expression when they saw me said I looked a whole lot different. I felt a whole lot different. Making mailboxes and being concerned about that had become as significant to me as the chirping of birds. I didn't say that to anyone when I was in the hospital.

A tube in my stomach was connected to a flexible clear plastic bag of brown liquid food. It hung over my head. One afternoon I awoke to the sound of two nurses talking. One of them was working hurriedly beside my bed with the food bag in her hand. I never saw her before or after that time. The other one was watching as if being instructed. That one was a young woman whose first job had been on the eighth floor. The older one emptied some of the content of the bag into a pan, and when she did some of it spilled on the floor. I asked her what she was doing as if I was interested in a new medical procedure. She poured a small amount of red liquid into the bag. Her reply was not typical of that place. She answered as if whatever it was it was inconsequential to me. She said, "What do you care?" I was in a drug-induced stupor most of the time, and the fact was I didn't care. She never looked at me the whole time, not when I asked that question or when she answered it. When the red-colored liquid was added she reconnected the tube and shook it up. The brown became red. She hung the bag on the hook, and as they both left she drew open the curtain. The stroke victim in the bed next to mine was watching television as usual.

The brown liquid on the floor didn't get wiped up. A week later the sight of it was a surprise to the man pushing a mop bucket on wheels. I said to him I leaned over twice last week to see if it had been cleaned up. By that time the food bag was brown again, the same color as what was on the floor. After he wrung out the mop he stood there and looked up and down. In so many words he said he had been mopping floors in that hospital for years and the stuff on the floor plus the length of time it had been there was not like anything he had seen. He must have reported it to the nurses, because several of them at different times looked where the spill had been. It was a very narrow place between my bed and the curtain. When the curtain was drawn back it covered the place where the spill had been. On the other side of my bed was a table and chair. Any visitors, doctors, and nurses stood there.

The day after the nurse changed the color of the food to red a hospital doctor who saw each rehabilitation patient every morning looked at the bag and then quickly at the papers in his hand. He didn't say anything medical. He told me a decent joke and left. The brown liquid food was not made red another time.

Before my accident I went to three or four meetings of Jehovah's Witnesses. I befriended several people there, some of whom came to the hospital. At the meetings in the "Kingdom Hall" (that is what they call the building) I always sat up front by myself. I was there to learn about God, not get in one big ice-cream social with the people.

I told a longtime friend that I was studying the Bible with Jehovah's Witnesses and that I was startled to find many of the customary ideas that are said to be written in that book aren't there at all. One of them is the popular notion that Christ was executed on two pieces of wood in the shape of a cross. It cannot be proven as fact one way or the other, but the method of execution at that time and place was by hanging a person on an upright piece of wood until they died. Christ died as a common criminal. There wasn't an abundance of wood in that area and the word indicating an upright piece of wood is translated as *cross*. Long before Christ walked on this earth a cross shape was the symbol of another long-lost god. A prominent modern-day historian wrote: "Christianity didn't replace paganism, it adopted it."

When I told my friend about this and that I learned it from the Jehovah's Witnesses he said, "What are the people like?" At that time before my accident I didn't want to abandon my past, and although I thought I must be missing something that would explain why he wasn't as concerned as me, I said, "If all the Jehovah's Witnesses are going to heaven then I don't want to go there."

It is a safe guess that the nurse changed the color of the food bag so the Jehovah's Witnesses would stay away. The Witnesses were in the habit of, and probably did, stop people in their tracks to talk to them about the Bible. I would guess they talked to the young nurse who subsequently questioned the older nurse about the propriety of having such a discussion in the hospital. The older nurse probably got livid when she found out that under the circumstances she could not flatly tell them to get out. She probably decided the same thing could be accomplished if she made the food bag look like blood.

Over the years quite a few Jehovah's Witnesses when presented with a live-or-die choice about whether or not to be hooked up to a bag of blood have reacted like three youths in the Bible who when faced with the prospect of either denouncing God or being thrown into a fiery furnace said in so many words whatever happens, happens, and that it was unthinkable that they denounce God. Jehovah's Witnesses consider taking blood contrary to Jehovah's (Almighty God's) direction in the Bible, and to them doing so would be the equivalent of denouncing God. For a Jehovah's Witness to come to the bedside of someone visibly hooked up to a bag of blood would be like trying to have a normal conversation with someone who was in the process of mutilating themself.

The people in the hospital could see I was not a Jehovah's Witness by my medical history. The fact that Jehovah's Witnesses were coming to the hospital to visit me might have been understood by at least one nurse as their taking advantage of my condition, but I was capable of telling someone not to be there.

I got a whole lot smarter in there. I could not clean myself, but I was tremendously strong inside. I was like a large body of water with a stream going out of it at one end. The water in the stream is free from contamination if the large body of water is clean. I never had to consider what I said might be the wrong words. Whatever I said came out right. That condition came from my understanding and taking to heart what the Bible terms "the force actuating the mind," "putting on the new personality," and "the more important things." The Jehovah's Witnesses were responsible for clarifying this and making it happen. Naturally, when any of them showed up at the hospital I was happy to see them.

Another visitor I had was a young woman who once watched our children. She told me she was about to finish nursing school and wanted to be a nurse. When she was a small child she took care of a pet rabbit at her house. A few years after that she took care of our children when we were gone. A few years after that I saw her in the hospital, and a few years after that she got married. At her wedding in Cincinnati two people traveled 800 miles to be there. They went on and on about the personal interest she had in their boy when he was in an Atlanta, Georgia, hospital for a long time. They said she was the best nurse they could imagine. There was no doubt they were also her dear friends. I could understand what they said about her.

I only meant to humor a nurse when I asked if every bed in the hospital had a horsehair mattress. Soon after that I got a new mattress. I was doing therapy when it was changed. The one I got had an electric blower on one end that was turned on all the time to keep the mattress full of air. It must have cost extra. I didn't have the slightest thought about money, and no one brought up the subject.

Another time, for no particular reason I asked the main day nurse quite matter-of-factly if she thought I lived in a grass hut. She left without replying.

The stroke victim in the bed next to mine was moved to a nearby county hospital, and the next day another stroke victim was in that bed. Meanwhile a man who represented a company that rented wheelchairs came to ask me some vital questions. His being there implied I was going to need a wheelchair even though he was the first person to bring up that subject. He never said what it cost to rent one, and it never crossed my mind to ask. He started to talk, and when he stopped to take a breath I asked which one had the most get-up-and-go. The one I got was top-of-the-line. It was like driving an expensive car. I used it to go to therapy each day. At night it was plugged into an electric wall socket to recharge the batteries. It was self-propelled.

The new preacher from the church I attended as a child came to the hospital. That was the church where right after my accident the name "Jocko" audibly bounced around the congregation during a moment of regularly scheduled silent prayer. He came several times. We never talked much, and he didn't stay long. The last time was when I was doing physical therapy in a room full of people doing physical therapy. When he arrived I was in the wheelchair just about to leave. It had one toggle switch where my right hand went. Depending on which way the switch was pushed the chair on its own would go in one direction or the other.

When he came in he was wearing a clergy collar. The physical therapist said I had a visitor. I pushed the toggle switch to the left, the chair pivoted in that direction, and there he was. Nobody else had a visitor in there then or any other day. I was embarrassed by his presence. I thought he was going to talk about the meaning of life right there in front of God and everyone. I was done doing therapy. I wanted him to make it short and sweet for everyone's sake. I looked up at him and said, "Say a benediction." He took me seriously and right there over my head commenced to say something that was what a benediction is. It seemed to take an eternity. When it was over I pushed the toggle switch full speed ahead and zoomed off without a word. The next day the physical therapist told me when I was gone the preacher said, "Where did he learn that?" Perhaps I was too short with him, because that was the last time he came there. The next time the preacher who married Jenny and me came to visit. He was from the same church, and didn't stay long either.

The physical therapist was rather nice-looking. We didn't have much personal conversation. She did tell me she was going to get married that autumn. I didn't ask her anything about it except to say something antiseptic like "congratulations."

A few times during the last month I was not as professional as she was. I didn't want her to be aware of it, but I think she was. In the morning people in wheelchairs were lined up on one side of a corridor leading to the physical therapy room. We waited until our therapist came and got us. This time she was not there yet. While I was sitting in the wheelchair in a line of people in wheelchairs she put her hands over my eyes and said, "Guess who?" It was so sudden. Before she spoke I didn't know who it was. I couldn't say anything. She moved around to the side of the wheelchair, said good morning, and what we were going to do that day. She lowered herself so our eyes were on the same level, and because the corridor was narrow she was not far from me. I sat very still looking attentive, breathing in slowly the whole time she was talking. I could smell her breath. I wanted to exhale, but I didn't. I tried not to show what I was doing, but she must have perceived something like my breathing was not normal. An inquisitive look came over her face as if to say are you dying or what? She stood up, and we went into the room.

Not long after that she was on her knees and elbows reaching far under a one-foot-high square table to get something that had gone under there, and when she did her posterior was high in the air. There was a definite delectability about her. When she got the block, or whatever it was, she looked at me for a split second. I tried to maintain a comatose look on my face.

The first time I went entirely vertical was in that room. I was strapped to a flat surface that moved to an upright position. The therapist went to do something else. The rehabilitation doctor was in the room checking on this and that person. When he got to me I felt kind of ridiculous strapped to that board high in the air. He asked me how I was doing. I said I was hanging around. That cracked up one of the stroke patients nearby, but the doctor wasn't visibly moved. He and his clipboard went elsewhere. Then the therapist came back. The rest of the time I practiced transferring back and forth between the wheelchair and one of the low tables.

Jenny came to the hospital every day and stayed as long as an hour. More often than not she would sit on the edge of the bed with one leg pulled up so she faced me. When there was a visitor the curtain was drawn. We talked about people, letters, thoughts, and things. Sometimes we didn't talk at all, and when I closed my eyes she would say it was time for her to go.

There is a familiarity that comes from being with a person a long time. No words are required to communicate. A time like that was when Jenny was sitting on the bed. She slid her hand under the sheet and grabbed my penis. It swelled in size. She pushed back the sheet. It had been a long time. She looked behind her wondering if the nurse might see. Nurses had seen it all. She started rubbing it, and soon I had an orgasm that spurted all over the place.

On the side table there was a self-dispensing box of soft pieces of paper that I always thought was there for people who wanted to cry or blow their nose. Maybe they had one more intended use.

I also went to speech therapy and occupational therapy each day. When it was time to go a male nurse would come to the room. Their job was to get patients to therapy on time. I had no strength in my legs. With help from one of them I managed to sit up with my feet on the floor. He would roll the wheelchair over to where I was, and lift me into it from the bed. Even though I had lost forty-five pounds since my accident it was still a physically demanding job. When I learned how to "transfer" from the bed into the wheelchair one of them still had to be there to position the wheelchair and lock the wheels. Then he would take me where I was supposed to go. When one therapy was over they would follow me back and get me in bed.

One day two of them were standing together in the hall when I went past. The one facing me looked aside like he was thinking what he was going to say next to the person standing with him. When he did he was looking at me. I held my hand up with my arm on the armrest of the wheelchair, and said, "Hey, brother man." Then I was past. A few weeks later when I was going down the same hall on crutches with one of the male nurses beside me the one I said that to stopped me. He said something about how he noticed I went from a wheelchair to crutches. He said he had not seen that happen very much. It was nice that he said that, especially since talking to me that way was not part of his job. I called him Jim, and by the way he looked that might have been his name.

Speech therapy was in a small office where I sat across the desk from a speech therapist who lived in Bright, Indiana, and traveled by car each day. We talked about life and everything else under the sun. Many times I responded to written questions that she said had no right answers. She said the first time I was in her office I said in a matter-of-fact tone that being there was a waste of time. I told her the drugs must have made me mean and now I didn't feel that way. Was that a question and answer? She wrote something down.

Occupational therapy was in a big room across the hall from the physical therapy room. It was full of colorful rubber balls and people trying to put round pegs in square holes. I was to learn hand-eye coordination. Often my time in that room was rounded out playing a detestable board game all about battleships. I told the professional person I played the game with that no matter what happened I was not going back into the military. She thought I was quite insane. I no longer made the effort of trying to present myself as being in a state of normalcy.

Three times a male nurse took me to the resident psychiatrist's office and once, without me, Jenny went with our three children. Jenny said Whit and Gretchen didn't have much to say, but Sam sang like a canary. He went on about the weather and all sorts of impertinent things. When I was in the psychiatrist's office he asked me questions from standardized tests.

A few months earlier my sister successfully got my mother to undergo a "mental competency evaluation" for unrelated reasons. That child of hers was in the room with the doctor who was asking her a battery of questions. In relating to me what it was like my sister said Mom was asked, "What is the similarity between a dog and a wolf?"

She answered uncharacteristically, "They are both quadrupeds."

So when I was asked the same question I knew I was taking the same test. For a moment I was both amused and thrilled. I would have said they both have sharp teeth or something like that, but I gave the same incredible answer my mother did. The psychiatrist asked a few more questions and then went back to that one and said, "You don't have to be so specific."

A recurring physical problem I had in that hospital and for a year afterward was vomiting. No sooner did I eat than I would feel nauseous and vomit. The first time I vomited on myself. The next time a nurse held a dish made for that purpose under my chin. After that, one of those dishes was always beside my bed. I carried it everywhere I went. The doctor told me to eat slower, and that helped some.

One day I was vomiting continuously. When the male nurse came to get me for physical therapy I told him to forget it; I was too sick. If a patient didn't want to go to therapy the male nurse was not supposed to make an issue of it, but the therapist was. Later that afternoon the physical therapist came into the room. It was the first and only time she was there. She asked why I didn't show up that day. I told her not to take it personally; I didn't want to puke on the floor. During the entire exchange of words she kept walking and looked at me very seldom. She walked in a straight line past the foot of the bed to a chair where she practically did a military-style 180-degree turn and left without waiting for a reply to her saying she hoped I would be there tomorrow. She was in the process of teaching me how to use crutches.

Toward the end of my time in the hospital I got to go home every Sunday. I went there flat on my back and returned the same way. Two people who rode around in an ambulance all day brought a gurney up in the elevator, lifted me onto it, and went to the farmhouse at normal speed without using the siren or emergency lights. When we got there I went into the house and was put on a couch where I remained until they returned at the end of the day. I would lie sideways on the couch with pillows behind my back so I could read, watch television, listen to music, take pills, eat Jell-O, and throw up. Jenny was in and out of the room all day. She was attentive, to say the least.

When I left the hospital they gave me a prescription for two antinausea drugs. Those were the only two pills I was on when I left there. In the morning at home we all had breakfast together. The children went to school, and even with the pills I got sick most mornings. I told the children I threw up a lot and if I had to vomit while they were getting ready not to mind because I didn't.

When I could walk without crutches and was painting mailboxes with an external air supply several times I got the hood off just in time to vomit in a rubber garbage can full of empty one gallon paint cans, used paint strainers, and puke. The others making mailboxes in the outer room didn't know.

The farm implements place where my brother and me bought nuts and bolts when we were children was gone, and a restaurant was on the same ground. It was at the head of the road where the Apple Barn was. I ate lunch there when it was not so certain I was going to get sick. By then vomiting had become a mind game. I was losing the day a person who helped me make mailboxes appeared to ask me something. He saw my truck outside. It was the weekend, and his wife was with him. I didn't know her very well. Once we talked on the phone and I told her he should lay off the sauce. He was the one who put his fist through a fish tank on a Friday night.

He asked me if he could use my trailer to haul a small tractor he was going to buy. Both he and his wife sat down across the table from me. Now I really felt like I was going to puke. I did not call on God for incidental, self-serving things, but at that moment there was no way I could do anything to prevent what was going to happen. It was too horrible to think I was going to get sick in front of them just when they sat down. A clear thought went through my mind; *Please, God, don't let me puke now.* I can't say I felt better instantly, but I was able to make a showing of myself and go over the details about his using my trailer. I did not throw up.

Jenny and I were eating at a fast-food place. Half way through the fried food I told her it was time to go. She got my meaning, and we went out the door to the car. She drove. I went around to the other door, but before I got in I threw up beside the car. I thought I was being discrete about it, but after the first part of what I ate splattered on the ground I noticed a pickup truck facing our car with what appeared to be two workers sitting inside eating lunch. They saw the whole thing. Jenny was such a lady. They laughed and were still laughing when we drove away. They must have thought it was the food.

Jenny and I didn't own the farmhouse. The industrialist who once did was dead and his four adult children were the owners. Technically a "foundation" was owner, and they were the directors. That was a legal arrangement between them and the tax people. When the farmhouse was built it was on ground known as the Hog Back Farm. Then it became part of Peterloon Farm. After that it was Peterloon Foundation.

When it was Peterloon Farm the industrialist was alive. It didn't concern anyone when he said I could live there. When it became part of a foundation the informality slowly changed. There never was a landlord–tenant agreement written down, but things like mowing with the Peterloon Foundation tractor had to be done in consideration of others even though some of them would never see the field.

To me ownership is one of life's biggest illusions, and some of that must have permeated Jenny's thinking. When I was in the hospital she and her friends put an entire addition on the farmhouse, a house we didn't even own. People gave us money, their labor, or the necessary building materials. It didn't cost us a thin dime. Jenny said they were my friends. I said they must be her friends, because I didn't think I had that many friends.

There were no stairs in the addition. The shower was big enough for a wheelchair. A ramp went to the back door. There were plans to build another ramp outside to a wood deck. It never got built. By then I had graduated to crutches. There were no closets in the original part of the farmhouse, but in the addition there were big ones and little ones everywhere.

What happened is this: A lifelong friend of Jenny sent a letter to people we both knew telling them of our situation and asking for their help. Our situation was that we cared very little about money and consequently had very little of it saved for a time like this. The letter didn't tell about that specifically, but it did talk about our "simple life," which wasn't exactly a choice.

The result was a large outpouring of help. One person gave us the concrete for the foundation of the addition. Another took our children on vacation with them. Another who was an architect designed our addition free of charge. A person we knew very little owned a building supply store, and he donated the lumber, dry wall, nails, windows, shingles and many other things at cost.

The job supervisor was a lifelong acquaintance. We knew each other growing up but were no more than casual friends. He was an independent contractor between jobs and had always done some kind of construction work since he left school. He donated all his time to run the job until the addition was finished. His wife worked at a big company downtown.

A person who built decks built one on the back of the addition.

An accomplished carpenter, and cousin of Jenny while on his way from New Hampshire to Florida stopped at our house. He was passing through after visiting his sister in Detroit. He saw the addition and a space where bookshelves were meant to go. He stayed an extra day and built some very nice ones. His dog traveled with him.

Two other people did all the dry wall work, which means they made smooth interior walls. There was one paid carpenter. He and the job supervisor were the only ones who could hit a nail on the head every time. Other paid professionals were a plumber, an electrician, two painters, some vinyl siding people, and a heating contractor. Thirty or forty other people gave us the money to pay them. A wealthy woman whose paddle tennis courts I once kept clear of snow gave Jenny a huge amount of money. There was no stipulation about how it should be spent. She just gave it to her, and asked it be anonymous.

Our refrigerator stopped working, and two people installed another one. Their time and the refrigerator were free. In the same way a large deep-freeze appliance was put in the basement. It was the first one we ever had. We used it to store food.

A lady friend who got a big brand management job a few weeks later put wallpaper in one of the front bedrooms free of charge. During that time and for a month after I got out of the hospital a different person brought dinner every night. They were assigned a day, and when I was home it didn't seem like anyone did it more than once.

Once the concrete foundation was set in place many people converged on the farmhouse, worked all day, and completed most of the addition. Jenny said only about three people knew what they were doing. The others had much energy and did what the job supervisor told them.

Someone had a video camera and recorded the event. I was at the hospital that day but saw the videotape when I got home. People put up walls and crawled on the roof like army ants. There were bankers and lawyers hammering nails. It was like an old-fashioned barn raising. People with little or no experience on roofs were nailing down shingles. Nobody rolled off. Nobody got hurt.

There was food set up on tables outside. Children played everywhere. Jenny said she thought only a few people would show up, but so many did that the addition was mostly done that day. The dry wall still had to be hung, and the professional people had their work to do.

That same day I was wheeled into the operating room where an orthopedic surgeon cut into my wrists in order to remove steel pins that were put there by the surgeon in Missouri. It was explained to me that the wrist joint is one of the most, if not the most, complicated bone structure in the human body. The hand can move in every direction because of the wrist. I was told the steel pins were put there temporarily until the bones healed. My wrists were in a "cast" before the operation. After the operation I got a new cast on each wrist.

I was anesthetized so I would have no feeling. It put me asleep. When I woke up it was night and I was back in my familiar hospital bed. I wasn't aware of much, but I knew where I was.

Apparently I was causing an uproar, because I was lovingly put in a "straitjacket."

I knew what a straitjacket was from old movies about insane asylums. I thought they were part of history along with frontal lobotomies, but one was tucked away in the far reaches of that hospital. When it came there were numerous people who came with it like seamstresses who were going to make it fit. Those four big ugly Yugoslavians were in the back. They must have been flown in that night. It was a white canvas jacket with sleeves stitched to the body cloth. There were no openings for my hands. When the nurse with all the people behind her said in a sweet tone of voice something like, *"Here, let's put this on."* I helped in whatever way I could. I didn't realize what it was until I was wearing it, and even then I didn't care much. My arms were against my body. It was made of the same material as a fencing jacket. I hoped they weren't going to ask me to sword-fight.

All the drugs had definitely modified my mood, and they gave me more. Jenny said that around midnight she got a call to get down there immediately, because I was out of my tree. Jenny said by the time she did get there in the middle of the night I was so full of drugs that there was no need for her to stay and calm me down.

I was having an adverse reaction to the drug or drugs the surgeon prescribed for me. The correlation between my behavior and the surgery was not identified until two days later when Jenny finally got through to them that I was different.

The morning after the operation I gained a small amount of sensibility. The straitjacket was removed. I was still insane, but it was not apparent. I was certain the hospital staff was secretly trying to freeze to death everyone in that wing of the building. I learned later that an ice pack on my wrist might have contributed to that deranged notion. There were big picture windows across one wall of the room. That was where my bed was. It looked like a sweltering summer out there. The windows weren't meant to be open. I thought if they were opened it would prevent the others and me from dying.

There was a nurse there I named Attila the Hun. She was a short older lady who was so wide that when she walked she moved from side to side. She relied on her own understanding more than what anyone taught her. I needed an ally. I couldn't move without help. I didn't want the other nurses to know I thought there was a conspiracy to freeze us to death. When Attila the Hun was in the room I said with the utmost seriousness and very quietly so no one else would hear that they were freezing us to death. I asked her to throw a chair through the window. We were on the eighth floor. She didn't say yes and she didn't say no. She just left and probably mumbled to herself something about how I had gone berserk. I thought it would be a matter of time before she broke open the window. When it didn't happen I figured she was afraid of losing her job.

It may have been time to take me off the painkiller, because when they did I felt no pain. The reason could also be that when I was on it I tried to break the window myself. In the afternoon the day after the pins were removed from my wrist I was alone in the room. The cast covered my wrist and most of my hand. It was heavy and hard. It felt like a demolition ball. I was sure if I got in the chair I could open the window by breaking the glass. The railing on the side of the bed was down, and with much exertion I managed to get to the chair. I tapped on the window with the cast. It was thick glass.

The reality of what I was doing became clear to me. I couldn't have done it even with a hammer in my hand. I just sat there with no desire to move anywhere else. The main day nurse, the grandmother who retired, appeared in the doorway. We looked at each other, and a horrified look came over her face. She didn't know why I got in the chair, but she knew I was there. I don't remember what I told her, but a few days later speaking about that moment she said she was down the hall attending to some other business when for no reason all of her attention went to me. She couldn't figure it out and said once before in that hospital a person fell to their death. Did she think I was going to jump?

Later that afternoon I opened my eyes and saw Attila the Hun sitting in a chair between the window and me. She looked at me crossly and said she wasn't moving. I said, "Good," and went back to sleep.

While I was flat on my back Jenny kept the mailbox business alive. She did the paper and numbers. People in the shop oversaw production, and between the two of them orders were filled. A few weeks before the accident happened I taught one other person to paint. If there hadn't been someone to paint the whole thing would have screeched to a halt.

Jenny didn't talk much about mailboxes, but every once in a while she would ask me something. One time it was about disposable clear plastic stick-on lenses for the paint hood. I had always bought them ten or twelve at a time. Now the supplier was saying they only came in boxes of 2,000. That quantity would last me ten or fifteen years.

Another time it was a weightier matter. She had made a command decision, but it was not entirely irreversible. She told me what happened.

The top marketing man at the first mail-order company had been fired, and he wanted to sell the mailboxes through a second mail-order catalog company he and another person were starting. Jenny called the owner of the first company and told him we needed more money and that we were going to sell mailboxes through the second company. When they were talking on the telephone several other of his people were on the same line. Jenny said the whole thing was rather intimidating.

On the telephone with the mail-order company owner and his cronies Jenny kept saying we had to sell more mailboxes, and the owner's last words were, "You do what you have to do and we will do what we have to do." That was the end of the conversation.

When she told me about this it sounded like she was taking care of business. She said she didn't know what meaning the word "exclusive" had with mailboxes so I told her.

Right after I went from using a paintbrush to using a paint sprayer I got a letter from the marketing man while he was still at the first company. In the letter he said he saw the mailboxes at the home and garden show. He asked to see another mailbox, and a few days later he wanted to talk about details. A meeting was set up. I met with him and another person who took pictures for the catalog with a large-format Swedish camera. The photography person and me were in two chairs in front of the desk. The marketing man said he wanted an agreement with me (probably written) that said I would not sell mailboxes to any other catalog. I told him if my mailboxes were sold exclusively by them I would be like one of their employees except I'd be one without a retirement plan. He said he only wanted the exclusive for the mail-order business.

The owner of the company opened the door, and leaned into the office. He said something about a story he read in the local daily newspaper that morning. He left pulling the door shut behind him. The marketing man and the photographer looked at each other when he was gone.

We got back to business. I said a lawyer in a suit who wanted to be an outrageous rock-and-roll star when he grew up told me the most important thing to have in any agreement is a way to get out of it.

Also I said their idea sounded like a treaty between two countries. As long as both sides were happy it worked. As soon as one side isn't happy the treaty is worthless.

Then the marketing man said it would be an agreement just like the one with, and he named a huge international Japanese company. He said they had an exclusive with them for a handheld airport "scanner" radio. He said the agreement was "cancelable" by either side with thirty days' notice. That seemed like no agreement at all to me. I told him we could have one cancelable by either side with Three-months' notice.

When I was in the hospital the second catalog company was in the inception stage. I told Jenny we had no exclusive with the first catalog company or anyone else. We decided to send them a piece of paper suitable for framing that said in four months we were going to sell mailboxes to another mail-order company. Then we talked about other things.

I had one more operation on my wrist by the same orthopedic surgeon. That time I was given a "local" anesthetic which meant I was awake during the operation. The area where the doctor was cutting was numbed. While the doctor was working on me he was talking to another person who was standing on the other side of the table where I was lying. When I joined in with a few words of my own the doctor said, "What?" like he didn't expect me to talk. After that no one talked the rest of the time.

I was in that hospital three months. Shortly before I left the occupational therapist, Jenny, and me met by my bed and talked about adjustments at home. Those adjustments primarily concerned access to the house and questions about stairs. I was learning to walk with crutches across smooth linoleum floors, but when I went from one place to another I went mostly in a wheelchair. The therapist said she would go to our house in order to recommend this or that about a passage, but when she heard a room addition was almost finished with a wheelchair ramp leading to the back door she said there was no need for her to go there.

The occupational therapist loaded me up with torsion springs and other gadgets that would strengthen parts of my body. She was standing at one side of my bed, and Jenny was standing on the other side. I had the awful habit of interrupting people when they were talking, and I did it enough times to the therapist that she finally interrupted me and said, "Shut up or I'll smack you."

There were no farewells expressed or implied when I left. It was a matter of routine, like going home on Sunday. I just left! By then I had enough strength to get in our car. It had enough legroom. We used it on several previous Sundays when an ambulance was no longer needed to take me home for the day. But that day the friend who shaved my face drove his car. I didn't have what the medical people call the full range of motion in my knees so whatever car I used the size of the door opening was a concern. Jenny came up to the room. She opened a folding wheelchair, put it beside my bed, and locked the wheels. I made the switch with my trusty transfer board, and off we went. She wheeled me down the hall to the elevator. We went through the lobby and out into the summer heat. It felt good to be alive once more. My friend and his car were waiting by the front doors. After I got in he put the folding wheelchair in the cargo space. I was in the front, and Jenny got in the back. He drove.

The bed next to mine in the hospital room had three different people in it (at different times). Every one of them was an older male who turned the television on in the early morning, and, if they had their way would keep it that way all day. A nurse turned it off if they were gone to therapy, or if they were asleep. I also had one. The television for each person was located high on the opposite wall, and was held there by a specially made bracket. When we sat up in bed we were looking directly at the thing. A person in bed without getting out of it could turn their television on or off, raise or lower the volume, and change channels.

On Saturday mornings the other television had one program after another about fishing. Topics discussed were how and where to fish. I saw so many of those shows I felt as if I could find a desolate lake or stream in the mountains and fish like a pro.

The week before I left the hospital there was a commercial that appeared repeatedly about six burritos and a choice of sauce. On the way home all I wanted to do was go to a "drive-through" and get some. The three of us were all going to have the same thing, but until I talked about it neither Jenny nor my friend had heard the burrito advertisement.

At the restaurant my friend stopped the car beside a large sign. It had pictures of food and listed the food for sale there. It also had an electronic device in it that enabled him to talk with a person in the restaurant. He asked for burritos and sauce. A voice repeated the order, said the cost, and told him to drive forward to a sliding window where money and food were exchanged.

At the window a young woman said they were out of one sauce, but they had the other two. I was very upset. I leaned over from the other side of the car so I could see her. In a furious manner, with saliva coming out of my mouth, I said crossly that all month there was advertisement after advertisement about the sauce they didn't have. She was shaken by my loss of temper. She called another person to the window who repeated that there was no more of that sauce. I also repeated what I said about the advertising. I added it was against the law, in the United States of America, for anyone to advertise something for sale they didn't have. She said there was a case of it in the building, but it was not opened. I told her to go open it and said we would wait right there in the fast lane until she did. A few minutes later she gave us all the sauce we wanted.

We took the food home to eat like a wild bird with something in its claws. It was tasty, but I never got it another time. My friend and Jenny had been quiet during my exchange with the drive-through lady. I felt there was a need to explain myself. I said the sauce really looked good on television.

I had gotten in a rage over burrito sauce. Later I was told outbursts like that were typical of people who had strokes and/or closed head injuries. Another time it happened was in a restaurant that had white tablecloths on all the tables. Jenny and I had too much wine and bourbon. I was speaking loudly about my nephew. He was going either to live with us or live in an orphanage. I had been studying the Bible, and one of the things in there was that someone who didn't help their own had a lot of nerve asking Jehovah for help. Jenny thought my whole obsession with the Bible was part of the accident and had to be dealt with like a broken bone. I didn't go into the Bible with her. I simply said there was a moral obligation. She said it would ruin our family. By then I was in the midst of a rage. I said our family was already ruined. My temper got worse. Jenny got up to go to the toilet. I was staring at the plate when someone said, "You shouldn't air your laundry in public." There had been a large group at the table next to us. They had just finished eating and left. This one individual was from that group. When the others were gone he came over and said what he said.

I looked up at him like I heard him wrong and asked, "What?" He said it again about the laundry. I said, "You know what you can do?" It was a rhetorical question. I didn't wait for an answer. "You can go fornicate yourself," but I didn't use such a nice word.

Then he was the one who said, "What?" I said it another time. He clenched his fist and said he would like to hit me. I had images of us tearing up the restaurant breaking tables and chairs over our heads. We would smash everything just like in the cowboy movies. But like my inability to break the window in the hospital what I did was say if he hit me I would sue him. Then he said, "What is she going to sue you for?"

I said, "I hope for divorce."

After that he walked away from where he was. Then he was talking to me again from the next table. He said, "Even he agrees with me," and he pointed to a man with his back to me who didn't turn around.

I said, "Tell him to go fornicate himself too."

When Jenny came back to the table she showed me a business card he gave her. The card said he was the preacher of what sounded like a one-of-a-kind church. Jenny said he stopped her in the front room and told her to call if she needed help. She wanted to know what happened. Perhaps he was sincere, but I told her all he probably wanted was to get into her pants. She said at least someone did. We both laughed. Our sweet little waitress came over to the table and as sweet as could be I asked her if she had any ice-cream products for dessert. She looked at me in a way that said she knew everything that just happened and it was sickening the way I was trying to be so sweet all of a sudden.

Eventually I was able to control my fits of anger, but not before I hit Jenny. It happened when Jenny and I were going back home after a cookout. Our whole family was invited and went. The person who asked us also asked twenty or thirty other people. We all grilled dinner under shade trees that were near a large swimming pool. It was a swim club, and that meant everybody at that place was either a member or a guest.

Most of the people knew nothing about our group. Children were splashing and playing games in the water. Others were talking across round tables. Some were sprawled in the sun as if asleep, and some sat motionless peering through dark glasses at people who could not see their eyes.

On the way there, less than a mile from the swim club, we passed a church where it was plain to see that a temporary festival with strings of lights, carnival rides, tents, and booths was about to begin. If it was like all the other church festivals that sporadically happened in the summer, most of the booths were "schemes of chance such as number games or lotteries. Games of chance such as poker, craps, roulette, slot machines, or other games where the player gives something of value in the hope of gain, the action of which is determined largely or wholly by chance." That's how gambling is defined by the Ohio Revised Code Sec. 2915-01E.

It would be commonplace anywhere else, but on church grounds, a place that claims to promote the values of God, they gamble there. I was not capable of convincing anyone what they did. I tried to explain to Sam I knew it was wrong. He said, "Did you see a burning bush?"

Not long after that I was trying to explain my obsession about writing this book to my oldest son. He saw it as an achievement like a wrestling championship. He told me be prepared to lose. He was a wrestler. His senior year he was undefeated at the district level. He worked extra hard preparing for the state finals. Every day he ate right, ran, and practiced wrestling. He lost at the state level. When he lost we sat in the stadium pretending to watch other matches being won and lost. Then I broke the silence with a story about something I saw years earlier. I said to him, "A person who won an Olympic marathon was unknown. He was from an English-speaking country. He was still out of breath when a television reporter stuck a microphone in his face and asked if he came prepared to win. He said, 'Yes, but I also came prepared to lose.'" Whit remembered those words from a year earlier. Now, with my being obsessed, I couldn't logically explain to him it was not something I could win or lose. It is something I do like a bird goes South every year.

Just the two of us were in the car when we returned home from the swim club. The children had met friends. Their parents were our friends. Our children were going to spend the night at their house and go to the festival. The first time we drove past the festival I had talked about it like it was far off and how awful it was. Little did I know our children were going there. Returning home, going past for the second time it was dusk. Children were walking rapidly through the road intersection to get there and meet their friends. Jenny and I were not exactly talking peacefully about the situation. We were having what is pleasantly referred to as a heated discussion in the car about the pros and cons of the festival. There were mostly cons coming from me. It was difficult for me to speak clearly. Over and over again she talked when I talked. She was infuriated that I was infuriated over what seemed to her like harmless fun. I told her not to talk when I was talking. She talked even more. I couldn't talk over her. I yelled uncontrollably something along the lines of, "Shut up, bitch," and smacked her across the face with the back of my hand (literally a bitch is a female dog, but more often it is a derogatory term applied to human females). Her lip was bleeding and she was quiet while she patched that up. We talked no more. After several miles she broke the silence and said, "You hit me."

The scene in the restaurant and after hitting Jenny, I became aware that losing control so easily was a problem. Our life together had always been volatile. We went from one extreme to the other. I got rid of the last door Jenny slammed. She was looking on the bright side when she said there was never a dull moment.

I told one of the older men in our congregation about losing my temper in the restaurant. I was a newcomer. Perhaps he didn't say anything because he didn't want to discourage my interest in the Bible by telling me my behavior toward the other person was base and despicable by Bible standards. Sometimes I felt like an Egyptian crossing the Red Sea with a bunch of Israelites.

The brother who once a week studied the Bible with me had something to say. He always brought another person with him. This time his wife was there. They were young adults. It seemed appropriate that I use the same four-letter *f* word I used in the restaurant to describe what happened there. Right after I did I was sorry. It made her uncomfortable. Without making any expression she kept looking at her lap. Actually, her reaction was definite, because without intending, she made it quite clear she could not deal with that word in any way, shape, or form.

Her husband said, "We try to set a good example," and he said, "The example we follow is the one set by Jesus Christ."

Jenny told a friend about my outbursts and when I hit her. In a genuinely concerned way with smiles and kindness, the friend told me about a doctor her husband saw once a month. She said the doctor was a tremendous help to her husband. She was certain he would be as much help to me. She told me the doctor's name but said she would have to call me with his telephone number.

I went there and filled out the necessary forms. I spoke with a lady in a room off to the side about the nature of my problem. I said it was typified by a recent situation in a restaurant. When I told her what I said to the preacher man she as much as asked if that was a problem. I don't think she was a doctor, but I didn't ask. I told her that according to the Bible I had a problem. I told her I was studying the Bible with Jehovah's Witnesses. She wrote on a pad of paper a long time. She stopped writing, put her head in her hand, and was staring at the paper. I expected her to ask something about the Bible just like I once did, but she didn't. She made an appointment for me to see a doctor.

The doctor and I sat in his office in two chairs that were the same. In the beginning of the very first visit I used the word *self-control*, and said the Bible was a source of guidance for me. Then he asked, "What does the Bible say about self-control?" I didn't expect he would ask that question. I wasn't able to tell him all nine fruitages of the spirit mentioned in the Bible, but I said self-control was one of them. We were having a nice time talking about the Bible, or at least I thought both of us were having a nice time. I don't know, because very abruptly our session was over. He wrote down a time for me to be there the next month.

I went several times. The last time he requested that Jenny also be there. He wanted her to say what it was like living with a Jehovah's Witness. She said from the edge of her seat that there wasn't a dull moment. The doctor scheduled me for another appointment a month later. I forgot that one, and for no particular reason I never went back.

In the Bible there is a difference between men and women that goes beyond the obvious sexual difference. It begins with Adam and Eve, who are in a three-way relationship with God. When Christ is on earth the relationship between men and women does not change. Women are in subjection to men. After the Garden of Eden, when mankind goes his way without God, the subjection becomes domination, even injurious domination. The godly relationship between men and women gets lost in a sea of confusion, conflict, and abuse.

The very first man and woman, Adam and Eve, had an unusual beginning. The man was formed out of the dust. He was given the breath of life and became a living soul. The Bible says: Now Jehovah God was forming from the ground every wild beast of the field and every flying creature of the heavens, and he began bringing them to the man to see what he would call each one; and whatever the man would call it, each living soul, that was its name. So the man was naming all the domestic animals and the flying creatures of the heavens and every wild beast of the field, but for the man there was found no helper as a complement of him.

And Jehovah God went on to say: "It is not good for the man to continue by himself. I am going to make a helper for him, as a complement." God had a deep sleep fall upon the man, and while he was sleeping, he took one of the ribs and then closed up the flesh over its place. And Jehovah proceeded to build the rib he had taken from the man into a woman and bring her to the man. Then the man said, "This is at last bone of my bones and flesh of my flesh. This one will be called woman because from the man this one was taken."

The Bible account continues, "That is why a man will leave his father and his mother, and he must stick to his wife and they must become one flesh. And both of them continued naked, the man and his wife, and yet they did not become ashamed."

That was a family. The man named the woman like he did the beasts in the field and the flying creatures in the sky, but he was not superior or inferior to her. The woman was the "complement" of the man. Together they were "one."

Everything ran amok. "And Jehovah God also laid this command upon the man: 'From every tree of the garden you may eat to satisfaction. But as for the tree of the knowledge of good and bad, you must not eat from it, for in the day you eat from it you will positively die.' "

Satan, later described as the original serpent, found a weakness in them, and they ate from that tree. Then here is what happened: "And Jehovah God kept calling to the man saying to him, 'where are you?' Finally he said: 'Your voice I heard in the garden, but I was afraid because I was naked and so I hid myself.' At that he said: 'Who told you that you were naked?' " The rest is a history of turmoil, not just for women but also for mankind.

In early Bible times after Adam and Eve were expelled from the Garden of Eden it can't be denied the treatment of women is sometimes horrible, even when it happens in a five-thousand-year-old civilization. A lady friend earnestly attempting to read the Bible upon reading the story of Lot read no further. She ended up rejecting the Bible in part or in whole and continued with her own personal idea of goodness. Contrary to popular opinion, according to the Bible there is no good in our flesh. Being good without God is impossible. One thing for sure: God doesn't use high-and-mighty public relations techniques to get his point across.

Lot's story is an example. God always provides an escape route for those who listen, and from the story a person may see it is a good idea to follow God's directions, especially the one about looking back.

The woman I know who abruptly stopped reading the Bible when she reached chapter 19 of Genesis saw something else and later said, "Is the Bible the way to live or the way not to live?" In the story, men and boys in the city of Sodom and Gomorrah surround Lot's house. They call for Lot to send out two men so they can have "intercourse" with them. The two men are angels. When they arrive in that city Lot knows who they are, and repeatedly he asks them to stay the night at his house. They accept, and like any right-minded person who knows two angels are in his house, Lot shows them the utmost hospitality. He washes their feet and prepares a feast for them. That is when a mob surrounds his house. Lot goes outside, closing the door behind him. He doesn't say the two men inside are angels. The mob might think he is insane. Lot tries to appease them. He calls them "brothers" which is a friendly greeting. He tells them not to act "badly," an understatement if ever there was one. Lot tries to relate to these people. He tells them, "Only to these men do not do a thing, because, that is why they have come under the shadow of my roof." Hospitality is understood to be a virtue.

Here is what stopped my friend from reading any further in the Bible. Lot says to them, "Please, here I have two daughters who have never had intercourse with a man. Please let me bring them out to you. Then do to them as is good in your eyes." It is rather obvious nothing about those people is good. Lot was suggesting they gang-rape his two daughters instead of gang-raping his two male guests. Then the mob threatens to gang-rape Lot. That is when Jehovah intervenes. The angels pull Lot inside, and everyone outside becomes blind. The account says Lot told his "sons-in-law" that Jehovah was going to destroy the city. Either Lot had other daughters or the two virgin daughters were engaged to be married. In the ancient Jewish culture engaged men are sons-in-law. The Bible says the sons-in-law thought he was joking.

The next morning the angels promptly lead Lot, his wife, and the two virgin daughters (Lot's family) by the hand out of the city. As soon as they are outside the city Jehovah makes it rain sulfur and fire on Sodom and Gomorrah. All the people are destroyed. Even the plants are destroyed. The two angels insisted they move quickly. Lot and his two daughters escaped the destruction of that city with nothing but the shirts on their backs. On the outskirts of town Lot's wife wants one last look at what is behind her. She gets that look and becomes a pillar of salt. That was the end of her. She is gone. Jehovah's direction through one of his angels was that no one look back.

After what happened Lot must have been jumpy. He goes to live in the city of Zoar. The Bible says that he is afraid to live in the mountainous region where some calamity might "keep close to him." Without giving a reason, the Bible says Lot soon was afraid to live in Zoar and began dwelling in the mountainous region in a cave with what remained of his family, his two daughters.

Then in the same chapter the Bible says: "And the firstborn proceeded to say to the younger woman, 'Our father is old and there is not a man in the land to have relations with according to the way of the whole earth. Come let us give our father wine to drink and let us lie down with him and preserve offspring from our father.'" The two daughters wanted to have sexual relations with a man according to the way of the whole earth, and they reasoned having sexual intercourse with their father was necessary in order to "preserve offspring from our father." The Bible says Lot was drunk. It says: "He did not know when she lay down and when she got up."

The account continues: "And it came about on the next day that the firstborn then said to the younger: 'Here, I lay down with my father last night. Let us give him wine to drink tonight also. Then you go in, lie down with him, and let us preserve offspring from our father.'"

That story ended one person's attempt to read the Bible.

Since the day Lot's story was recorded, people, in an attempt to explain their personal philosophy have explained it their way.

It has become like an inkblot.

Lot's treatment of his daughters is not what someone would expect of a parent today. In the cave the subject of incest had not been defined, but today it would be foremost on our mind. It wasn't until later, in the Bible book of Leviticus, chapter 18, that Jehovah gave specific directions to his people about sexual relations.

Another story early in the Bible that details what on the surface seems to be the harsh treatment of women is about what Phinehas did. Leading up to his appearance in the Bible there exists a situation where the nation of Israel is attracted to another group of people especially to their women. The Bible account says their attraction extends to their having "immoral relations" with them. The Israelites then become attached to the foreign god of those people. Until then their devotion is going exclusively to Jehovah, who is helping them every step of the way. Why are they unfaithful? An explanation is in Matthew 26:41, "The spirit, of course, is eager, but the flesh is weak." Jehovah brought a "scourge" against Israel.

During that time a well-to-do Israelite waltzes into the tent of meetings with a well-to-do foreign woman. At chapter 25 verses 6-9 in the Bible book of Numbers it says what happened, "But, look! A man of the sons of Israel came, and he was bringing near to his brothers a Midianite woman before Moses' eyes and before the eyes of all the assembly of the sons of Israel while they were weeping at the entrance of the tent of meeting (it was a sad situation). When Phinehas the son of Eleazar the son of Aron the priest caught sight of it, he at once got up from the midst of the assembly and took a lance in his hand. Then he went after the man of Israel into the vaulted tent (bedroom) and pierced both of them through, the man of Israel and the woman through her genital parts. At that the scourge was halted from the sons of Israel. And those who died from the scourge amounted to twenty-four thousand."

There are no spears in the coatroom anymore, but human nature and sexual understanding do not change. In the last book of the Bible, Revelations 17:18 & 18:1-3 it talks about symbolic Babylon the Great (corrupted religion) fornicating with the kings of the earth (governments). According to the Bible, they both will be destroyed.

In early Bible times the law of Israel said a wife and children were the possessions of the male head of household. The law was in the form of the Mosaic code provided by Jehovah through Moses to the nation of Israel. All together there are more than 630 of them. The Mosaic code served as a protection for the Israelites leading to the Messiah.

The Mosaic code allowed for divorce of women by men but not the divorcing of men by women. Under the law (Mosaic code) the woman was a possession. Grounds for divorce was if the woman did "something indecent." It was not adultery, because the punishment for adultery for both men and women was death.

A Jehovah's Witness Bible reference work titled *Insight on the Scriptures* says this: "Doubtless, originally the 'indecency' that would have given a Hebrew husband some basis for divorcing his wife involved serious matters, perhaps the wife showing gross disrespect for the husband or bringing shame on the household. Since the law specified, 'You must love your fellow as yourself,' it is not reasonable to assume that petty faults could be used with impunity as excuses for divorcing a wife. —Leviticus 19:18."

The reference work continues, "In the days of Malachi many Jewish husbands were dealing treacherously with their wives, divorcing them on all kinds of grounds, ridding themselves of the wives of their youth, possibly in order to marry younger, pagan women. Instead of upholding God's law, the priests allowed this, and Jehovah was greatly displeased (Malachi 2:10-16). That the Jewish men were using many grounds for divorce when Jesus Christ was on earth is indicated by the question the Pharisees put to Jesus: 'Is it lawful for a man to divorce his wife on every sort of ground?'—Matthew 19:3."

The answer in Matthew 19:8-9 is, "I say to you that whoever divorces his wife, except on the ground of fornication, and marries another commits adultery." The only indication in the Bible that a women can divorce a man is at Matthew 10:12 where Jesus Christ, who the Bible says replaces the law code (Romans 7:6 & 10:4) said, "If ever a woman, after divorcing her husband, marries another, she commits adultery." Jesus Christ in his Sermon on the Mount said the only ground for divorce was fornication. A person is not obligated to divorce an unfaithful mate, but the only scriptural basis for divorce is fornication.

The Bible does not define *adultery* and *fornication* in one place, but from all the places where those words occur it can be understood that adultery happens when a married person has sexual intercourse with someone of the opposite sex other than their marriage mate. Fornication happens when a married or an unmarried person has any type of sexual relations with another person (not a scriptural mate) or persons or a beast.

The man is head over the woman, and the Christ is head over the man. Headship is described in 1 Corinthians 11:3, "But I [Apostle Paul] want you to know that the head of every man is the Christ; in turn the head of the woman is the man; in turn the head of the Christ is God."

A woman prancing down the street with a fancy attaché case can be happily married to a local coal miner with soot on his face. Neurotic as we are, it is unlikely that relationship could exist, but if it did it would not conflict with God as long as the man is the family head and its spiritual leader.

The Bible says a married man and woman are to be aware of the sexual needs of the other person. In 1 Corinthians 7:3&4 the Bible says, "Let the husband render to (his) wife her due; but let the wife also do likewise to (her) husband."

Patience and self-control is a big part of it. Ephesians 5:25,28 &29, "Husbands, continue loving your wives, just as the Christ also loved the congregation and delivered himself up for it. In this way husbands ought to be loving their wives as their own bodies. He who loves his wife loves himself, for no man ever hated his own flesh; but he feeds and cherishes it, as the Christ also does the congregation, because we are members of his body."

The Bible tells women in 1 Peter 3:3, "And do not let your adornment be that of the external braiding of the hair and the putting on of gold ornaments or the wearing of outer garments, but let it be the secret person of the heart in the incorruptible apparel of the quiet and mild spirit, which is of great value in the eyes of God. For so, too, formally the holy women who were hoping in God used to adorn themselves, subjecting themselves to their own husbands, as Sara used to obey Abraham calling him 'lord'. And you have become her children, provided you keep on doing good and not fearing any cause for terror."

Then in verse 7 it says, "You husbands, continue dwelling in a like manner with them according to knowledge assigning them honor as to the weaker vessel, the feminine one, since you are also heirs with them of the undeserved favor of life, in order for your prayers not to be hindered."

Verse 8 speaks about men and women together: "Finally, all of you be like minded, showing fellow feeling, having brotherly affection, tenderly compassionate, humble in mind, not paying back injury for injury or reviling for reviling, but, to the contrary bestowing a blessing, because you were called to this course, so that you might inherit a blessing."

The apostle Paul was not married. Under inspiration he wrote more books of the Christian Greek Scripture than anyone else did. He said he was a slave of the true God. There was no doubt in Paul's mind that God was a reality. God's own Son appeared to him on the road to Damascus and spoke directly to him. Until then Paul was involved with killing Christians. Jesus Christ began by asking Paul why he was persecuting Him. That incident made Paul a firm believer. From then on nothing, not even bad health, stopped his zeal. He wrote in 1 Corinthians 7:9, "Now I say to unmarried persons and the widows, it is well for them that they remain even as I am. But if they do not have self control let them marry, for it is better to marry than be inflamed [with passion]." It is God's direction that their be no sexual activity outside marriage.

Jenny drove me to a place where each day I spent time learning to walk and make sense on the job. Other people there were recovering from a stroke or from an accident of some kind.

I was in a wheelchair the first few weeks. Jenny signed me in and left. The physical therapist who worked with me every day came to the waiting area. She was very pregnant. She left during that time, and the word was she had a baby girl. She walked behind me while I propelled the wheelchair from the waiting area to a big room where five or six other people were working on their mobility.

The first thing I did was transfer from the wheelchair to a low table. These tables were just like the ones in the hospital. Lying flat on my back I would stretch muscles in my arms and legs. I did the same exercises every day. The physical therapist always told me which one to do next. She would then measure and write down how well I could bend my knees and other joints.

Once that was done I worked on walking, which eventually involved moving with the help of crutches in the parking lot, opening doors, and going up one or two stairs. Even when we were talking she walked behind me. One time we were going down a hallway in the building and she said I would be walking on my own in a few weeks.

That was the first time in a long time anyone had mentioned my future. I hadn't thought about it one way or the other. I expressed something along the lines of polite disbelief. I couldn't imagine walking without crutches. It wasn't clear to her what I said. She came up beside me. Then I said something that paralleled what I considered her overly optimistic statement.

After the physical therapy I saw a speech therapist in a much smaller room. Invariably she had me do computer games to exercise the muscle between my ears. I didn't do well at those games. I think that is why I had to keep doing them. I needed improvement.

Another thing she asked me to do was make change with coins. I could do it, but overall I didn't do very well. Jenny told her my poor performance wasn't a result of the accident, that I never could count money.

The therapist had me read advertisements. The advertisements were designed by medical people to determine if someone would be the lawful game of someone else. It took a few minutes to read each one. When I was done the therapist would ask me what I thought. One advertisement was particularly blatant about asking for large amounts of money for little or nothing in return. I told the therapist if I got anything like that in the mail I would unbolt the kitchen sink and send it to them. She asked me about that over and over again, and I kept saying over and over again they wanted the kitchen sink. The advertisement didn't say anything about the sink in the kitchen, and I suppose that concerned her.

The last few weeks I saw a psychiatrist who asked many of the same written questions the psychiatrist in the hospital did. Based on that she wrote an eight- or nine-page paper. No one had ever written that much about me in my entire life. It was very academic sounding. It made me feel very special. It said I had the equivalent of an eighth-grade education in mathematics, and that my vocabulary was up there near the 100th percentile.

The last segment of instruction each day was occupational therapy. Among other things it involved developing hand-eye coordination. The amount of time it took me to invert a row of blocks was recorded. The person who was telling me what to do said my right hand was much slower than my left hand. I did it several more times, and each time she said how one side was faster than the other.

We held a rope between us, and knocked an object with a hole in it back and forth along the rope. Once I batted the object too hard with my right hand. It whizzed along the rope very fast and knocked loudly into the wooden handle she was holding. Very quickly she fired it back to me with just as much force. She thought I did it on purpose. I apologized several times for sending it so hard. When I said that, she didn't look at me but at a nearby therapist, who might have been listening.

The last week I was there she got in a chair next to the chair I was sitting in and gave me a piece of paper to sign. It seemed she wrote it herself. She talked quietly and looked to see if anyone else was near. The paper said I was able to return to work. She asked if everything was correct. She reminded me of the army induction officer who asked me where I wanted to be stationed. I signed her paper without hesitation and said, just like Goofy in the cartoons, "Yup, that's me, a-ugh a-ugh a-ugh." She was not capable of altering what was going to happen.

A few months after I was finished with that place I was walking across a parking lot at a mini shopping center when I saw her locked out of her car. By then I had enough strength to push down the clutch pedal of my truck. The great state of Ohio said I was allowed to "operate a motor vehicle." We recognized each other immediately. I told her I had done the same thing many times. The solution was keeping a spare key in a magnetized box somewhere under the car. She didn't need my help. Later that week I took a new magnetized box to the medical place where she worked. I asked a woman at the front desk to give it to her, and then I left.

17

Secular Work/Spiritual Exposure

I made mailboxes longer than I did anything else in my life. When I started in the Apple Barn we depended entirely on the mailbox business for money. That changed a few years after my accident when the mail-order companies stopped buying from us. It was also when the business moved to a new building that had a dry, well-lit office that was heated in the winter and air-conditioned in the summer. A toilet and sink were in a small room connected to the office. There was another toilet and sink in the shop area. With additional comfort came additional expense. After a few years the business no longer supported itself or us, and at the same time we started getting money from dead relatives. We lived on that money and against the best professional advice kept the business going.

Instead of going into the facts of the situation with my children which would only lead them to think I was quite insane, I told them I had the capacity to wash dishes and cook dandelion greens. In light of what was going on I was secretly convinced my individual problems were nothing.

Again and again things seemed to take care of themselves. We got a letter from the tax people saying we owed a rather large sum of money in back taxes. There was no way we could pay it, and if we divided it into twelve installments we would have no money left each month. We put the letter in a pile of other bills. I had no idea what we were going to do. That same week we got another letter from the government. It said the disability application Jenny sent a year earlier had been approved and we would get money each month. When that money arrived we turned it right around and sent it back to the government. The whole tax bill got paid that way.

Legally I was classified as an unemployed disabled person. I got to like that status, because when you have nothing you find out who your friends are. The telephone rang, and it was a person from a collection agency trying to get more of the money I owed in Missouri. I said I had no money or a job. I said I was an unemployed disabled person. He asked, "How are you getting by?"

I said, "My wife brings home a check," and added, "I guess I am just a kept man." He never called back. When the business was still earning money, as a legal matter the paycheck had to be in Jenny's name, not mine.

The first year I went to a district convention of Jehovah's Witnesses our congregation was assigned to the one in Louisville, Kentucky. Nearly 15,000 people were there. District conventions happen the best time of year in the country where they are. A yearbook told about a person in a remote part of the world who paddled a canoe two days to get to one.

In the Bible, Christ says you can recognize a tree by its fruit. The convention was in a large indoor arena in Louisville, Kentucky. The place was filled with Jehovah's Witnesses. I never saw so many.

A wheelchair-bound person wheeled himself into one of the men's rooms when I was in there. I was facing the other way, but I heard someone ask him by name if he needed help.

The convention lasted three days and dealt with how to cope with the problems of life using Bible-based information. When it was over there was a puddle of green engine coolant on the pavement under a van belonging to a family in our congregation. Someone walking past stopped. He lived in Louisville and had never met the family. When he learned what the situation was he told one of them where to get a new pump. He said he would go home to get his toolbox and overalls. The man with the tools worked right there in the parking lot three hours into the night.

No one acted like anything unusual was happening. There were half a dozen of us standing around, and when everything about bolting on the new pump was going right we enjoyed being there. I got back to the house late. I explained to Jenny more about why I was late and what happened. She said it would be that way with any church group.

Jehovah's Witnesses are one worldwide group without national boundaries. There has never been anything like that. A traveling district overseer said the organization of Jehovah's Witnesses was like a multifaceted diamond, and from the podium he pleaded, "Don't smash the diamond." Many times, many ways, the Bible warns about the danger of contentions developing between brothers. Personality conflicts are a threat to the unity. The word *brother* in the Bible and among Jehovah's Witnesses refers to everyone who shares in the knowledge of Jehovah and acts accordingly.

A brother and his wife in our congregation went to Australia. When they got back, many members of our congregation went to a banquet hall to hear about the trip, see slides, and have a good time. The photographs were projected on a large screen. It showed brothers and sisters who lived on the other side of the world.

After looking at the pictures, everyone ate dinner and danced. When it was over I helped tidy up the place. I put the paper tablecloth on our table in a garbage bag. There were paper plates, empty paper cups, plastic cups, plastic knives, forks, and spoons rolled up inside the tablecloth. Apparently, there was also somebody's cake. A sister very different from me (skin color and all) was downright cross at me when she returned and saw her cake was gone. Later that week after the Sunday meeting (it isn't called a service like in churches) the woman came up to me and said, "I hope you're not mad at me."

I said, "Heavens, no. Why would I be mad at you?" At first I didn't remember the incident.

Then she said with a curious and embarrassed look, "It was my cake you threw away." That is what he was talking about when he said, "Don't smash the diamond."

Each year the program at the district convention is outlined at the world headquarters in Brooklyn, New York. Everything about the Jehovah's Witness organization is like neat rows of army tents. Branches are divided into districts, and districts are divided into circuits. Circuits are divided into congregations.

Meetings on every level, even the district one, have the same purpose. First, it is what the Bible says. "Let us consider one another to incite to love and fine work, not forsaking the gathering of ourselves together." The *us* refers to a spiritual brother or sister, or people "in the truth." There are many expressions like *in the truth* which have special meaning to one of us.

Moments before Jesus Christ endured a long, tortuous execution he told a governor who was questioning him, "For this I have been born, and for this I have come into the world, that I should bear witness to the truth." The governor said back to him, "What is truth?" When someone says they are in the truth it means they are certain about Christ.

Secondly, the district meeting is designed to keep people "spiritually awake." That is the goal of every meeting. Over and over the Bible stresses the need to stay spiritually awake, and it warns about the "spirit of the world." The Bible says the spirit of the world is passing away. That "spirit of the world" is the conglomeration of people entirely absorbed in themselves and in getting what they want for themselves. A spiritual person knows the truth, and that makes them selfless.

In the United States there are numerous district conventions every year. The one I went to lasted Friday, Saturday, and Sunday. Jenny and the children never got past the way we all felt during the first one. I heard from them about sitting in one place all day and how tiresome it was. I suppose at first I also felt that way, but as time went by things were getting clearer. Everything didn't have to be so mystifying. I was being moved in more ways than one.

One of the ways was by Holy Spirit. That is difficult to explain, because it cannot be proven. For someone who has some or is on the receiving end of it, it is unmistakable. Holy Spirit is defined at the very beginning of the Bible by the words *active force*. ". . . and God's active force was moving to and fro over the surface of the waters." Different translators may use different words. Maybe they unknowingly lean toward a certain doctrine, but if a person lists all the references to Holy Spirit they will come to understand what the Holy Spirit is. Knowing what it is, is nothing compared to knowing its effect.

It was not possible that I discontinue my interest for any thing or anyone. There were days when I went to Louisville alone. Forcing the issue at home, insisting that everyone do this or that was blowing us apart. If it was better we remain one family it was better left alone. Many families stayed in Louisville all three days. They got special lodging rates that were determined by a person in Brooklyn and someone at the hotel or motel near the convention site. Others went back and forth each day. I was one of those. One year, early in the morning several of us met in the Kingdom Hall parking lot. We filled two cars.

That morning in the parking lot we waited for everyone to arrive. It was starting to be another hot day. Some people were drinking coffee from paper cups. There was an old man from another congregation. I had not met him. We talked. I didn't think he would mind so I asked him how old he was. He said he was ninety-two years old. We talked some more about the price of eggs and the hot weather. He was much shorter than I was. He sparkled, smiled often, and moved about agilely. At the same time most of us still had sleep in our eyes. I sat next to him on the way down there.

Occasionally the driver talked to the other person in the front seat. It was always a conversation just the two of them were having. I didn't talk and neither did the old man. When we crossed the Ohio River Bridge I began to think maybe I should try to strike up a conversation with him. Sometimes idle talk had its purpose. He seemed content to sit there without saying a word. I asked him how he got to be a Jehovah's Witness. What he said wasn't ordinary.

He said he lived in Adams County, which is a rural area east of Cincinnati. He said it was "unassigned territory," and some "brothers" came up from Portsmouth, Ohio. He said they stayed overnight at his house and left some books. He looked at me, smiled, and said it was eight years before they made a return visit. In the meantime his family became the only Jehovah's Witnesses in Adams County. As far as he was concerned that was the answer to my question, but oh no, there were many more questions. It was a good thing we were in a moving car. He couldn't leave. There was nothing frivolous about him.

It was 1920 when the books were left at his house. At that time and until 1935 the Jehovah's Witnesses went by the name Bible Students. It began in 1870 when a small group of people in Pittsburgh, Pennsylvania, got together to find out if widespread popular Christian ideas were in the Bible. If those ideas weren't in the Bible, where did they come from, and why? What they found out led them to quit their jobs and dedicate their lives to spreading the truth. Their effort snowballed into what today is known as the Jehovah's Witnesses, with 93,000 congregations in 235 lands.

In the following years our circuit assembly was in London, Ohio. Several times I saw two of the old man's grown children with him. The three of them always sat together. Years before on the way to the district convention in Louisville he told me when they lived in Adams County more than once his children had to walk home from school after the morning assembly. He said they were sent home because they did not pledge allegiance to the flag. As grown men sitting with their father. I mentioned this on two different occasions a year apart and both times they looked at their "dad" without saying anything to confirm or deny that it happened.

In the car going to Louisville I kept asking him questions. He realized my interest and started to say more. He told me the official in charge of the school wanted him ruled unfit as a father and tried to have his children taken away from him. He said they moved to another county where the school superintendent was more tolerant. Jehovah's Witnesses do not salute flags.

Bible education and applying Bible principles to present-day life is the subject of reams of literature made available to us. The governing body of Jehovah's Witnesses prepares it. They do it the same way someone builds a house. They don't hammer every nail. They have help. The governing body is comprised of between ten and twenty men. The number changes. Among us they are the "faithful and discreet slaves." One piece of literature refers to them as "fallible people teaching the infallible word of God."

The Bible asks: "Who really is the faithful and discreet slave whom his master appointed over his domestics, to give them their food at the proper time?" The master is Christ. The domestics are people. The faithful and discreet slave provides spiritual food. They help us apply Bible principles to present-day life. Exclusive devotion to God, not pledging allegiance to a flag, anything, or anyone, that is a Bible principle. Just like the Beroeans in Bible times, we are encouraged to verify what is being taught with the Bible.

A good example of how this works happened in what for a short time was Nazi Germany. Half a century after the fact, most people, or those who are not the same way, regard the person who formed that government as a totally evil person, but back then the man who oversaw the Witnesses' branch office in that country wanted to know what to do. He was told to do what his conscious dictated. Having a good Bible-based conscience comes from absorbing the literature. Everybody was told to follow their conscience. Meanwhile that government outlawed Jehovah's Witnesses.

The Bible teaches people to obey human governments, and while God didn't create those governments, according to the Bible they exist because God lets them exist. It doesn't specify that the Nazi government was an exception. The Bible also says: "We must obey God rather than men." Add to that Christ's comment, "Pay back Caesar's things to Caesar, but God's things to God," and all together there are some principles. A good Christian pays taxes honestly and obeys the government where they live, but that will only go so far.

With the Nazi government it wasn't very far. When a government expects an individual to violate God's law that is going too far. Jehovah's Witnesses would not involve themselves in the nationalistic fever. Like the Vietnamese rice farmer, all they wanted to do was brush their water buffalo.

Jehovah's Witnesses will not directly or indirectly go around and kill people, not even people who are from a different race, have a different religion, ethnic background, or are from a different nation. The Nazi leader couldn't deal with that, and as a result during the years he was in power Jehovah's Witnesses were beheaded, shot, transported to Nazi concentration camps, and in general treated as undesirable human beings, all because they wouldn't do what the Nazi government wanted. To express loyalty to the government they only had to sign something, do an act of obeisance to the leader or to a flag. Their only loyalty was to Jehovah. Many of them did what we call, "endure to the end." The Bible principles they expressed by the way they lived are defined again in the Bible this way, "Do not put your trust in nobles, nor in the son of earthling man, to whom no salvation belongs. His spirit goes out, he goes back to the ground, in that day his thoughts do perish."

Wherever Jehovah's Witnesses live, in whatever country it is, they explicitly obey the laws and rules of that government but do not get involved in any sort of political activity. In a country like this one, where the population votes to elect a government authority the prevailing attitude toward a person who doesn't vote is that they are getting a free ride, they are un-American, they are unappreciative, or all of the above. One angry lady said this: "You're Jehovah's Witnesses? My best friend's son died for this country."

The lady didn't want anything to do with us, but the person standing beside me got a few words out. He said something about tragedy, and as she shut the door he said, "Your friend's son wasn't killed by a Jehovah's Witness."

When I first started studying the Bible with the Jehovah's Witness lady I clearly remember thinking I could never be a Jehovah's Witness. I had seen people die for their country. I kept an American flag folded a special way for no other reason than to hang it against the front side of the farmhouse one day a year when American war dead were honored. Doing that made me think about moments in the past, and Jehovah's Witnesses didn't vote. I told the Jehovah's Witness lady their approach to the Bible was a good one, I wanted to keep the Bible study going, but I said I could never be one of them. She didn't try to talk me in or out of anything. I was adamant about voting. Not voting seemed like urinating on their grave. There was a swift current all around me and my attitude resulted more from that than from any clear thinking on my part.

What about all the other mother's children who were blown to kingdom come? The ones on the other side, what about them? Soldiers do "search and destroy" missions in the dark. A village is "pacified." A long time ago an English poet said the political leaders should slug it out to see who gets what. A Jehovah's Witness magazine quoted someone who said of all the "isms" the one that has caused the most human suffering, misery, and death is nationalism.

Today two nations struggle against each other and each one

thinks God is on their side. The truth is, if any supernatural being is on their side, it is Satan. That wasn't always the case. Again and again the Bible describes how Jehovah helped ancient Israel in a big way. Jehovah made a promise with them, and the "greater fulfillment" of that promise was Jesus Christ, who was to come from them. Jehovah was like a parent to a child.

One of the times ancient Israel was helped by Jehovah is in the Book of Judges, chapters 6 and 7. First it says: "Then the sons of Israel began to do what is bad in the eyes of Jehovah. So Jehovah gave them into the hands of Midian for seven years."

The Midianites would set up camp next to the Israelites. Verses 5 and 6 says: "They would come as numerous as the locusts, and they and their camels were without number; and they would come into the land and ruin it. And Israel became greatly impoverished due to Midian; and the sons of Israel began to call to Jehovah for aid."

They were helped. Verse 12 says; "Then Jehovah's angel appeared to him [Gideon] and said to him: 'Jehovah is with you, you valiant mighty one.'" At this Gideon said to him; "'Excuse me, my lord, but if Jehovah is with us, then why has all this come upon us, and where are all those wonderful acts that our fathers related to us, saying, was it not out of Egypt that Jehovah brought us up? And now Jehovah has deserted us, and he gives us into the palm of Midian.' Upon that Jehovah faced him [faced him by proxy through the angel; none has seen Jehovah and lives], "and said, 'Go in this power of yours, and you will certainly save Israel out of Midian's palm.'" Gideon is human. In verse 15 he asks what to him is a highly relevant question. "Excuse me, Jehovah, with what shall I save Israel?" Then Jehovah replies, "Because I shall prove to be with you, and you shall certainly strike down Midian as if one man."

That conversation took place while Gideon was sitting under a big shade tree in Ophra. Quite naturally he wants more to go on. After all, how many times does an angel sit down under a tree with you? Saving Israel involved others, possibly others who would die. Gideon might have considered that he had some screws loose or something of that sort. So Gideon says, "If, now, I have found favor in your eyes, you must also perform a sign for me that you are the one speaking with me."

Here is the sign: "Then Gideon said to the [true] God: 'If you are saving Israel by means of me just as you have promised, here I am keeping a fleece of wool exposed on the threshing floor. If dew comes to be on the fleece alone but on all the earth there is dryness, then I must know that you are saving Israel by means of me, just as you have promised.' And it turned out to be that way. When he rose up early the next day and wrung the fleece, he got to drain off enough dew from the fleece to fill a large banquet bowl with water. However Gideon said to the [true] God: 'Do not let your anger blaze against me, but let me speak just once more. Let me, please, make tests once more with the fleece. Let, please, dryness occur to the fleece alone, and upon all the earth let there come to be dew.' So God did that way on that night; and dryness came to be on the fleece alone, and upon all the earth dew occurred."

In chapter 7 Jehovah tells Gideon exactly what to do and with 300 men Gideon permanently chases away all of the Midianites.

When ancient Israel did things their way and not Jehovah's way calamity was right around the corner. One of the times this happened is explained this way in a Jehovah's Witness publication: "Social injustice, tyranny, greed, dishonesty, bribes, sexual perversion, criminal attacks, bloodshed, as well as religious hypocrisy that converted God's temple into a " 'cave of robbers' "—all of these things were decried by Jehovah's prophets in their warning messages delivered to rulers and people. (Is 1:15-17,21-23; 3:14,15; Jer 5:1,2,7,8,26-28,31; 6:6,7; 7:8-11) Neither the support of the apostate priests nor any political alliance made with other nations could avoid the coming crash of that unfaithful kingdom. (Jer 6:13-15; 37:7-10). The capital city, Jerusalem was destroyed and Juda was laid waist by the Babylonians in 607 B.C.E.-2Ki 25:1-26."

The Israelites who survived were slaves in Babylon for quite some time. Jehovah eventually returned them to the land where they once were. The first thing they did was rebuild the temple.

The Messiah had not been born yet. The ancient Israelites were descendants of Abraham, and Jehovah directly told Abraham that the Messiah would come from his descendants. When

Jesus Christ was born and every sign identifying him as the Messiah was fulfilled, he was rejected. After that Jehovah did not treat one kingdom or nation in the parental way he did that one. Now, according to the Bible, Jehovah seeks "people out of all nations, tribes, and peoples and tongues."

When David moved the ark of the true God to Jerusalem and decided to build for it a house of cedars. Jehovah tells David through the prophet Nathan in 2nd Samuel 7:11-14 that not him, but one of his descendants will build a house for Jehovah that will last to time indefinite. David doesn't know the details of what Nathan said, but those details are now known from parts of the Bible written after David's time. The descendant is Jesus Christ and the house is the Congregation of God.

The apostle Peter explains this when he talks to religious leaders about a cured lame beggar. In Acts 4:10-12 he says to them, "Let it be known to all of you and to all the people of Israel, that in the name of Jesus Christ the Nazarene, whom you impaled but whom God raised up from the dead, by this one does this man stand in front of you. This [Jesus] is 'the stone that was treated by you builders as of no account that has become the head of the corner.' Furthermore, there is no salvation in anyone else, for there is not another name under heaven that has been given among men by which we must get saved."

Saved from the condition of all people. We are the offspring of Adam and Eve. All of us have inherited their sin, and like them we grow old and die.

In the very beginning, when Adam and Eve chose to willfully disobey God, God told them in that day they would surely die. They lost the prospect of living forever on a paradise earth.

Out in a world without God they began aging and died. It was God's original purpose that righteous people inhabit the earth, and that purpose has not changed.

When God was sending Adam and Eve out of the Garden of Eden the first prophecy appears in the Bible. In Genesis 3:15 God says, "And I shall put enmity between you [Satan] and the woman [heavenly Jerusalem]. Between your seed [Satan] and her seed [Christ]. He will bruise you in the head [do away with Satan] and you will bruise him in the heel [kill Jesus Christ while he is on earth]. Christ hasn't "abyssed" Satan yet, that will happen at Armageddon, but Satan has bruised Christ in the heel.

Nobody knows the time of Armageddon. In the Bible Christ says he doesn't know, but only the father (Jehovah) who is in heaven knows, and Christ goes on to say it will come just like a thief in the night. After Armageddon, the Bible says, Christ will rule a cleansed earth. Christ is the only escape route. Now more than ever mankind has proven beyond a reasonable doubt that we cannot live without God in a manner that God approves.

A manner God approves is the example provided by Christ, and it is in all that he said. No longer will people run around hacking each other up with machetes. It will be a world where there will be enjoyable work for everyone. If we can't understand that or think it is too far-fetched that is because we are leaning on our own understanding. With God all things are possible.

Without any preconceptions resulting from what I knew but could not prove I reconsidered God. Very soon after that I had to admit even by normal standards a supernatural being was involved with the Bible. One of the laws Jehovah gave to the ancient Israelites was one that said they had to wash their hands before eating. Another one was a law that they were to bury human excrement outside camp. There was no explanation. An ancient Israelite would have figured an all-knowing God said so and that was good enough for him. Also, there was the implication that it would go well with them to do so. Today, through modern science, we know there are some health benefits to those two laws. They didn't know that back then, but they did it anyway. Were they told to do it for their own good?

The Bible was written over a period of 1,600 years by forty people, who, it says, were "inspired" by Jehovah. If they weren't, how did they know what they wrote? No human source could have provided the details they have. Historical events are described that hadn't happened. Some critical people say that proves it was written after the fact. That would make the Bible writers conniving liars. Is it beyond the critical people to at least speculate that a supernatural being was involved?

In 1492 a Spaniard said he could get to the East by sailing west. He speculated the Earth was round. That was a different idea from prevailing thought, scientific, religious, or political.

Thousands of years earlier a Bible writer made an obscure reference to the "circle of the Earth," and at about the same time another one in the same way mentions off to the side: "The Earth is hanging on nothing." How did they know that?

I told Jenny I wasn't going to vote anymore. She asked why like I wasn't altogether serious. I said I learned the obvious from the Bible. It is impossible for humans to rule other humans. Even when political leaders have good intentions, hurtful desire always gets in the way. Look for yourself. Some governments might be more successful than others in attempting to bring lasting peace and happiness to the people they govern, but all of them have failed. Isn't that what it is all about, and if it isn't, what is the purpose of government?

Jenny said, "What if everyone did that? What if no one voted?"

"What if a duck charged you?" I said.

If God is so powerful, why don't we get absolute, indisputable proof that we can see, hear, touch, smell, and taste? Christ raised the dead, cured the sick, and fed the multitudes; that "proof" lasted only a short while into the early part of the first century. The ancient Roman government killed two birds with one stone, providing entertainment in the Coliseum and getting rid of a pesky people by feeding them to lions. To avoid a gruesome death a Christian only had to go over to an altar and sprinkle some incense over a flame. That was an admittance that Christ and the resurrection was a lie. It was also a sign of token appreciation for the ruler of Rome. The ones who died must have known something absolutely, even though they couldn't prove it to their jail keeper.

Does being spiritual mean believing in something regardless of whether it makes sense to anyone else? The Bible says: "Happy is the person aware of their spiritual need." In this day and age there is a litmus test for everything. In the door-to-door work I talked to a man watering his garden. He was a nice man who wanted to talk. Another person, the man, and I stood there watching the water fall on the ground. We talked about what made plants grow, and from there the conversation got into creation. His last words were that he was a biologist with a degree. He said when we had a degree come back and talk to him. I don't think spiritual matters were pertinent to him. No matter how much we say spiritual matters are not for us, or repress it, we have this spiritual need not entirely unlike every motorized car has a drive mechanism. Secular education, and adherence to courtroom evidence does not prevent one from realizing their spiritual need, it just makes it much more difficult.

Between 450 and 60 million years ago did dinosaurs lay eggs and leave? Or did they return repeatedly to bring their young food? Did God create mankind 6,000 years ago? If a scientist could hide in a tree and watch the behavior of dinosaurs for just one afternoon, upon returning, he or she would be fortunate if in the remainder of their lifetime they could gather enough fossil evidence to convince others what they alone knew were the facts. Everyone would criticize them saying they were unscientific. If a juror of an accused person, unknown to everyone else, was at the crime scene, to him or her, would evidence or the lack of it make a difference? If, on the basis of what they knew, they tried to explain innocence or guilt, the other jurors would say they were biased.

One side says the Earth started as one big hot rock in outer space. It went, and still goes through, evolutionary change. That satisfactorily explains for them how this place got to be the planet where we now reside. The other side says a Creator made the Earth and everything in or on it.

For the moment remove the element of time from what these two sides say. The one side "theorizes" a particular species became something else. The amoeba, a one-cell creature that lives in water, both remained the same and evolved into a more complex animal. The fern, the simplest of green plants, both stayed the same and changed into a more complex plant like a tree or a daffodil. People who suppose this theory is accurate are unable to explain in the scientific terms they love so much why a plant or animal, whether it sticks around or suddenly disappears, leaves no indication in the fossil record that it became something else. There is no evidence that a turtle crawled out of the water and eventually became a human.

Beyond this planet, the more we find out, the more we find out there is no life but on this place. There is no scientific explanation of where living matter came from or how it evolved from nonliving matter. No human, try as we may, has been able to take nonliving matter and from it make living matter. People have tried to create life in electrically charged bell jars on laboratory tables. They can't produce the smallest microorganism. They explain that the biological distance between a microorganism and a human is nothing compared to the distance between the microorganism and nonliving matter.

The other side holds fast to there being a Creator. They disregard all the schooled thought that says impossible without saying impossible. They believe if the Creator simply wants this or that in a particular way, this or that becomes that way. Like the parting of the Red Sea, it cannot be explained scientifically.

So the Creator wanted light and there was light. Every creature was deemed necessary so they happened, the giraffe with its long neck and all the others big and small.

Once the evolution foundation is in place that we evolved from animals it is smooth sailing to say we are animals and "survival of the fittest" applies to us also. When that notion was first presented more than 100 years ago it pleased many to think it applied to them. It justified the way they were or wanted to be.

In recent times more than a few well-meaning people apparently consider this notion a fact even though they don't say so. One of them, typical of the rest, backs into the idea of improving our humanity by saying we should understand animals. Recording the behavior of a flock of Grey Leg Geese, he notes striking similarities between animal behavior and human behavior. At the end of the book he moralizes and says, if ever we are going to understand ourselves we have to understand animals.

Bones cause many people to consider the evolution theory a fact. Their thinking is that our bones are like the bones of animals so, of course, we must also be animals. It has been demonstrated, at least once, that a hungry orangutan, when given enough time, without assistance unscrewed the top of a clear glass jar to eat an orange all up. Does that imply the animal can reason?

Our bones and biological functions are not different from animals'. It is our ability to reason that is different. Reason is this: If *A* equals *B*, and *B* equals *C*, then *A* equals *C*. The ability to reason, not bones, sets human beings apart from animals.

There is no courtroom evidence and never will be that the ability to reason was the product of evolution. A bunch of people will never be able to stand around looking at reason and say it came from this or that rock formation.

The creation account does not rule out that mountains wash to the sea or that a predatory bird soaring on high gets more to eat than one that doesn't see as well. That is "natural selection." Where the two sides part company is whether or not the bird will ever become something entirely different like a fish.

Enter time. Time is the most conflicting piece of evidence there is. By our own understanding it cannot be resolved. This is exactly the situation of someone who has only a technical knowledge of God, but doesn't know the power that is there. Understanding God by scientific standards is not possible. When Holy Sprit hits there is no question that God exists. Courtroom evidence like the time thing is meaningless because, in effect, you were there.

Many people stood at their front door and said they were happy with their religion. They knew we were Jehovah's Witnesses. Most of them were too busy to explain why they were so happy with their religion. The few who did explain seemed to think we were trying to recruit Jehovah's Witnesses and that our purpose was to make them a Jehovah's Witness. I said our purpose was to draw attention to the Bible as a source of guidance and power and they could decide the rest for themselves.

One lady clasped her hands together against her chest and with a big smile said, "You're Jehovah's Witnesses." She went on and on about how we were where it's at, although it was clear she was not a Jehovah's Witness.

She was still talking. I managed to get a word in edgewise. I said, "Ma'am, if you think Jehovah's Witnesses are so great why aren't you a Jehovah's Witness?"

She said she was a Methodist. I asked her why she was a Methodist, and she said, "Because my mother was a Methodist."

Another woman who had time to talk also said something about her mother. In a very friendly manner she said her sister was a Jehovah's Witness. I asked her what she thought of her sister, and this gray-headed woman said, "She is a disgrace to her mother."

Many people had an adverse reaction to the idea of organized religion but identified in themselves a spiritual need. They said God was something undefined in them. When I mentioned the Bible or Jehovah I could see all kinds of warning flags pop up in their minds. When I first became a Jehovah's Witness there was much said about other religions. People tended to shut down when I talked about their religion. It was like I was criticizing their house or the way they lived. Drawing people's attention to the Bible was an indirect way of saying how sick their religion is.

When I was in the military I was standing in a movie ticket line at Fort Benning in Columbus, Georgia. An airborne trainee in front of me wearing civilian clothes had words printed on his shirt that said: KILL THEM ALL AND LET GOD SORT THEM OUT. He bought the shirt off base. It was not Government Issue. Thirty years later I read practically the same words in a Jehovah's Witness magazine. This is what it said: "'Slay them all; God will recognize His own.' On that summer day of 1209, the population of Beziers, in southern France, was massacred. The monk Arnold Amalric, appointed as papal legate at the head of the Catholic crusaders, showed no mercy. When his men asked how they were to distinguish between Catholics and heretics, he reportedly gave the infamous reply quoted above. Catholic historians have watered it down to 'Do not worry. I believe very few will be converted.' Whatever his exact answer, the result was the slaughter of 20,000 men, woman, and children at the hands of some 300,000 crusaders, led by prelates of the Catholic Church."

For several weeks beginning on April 6, 1994, in the country of Rwanda in Africa, a country that is said to be predominately Christian, people hacked up people with machetes because they were either Hutu or Tutsi. Five hundred thousand people were killed. One well-documented incident involved a group of people who hid in a church. Meanwhile the person with the key, a priest, summoned the rival ethnic group, and they killed everyone there.

Not long ago I was getting some mailbox paint and I heard a telephone conversation on the radio. On one end a radio talk show personality assumed the manner of a person who didn't use the King's English very well. This time the call was to someone advertised as being a person who would pray for the caller. In a sincere unschooled tone the radio personality explained a problem and asked over and over in a sorrowful way, "Would you pray for me?" After talking a while the voice on the other end finally said how he would pray for him, but first the sincere unschooled person had to send $50.

Many people said God was inside every living thing, including them. They wanted nothing to do with religious people, especially Jehovah's Witnesses. Just the mention of a word like *government* when talking about God's Kingdom caused them to throw up their hands, shake their head, or terminate the conversation. The name Jehovah or the word *Bible* and *organization* often had the same result. Those who talked said "God" was in them. Who or what that God was depended on the person talking. Parts of the Bible they liked, but the whole of it was not a concern to them. When I mentioned Christian standards they thought I was talking about a Jehovah's Witness "interpretation." The spiritual dimension of their life was private. Putting a name on it was the same as being associated with a particular religious group. They didn't want to be like religious people. None of them talked about the behavior of past or present religious people. The ones who responded said in one way or another "to each his own." I told them the most wicked people on earth could have a private understanding of God.

People who say God is in them make good to be whatever they want. They are like the woodcarver in the Bible: "Half of it he actually burns up in a fire. Upon half of it he roasts well the flesh that he eats, and he becomes satisfied. He also warms himself and says, 'Aha! I have warmed myself. I have seen the firelight.' But the remainder of it he actually makes into a god itself, into a carved image. He prostrates to it and bows down and prays to it and says: 'Deliver me, for you are my god.'"

A movie I saw as a child was about a government official in a dark suit and a barefoot farmer's daughter. The government was going to make huge lakes in rural Tennessee, and people had to move. She had outgrown the dresses she wore. Their relationship was the movie. When he left she did not go with him. He gave her a coin, saying it was a good luck piece that would help her when he was gone. She always kept it close to her.

Like the young woman, and the woodcarver many people are

certain they get help from foreign objects, but the help is their own. Self-help and help from God are not even close to being the same thing.

I hadn't seen the preacher who married us in a long time. He married and buried quite a few of my relatives. He was a young man when I was a small child. I told him I fondly remembered his fiery sermons about how it was easier for a camel to get through the eye of a needle than it was for a rich man to get into heaven. He said he never made sermons like that and was embarrassed by the thought. Now he was old, retired from his job at the church, but he still officiated at some church events.

On the telephone I asked him to have lunch with me. I could hear him turning pages in his date book. He said he was in so many wrecks that his son convinced him not to drive anymore. On the set day and time I went to his house to pick him up. We had lunch at an Indian restaurant. We talked about life in general. He said his friends were dying and he buried them. I could tell, by the way he said it, it wore him down. We talked about the resurrection.

He knew I didn't go to church anymore, and that I was a Jehovah's Witness. He asked me how the "Jehovahs" were. I said fine like a child whose parent asks about a day in school. Then I said in all recorded history there has never been a worldwide group of people who didn't follow a flag until there were Jehovah's Witnesses.

We talked about war, nationalism, and bloodshed. He said, "What about the Old Testament [Hebrew scripture]. That is part of the Bible too." He was talking about war and how because it happened so much in the Bible it was therefore OK with God. He thought a while about my worldwide brotherhood comment and said, "Quakers are very much like Jehovah's." I didn't reply. We had a good lunch. I drove him home. It was a sunny day. He got out of the car at the end of his driveway to get his mail. It was a long driveway with one big shade tree near the house. He walked to the house. I turned around and drove home.

A man at his door talked gruffly. He said he was very involved in *his church*, that he was in some sort of leadership capacity. We could say nothing about religion he didn't already know. I asked him, "Didn't Christ teach all of us to love each other? In the Bible doesn't Christ say people everywhere will recognize his followers by their love among each other?"

He gruffly said, "Yes, of course."

I asked him what he told his son or a member of his congregation who wanted to join an army and go off to kill people.

"Oh," he says, "that is different."

I asked him, "What is the difference?" He had to go. He closed the door between us.

During a gathering of people I had a conversation with a person who said he was a schoolteacher studying the ancient philosophers and working for a graduate degree. He was doing a paper on the "philosophy of religion." I asked him if that wasn't a contradiction in terms. It seemed to me that a religion that became a philosophy was no longer a religion. When I mentioned Christ and the Bible he was quick to remind me there were other religions. I didn't want to fragment the conversation by saying there is a story in the Bible about how Elijah made all those in attendance aware who the true God was, and I didn't want to hear him say I couldn't logically use the Bible to prove what the Bible said. I didn't want to insult his sense of academic procedure by saying the true God cannot be proven, and is only apparent to individuals, all of who have three things in common: they are humble, honest, and spiritually hungry. Instead of getting into that I asked him where the notion came from that people are good. He named a fifth-century B.C. Greek philosopher who he said put forth that idea, and he said it probably came from a philosopher before the one he named. Then he said the ancient philosopher established many Christian ideas. I asked him what ideas those could be, because the idea that people are good is not a Christian one.

He said, "I'm sorry, but if you're trying to tell me that God created people who by their nature are bad I cannot accept that idea." I said people aren't created bad, but people all by themselves, without God, are bad. I said that wasn't a philosophical idea. It was a fact, one that is spelled out in the Bible, no place better than the one where the apostle Paul says in his flesh there dwells nothing good. I told him an honest look at man's treatment of man since history began would answer any philosophical questions he might have about the goodness or badness of mankind. It sits well with us to say we, all by ourselves, are good. Today in both hemispheres humans have heard that stated or implied so much it is assumed true.

"Original sin." He said, "Is that original sin?"

I had to think what that meant, because I hadn't heard that expression for a long time. "Yes it is," I said. "If you mean Adam and Eve in the Garden of Eden, that is exactly what it is. That is why the Apostle Paul says nothing good dwells in him. It's original sin."

We started going around in circles. He repeated, If God is the creator of people, why would he create everyone a bad person? He said it like there was no real explanation and the matter of good and bad was a subject to explore, a mental gymnastics for the future, a philosophical topic just like it was in the past. He wanted to grapple with the thought and was thinking about it when I told him there is an accurate explanation, which is the theme of the entire Bible. As I began to say what that is he was looking across the room. He would go there in a polite way. I was trying to make it short and sweet. He was somewhere else. He was like so many people: preconceived notions overwhelmed him. I was trying to explain why there is a good and bad person. I was going to tell him where God was when a Cossack shot a baby in the face at point blank range while it was in its mother's arms. I never got to finish or even get started.

The Bible says the one called Devil and Satan is misleading the entire inhabited earth, and the Bible calls him the "God of this system of things." In the account of Christ's temptation, the Bible says; "The Devil took him along to an unusually high mountain, and showed him all the kingdoms of the world and their glory, and said to him, 'All these things I will give you if you fall down and do an act of worship to me.'" Christ did not deny they were Satan's to give. He told Satan to get away.

According to the Bible, Satan was an angel created by God but one who challenged God's leadership. Using a serpent as a mouthpiece, Satan got Adam and Eve to disobey God. The Bible also tells us that Satan set out to turn all of Adam and Eve's unborn offspring away from God. God allowed time for Satan to prove his point. We're still in that time, still in that mess.

Satan is not alone in his leadership of the world. Other

angels joined him in the rebellion against God. Demons are the name given to them in the Bible. The Bible speaks of them when it says to Christians: "Stand firm against the machinations of the Devil; because we have a wrestling, not against blood and flesh, but against the world rulers of this darkness, against the wicked spirit forces in the heavenly places."

The Bible over and over refers to Satan as being as real as Jehovah God is. Christ says this when he is talking to the religious leaders, "But now you are seeking to kill me, a man that has told you the truth that I heard from God . . . You are from your father the Devil, and you wish to do the desires of your father. That one was a manslayer when he began (Adam and Eve were the first victims), and he did not stand fast in the truth, because the truth was not in him. When he speaks the lie, he speaks according to his own disposition, because he is a liar and the father of the lie."

Satan spoke the first lie when he told Adam and Eve, "Surely you will not die." Jehovah had previously told them in the day they ate the fruit they would positively die. Somebody had to be lying.

I often heard a friend say in the halls between classes, "The serpent *beguiled* the fair maiden." Adam and Eve had the prospect of living forever, filling the earth, and being perfect tenants. They only had to stick with Jehovah. They lost what they had. They began aging and died. They thought they could live better without God.

So why all the time? Why weren't Adam and Eve swatted like flies and someone else given a try? It wouldn't have settled a thing. Man's ability to live without God would still be a question in the minds of people. Much time has gone past for us. Our condition is described once this way in the Bible: "Man has dominated man to his own injury."

In the big picture God is in charge, and that makes personal problems seem small. It is a good thing, because in a one-year period my mailboxes got copied and we lost our two biggest buyers. That would have been a crisis several years earlier, but when it happened it was just another day. One thing happened and soon enough another thing happened to counter it, and all the time I was prepared to wash dishes. It wasn't important how glorious a job I had. I even told that to the number two guy when he was on top at the second catalog.

The mailbox business was not making it. That became truer after the two mail-order companies dropped us. When we were still doing business with them I wrote distressing letters about how I made a good mailbox but wasn't very adept with paper and numbers. The letters were far apart and unrelated, but in different ways they said the same thing. If they liked the mailboxes, we needed help on the financial end. The letter to the first mail-order company said the price of a mailbox was going to increase 20 percent every six months for the next two years. The second mail-order company (by then the first was gone) was told we would keep bringing them mailboxes, but could we also bring them all our bills? They could then pay us a fair amount for our labor. Most months we couldn't pay all the bills. If the mail-order company took care of the bills they would be certain of an uninterrupted supply. As it was, the only ones making money were the government and the employees. It wasn't a long time after those letters that both companies were either having their own copies made or buying a lower-cost, lighter-weight copy.

Veeders Mailbox was just another vendor to them. One or the other company wasn't going to become involved in the financial management of a vendor. To them I was unprofessional, but if the space given to a product in a catalog is any indication of its profitability the Veeders Mailbox must have been one of the most profitable items in both catalogs. One whole page was devoted to the mailbox. My saying in a letter how there would be a price increase every six months for the next two years was all the push they needed. They each thought anybody could make a mailbox for the same money, which wasn't true. They would find that out for themselves. The first company dittoed the mailbox and called it their own. They even copied the mailbox flag design which I always thought was unique to our mailbox. It was the Veeders trademark. We used it on our letterhead and on printed material. They knew that but used it anyway. They thought it was theirs. Before that we tried to have it legally protected by the federal government in the trademark office. They denied the application. The examiner said the reason was because the flag was part of the mailbox. It didn't make sense to me, but very little ever did. When the mailbox was copied by the first mail-order company, they turned it around backward so the design was reversed.

During the short while I was doing business with both mail-order companies the first mail-order company was late paying me a big chunk of money that I needed to make payroll that Friday. I called their finance person on the telephone. I arranged to get there that day and get paid. We would meet on the shipping dock. Veeders Mailbox policy was that each invoice was due in ten days. In exchange we delivered for free to their dock. Finance people had the same excuse. "The mail delivery took a long time" was the one I heard most often. The postmark indicated when the piece of mail had been sent. Big companies had a machine in their office that was owned and controlled by the post office. The machine would postmark each piece of mail. After it went through the machine it was up to the company to mail it at the post office. My money often took two weeks for no apparent reason. Purchase orders or other written communications from them took two or three days. From me to them was twenty-five miles. I called the postal superintendent at the post office where the mail-order company was located to ask him why it took so long to get mail that had a check inside. In so many words, he said it didn't. When I told the finance person about this exchange he was not very pleased with me. My intention was to get my money on time, and in attempting that I failed.

The day I went to the shipping dock to get my money I waited in the receiving department where there were four big rolling doors. On the other side of the building packages were sent out. It was a huge operation. The marketing man who started the second company told me when he worked at the first company they mailed out millions of catalogs each year. The first company began one year before I started making mailboxes. The owner must have made all the right moves. I think he owned it entirely. I heard from a person in the receiving department that more and more trucks were arriving there every day.

By telephone someone told the finance person I was there. I watched people move large bundles to well-lit worktables. Smaller packages inside the bundles were neatly stacked on carts. The carts were moved into the main part of the building where the packages were restacked on high steel shelves. The catalog said everything for sale would ship the next day.

While I watched I saw the owner coming toward me. The main finance person was on one side of him and the main purchasing agent was on the other side. The building was so big it was a while before they got to me. I decided it was better to wait where I was. When they got to me I shook the owner's hand first. I was in my work clothes, and I hadn't shaved that morning. I apologized for the way I looked and said to the owner if I knew he was going to be there, I would have shaved. He was friendly in a very professional manner. He had the check in his hand. He gave it to me and at the same time mentioned the second mail-order company by name. He asked if they paid their bills on time. Those were the first words out of his mouth after hello. I said I had three children and from the middle one I learned how to make things fair. I said the other company paid on time and, just like them, was on ten days net. The finance person was standing behind the owner. I could see by his expression that I said the right thing mentioning the ten days net. The owner must have wondered what the finance person was doing behind his back, because he turned to see him. The finance person immediately assumed a cold, disinterested expression. We were by the work-tables. When he glanced at six or seven people standing under lights they worked extra fast.

The second company selected a special color for the mailboxes. They were the only ones selling that color. The owner said he wanted it also. I told him I promised a main person at the second company that they would be the only ones to have that color. I said to the owner if he wanted his very own color I would be more than happy to paint mailboxes whatever color he wanted. I suggested hot pink as a possible color he could have all to himself.

He looked out toward the receiving docks where trucks backed up to unload. When he found out I didn't have any mailboxes for him he said I had better get back and weld. I said he would get more on Monday. I told him over the weekend the paint would dry and I would pack them in cardboard boxes. Also that weekend I wrote him a letter asking whether or not he wanted hot pink mailboxes. He wrote back that he didn't.

The first time we met after my accident the main purchasing agent telephoned to say the owner wanted to meet person-to-person. Jenny and I both went. I, Jenny, the purchasing agent and the owner went to a cafeteria in the building that was full of employees eating lunch. It was a large rectangular room with a polished linoleum floor. People sat in bright-colored plastic chairs at long tables with plastic-coated tops. The ceiling was very high. A concrete block wall painted a light color separated the cafeteria from the inside of the building. The opposite wall was glass. The cafeteria overlooked the airfield of a county airport he also owned. Vending machines were lined up on another wall. Next to them was a countertop with a solid base. A stack of red plastic trays was on the right side of the machines.

The building was new. It smelled new. If the owner felt he had accomplished something he didn't let it show. When I first started delivering mailboxes to his company five or ten years earlier I delivered to a much smaller building a short distance away. Several times he came out on the receiving dock in the winter cold wearing a white button-down shirt sweat-soaked around his armpits. He would tell me to make mailboxes faster. Once he asked why I didn't bring them to his attention earlier. Without stopping unloading my overloaded car trailer I told him I painted with a brush back then. When he started ordering, even with a paint sprayer some night, I would sleep on the shop floor, and he wanted them faster.

In the cafeteria he got trays and asked us what we wanted to eat from what was available. The purchasing agent helped himself. The trays were not clean to the owner's satisfaction, and he made that plain without saying anything. In a disgruntled fashion he washed the trays himself in a sink, and he dried them with paper towels. He lined them up on the counter and turned around to pump some money into the machines.

We were on the other side of the counter. The four trays on the countertop were unattended during the moment he was getting food. During that time one of the employees, a young man, put his lunch on one of the trays. Then he left to get a canned drink. While the young man was gone the owner returned with his hands full of food. He asked the purchasing agent who also had just returned if the food on the tray was his. The young man in a crowd of people with his drink in hand realized from a distance that he had put his food on one of the four trays set out by the owner. At that point he started to walk in another direction abandoning what he had just bought. The owner looked down the counter to see whose food it was. When no one appeared to belong to it he took it off the tray and put it on the counter. We all went to sit down.

We didn't talk much. After eating in that impressive place we went to a conference room with one long table. Quite naturally, Jenny and I sat on opposite sides of the table, which forced them to do the same. The purchasing agent and me were on one side. He was four chairs away from me. The owner was directly across from me at the middle of the table. Jenny sat one seat away from him on his left side. She had a pencil and paper. The purchasing agent had many pieces of paper. I had brought the eight-page medical report. The owner didn't have anything but himself.

Before we ate lunch, going up the stairs to the cafeteria he asked me if I was still riding motorcycles. I told him in no uncertain terms I was not. Sharing the road with 2,000 pounds of sheet metal going the other way with nothing but a yellow line between us was something I could live without. When we were seated in the conference room he asked me if the letter I sent was a list of demands. It immediately became apparent the reason he wanted the meeting was to establish some sort of footing for the future, to see what my attitude toward him was. Always before I had dealt with the number two man who was no longer with the company and who had started the second mail-order outfit. The letter he called my list of demands was a list of what the number two man and me had agreed upon as a way of doing business. Before the letter there was nothing in writing. The letter said the owner could change anything. For him to begin abruptly saying the letter contained a list of demands was not good by any stretch of the imagination. He certainly didn't believe in small talk.

When he began with that comment I quickly replied that I had never made any demands in my entire life. One of the items that he called a demand was that they would pay in ten days if I delivered for free.

I was already selling mailboxes to the other company. The letter explained what happened to the exclusive. It said the exclusive was cancellable by either side with thirty days' notice. He questioned that, and I explained how the exclusive evolved. I named the international Japanese company that sold them the scanner radio and said we agreed the exclusive would be just like the one they had with them.

He said, "How do you know what agreement we have with ____?" He named the international company.

I told about the time when I sat in the number two man's office. I forgot the name of the other person. I turned to the purchasing agent for help. I described the man whose name I forgot as having a pockmarked face and added that he took pictures for the catalog. The man had been gone from there for many years. The purchasing agent knew exactly who I was talking about, and with no hesitation, without looking up, he said the man's name. Every time I looked at him he wasn't looking up. It seemed like the whole time he was facing straight down at the papers in front of him. The purchasing agent was in charge of the purchasing department. I had talked to him many times. When he was by himself we could joke about things. He wasn't so serious. He could be very serious. He had a wonderful smile. The owner was all business. When the purchasing agent said the man's name so quickly that subject ended then and there. There was no doubt in the room that I knew what their agreement was with the international company.

The owner said firing the number two men was the hardest thing he ever had to do. It surprised me how human he was all of a sudden. I said I was sorry it was so hard for him. I really meant it, but it sounded like I didn't really care why he fired the number two man. I think he thought the man he fired who went on to start the second company and me were best friends. The fact was, I could relate more to the owner sitting across the table from me than I could to the other guy. The owner was consistent and predictable. When he said it was the most difficult thing he ever had to do, and I replied that I was sorry it was the most difficult thing he ever had to do, he looked at me sternly and said, "What?" Business life was one big fencing match, parry and repose. I said again, sincerely, compassionately, with better diction and syncopation that I was sorry firing the other guy was the most difficult thing he ever had to do. I am not sure he believed me that time, either.

There was a folder in front of me, and from it I got a very impressive eight page medical report, and gave it to the purchasing agent who had all the other paper. In a very technical way it said I was competent to stand trial. In some areas, it said I had the equivalent of an eighth-grade education. When I handed it to the purchasing agent I said to the owner it proved beyond reasonable doubt I was back and could make mailboxes. A few days later they sent the medical report back to me with no explanation whatsoever. For them to go to the trouble of sending it back the way they did made me think it was done for some legal reason like down the road, later on, they might want to disavow that I ever existed. Eventually that is exactly what they did.

Each winter I would go to the island in Maine for a few days. All the tourists were somewhere else that time of year. It was unusual I would go there by myself in summer, but before my accident that is what I did. No matter if I was alone or not, the first stop was a one-night visit at my brother's house on the mainland.

Jenny said I should laugh more often like I did when I was with him. She said she never heard me laugh like I did when we were together. When we were small children I got him used to the rain. For a long time he thought rain was like a bucket of cold water. He was my slave after that, running to fetch this wrench or that piece of bailing wire. When he got older he became more self-assertive in a healthy way. He did not get tools for me anymore.

When we were children we started sending a model of an American riverboat back and forth each Christmas. It stayed in the box. Neither of us ever put it together. Year after year it went back and forth. Some years it missed a year. When we met and when he or I thought about it, we would ask who had it or where it was.

I bought it the first year from a man who had a hobby shop in Montgomery. His store had top-notch models for sale. The box had the word MOTORIZED across the top. I bought it with the intention of building it myself, but I never did. At Christmastime

I wrapped it up and gave it to my brother. He knew I had bought it for myself several months earlier. The Christmas after that one he wrapped it up and gave it back to me. Every year since then it has gone back and forth. Very seldom either of us mentions it, but the model keeps going back and forth.

Jehovah's Witnesses don't want any part of Christmas. For one thing December 25 in ancient times was a time to celebrate the return of a sun god and was selected as the time to celebrate Christ's birthday. The merchants and religious institutions that promote December 25 as the time to celebrate Christ's birthday disown him by their works. Christ has been sold out.

All birthdays are an expression of vanity. One time a lady said to me, "I am a retired schoolteacher. I know you don't believe in birthdays."

I said, "You know why that is? Christ never commanded anyone to celebrate his or her or anyone else's birthday. A birthday puts a person in the spotlight, a place no humble God-fearing person wants to be. Two birthdays are mentioned in the Bible and they are hideous events. People get their heads cut off at birthday parties."

At that she said, "You should get your head cut off." She was getting upset. Her husband came beside her to calm her down. He put an arm around her. She was getting wound up inside. That is easy to do after a stroke.

Long after I became a Jehovah's Witness the riverboat model kept going back and forth between my brother and me. I never sent him or anyone else Christmas presents. I do not know what the riverboat was, but it definitely was not defined by Christmas.

The summer before my accident when I was in Maine by myself, my brother and I sat at the table in his house talking. At home I had been studying the Bible with the Jehovah's Witness lady and going to a few meetings at the Kingdom Hall. I told my brother about this and how amazing it was that some of the ideas about God and Christ that for a long time have been accepted as truth are not in the Bible. I asked him, "If widely held ideas didn't come from the Bible then where did they come from?"

He said to me, "That is ——[toro feces]. You've been brainwashed." I said he didn't have to swear. He said, "It's my house. I'll swear if I want to."

I told him, "If you want to swear in your house tell me before you do so I can go outside. This whole house might get struck by lightning."

He said, "If it is struck by lightning would you feel the effect of the lightning?"

I said, "Yes, that is why I want to go outside." Then we talked about other things. Late that afternoon I went to the cabin on the island. It was Saturday night. The next morning I planned to go back to the mainland and drive to a nearby kingdom hall for the Sunday morning meeting.

That was the second Kingdom Hall I ever went to after the one in Ohio. The mechanic in overalls could have been there. The word *unified* describes that phenomenon.

That Sunday morning, the next day, my brother was on the coast. He saw my boat tied up to a float on the mainland. He and his wife were getting in their boat to go out to the island. As they walked down the steep ramp at low tide his wife said to him, "Why is Jocko's boat here?"

He said to her, "He was probably scared by the lightning."

Later that day when he told me about that conversation I asked him, "What lightning?"

He said, "Wasn't there a storm on the island?"

I said no. He said in the middle of the night an electrical storm woke them both. He lay in bed with the covers around his neck. His exact words were, "The lightning was so bright I could see it through my eye lids."

Back home in Cincinnati I took pocket money out of the business each week. Aside from that money was the satisfaction of making a good product in an efficient manner and for Jenny doing the numbers and paper provided the illusion of having a real job. At the end of the month we often used personal money in order to pay all the bills. When Jenny's father died and a short time later my father died we started getting free money on a regular basis. A financial person said it would be a good idea to close the business. He said it was costing us money. When I told him everything would change when the book was finished he looked at Jenny.

I knew Jenny's father the last ten or fifteen years of his life. We saw each other often. Jenny really listened to him. She listened to me, but not like she did to him. He did not pry into our life, but in a very sincere and loving way he knew exactly where we were. When there were problems she always consulted him. The time I hit Jenny she told him, and soon after that he wanted to have lunch with me. We had lunch several times before for no particular reason, but that time there was a reason even though he didn't say so. He didn't ask me what happened. I told him anyway. I just said it like it happened and let the chips fall where they may. As I was talking he didn't speak about the incident. We had a casual lunch the rest of the time. It was a given that he was aware of the situation and cared about her very much. A while later I asked her what he said to her about what happened, and she said he said, "It takes two." Beyond saying that she didn't tell me what he said.

He was never thought of by businessmen as a successful businessman, but he had an unusual quality that attracted people to him. I could never put my finger on what it was. One time coming out of a restaurant a total stranger who ate there was speaking with him and the stranger said, "I have a case of the dickey-dos." Jenny's father asked the man what that was. The stranger said, "That is when you can't see your dickey-do anymore." Jenny's father had a robust middle area too.

Jenny's father did not attend church during his life, at least not when I knew him. He died of cancer. When he was dying he didn't bring it up about God, but I did. He said just as briefly as I that it was all true, and that was the end of conversation on the subject of God. His death announcement didn't appear until after the funeral. There was a mistake at the newspaper. The funeral service was in a local church, and even though there was no official announcement of the time and place, the church was packed. People were squeezing into every corner, and it was not a small building.

The funeral service for my father was at his graveside in Maine. That is where he lived the last part of his life. The preacher said what he remembered, and then he asked for anyone else in the small group to say what they remembered. A few people said something. I said he was a good man, and that I hoped God would remember him.

When they first moved to Maine he walked back and forth to a little office he had above a corner grocery store. He had a copy machine in there and a manual typewriter with a spool of ribbon that had to be replaced every so often if it ever got used. As far as anyone could tell he spent his days reading magazines and calling 900 numbers to claim free gifts. He had a stroke and that was the end of going to the office. Two people carried him out the door on a stretcher. My brother was there and said to our father, ."Just lay there." He looked at him from the stretcher and said, "Only chickens lay eggs."

After the stroke my sister asked a preacher in town if he would stop by once a month and "give him Communion" (a religious ceremony), and that is how the preacher got to know him. Also after the stroke two Jehovah's Witnesses stopped at the house and started a Bible study with Pop. After their second or third weekly visit my mother who was in the next room yelled, "Get out." I asked her if she would feel differently if two other people did the Bible study. Her reply was, "No, I just don't like that sort of thing." Her reaction was surprising. It was not directed at Jehovah's Witnesses but at two people who went around preaching. She knew I was a Jehovah's Witness but didn't think I went from house to house like them. Going by twos from door to door is how Christianity was spread in the first century. The organization of Jehovah's Witnesses copies that model.

The Bible says in Luke 10:1, "After these things the Lord designated seventy others and sent them forth by twos in advance of him into every city and place to which he himself was going."

When my father died there was a void in my life. I always had a father, but now he was gone.

In the Book of Ecclesiastics 9:5 the Bible says, "For the living are conscience that they will die; but as for the dead, they are conscious of nothing at all, neither do they any more have wages, because the remembrance of them has been forgotten." Verse 10 says: "All that your hand finds to do, do with your very power, for there is no work nor devising nor knowledge nor wisdom is Sheol, the place to which you are going."

Another translation puts it this way: "For the living know

they shall die; but the dead know not anything, neither have they any more a reward; for the memory of them is forgotten. Whatsoever thy hand findeth to do, do it with thy might; for there is no work, nor device, nor knowledge, or wisdom, in the grave, whither thou goest."

The word *Sheol* (Hebrew) or *Hades* (Greek) refers to the common grave of mankind not to a place of eternal torment. One popular English-language Bible translates the word *Sheol* thirty-one times as hell, thirty-one times as *grave*, and three times as *pit*. The same word is translated three different ways.

Grief-stricken Jacob thinks his son Joseph has been killed by a wild beast. He laments at Genesis 37:35, "I shall go down mourning to my son into Sheol." In the Bible good people go to hell. In Job 14:13 the good man Job at the height of his suffering prays, "O that in Sheol you would conceal me, . . . that you would set a time limit for me and remember me."

The Christian Greek Scripture says Jesus Christ was in Hades. In Acts 2:31,32 it says: "His soul was not left in Hades . . . this Jesus God hath raised up." Jesus was in his grave where he remained three days until he was resurrected.

People get out of the grave only by the power of Jehovah. Revelation 20:13 says, "The sea gave up the dead who were in it; and death and Hades delivered up the dead who were in them: and they were judged every man according to their works."

The Bible character Jonah was delivered out of his would-be grave. He was swallowed alive by a large fish, and in Jonah 2:2 he prays: "Out of my distress I called out to Jehovah, and he proceeded to answer me. Out of the belly of Sheol I cried for help. You heard my voice."

There is a story in the Bible about Phillip and an Ethiopian eunuch. Here's what it says, ". . . but he was returning and was sitting in his chariot and reading aloud the prophet Isaiah. So the Spirit said to Phillip: 'approach and join yourself to this chariot.' Phillip ran alongside and heard him reading aloud Isaiah the prophet, and he said, "'Do you know what you are reading?

"'He said, "'Really how could I ever do so, unless someone guided me?'" And he entreated Phillip to get on and sit down with him. Now the passage of Scripture that he was reading aloud was this: 'As a sheep he was brought to the slaughter, and as a lamb that is voiceless before its shearer, so he does not open his mouth. During his humiliation the judgment was taken away from him. Who will tell the details of his generation? Because his life is taken away from the earth.'

"In answer the eunuch said to Phillip: 'I beg you, about who does the prophet say this? About himself or about some other man?' Phillip opened his mouth and starting with this Scripture, he declared to him the good news about Jesus."

There are four terms in the Bible connected with death. They are G*ehenna, hellfire, the lake of fire*, and the word *tormented.*

The word *Gehenna* is often translated as *Hell.* Gehenna was a garbage dump outside Jerusalem where every sort of refuse was thrown. Fires were kept burning there by adding brimstone (sulfur) to burn the garbage. Anybody who lived there knew what Gehenna was. Christ talked about it as a symbol of everlasting death, of being completely destroyed, as a place from which there is no resurrection. In Matthew 23:33 Jesus told religious leaders, "Serpents, offspring of vipers, how are you to flee from the judgment of Gehenna?" Being thrown in Gehenna meant being completely destroyed, like so much garbage. It meant everlasting death, no resurrection.

In the Bible before Gehenna became a garbage dump it was known as the "valley of Hinnom." At that time Israelites with pagan influence had the ungodly practice of sacrificing live children in fire. About that Jehovah said in Jeremiah 7:31 "a thing I had not commanded and that had not come up into my heart." Burning alive in fire was not in Jehovah's heart.

Fire is associated with Sheol or Hades. There is the expression "lake of fire" in the Bible. Revelation 20:14 says, "And death and Hades were hurled into the lake of fire. This means the second death, the lake of fire." The first death is the absence of vital signs. The second death, the lake of fire, like Gehenna is the death from which there is no resurrection. Death and Hades are thrown into the lake of fire. They are no more. They are completely destroyed in the lake of fire.

The word *torment* describes what is imagined to be a key

ingredient of Sheol and Hades. In Revelations 20:10 the Bible says the Devil will be hurled into the lake of fire and tormented day and night forever. Jesus said in one of his illustrations in Matthew 18:34, "And his lord was wroth, and delivered him to the tormentors, till he should pay all that was due unto him." Back then jailer and tormentor was the same person. When people or places are thrown into the lake of fire it is total destruction like being in jail forever, removed from the picture.

There was a man at his door. The first thing said by either of us was by him when he abruptly said, "You are the son of Satan."

I said, "Why is that?"

He replied, "Because you changed your Bible," and he pointed to the bag I carried.

I said, "What Bible is that?" I could be bringing him much refined gold or a million U.S. dollars in the bag.

He answered, "The Jehovah's Witness Bible." His house was in what we call often worked territory. He knew what a Jehovah's Witness was, and here was another one. I got him to stop closing the door long enough to tell me why he thought the way he did. He said two things. First, that he had talked to Jehovah's Witnesses before at length about what kind of place hell was. From that exchange he had all kinds of questions, which he promptly asked at the church where he went several times a week. The preacher told him not to talk with Jehovah's Witnesses anymore and to do so was the equivalent of talking to the Devil. Second, he mentioned a Bible story about a rich man and Lazarus as if to say that story reconfirmed all he thought about Hell before he ran into Jehovah's Witnesses. The story is in Luke 16:19-31. Here is what it says:

"But a certain man was rich, and he used to deck himself with purple and linen, enjoying himself from day to day with magnificence. But a certain beggar named Lazarus used to be put at his gate, full of ulcers and desiring to be filled with the things dropping from the table of the rich man. Yes, too the dogs would come and lick his ulcers. Now in the course of time the beggar died and he was carried off by the angels to the bosom of Abraham.

"Also the rich man died and was buried. And in Hades he lifted up his eyes, he existed in torments, and he saw Abraham afar off and Lazarus in the bosom with him. So he called and said, 'Father Abraham, have mercy on me and send Lazarus to dip the tip of his finger in the water and cool my tongue, because I am in anguish in this blazing fire.' But Abraham said, 'Child, remember that you received in full your good things in your lifetime, but Lazarus correspondingly the injurious things. Now, however, he is having comfort here but you are in anguish. And beside all these things, a great chasm has been fixed between us, so that those wanting to go over from here to you people cannot, neither may people cross over from there to us.' Then he said, 'In that event I ask you, father, to send him to the house of my father, for I have five brothers, in order that he may give them a thorough witness, that they also should not get into this place of torment.' But Abraham said, "'They have Moses and the Prophets; let them listen to these.'" Then he said, 'No indeed, father Abraham, but if someone from the dead goes to them they will repent.' But he said to him, 'If they do not listen to Moses and the Prophets, neither will they be persuaded if someone rises from the dead.'"

The image of the rich man and Lazarus is one of Christ's many illustrations about acting right. To us it is not visible what a person is, but to God it is visible. The Bible teaching about death is that when the resurrection occurs the wicked will be forgotten in their grave.

The Bible says heaven is a place a few go right after they die "in the twinkling of an eye." The Bible book of Revelation puts their number at 144,000. They are part of the kingdom government in heaven named Spiritual Jerusalem. The kingdom government will provide leadership over the earth where the "the other sheep" will be. Christ refers to the ones in heaven as his "little flock." Those who go there go as spirit persons. First Corinthians 15:50 says, ". . . blood and flesh cannot inherit God's kingdom."

Heaven is made up of people who died after Christ died on earth. Christ said in John 3:13, "Moreover no man has ascended into heaven but he that descended from heaven, the Son of man." Christ was the first one resurrected. Job, Rachel, Moses, John the Baptist, Jacob, the Shulammite maiden, Noah, Abraham, and all the other righteous people who died before Christ are not up there. They are in the grave where they remain until resurrected to everlasting life here on earth.

In John 10:16 Christ talks about the other sheep who will be resurrected to a life here on earth, "And I have other sheep, which are not of this fold; those also I must bring, and they will listen to my voice, and they will become one flock, one shepherd."

When the other sheep are resurrected to life here on earth Jehovah's original purpose will be fulfilled that the earth be a Garden of Eden paradise. Until then we play out man's inability to rule man.

There is a prophecy about this in Daniel 2:44. It reads: "And in the days of those kings the God of heaven will set up a kingdom that will never be brought to ruin. And the kingdom itself will not be passed on to any other people. It will crush and put an end to all these kingdoms, and it itself will stand to time indefinite." So far Jehovah's prophecies have a 100-percent fulfillment rate.

When Jehovah's kingdom takes control of the earth it will happen all of a sudden like a "thief in the night." The Bible calls that event Armageddon and says everyone will know it is Jehovah. That rules out cataclysmic events such as collisions between the Earth and other objects in the universe. It rules out that mankind in one way or the other will bring about the demise of this system of things all by himself. The Bible describes people, some people, as sliding into oblivion gnashing their teeth.

Christ speaks about the time of Armageddon in Matthew 24:36-39, "Concerning that day and hour nobody knows, neither the angels of the heavens nor the son, but only the Father. For just as they were in days of Noah, so the presence of the Son of man will be. For as they were, in those days before the flood, eating and drinking, men marrying and women being given in marriage, until the day Noah entered into the ark; and they took no note until the flood came and swept them all away, so the presence of the Son of man will be."

At Armageddon the earth will not be vaporized or in some way made uninhabitable. The prophet Isaiah says in Isaiah 45:18: "This is what Jehovah has said, the Creator of the heavens, He the true God, the Former of the earth, and the Maker of it, He the One who firmly established it, who did not create it simply for nothing, who formed it even to be inhabited: 'I am Jehovah, and there is no one else.'" Other Scriptures that say this piece of real estate we call earth will always be here are not few.

In Psalms 37:29, "The righteous themselves will possess the earth, and they will reside forever upon it."

In Matthew 6:10, "Let your kingdom come. Let your will take place as in heaven, also upon earth."

In Ecclesiastics 1:4, "A generation is going, and a generation is coming; but the earth is standing even to time indefinite."

Psalms 104:4, "He has founded the earth upon its established places; it will not be made to totter to time indefinite, or forever."

Matthew 5:5, "Happy are the mild-tempered ones ["meek" in some translations], since they will inherit the earth."

Proverbs 2:21-22, "For the upright are the ones that will reside in the earth, and the blameless ones are the ones that will be left over in it. As regards the wicked, they will be cut off from the very earth; and they will be torn away from it."

Psalms 115:16, "As regards the heavens, to Jehovah the heavens belong. But the earth he has given to the sons of men."

All the major religions say that in one way or the other people never die that death is a transition to some other realm; at death everyone, or their soul, immediately gets whisked away to some other place.

In Genesis 2:7 the Bible says: "Jehovah God proceeded to form the man out of dust from the ground and to blow into his nostrils the breath of life, and the man came to be a living soul." Adam didn't *have* a soul; he *was* a soul.

In the Hebrew Scripture of the Bible (commonly called the Old Testament) the word translated *soul* is *nephesh* and it appears 745 times.

The word translated *soul* more than a hundred times in the Christian Greek Scripture (commonly called the New Testament) is *psyche*. Like *nephesh* this word often refers to a whole person.

Humans and animals are in the same condition when dead. Ecclesiastics 3:19-20 says: "For there is an eventuality as respects the sons of mankind and an eventuality as respects the beasts, and they have the same eventuality. As the one dies so the other dies; and they all have but one spirit, so that there is no superiority of the man over the beast, for everything is vanity. All are going to one place. They have all come to be from the dust, and they are all returning to the dust."

A Jehovah's Witness Bible aid on the subject puts it this way: "The spirit that makes animals live is the same as that which makes humans live. When this spirit, or invisible life force, goes out both man and beast return to the ground from which they are made, but this does not mean that our life force literally leaves the earth and travels through space to God. Rather, the spirit returns to God in the sense that now our hope for future life rests entirely with God. Only by his power can spirit, or life force, be given back so that we live again.—Psalm 104:29,30."

The soul and the spirit are not the same. The soul is blood and flesh. Spirit or life force belongs to Jehovah. Every living thing has Jehovah's spirit or it would not live.

A long time before Christ came to earth people said the soul is immortal. The idea goes back at least as far as Babylon. It was polished by ancient Greek philosophers and either started spontaneously or crept into Eastern religions from the West. According to one historian, the idea of an immortal soul might have spread to the East by way of the Eurasian nomad society, which in the eighth and seventh centuries B.C. descended upon India, southwestern Asia, the Steppe country along the north shore of the Black Sea, and the Balkan and Anatolian peninsulas.

The older I got the more funerals I went to and at most of them someone reassuringly recites John, chapter 11, verse 25, as if to say the person is not really dead. In that Scripture, Jesus Christ says, "I am the resurrection and the life. He that exercises faith in me, even though he dies, will come to life; and everyone that is living and exercises faith in me will never die at all."

Another time Christ says, "Let the dead bury the dead." On the surface that doesn't make sense, but understanding Christ means understanding what he says. There are two kinds of dead people: the spiritually dead and the biologically dead.

When Christ says a dead person will come to life he means that a dead person (one with no vital signs) if while alive (with vital signs) exercises faith in him. Then when they die (have no vital signs) they will be asleep (not dead in both ways) in the grave until the time comes when Jehovah God resurrects them. In that way they never die. For those exercising faith in Christ, death (having no vital signs) is sleep.

The story surrounding the verse so often said at Christian funerals is in the eleventh chapter of John. This is what it says: "Now there was a certain man sick, Lazarus of Bethany, of the village of Mary and Martha her sister (not the beggar Lazarus). It was, in fact, the Mary that greased the Lord with perfumed oil and wiped his feet dry with her hair whose brother Lazarus was sick. Therefore: his sisters dispatched words to him saying: 'Lord, see! The one for whom you have affection is sick.' But when Jesus heard it he said: 'This sickness is not with death as its object, but is for the glory of God in order that the Son of God may be glorified through it.'

"Now Jesus loved Martha and her sister and Lazarus. However, when he heard he was sick, then he actually remained two days in the place where he was. Then after this he said to his disciples: 'Let us go into Judea again.'"

A few verses later the story continues: "He said these things and after this he said to them: 'Lazarus our friend has gone to rest, but I am journeying there to awaken him from sleep'. Therefore the disciples said to him: 'Lord, if he has gone to rest, he will get well.' Jesus had spoken, however about his death. But they imagined he was speaking about taking rest in sleep. At that time, therefore, Jesus said to them outspokenly: 'Lazarus has died, and I rejoice on your account that I was not there, in order for you to believe.'"

"Consequently when Jesus arrived, he found he had already been four days in the memorial tomb. Now Bethany was near Jerusalem at a distance of about two miles. Accordingly many of the Jews had come to Martha and Mary in order to console them concerning their brother. Therefore Martha, when she heard that Jesus was coming, met him; but Mary kept sitting at home. Martha therefore said to Jesus: 'Lord, if you had been here my brother would not have died. And yet at present I know that as many things as you ask God for, God will give you.' Jesus said to her, 'Your brother will rise.' Martha said to him: 'I know he will rise in the resurrection on the last day.' Jesus said to her: 'I am the resurrection and the life. He that exercises faith in me, even though he dies, will come to life; and everyone that is living and exercises faith in me will never die at all. Do you believe this?' She said to him: 'Yes, Lord, I have believed you are the Christ the Son of God, the One coming into the world.' ... And he said: 'Where have you laid him?' They said to him: 'Lord, come and see.' Jesus gave way to tears. Therefore the Jews began to say: 'See, what affection he used to have for him.' But some of them said: 'Was not this man that opened the eyes of the blind man able to prevent this one from dying?'

"Hence Jesus, after groaning again within himself, came to the memorial tomb. It was in fact a cave, and a stone was lying against it. Jesus said: 'take the stone away.' Martha, the sister of the deceased, said to him: 'Lord, by now he must smell, for it has been four days.' Jesus said to her: 'Did I not tell you that if you would believe you would see the glory of God?' Therefore they took the stone away. Now Jesus raised his eyes heavenward and said: 'Father, I thank you that you have heard me. True, I knew that you always hear me; but on account of the crowd standing around I spoke, in order that they might believe that you sent me forth.' And when he had said these things, he cried out with a loud voice: 'Lazarus, come on out!' The man that had been dead came out with his feet and hands bound with wrappings."

This account demonstrates the power of God to raise the dead, and notice Lazarus didn't talk about being somewhere else.

When the two mail-order companies were selling our product several small-time dealers in different parts of the country started selling them also. They learned about the mailboxes after installing one for someone who bought it from one of the mail-order companies. A mailbox installer would telephone long distance, and say they could sell them out of the back of their van with bald tires. They were right. They bought one at a time at our lowest price. None of them had a big operation.

A few times someone presented themselves, or their company as a big operator. They talked about being a regional distributor. They wanted me to believe they would sell many mailboxes. The first few times I believed them. I got wise about who could or couldn't sell them.

I asked one prospective distributor what I should do about dealers in their territory? They said they would distribute mailboxes to them. The dealer price would increase forty percent. Distributors had multi-page contracts detailing their terms.

The mailbox was already expensive. It was not a mass-market item. It was a deluxe item. A person had to be wealthy to afford one. There never were any distributors, but we kept getting more and more dealers. Our price to them must have been too low, because we weren't making any money. It was costing money.

The telephone rang in the new building and the person on the other end said he wanted to buy eleven large stainless-steel mailboxes. Each one had to have a custom-mounting bracket. All of them were going to be grouped together. Eleven different people sent money. The person who first called was a commercial airline pilot who described himself as the low man on the totem pole in an "exclusive" development. He said one individual living there was the chief executive officer of a well-known international company. He did not name which one of the people it was.

I talked with the pilot several times. He said we should sell the mailboxes on the Internet, and he said if we sent him information and photographs he would set up a display for the practice. The airplane he flew was computer-operated like the space shuttle. He had to know all about computers. The Internet was computer technology. We sent him information, and glossy photographs. What he came up with was a very good representation of the mailbox.

I know very little about computers, but I know one that is properly connected enables a person to view goods and services for sale on a worldwide medium called the Internet. The difficulty is in finding items or information wanted. There are categories and subcategories. There are "domains" and "search engines." Can a person see or hear a search engine? Does it have billowing smoke? Does some unseen person yell, "All aboard!" as it searches every dimension? An actual Internet address avoids the search engine altogether. The Internet address the pilot established for us is http://www.veedersmailbox.com.

When things weren't going so good with mailboxes a steel salesman I had known for more than ten years asked me why I was buying less steel. Our relationship was a little bit beyond the niceties of buying and selling steel. I told him the situation. With a troubled look he asked me how I was going to advertise. I told him I was going to write a book and in that way I was going to advertise, advertise, advertise. He had a hard time concealing the strangeness that suddenly came over him.

Sales from the Internet were retail sales. Half the money coming into the business was from people who bought the mailbox on the Internet, but much more than half the number of mailboxes made went to dealers at the wholesale price.

Selling retail helped our business break even. Spare change was all we took out. The money we lived on was the free money. That money was like manna from heaven. We worked on the mailbox business for nothing. When the free money came each month we felt it was earned.

It is as if a huge complicated machine moved in front of me. There is thick vegetation, cliffs, and steep hills. For me it would be impassable, but the machine makes a smooth road. I follow where it goes.

18

Where the Road Goes

The road ahead goes up a hill. On top I see a building with spires, walls, and towers. On the other side a cliff is overlooking the ocean. I cannot see the ocean from where I am. In the afternoon waves smash against the rocks. In the morning the water is calm. At night I shout into the wind, "Three foggy mornings and one rainy day will rot the best birch fence a man can build!"

I wonder if they need help gathering hay. They probably have the wagons they need. The oxen are slow. It is almost too far, but since I am here I will go.

The door on the side is the one most people use. It is thick oak. The hinges are enormous. The end of each one curls back in two pieces. Whoever made them took the time to hammer them smooth.

No one is outside. I look around imagining long ago when all this was defended against bands of marauders or whoever wanted to take it by force. They are all dead by now. At the center of the door is a heavy knocker. I raise it and let it fall several times. It makes a definite noise. I wait a long time, step back, and look at windows near and far. I shout to make myself known. It cannot be that no one is inside and I have come all this way for nothing.

Then I hear the latch on the other side of the door, and it opens. It is massive indeed. A tidy person with his sleeves rolled up appears. He looks behind me at the animals and in a bothered way asks what business I have there.

I say the haying work below is done, and would another wagon be needed up here? He says the only one who knows, the one in charge of the fields, left in the morning to hear the bishop speak and will be back that day.

The sun is getting low. Soon I must start back, but I ask if I may wait. Looking quickly at my shoes, he says there is hot soup on the stove and there is enough for me. He is more than kind. I turn and look at my animals. Then I go inside.

There is a wonderful smell that is not from one kind of food. It is from all the days and what is there. There is an oak floor polished by years of use and a kettle on the stove. Beside the stove is a fireplace. The fire has gone unattended for some time. Smoke from smoldering pieces of wood trail up the chimney.

The ceiling is high. Evenly spaced hewn beams support wide planks. They are so square and smooth they could have been cut by machine. On the side of the kitchen where I am standing it opens into another room. A long table in the middle is where people who work there and live there eat. Across the kitchen near the stove there is a closed door that leads to a hallway that servants use that leads to another room that servants use that leads to the magnificent dining room where the beautiful people eat. He puts a tray on a large table in front of the stove where a person stands to fix food. Everything is in drawers, in cabinets, or on shelves. He walks with the loaded tray toward a table between us where we sit. He says about the quiet that the others are gone for the day.

"They left early this morning," he says. "They left with the one you want to see. The day the bishop is here, that is the day they all leave."

"What about you," I say.

After swallowing from his cup he says, "Someone has to be here. Besides, I heard it all. I do not think I could hear it today. I hope God understands."

"What does the bishop talk about?" I ask.

He answers, "I suppose the bishop will say all the things bishops say in their own eloquent way. Did you know we are sinners dangling by a thread over the fire of an angry God and that it is better to give than receive?" Then he stops himself. "Oh dear, I better be careful. When was the last time they burned someone at the stake?" Then he asks me what I am about and what I say.

I tell him I have a fine wagon with a strong team that can haul a much heavier load than hay. I say the work nearby is done and because it is that time of year, if nothing else, I will haul hay.

He asks if the wagon and animals are mine. I say I recently agreed to buy them, but it will take some time. I say I haul mostly heavy things. He asks where I live, and I say beyond the village.

I ask if he has lived here long.

"Yes." he says. "I am the finest indentured servant you will probably ever see. I was born here. It is my sincerest hope that I die here, as did my father and mother. Just the thought of toiling with suffering humanity is unbearable. Everything is provided in this place. True, I have nothing, but I find no difficulty in having nothing. Sometimes I wonder if I have any ambition. Sometimes I wonder if we're born, live painlessly, and die. Have we lived?"

I tell him it might seem strange to say, but I have wondered that same thing only in some other way. Silence prevails. Then I say, "In one way or another all of us strive to avoid pain, and if we are successful what do we put in its place? Pain of another sort? Pain that makes us feel alive? Pain that has a purpose? Pain of our own choosing? The pain I chose comes from living intensely with God. There was pain at first. That cannot be denied, but now it is gone. It came from being alone in my understanding of God, and there were other things. Once I wanted to jump in the hayloft with a searing milkmaid, pail and all. I did not, not entirely to keep the anger of God from blazing against me, but because that One, our maker, says a person who listens and hears will have a happy life. That One knows human nature like no other. When I denied myself what, to me, was a major event because it conflicted with a godly way of life at first it was painful, but time after time when I realized what was happening I became certain something was there. What happened is my life improved, and as it did the pain disappeared. My own selfish desire to do something detestable ceased."

I lean toward him and quietly say, "My understanding of God did not come from anything a bishop said. I have an English-language Bible, and very little of what they say comes from there."

"You better not be caught dead with that book," he says. "Somebody might think you are trying to start something."

We both know it is against the law to own or have a Bible. I say it is well hidden. I say my wife would not tell anyone where it is, although she thinks my preoccupation with God is a dangerous fantasy of some kind.

"What about me?" he says. "I know you have it. Why did you tell me?"

"This is the conversation we are having, but if you are not the sort you seem to be, unlike you, I will die in the village square."

"And where will I die?" he asks.

"Probably in a place of your own choosing," I say.

"What is in the Bible that is so different from what we have heard?" he asks.

"It is a communication from God that deals with the past, present, and future of this earth. It is the God of Abraham, Isaac, Jacob, and the Father of Jesus Christ. The name of that God is Jehovah.

"Says who?" he asks.

"Says God, through his prophets. When the time is right for God everyone will know that name.

"None of the Bible will ever be proven false," I say, "and sooner or later the rest of it will come true. A person is moved to translate it into a language a common man can read. Why does he take that risk? For his effort authorities will publicly kill him. The Bible survives like nothing else. It has backing beyond what is normal. It has a life of its own."

He asks, "The rest of it that will come true, what is that? Really now, how can anyone in all seriousness say they know what the future will be?"

"God is not anyone," I say. "But, if by anyone you mean one of us muddling around this earth, we know only as much about the future as God wants us to know."

I tell him, "Many say they can tell what lies ahead of a person. Soothsayers, astrologers, and people who glare into crystal balls are a few of them. In the Bible, God does say that to avoid ruin stay away from what they do. Their power comes not from God but from creatures opposed to God. It may sound far fetched to say, but once these spirit forces invade a victim an entrenchment begins with the singular purpose of keeping that poor soul away from God. That is the equivalent of ruination, because salvation belongs only to God."

"And what is it we are to know about the future?"

"God will rule the earth. That is the future," I say, "and anyone who does not like it will not be here. It is that simple. The wicked will be so much dust. The villainous character and everyone not doing the will of God will be gone. That event is referred to in the Bible several times as a 'new heavens and a new earth.' Quite a few times it is called 'the great day of Jehovah,' and once it is referred to as 'Armageddon.' Take your pick."

"What about the ones on the other side of the world," he asks, "the ones who know nothing about the God of the Bible?"

"There is no injustice in God," I say. "The Bible says there will be a resurrection of the righteous and the unrighteous. Christ will decide who has a good heart. Those who are resurrected have the free choice to be one of God's people or not to be one of them. We all make that choice at one time or another. The ones who are not one of God's people or chose not to be one will be destroyed. That is what the Bible says."

"That makes the choice rather obvious," he says. "What fool who is here after Armageddon and is aware of the past would choose to be destroyed? However, I must admit living forever on earth would take some major adjustment."

"You assume living on the earth will be the same as it is now. Nothing will be the same except your consciousness. Early in the Bible the nation of Israel is wandering around in the wilderness. They are God's people. Moses, their leader selected by God, speaks to God and says the people are hungry and have nothing to eat. After that every morning a food called manna is on the ground around their camp. A few years earlier those same people saw the parting of the Red Sea. You would think if there was any doubt in anyone's mind about God, about God being in control of the situation, it would have vanished the day food fell out of the sky. After that day you would think everyone in camp would be a true believer, but a short while later those people were turning their back on the One who brought them out of Egypt, parted the Red Sea, and gave them food. Likewise, people on the other side of Armageddon, people aware of their past, will end up turning their back on God."

"After Armageddon what happens?" he asks.

"God's people are from all nations, tribes, people, and tongues. God's promise to those people is that the way he is setting things up this time will last to time indefinite."

"Is God a he?"

"God is said to be a he in the Bible. The Bible also says all people are made in God's image. Several times it talks about something as seen in God's eyes. That may or may not be exactly the way it is, but those words make our ability to understand what God wants us to understand within our grasp. There are parts of the Bible no person can explain right now. One of God's prophets writes these words from God describing the future: 'The wolf and the lamb themselves will feed as one, and the lion will eat straw just like the bull; and as for the serpent, his food will be dust. They will do no harm, or cause any ruin in all my holy mountain, says Jehovah.' If that is seen as exactly the way it is, or as a comparison of the way it will be, it makes no difference to understanding that things will be very different. Lions do not have the teeth for chewing straw. We can no more understand the intricate details than a dog can add two and two. There will be no want, not just by the ones sitting pretty, but by absolutely everyone. That is what Jehovah says."

"Why do you keep saying Jehovah?" he asks.

"It is the name of God. In ancient Hebrew the name of God is Yahweh. Today in English it is Jehovah. Any god is god. It could be a plug nickel or a person."

"What is a plug nickel?" he says.

"It is a metal coin made worthless by someone who removes most of the metal in the center by putting a hole in it with a projectile triggered from a handheld device called a gun. I am getting way ahead of myself, but while on the subject let me add that several hundred years from now in the same land where people will talk about plug nickels there will be a small group of people called Jehovah's Witnesses. Their numbers will grow quickly and they will cover the inhabited earth with the Bible message. Then the end will come."

"The end of what?" he says.

"The end of this system of things. No longer will the unrighteous swallow up the righteous. No longer will there be sickness and death. 'The former things have passed away' is what it says."

"Do you really believe that?" Amazed, he is certain I am crazy. He stands up, and without moving beyond his chair, shouting, he asks, "Does all you say serve merely to answer questions?"

"No," I say in a tired way. I know what he thinks. "The truth is from God. It is bigger than both of us." He sits down. I am reminded of something and tell him, "There is a story in the Bible about a king who is given a scroll from Jehovah. Call him God if God's name is an obstacle for you. The king does not like what it says, so he burns the scroll. It is his idea that doing so will stop what it says. That was stupid.

"The Egyptian pharaoh and all the ones with bows and arrows who charged into the Red Sea against whoever parted all that water were also stupid. In the Bible the word stupid does not mean someone with little intelligence or someone without position among people. It means someone who does not know the work of Jehovah when it is in front of their face."

"Our master would burn the scrolls," he says. A grin of fondness comes across his face. Then, coming back to where we are, he says, "He has been gone for almost a year. What he would say is they are so much hogwash. That is what he would say."

I reply, "People with wherewithal have much difficulty grasping the Bible message. They are accustomed to relying on their own understanding. If doing things their own way delivers what they want here and now what good have they done if it also delivers to them death?"

In early Bible times God's people were slaves in Egypt. People attracted to Christ are seldom nobles or gentry folk. Christ describes a crowd of people as skinned and thrown about like sheep without a shepherd. People who are attracted to the Bible message are very ordinary people.

"What is the Bible message?" he asks.

"Repent, because the kingdom of God has drawn near."

"The kingdom of God has drawn near for many lifetimes. Why should I believe it now?" he asks.

"When Christ was on earth his closest followers asked him when the end will come, and Christ said nobody knows, not him or the angels in heaven, but only the Father Jehovah. A person loyal to God may die first, but the kingdom of God is still near for that person. A person's death for a thousand years is one night's sleep if God remembers them. The Bible says many times many ways be ready, stay awake, and endure. That is because nothing a human does can compare with what God can do. Our struggles are small and meaningless in light of what really is."

"Why should I repent?" he asks. "I have done nothing wrong."

"You should repent because God is about to pull the plug on this old system of things," I say.

"Plug?" he asks.

"Think of it as a drain plug in a trough full of putrid water."

"I have not done anything wrong. Should I feel guilty just so God can remove the guilt?"

"That would be a start," I say. "Repenting is a posture, a way of life, not something to be taken lightly. Repenting is seeking forgiveness but not all about guilt. It is a forgone conclusion that you, by yourself, are not right. Feeling guilty is futile. If you look at it that way, you were guilty of being born. At this point there is absolutely nothing you can do to change what is. You may dress up and present yourself proudly in front of people, but to God you are naked. There is nothing grandiose about you or any other human being.

"In the Bible there is an account of a man watching a woman bathe on a rooftop. They end up having a sexual relationship. The woman's husband is in the army. The man, because of his high position, has the woman's husband sent into battle, where he is killed. A messenger from God goes to the man saying God knows everything. There is nothing casual about the man when he seeks forgiveness. That is somebody who did something wrong.

"Honestly saying to God you are the miserable man that you are is acknowledging the truth of the matter. Some find that easier to do than others. Some never do. The very thought of it is contrary to most thought. Being humble is part of being with God. Benefiting yourself is what it is. Improve in God's eyes and there comes a freedom and power. It does not win contests or battles. It does not help get things or earn money. What it does is makes big problems small."

"How will God rule? People burn people to death and say

they are doing it in God's name. How will God keep matters straight?"

"Rule by God does not mean priests and clergy rule. It means God will rule the earth His way. Everyone here, by the very fact they are here, will recognize God's headship and authority, as did Moses. If God's appointed leader or leaders get self-righteous, God Himself will remove them. That is what happened when Moses took the credit for getting water from a rock.

"God will rule the earth, and that rule will be perfect in every sense. After all, this place called earth and everything on it belongs to God. That makes God the rightful ruler."

"If the earth belongs to God," he says, "why is there so much havoc? Why is death something we have to reckon with all the time?"

"The Bible explains why wickedness and suffering abound. It says the ruler of this world is Satan, not God. That is why there is so much turmoil. It began in the Garden of Eden when Adam and Eve chose not to do what God told them. It has been that way to this day. The result is irrefutable: man has dominated man to his injury. That is how the Bible describes the situation, and it will be that way until God takes over. Satan would have us believe we can do without God. By the time Armageddon hits it will be plain to see man cannot rule man. No bishop I ever heard talks about God's purpose the way the Bible does."

"What is God's purpose?"

"That those who want to be saved be saved."

"That is not different. Saved from what?"

"Satan's grip, and the wrath of Jehovah at Armageddon. The reason makes sense in the Bible. That is the difference. The truth makes sense. When that sinks in physical needs cease to be needs. I have to show you something." I spring from my chair and return out of breath with the English-language Bible. It is hidden in the wagon. His elbows are folded on the table, and the cup he pushes to the side.

Flipping pages I find the place. "Look what Christ says about physical needs. For me this is true." I read, "stop being anxious about your souls as to what you will eat or what you will drink or about your bodies as to what you will wear. Does not the soul mean more than food and the body than clothing? Observe intently the birds of heaven, because they do not sow seeds or reap or gather into storehouses; still your heavenly father feeds them. Are you not worth more than they are? Who of you by being anxious can add one cubit to his life span? Also, on the matter of clothing, why are you anxious? Take a lesson from the lilies of the field, how they are growing; they do not toil, nor do they spin; but I say to you that not even Solomon in all his glory was arrayed as one of these. If, now, God thus clothes the vegetation of the field, which is here today and tomorrow is thrown into the oven, will he not much rather clothe you, you with little faith? So never be anxious and say, 'What are we to eat?' or, 'What are we to drink?' or, 'What are we to put on?' For these all are the things the nations are eagerly pursuing. For your heavenly Father knows you need all these things. Keep on, then, seeking first the kingdom and his righteousness, and all these other things will be added to you. So never be anxious about the next day, for the next day will have its own anxieties. Sufficient for each day is its own badness.

"What do you think about that?" I ask.

We both sit back in our chairs. The Bible stays open on the table.

"Where did you learn to read?"

I have to think where it was. Then I tell him, "At Cincinnati Day School." A bewildered expression comes across his face. He is about to ask another question. I interrupt to say I was kicked out in the sixth grade and that it is a long story not worth repeating. Once again, I ask him, "What do you make of that?"

"It sounds good," he says, "but in practice does it mean forget the leak in the roof, God will get it done? Does it mean if God is on my side I can spend the afternoon in a field of luxurious clover hay smelling the blossoms? Does the leak get fixed? Is that what it means?"

"You get up on the roof to fix the leak," I say. "It is something you have to do. The roof has a steep pitch. The ladder may be shorter than you would like. Going from it onto the roof might be treacherous. In a situation like that you might say something clumsy like 'please God, don't fail me now.' You are a beginner with God, but you called on God. Assuming you're not detestable to God, God might see you through. Even a casual understanding of God might have momentary results, but a long-lasting, strong relationship, not one that is simply spur-of-the-moment, comes from loving God, and that comes most easily with an accurate Bible understanding. It is hard to love something you do not understand.

"On the roof you have communicated with God in your own feeble way, and maybe God heard you that time. There is nothing to say he did not. You do not slip. Now, the real test of your faith comes later as you fall asleep; do you want to think you would not have slipped anyway?

"Think of this. If we have been faithful to Jehovah and we slip and fall, do we curse God and die? These are things that constantly went through my mind when I started out, but soon there was no question: if we fall or do not fall, God is there. It is foolish to question if God is there."

"Can God see through walls," he asks. "Does God know about me?"

"None of us need a letter of introduction to get the attention of the creator of the universe. That in itself is amazing. The Bible says God knows how many hairs are on our head. People who think they are lost in a sea of humanity are making a terrible mistake if they imagine there is something God cannot do including know how many hairs are on our head. God's power is limitless. The Bible plainly says, at least twice, 'With God all things are possible.' "

I say to him, "If you fall off the roof or if something about something does not go the way you would like, understand accidents still happen to faithful Christians. There is a story in the Bible about how Christ is standing within sight of a tower that falls over killing eighteen people. Someone with Christ asked him, 'What is their sin?' Christ answers that their sin is no more or less than anyone else's and that they are in the wrong place at the wrong time. Also understand what you think should happen might not be what should happen. The Bible says trust in Jehovah with all your heart and do not lean on your own understanding. A little example of this is the last day at work before going on a long trip I say to a fellow worker, 'If all goes well I will see you in two weeks.' That is my understanding. Maybe if things go well I will see him tomorrow."

"Is that blind faith?" he asks. "Is everything that happens meant to happen?"

"No, it is not like that. Trust in God goes far beyond what happens. After Christ's resurrection Thomas finally had to admit to himself that it was Christ who was standing in front of him. Christ then said to all those present, 'Happy are those who do not see and yet believe.'

"Those who believe trust, and that comes easily to those who make the effort to learn about God. They learn about God. They trust in God, and with that comes God's help. By their effort they help themselves. At that point a person does not need to see God to know God is real. In the beginning there is something like blind faith, but it does not last very long. A relationship with God began for me when I started intently striving after what the Bible calls 'the more important things.' A strong relationship involves love. God's love is always there, but it is like tapping maple trees. It just does not happen. It is there for those who know how.

"Even the first humans," I tell him, "were not made to love God like programmed robots. If they did it would not be love."

"Like what?" he asks.

"By instinct," I say. "It is by free choice we side with God. That is the way God wants it to be. Following God will happen most completely when it is based on love. Obey out of love. At first some healthy fear comes with knowledge of God. God is more powerful than anything we will ever know. The fear might get us going, but it is the love that keeps us going."

"Obeying sounds childish. Do adults obey God?"

"If they are smart they do. A parent might tell a child not to touch a hot stove or play near a cliff. The child does not know the reason but obeys out of trust. A lot of it has to do with trust. I obey God's directions in the Bible because I trust God. The trouble is, people want to think they, as adults, are able to decide for themselves what is right and wrong. All you have to do is look around to see the effect of everyone doing what they think is right. Then there are people who say they speak for God, but really it is for them. Nobody knows the difference. We think the injustice they do comes from God. Christ has some choice words for people who mislead others. It is Satan's design that things are the way they are. There is much misinformation out there. Suffering humanity is proof, and suffering humanity is the victim. The Bible would stay in Latin if certain people had their way. There are well-meaning people, good-hearted people who swallow dogma handed down from one generation to the next. The situation will not change until God changes it."

"Is dogma a quadruped?" he asks.

"No," I say. "This kind of dogma is a religious teaching that is passed from one generation to the next so many times that where it began becomes irrelevant.

"There are false Christian religious dogmas that extend far past this time. Many are just plain not true. One is the idea that God the Father, God the Son, and the Holy Ghost are one, and the other is the idea that the soul is immortal. Neither has any scriptural basis, and that leaves only one other source, people.

"Numerous times Christ makes definite distinctions between himself and Almighty God. One time he says, 'The Father is greater than I am.' In prayer to his Father shortly before his arrest and death Christ prays to Almighty God, 'Father, if you wish, remove this cup from me,' and then He says, 'Not what I want, but what you want.' One of the Bible writers writes that Christ 'gave no consideration to a seizure, namely, that he should be equal to God.' A person is not apt to develop a strong relationship with God when there are untrue dogmas that can neither be sensibly explained nor understood. The one that says the soul never dies, that it goes straight away to heaven or to eternal torment in hell, is a lie. The Bible says the wages sin pays is death, not eternal torment. If the soul never dies in the first place why is there a need for a resurrection? The Bible says: 'The dead are conscious of nothing at all' and that the ones He, Jesus Christ, chooses will have their life restored by means of a resurrection on earth that occurs after Armageddon."

"What about heaven?"

"One hundred and forty-four thousand are corulers with Christ in heaven. In the Bible, Christ calls them his 'little flock.' Someday God's will, will come to earth as it is in heaven. Then, those resurrected to a life here on earth will be what Christ calls his 'other sheep.' There will be one flock with one shepherd."

"Now that is different. Do you honestly believe all these

years there has been a grand conspiracy afoot to suppress this information? It would involve all kinds of people."

"The Bible says: 'The one called Devil and Satan is misleading the entire inhabited earth.' The conspiracy is not a conspiracy at all but involves one."

"Does it say why people die over opinions? You read it."

"The Bible tells the story of mankind's involvement with God. It says: 'All Scripture is inspired by God.' What that means is, all we need to know is in there. Once, one time, the Bible personifies the Holy Ghost. An inspection of the Scriptures shows the Holy Ghost is not a person, but that does not stop people from being told otherwise, or having an opinion otherwise, or insisting otherwise."

"Why does an all-knowing God leave details open to argument? People are always convinced of one thing or another. People kill people over details like that," he says.

"Christ reduced more than six hundred details down to two principles. When the Bible story begins, one group of people is God's people. They revere the true God. Jehovah God declares to them early in the story that from them a 'seed' will come who will give back what Adam and Eve lost: a paradise earth free from sickness and death. God gives those people more than six hundred laws that govern what they are to do and not do. It is called the Law. As time goes by, the people in charge of administering the Law bolster their own importance by adding laws onto the laws. When the promised seed, Christ, comes along he lives according to the Law but condemns the religious leaders for making the Law burdensome and petty.

"Here is what Christ told them: 'You hypocrites, Isaiah aptly prophesied about you when he said, 'This people honors me with their lips, yet their heart is far removed from me. It is in vain that they keep worshiping me, because they teach the commands of men as doctrines.'"

"He also told them that they resemble whitewashed graves." I read him the place where Christ says, "Whitewashed graves that outwardly indeed appear beautiful but inside are full of dead men's bones and every sort of uncleanness. In that way you also outwardly indeed appear righteous to men, but inside you are full of hypocrisy and lawlessness.'

"What he told just plain folks is something else entirely. He said, 'Come to me, all you who are toiling and loaded down, and I will refresh you. Take my yoke upon you and learn from me, for I am mild-tempered and lowly in heart, and you will find refreshment for your souls. For my yoke is kindly and my load is light.' Christ said he replaced the Law. He replaced it with his very person. He replaced the Law with two principles: that you love Jehovah God with all your heart, mind, and soul and that you love your neighbor as yourself. Christ said all the Law and the prophets were about those two principles."

"So why do the people in power ignore what Christ said? They can read."

"It is the same situation now as in Christ's day. Back then people were aware the Messiah would come. Their thinking was the Messiah would save them from Roman domination. Actually, if Christ wanted he could do that and a whole lot more.

"When Christ did come all prophecies pointed to him as the Messiah. There is a conversation between two religious leaders that reveal why people had Christ executed and why he is ignored now. One says to the other, 'If we let him alone this way they will all put faith in him and the Romans will come and take away both our place and our nation.' They did not want to lose their job. If the Messiah got there they would be out of work. Now it has become tradition. There is always a personal reason.

"Christ called them hypocrites many times, and one time Christ called them 'blind guides who strain out the gnat but gulp down the camel.' They were more concerned about the letter of the Law than about what it all meant."

"People are concerned about details so much," he says. "They burn people alive to prove it. The people who burn them are just like the religious leaders around Christ."

"Yes, but a Bible-based understanding of details make having a firsthand knowledge of God a whole lot easier. Being a footstep follower of Christ is what matters."

"Why does it matter so much?" he asks. "Should we drop everything today and live for what is not here? Is God that radical?"

"Yes and no," I answer. "Jesus Christ put out some radical thoughts. He was radical. But if by *radical* you mean politically radical Christ was not that way. In Bible times Christ fled when people tried to make him a king. Another time he said, 'My kingdom is no part of this world.' In the Bible, Christ's followers are told to obey government authorities, and if a government adversely effects another person's—"

"They are back. Hear them?" he says. "They took two coaches and horses." He tells me to put the Bible in my shirt. He gets up to inspect the soup, and says, "They will come in here to eat."

A little nervous, I stand up to see who is coming. Someone wiping his feet opens the door. When seven or eight people have come inside, the last one closes the door.

"Here we are," says a person among them who appears to be in charge. "Willy and Chandler will be in. They are bedding down the horses." Looking at me, he says, "Is that your team out there. They look well kept. Put them in the barn." Everyone is taking off their coat, and moving around the kitchen. He tells me to hurry and that Willy will show me where to put them. Once more he says they are good-looking animals.

While we are putting the animals away I say I am looking for work. They talk hurriedly while unfastening buckles and removing this piece of harness or that saddle. We finish and go inside. The others are sitting in the servants' dining room. It looks more like stew in their bowls than soup. I see pieces of meat, carrots, onions, and potatoes. It must have been on the bottom of the pot. Our bowls are stacked on the table by the stove. Also bread is there, and so is cheese. On the big white table where the others sit there is wine, cups, spoons, and cloth napkins. When I walk into the room, more than anything else I am trying not to spill what is in my full bowl.

The one who talks the most says to me that they have no need for a rig like mine. Finally I reach my place and sit down. "We have plenty of scythes," he says. I tell him it has been a while since I used a scythe. "After it is cut," he says, "it has to dry. Hopefully it will not rain."

I thank him for his consideration and say I have to get home. I will head back in the morning. It will be several days before they stack hay.

Then the one I was talking with earlier says to no one in particular, "What did the bishop have to say on this fine day?"

"He said the Bishop of Gloucester is going to be roasted alive." Just as quickly as it is said, the one who said it looks around the table to see who is going to tell him to pipe down. It was on his mind all day and could not be contained another moment. He sits beside a girl. They are just old enough to be in love. Except for those two lovebirds, everyone is exhausted.

"What did he do that is so terrible?" I inquire politely.

The child does not answer. Finally someone else does. "He insists it is lawful for the clergy to marry and he says Christ is not physically present during the mass. That makes him a heretic."

Another one says, "Do not breathe a word of this to anyone, but why does a religion need to burn people to enforce its teaching? I swear I do not know."

"It is Satan's fault," I say, and that falls on deaf ears.

Again the child speaks: "Pestilent popery is gone. Now woe unto anyone who does not go along with the pope."

Another one speaks: "The best thing to do is keep silent about these things until we know what to say."

"All the bishops may burn each other up as far as I am concerned," says Chandler, and without pausing he asks to have another piece of cheese.

My newfound friend says to him, "What you have is all you get, and let me tell you, fool, if you keep sounding off like that you might be the first person we know who dies that way."

"Am I a fool? That is the pot calling the kettle black."

In a calm, mitigating way my friend's wife says, "Please, it has been a long day. It is so tiring to hear you talk that way."

About me he says to the one in charge, "Is there room for him in the bungalow?"

Everyone is finished eating. They get up. I follow someone to where I will sleep. Before I go, I tell my friend good-bye. I say I am leaving at dawn. He is busily collecting bowls and from across the table looks up to wish me well.

The next morning as the others get up they go back to the kitchen. I need to get moving and go to the barn to harness Horatio and Talemecus. I have to push them to get them to move. They have enjoyed the lodging. On the way out I take them to water. Watching one, then the other with their heads lowered over the bucket I realize the wine from the night before has made me thirsty. They stand still while I raise water to my mouth with cupped hands. Outside, I hook them to the wagon and climb up. I sit on an empty thirty-gallon water barrel. A slap of the reins plus the words "come on" and we move on down the road, Horatio, Talemecus, and me.

The air is cold. There will be no more hot days this year.

The road slopes down through the middle of a field of long timothy grass cut twice that summer. It will be wet from the dew a little longer. I put the wagon brake on and leave it on. There is a creek in the distance. On the other side I can see the road goes uphill between fields and turns inland.

In the brightening sky there are ducks going south. They are blacks but from here dots in the sky. It will get cold once more.

Sycamore trees mark where the creek is. The creek winds out of low hills in the east and goes to the sea in the west.

Over the top of the hill on the other side a rider appears. His horse is moving at a gallop. No one back there would get a message delivered that way. Could this be the one?

We are closer now. If I did not know horses and riders are two by that sight alone I would think they were one. We will meet in the thicket by the creek.

He is intent with what he is doing. I hope he continues past unaware of me. Then we go behind trees. Before I see him again I am at the creek. He is foreign. I stand up in the wagon. His face is a shadow. The horse gallops. The oxen plow ahead. Quick as can be, without stopping, he lifts his hand and throws a spear into my body. I fall in the wagon. Soon I am lifeless. The oxen continue to plow ahead, but that is the end of me.